D0476023

This book is to be returned on or
before the last date stamped

A FREE WOMAN

Also by Libby Purves

Fiction
Casting Off (1995)
A Long Walk in Wintertime (1996)
Home Leave (1997)
More Lives Than One (1998)
Regatta (1999)
Passing Go (2000)

Non-Fiction
The Happy Unicorns (ed) (1971)
Adventures Under Sail, H. W. Tilman (ed) (1928)
Britain at Play (1982)
All at Sea (ed) (1984)
Sailing Weekend Book (1985) (with Paul Heiney)
How Not to Be a Perfect Mother (1986)
Where Did You Leave the Admiral? (1987)
How to Find the Perfect Boat (1987)
The English and Their Horses (1988) (jointly with Paul Heiney)
One Summer's Grace (1989)
How Not to Raise a Perfect Child (1991)
Working Times (1993)
How Not to Be a Perfect Family (1994)
Nature's Masterpiece (2000)

Children's books
The Hurricane Tree (1988)
The Farming Young Puffin Fact Book (1992)
Getting the Story (1993)

A FREE WOMAN

Libby Purves

Hodder & Stoughton

Copyright © 2001 Libby Purves

First published in 2001
by Hodder and Stoughton
A division of Hodder Headline

The right of Libby Purves to be identified as the Author of
the Work has been asserted by her in accordance with the
Copyright, Designs and Patents Act 1988.

10 9 8 7 6 5 4 3 2 1

A CIP catalogue record for this title
is available from the British Library

ISBN 0 340 79388 0

Typeset by Hewer Text Ltd, Edinburgh
Printed and bound in Great Britain by
Clays Ltd, St Ives plc

Hodder and Stoughton
A division of Hodder Headline
338 Euston Road
London NW1 3BH

To Priscilla Lamont

Chapter One

The storm was past. For the first time in days the clouds
scudding across the sky were white, high, harmless puffs; beneath
them the sea was deep blue and barely ruffled by a steady
westerly breeze.

Against the glare and dazzle of the noonday light, the
doorway of the galley made a darker rectangle. From the hot
shade of its interior a laden figure emerged, perspiring, dark
tendrils of hair plastered to its head, a ragged vest slipping on
tanned glistening shoulders. It would have taken a moment or
two for any outsider to recognize that the person advancing on
the rail with a bucket of slops was female; but then, there were no
outsiders on the *Evangelina*, and the men and boys of the little
ship's company had long grown indifferent to the gender of the
cook's mate. One flirtatious feint, one rebuff, were enough. A
thousand miles out from Panama, a kind of grudging kinship
bound them all together in a patient sexlessness. There would be
time for soft delights later, in some harbour town, when all were
clean and spruce in carefully hoarded shirts from the bottom of
kitbags. For the moment, the expression of each man's desires
was less pressing than the need to ensure he got a decent portion
of potato soup or an unbruised apple from the keepers of the
galley. The ship had come through bad weather during these past
days; food was more pressing than sex.

The woman vanished into the dim doorway again, where the slop bucket was heard clanging to the floor. Moments later she reappeared, and stooped to pick up another aluminium pail and lower it briskly on its long rope into the turbulence of the ship's wake. The new bucket jerked, filled, and was as rapidly hauled up and taken between two strong brown hands. Without ceremony the cook's mate upended the cold seawater over her head. She repeated the process, soaking her raggedly sawn-off jeans and cotton vest, shaking her shaggy mane of hair with angry energy; then threw the bucket back into the scuppers and leaned on the wooden rail while the sun began gently to dry her clothes.

'Maggie!' called a rasping voice from the galley. '*Komm! Ich möchte* . . .' His voice became indistinct as the sentence tailed off. She whipped round, the wet singlet plastered to her breast, her left arm hooked round a wire stay to maintain her balance on the shifting deck. Dark eyebrows knitted together, and big green eyes narrowed like an angry cat's.

'Fuck off!' she said, into the gloom.

A deep, rather drunken-sounding laugh came from the darkness, and a slurred, '*Ich liebe dich!*'

The woman turned, and taking hold of the tarred wires and ropes which rose above her to the topmast, hauled herself onto the rail and began to climb the rigging.

'*Wiedersehen!*' she called, from thirty feet above the deck. And added, in kitchen German, a routine obscenity. Two boys who were rubbing down the rusty side of the bridge looked up and laughed. Far aloft among the greying sails, the woman threw her knee over the yardarm and looked out ahead, eastward across the illimitable wastes of the Atlantic.

A thousand miles away, a pair of very similar green eyes were wide and soft, dreaming beneath dark arching brows as Sarah Penn wiped down her kitchen worktops. The house was silent, for it was a schoolday; it smelled enticingly of fresh coffee, because it was the day when Sarah worked at home.

'*From* home,' she would correct friends. 'You have to say I work from home because at home sounds as if you're doing housework.'

'But you do,' protested Nita, her neighbour and confidante. 'You use Fridays for cleaning and the weekend shop. I've seen you.'

'Sam Miller hasn't,' Sarah replied. 'And I can do the e-mails in half an hour, and catch up on the practice invoices in odd moments at the weekend.'

Now she finished her kitchen surfaces, threw the cloth into the sink, and crossed to the crowded noticeboard by the dresser. Among a chaos of timetables, notes, leaflets and bills there was a postcard pinned to the cork, half obscured by a yellow Post-it note saying, THE RICE CAKES ARE MINE. STRICT DIET! KEEP OFF! and signed with a self-consciously ornate 'Sam'. Sarah moved the note, and left it sticking to a curling parish magazine that hung limply near the bottom edge of the board. She took down the postcard, pushed its pin carefully back into the cork, and carried the card over to the table, looking at it all the way. There, reaching for the coffee pot and absently pouring her third cup of the morning, she read the small, neat writing.

'Acapulco Naval Base,' it said. 'May 13.' Out of habit Sarah turned it over, but there was nothing in the cheaply printed photograph of sky, beach and sea to distinguish it from a thousand other postcards. She turned back, to the message.

Got a free lift, hooray! Under sail, too. Ship is called *Evangelina*, has been doing film location work and now has to get to Europe for winter in Canaries, lucrative charter to build characters of French kids (forlorn hope from what I hear of their last trip). I am assistant cook but cook is German and mainly pissed. Small crew anyway, Chilean, Yanks and riffraff like self. Captain plays flute. Ten days max to Panama Canal, then eastward ho.

Sold the bike for US$50 and a waterproof jacket. Have brought kids really disgusting presents from Mexico.

XXXX Mag

Sarah smiled, and read it through again. As she put it back on the board, she glanced up at a small world map, torn by Jamie from an old diary months earlier when he decided to track his aunt's progress through the length of South America. She found Acapulco, and traced the way to Panama. She looked at the blankness of the Atlantic nibbling at the coasts of Europe and Africa, and thought wonderingly for a moment of her sister, out on the ocean.

Then she noticed, with a start, a scribble of black marker on the flimsy, cheaply printed football club flyer which hung beneath. MUM, REMBER CAKES, SALE IS TUEDAY. TEDDY.

'Bugger!' said Mrs Penn aloud, and crossed the kitchen to begin clanging out cake tins and ingredients. But while she tipped and mixed and cracked the eggs and deftly wiped saved butter papers round the well-worn tins, her mind drifted back to the long shared years of sisterhood.

Chapter Two

———◆———

The Reave sisters, Sarah and Margaret, were a piquant sight as children; elderly neighbours meeting the family on the wide, bland pavements of the Brackley estate would smile at how alike they were, even with the five years' difference between them. When Sarah doggedly pushed new baby Margaret in her buggy, they would say to her mother, 'Aah! Look at that little face, and the hair, and those black eyebrows already! It's like having baby Sarah back again! She *was* a beauty, wasn't she!' And Sarah would try not to mind, even though she privately felt that she had not gone anywhere, did not need to be brought back again, and certainly did not need replacing with a newer and more beautiful model.

Later, while the elder sister with continued doggedness pushed her way through public exams, growing pale and flabby with the effort of constant studying, Margaret continued to be a physical reminder of her younger self. A harassed Sarah would emerge from her books to see a revenant of her childhood: Maggie the brat, insouciantly nimble, as cheeky and skinny and wilfully disruptive as an elf. When she glanced up from her A-level work to see her sister practising handstands amid a pile of disregarded homework she would growl, 'Just you wait! Life isn't all fun when you get older!'

But Maggie would shake her shaggy head dismissively and

run outside to hang upside down like a bat, knees crooked over the top bar of the climbing frame, defying gravity and the academic future alike.

The same neighbours, frailer and greyer now, would glance over the garden fences from their tidy domains and say, 'She's a wild one – but you can't put old heads on young shoulders. I'm sure she'll settle down like Sarah. Oh, that's a bright girl: all A grades they say she'll get – and going to London University to study chemistry. Girls these days! They've got the world before them. It's wonderful, really.'

Sarah duly achieved her grades, her matchbox of a student room in the Imperial College hall of residence, and eventually her first-class degree and a promising traineeship at Intertech Industries UK, Paints and Wallcoverings Division. By contrast, when Maggie's turn came to be processed through the rites of teenage success or failure, nobody was predicting A grades for her. The head of their sixth form, a sour man with little tolerance of female fantasy, observed tartly that he was not even ready to predict that the youngest Reave child would turn up to sit her exams, let alone pass them. Maggie had by then acquired an impressive record of truancy.

'Though you have to admit that she's always been original,' said her father Ted after the third or fourth major crisis. He was sitting at the kitchen table, tired from a six-hour trip to fetch his seventeen-year-old daughter home from the Isle of Wight, where she had been intercepted and unmasked aboard an ocean racing yacht whose horrified skipper had believed her to be a 23-year-old veteran of the Fastnet Race. Maggie was upstairs now, fast asleep, and her father was yawning over his cocoa. His instinct was to defend her.

'According to the head, most of the girls bunk off so they can hang around Etam and Tammy Girl, and shoplift make-up from Woolies. At least Maggie's always had a reason. Ever since she was quite little.'

'I don't,' said her mother Nancy heavily, 'call going off with the circus much of a reason. Not for a twelve-year-old. Anything could have happened. Those men . . . two nights away . . .'

'It wasn't the men she went for,' said Ted stubbornly. Despite the stabs of terror she had so often inflicted on the whole family, he enjoyed his youngest daughter's wayward spirit. 'It was the elephant. She was learning about elephant-keeping.'

'The old man who did the elephants said she worked really hard,' added Sarah, who was home from university for a week-end. 'He thought she was sixteen.'

'Well, then!' said Nancy. 'Sixteen – yes! You know what that means. To a man. And as soon as she *was* sixteen . . .' She closed her eyes in pained memory for a moment. 'It was a whole fortnight. It was your fault, Ted. It was you who said they had to look after their own passports.'

'But she did phone home. We knew she was OK,' said Sarah gently.

'She was in *Turkey!*' exploded her mother. 'In the middle of *term!* With no *money!* We had the *council* round!'

'She was looking for the site of Noah's flood,' said Ted. 'Remember – it was in the papers that year, about someone in Turkey thinking they'd found the Ark. She said she wanted to see Mount Ararat.'

'Anything could have happened,' said Nancy tightly. 'I blame you as much as her. You never reined her back. You hardly even told her off.'

With practised diplomacy, her husband and elder daughter changed the subject. Although Nancy said 'anything' could have happened, they both knew that there was only one thing, fixed in her terrified brain, that the mother dreaded for her daughters. Through all those teenage years it was Nancy's daily fear that one of her pretty daughters would get pregnant. Sarah always thought it curious that their mother did not focus her dread on the danger that they would be raped, or murdered, or come off the back of a fast motorbike. As she grew older she privately decided that the fear of pregnancy might represent, rather than displace, those other fears. It was a kindly interpretation and typical of the elder girl's generous spirit. Maggie, meanwhile, stuck to her own theory.

'What she's trying to tell us,' she would say brutally, 'is that having us wrecked *her* life. Tough tit. As if anyone had to get pregnant these days, anyway. Gross.'

However it was, Nancy spent many mornings absorbed, scissors in hand, scanning the newspapers daily for terrible tales of girls who got knocked up, dropped out of education, and subsequently led graceless and sordid lives in council flats. The fact that this fate had overtaken none of her neighbours' daughters, nor any girl in living memory at Brackhampton High School, hardly reassured Mrs Reave. Nor did Sarah's series of earnest, respectful boyfriends or Maggie's tomboy scorn. The fact was that neither of them – despite Maggie's propensity for running away – ever showed the slightest tendency to get into that particular kind of trouble.

But still the mother fretted, and told the neighbours that bringing up boys would have been easy in comparison.

'Women,' she would say, 'live under a curse. A mother of girls can never really rest until they're safe.' By safe she meant married.

'Married alive. Ugh,' said Maggie, and grinned at her father, who would try not to grin back while his wife was watching.

The head of sixth from at Brackhampton High must have been, despite his sourness, an effective one. Somehow he coaxed Maggie Reave through her university application. Somehow he got her into the exam room, to emerge with a set of grades which, though not as starry as her big sister's, guaranteed her a place at a lesser university to read geography. It was a canny move on his part to point out to her the advantages of the subject for an adventurous spirit.

'There's a sandwich year,' he said. 'Fieldwork camps. There's a forestry project in South America, a survey they've got on in Iceland, and something about desert reclamation in Israel. You get your fares paid.'

So as Sarah moved decorously up through the ranks at Intertech, and conducted a slow, shy, happy courtship with an assistant bookshop manager called Leonard Penn, Maggie Reave gazed out of the windows of Midlands lecture halls and walked for miles, restless and bored, along canal banks. Her reward, in the year that Sarah and Leo became engaged, was to walk with a lighter step among grey boulders and steaming geysers in the far north, and camp at night beneath the Northern Lights.

Her father, who was privately amazed that his younger daughter had got through two years of ordinary student life and summer jobs without breaking free, read her ecstatic postcards from the icy edges of the world and said confidentially to one of his friends at the bank that he found it hard to believe that his Margaret would ever go back to a desk. 'She's my wild bird,' he said sentimentally to his kindly, greying, efficient secretary. 'If you try to hold her, she'll fly off. But if you wait with an open hand, she'll come to you in her own good time. I'm afraid my wife's never really understood that. She's a great believer in girls staying at home.'

He managed, however, to feign decent surprise and disapprobation for his wife's benefit when, at the end of her eight months in Iceland, Maggie fired off three missives: a postcard to her parents, a long letter to her sister, and a half-page one to the university. Each explained, in different terms, that she was giving up the course and travelling on.

Before this news was digested there was another bulletin: a crackling telephone call to Sarah. Maggie was edging along the Greenland coast as cook on an oil company tugboat.

'She'll come home pregnant!' lamented her mother. 'She'll ruin her life!' And, inconsequentially, 'She's a terrible cook, anyway!'

By the time Sarah had extricated herself from work and come home to discuss the crisis with the family Maggie was in Newfoundland, and represented at the family table by a grimy postcard bearing an incongruous picture of a leprechaun and shamrock with the words: 'Top of the morning from the top of a new continent. What a big world it is, to be sure. Too big to be wasting time at a desk. Why the leprechaun, do you think? Do you suppose there are expatriate Bostonian-Irish interests up here which form a customer base for leprechaun postcards?'

Sarah had brought her newly affianced Leo home with her, as she did most weekends. He had become a familiar of the tidy little house on the Brackley estate, and was tranquilly approved of by the elder Reaves. He was ten years older than Sarah, son of a long deceased North London doctor, an alumnus of both Cambridge and Harvard. Ted and Nancy, poring damp-eyed over the atlas volume of Ted's old *Encylopaedia Britannica*, found themselves instinctively turning for help to his apparent sophistication. Even the less impressionable Sarah said with reckless geographical unconcern, 'You know that part of the world, Leo. What do you think we ought to do? Do you reckon she'll be OK?'

In love, flattered, carried away by the moment, Leo said, 'I could go out there if you like. Speak to her. Persuade her to finish her education. I'm sure the university will hold her place.'

Slightly to his dismay, the Reaves collectively leapt on the idea.

Later that night, sitting on the sofa with his arm round Sarah, Leo said, 'Oh God. I'm going to have to do it, aren't I? How the hell do I get to Newfoundland?'

'Your fault for offering,' said his beloved, unkindly. 'It's a fool's errand. Nobody's ever persuaded Maggie to do anything she didn't fancy. She's been stir-crazy for two years, this was always coming. So it's going to cost a fortune, all for nothing.' She paused, and sipped at her tea.

'But yes,' she added, illogically. 'You've got to go. I don't think Dad is terribly well just now. They're not saying anything, but . . .'

Ted indeed, was looking thin and grey. It was, as it turned out, his last summer.

So Leo flew to Boston on the cheapest fare available, his long legs crushed uncomfortably against the seat in front, and took a train northward into Canada. By this time Sarah had had a brief crackling phone call from Maggie, saying that she had found a job cooking and cleaning up for some entomologists camped north-west of Halifax. She named the leader of the expedition, which was her big mistake. Once Sarah had telegraphed him the name, it took Leo, adept at using his old net of university contacts, a mere three days to track down his wayward sister-in-law-to-be.

He found her sitting, knees akimbo, outside an almost offensively picturesque log cabin in a forest clearing. She was mixing a panful of powdered mashed potato, and had the air of a stage gypsy with a red scarf wound round her head.

She looked up, and her big eyes widened.

'*What*,' she asked incredulously, 'are *you* doing here? Where's Sarah? Are you on holiday?'

But she knew within minutes that she was beaten. A family that could so rapidly and unprecedentedly dispatch an envoy into the heart of the great Northern forest was a force to be reckoned with. Leo slept for two nights on a hideously uncomfortable pine shelf in the entomologists' hut, and for two days steadily and relentlessly unrolled before Maggie the arguments for finishing her degree and not distressing her suffering parents any further. By the end of the first day she knew the sour taste of defeat. That night she wept, but kept up a show of resistance for a further twenty-four hours. When it was all over, and the scientists had begun to confer — with an insulting lack of concern — about where to find another camp mother, Leo made a mistake of his own. He produced, with a quite unnecessary flourish, her train and air tickets home.

'They're *dated*,' said the girl angrily. 'You were *sure* you'd get me home and you knew how long it'd take! You patronizing bastard!'

He was shattered by the emotional force of the anger he had unleashed.

On the plane back to Heathrow, Maggie did not speak one civil word to Leo Penn. She looked like a small furious wild animal, huddled in her seat, her big eyes hard and hostile. Leo thought, through the feverish weariness of the flight, that she was a scrawny feral version of his soft-hearted, gentle Sarah. Indeed there was an almost comical similarity in the two women's eyes, their straight dark brows, the way their hair fell, the timbre of their voices. He looked at her through half-closed eyes in the quiet of the aeroplane. It was a clear night, and among the slumped, dozing passengers she was sitting bolt upright, staring out of the window at the moon and the distant white specks of bergs thousands of feet below them. Leo marvelled that this ungrateful angry creature, compounded of fire and air, mountain and storm, could be the sister of his Sarah. She, he thought poetically, was rather earth and water: a gentle breeze through a cornfield, a stream through cool green woods . . . he was not worthy of such perfection. He fell asleep at last, to a troubled, happy dream of her.

Later, as they stood beside the baggage carousel at Heathrow, Maggie turned to him and spoke in a tight, small voice.

'I suppose you have to escort me all the way home? In case I bolt?'

'No,' said Leo tranquilly. 'You won't bolt. It was your decision to come home. I'm going back to my flat, and I presume you're going home to Brackhampton to sort out your kit for the new term.'

Maggie snorted, and ran her hand angrily through her shaggy dark hair. She was, he thought, still very young. He looked down at her, a tall, awkward figure in his black-rimmed glasses and crumpled jacket, and added, 'You've got all your life to go travelling. Once you've finished university.' Deftly, he hooked their bags off the carousel. 'Nobody's been forced to do anything. That's not what this is about. I'm not bringing you home tied to my chariot wheels.'

'Oh, thanks! For nothing!' Suddenly, for one treacherous

moment, the idea of Leonard driving anything more dashing than his old Ford Fiesta made the girl's lips twitch; all her life she had been easily betrayed into laughter at the most inappropriate moments. Then, reassuming her mantle of umbrage, she shrugged and walked away from him with her one light kitbag swinging. Leo watched her retreating figure for a few moments, then made his own way to the Underground.

She never sulked for long. Back home, Maggie saw her father's new pallor and threw her arms around him; she even took care to turn a reassuringly flat-bellied profile to her mother at every opportunity, and packed for the new term with every sign of meekness.

That was in 1983, the year before Ted died. Maggie became quieter during that year, almost (by her standards) withdrawn. The protracted farewell to her father took a heavy toll on her. To Sarah's surprise she spent the whole of her university vacations at home on the Brackley estate, sitting with her father as he grew weaker and tolerating her mother's tearful, capricious moods with a new gentleness. Her sister never doubted how much this forbearance cost her. When she came down at weekends from her job at Intertech, Maggie would chat for a while, then say with a sidelong glance, 'Take over?' When Sarah assented, she would vanish until Sunday night with the ragged old tent from their childhood, walking out of the straggling estate and along the verge of the roaring trunk road towards the sea. It took her the best part of a day to walk to the coast, where she pitched her tent on the beach with utter unconcern for by-laws and for the row of bungalows above, and sat by a driftwood fire. The next morning she would swim in the sea, whatever the season, and walk home.

'Why don't you get the bus? Or take my car?' Sarah asked once. 'It seems such a waste of your free time walking ten miles along that miserable road with all the container lorries when you could get there in half an hour and have proper walks along the beach.'

'Ugh!' said Maggie. 'That's like picking all the raisins out of a bun.'

Another time, she ventured a further explanation. 'You see, you have to measure out a journey,' she said. 'You measure it best in steps. And the shorter the journey is, the more important it is to use your own legs as a measure.'

'You mean,' said Sarah, intrigued, 'that you can turn any trip into an adventure provided you make it difficult enough for yourself?'

Maggie looked at her. Sarah saw that there were fine lines of disillusion, new lines altogether, spidering around the corners of her little sister's eyes.

'No,' said Maggie. 'Not an adventure. But you can pace up and down the cage a bit, can't you?'

'I worry,' said Nancy to Sarah during one of these absences, 'about her being out in that tent alone. Anything could happen. There was a girl in the paper who was – you know, violated – and she found she was pregnant. What a terrible thing.'

Sarah had suffered her mother's troubling obsession for too long to fall into the trap of responding. Instead, kindly, she said, 'Oh Mum, while you're here, I did want to talk through a few things about the wedding . . .'

So for a while the mist of Nancy's worries cleared, as her easier daughter led her up to the bright, safe, happy realm of weddingland, where nothing mattered but embossing and bouquets, fork lunches and the suitability of simple pearl necklets as the groom's present to the bridesmaids. Leo had taken his future father-in-law to the pub that evening because it was one of his good nights. He and Sarah were, their parents' friends agreed, a lovely and considerate young couple. Sometimes they added that it was a pity the younger sister was so odd.

Ted Reave lived just long enough to give away his elder daughter in Brackhampton church, amid great sprays of lilies and yellow roses. Sarah and Leo had their fortnight's honeymoon in France with no undue anxiety, but arrived home barely in time to drive down from London, say goodbye at a hospice bedside and arrange his funeral. It was the same church, and again Nancy ordered lilies.

'They made him sneeze,' said Maggie, *sotto voce*, to her sister when she saw the coffin lying tranquilly in the aisle between the white waxy blooms. The two of them had gone early into the church to make sure that all was well. 'Remember, at the wedding?'

'Well . . . Mum likes lilies,' said Sarah. 'If they do something for her, surely that's the point . . .'

Maggie turned her back on coffin and lilies alike and began suddenly to cry, not discreetly but with raw childish sobs. Sarah stood quietly apart, resisting the urge to hug her: Maggie hated to be pawed when she was upset. The surge of grief passed, and was replaced by a long, bubbling, unladylike sniff. Sarah handed over a wad of tissues.

'Poor Dad,' said Maggie, wiping her nose violently. 'I wish he'd had more of a life.'

'He was happy with it,' said Sarah. 'He had a family, he liked the bank, and they liked him. Mrs Minch cried when I rang to tell her, said he was the best boss she ever had. And they gave him that picture when he retired. He had Mum, and the garden, and us. It was a good life.'

'He never went anywhere,' spat Maggie with sudden vehemence. 'He never went anywhere hotter than Margate or colder than the Lake District. He never saw anything that lives wild in a jungle. He lived fifty-eight years and never saw coral, or coconuts on the tree. He never crossed anything wider than the bloody Channel on the ferry. He had to be a pillar of respectable society and smile at stupid old bats who got their accounts muddled, and then he died. It's desperate.'

She began to cry again. Sarah knew perfectly well that it was not only their father she was weeping for.

'You've been home too long, pacing the cage, Magpuss,' she said. 'You were lovely to him. He really appreciated the amount of time you spent at home. All you have to do now is a few more weeks at college, then finals, and you're free. Go and be a jackaroo or a pirate or a coconut farmer – whatever appalling life you fancy. I promise that I'll never, ever send Leo to bring you back again.'

Maggie almost smiled at that; for the intervening months had softened the Canadian forest outrage to a well-worn joke.

They walked out into the thin Easter sunshine, and shortly the organ began to play and the Reave sisters took their mother in to bury their father.

Chapter Three

The year of Sarah's wedding and Ted's death saw a sudden, startling reversal in the direction of Nancy's obsession. She was just as worried about pregnancy as before, but now the fever that consumed her was anxiety that her elder daughter should conceive as fast as possible. Almost every day the widow telephoned Sarah in London to ask, more or less directly, about the prospect of a grandchild. The newspaper cuttings that littered her kitchen table now were not about pregnant teenagers but about IVF and gametes and ageing ova and desperate women whose careers made them avoid conception until their fertility had waned beyond repair.

'You don't want to leave it too late,' the mother was crackling down Sarah's telephone line a mere month after the wedding. 'Women's, you know, *equipment* doesn't last for ever. And the older you are, the more tiring a baby can be. I was twenty-two when I had you, and twenty-seven when Margaret came, and there was a difference. Oh my word, there was. Well, you were too small to remember, but I was drained . . . I hardly had a moment's pleasure in that baby.'

Sarah, torn between pity for her mother's new loneliness and irritation at the absurdity of nagging a bride of twenty-three, would sit patiently in her bright new flat, tapping her foot on the carpet, grimacing humorously across the room at her husband to indicate that the subject had come up again. She and Leo were intensely happy in those first days, deeply at ease in one another's company; it seemed to her indeed that she had never been so much at home with another human being before. Each day they woke and smiled, embraced with easy passion, amicably split the morning papers and berated Mrs Thatcher together in total harmony. After a peaceful breakfast Sarah would shower, carrying on the conversation while Leo shaved. Then, in their neat business suits – Sarah's short-skirted, wide-shouldered navy blue and Leo's grey managerial pinstripe – they would embrace one last time and set off for their work.

They laughed together about that, too. Once the excitement of her real-life salary wore off, Sarah had begun to wonder whether departmental team leadership in the world of specialist paint marketing was really a goal worth being groomed for. Leo was increasingly disillusioned about the big chain bookstore where he had worked for close on a decade.

'Philistines,' he said. 'The books don't matter, only the numbers game. The customers don't matter, only their money. I might as well be selling burgers. At least there's less hype and tinsel in the burger trade. Do you know who they want me to have in for a so-called book event next month? *Fifi de Mornay!* The one who slept with two Cabinet ministers in the same week. No, I tell a lie, the bald one wasn't even in the Cabinet. When the book trade's sucking up to the discarded mistresses of *junior trade and industry spokesmen*, it's time for the Four Horsemen of the Apocalypse to step in.'

After a while his complaints ceased to sound like jokes and began to take on a genuinely querulous edge. When evening came, he had sometimes poured and finished his first drink before he could bear to discuss his day.

Sarah, happily in love and naturally of a more philosophical nature, was less inclined to complain of her lot. But then, as she secretly told herself, it was different for a woman. The idea of her being trapped for ever in Intertech, or on any kind of executive ladder, was an absurdity, even now, even in 1984. She was a married woman, her destiny awaited. At the moment she enjoyed her office, her team, the mildly exhilarating snakes-and-ladders challenge of commissioning and marketing new kinds of household paint. She had had a small triumph with a particular non-drip product, liaising brilliantly with a new advertising agency to bring in a hugely successful campaign on a cheap contract. She earned plaudits from her departmental chief. There was even an approach from the advertising agency, suggesting she discuss management opportunities there. She enjoyed earning well — she was paid more than Leo already — and took easy pleasure in the company of her colleagues and in the vigorous absurdities of corporate life.

But all the time, although she would have hesitated to say so in front of their more fashionable friends, Sarah Penn knew perfectly well that none of this would last. Some time — not as soon as her mother would like, but soon enough, perhaps when she was thirty — there would be a family. A baby, and a new kind of life. She rejoiced in the idea. Just as the fun of work began to fade and the office life to pall, she would find herself with a new and exciting function. She would be a Mother.

Probably, they would move to somewhere with a garden; fields, even. And although Sarah entirely applauded the idea of equal working rights for women, she had not the slightest intention of going into her fourth decade of life exhausted by working with a carrycot under the desk. Nor would she hand over any baby of hers to some hireling or nursery for ten hours a day. She knew with deep conviction what sort of mother she would be. She foresaw without repining that when she returned from the inevitable break, it would be to a different kind of work, a lesser level of commitment.

Sarah looked forward to this future of compromise, and rarely glanced beyond the child-rearing years to any future work. The child who had pushed her sister's pram knew beyond any doubt that motherhood would suit her; better, she suspected, than it had suited the pessimistic, anxious Nancy. Sometimes she allowed herself to consider a less sunny prospect, in which the babies did not come. But 'We'd adopt' she would say to herself firmly, pushing the fear away. Whatever tricks biology might play (and her mother's ceaseless keening did start to chip away at her confidence after a while), that second life of motherhood definitely awaited her. One way or another. Therefore it did not matter if Intertech was less than fulfilling: how could it fulfil her? It was only a prelude, after all, to the real tune of her life.

For Leo it was different. She was sure of that. A man's work went on and on until he retired. It was therefore more important for him to be well-suited and satisfied. And so, as the weeks went by, Sarah worried ever more about Leo's frustrations at work but bore her own with a shrug, because there was a time-release key on her shackles that a man could never have.

Thinking about all these things as she baked her youngest child a cake for school, Sarah shook her head in amused, indulgent disbelief. Sometimes, when she looked back from the perspective of the newborn twenty-first century, the attitudes and certainties she held in 1984 seemed ludicrous. Her daughter would not grow up with them, for certain. Samantha, already a moody, clever fifteen year old, would surely fight her corner, assert her right to her own career and expect equal partnership with her husband – if any – in every aspect of life. But at the time, Sarah told herself stoutly, her feelings and priorities had been perfectly reasonable. Especially, perhaps, to the favourite daughter of a woman who had never worked for money after her wedding day.

Anyway, she told herself in these rare moments of retrospection, there was no disgrace in having felt sorry for Leo. It was kindness, it was love that made her think his job mattered more. It was pity, because he would never be pregnant and therefore never be free from the daily commercial grind.

That was why, towards the end of 1984, Sarah said to her increasingly morose husband, 'Look, you don't have to stay with the company. You could set up as an independent. You've got the flair, you've got the contacts – have your own bookshop! I can support both of us easily for three years or so on what I earn. We can use my New Year bonus to help with the first stock. Why don't we just go for it?'

'I can't live off my wife!' said Leo, with a horror every bit as old-fashioned as Sarah's view of her maternal future. 'And suppose you had a baby?'

'I shall have a baby when I'm good and ready for it,' said Sarah. 'They don't just *happen*, you know. I'm only twenty-four. I've got six years before I need bother. And by then you'll be doing terrifically well, and I can take all my maternity leave and then go back part-time. And it'll be ever so much cheaper living out of London anyway.'

'Living out of London?' said Leo wonderingly. 'You've got it all worked out, haven't you?'

'Well, you aren't going to start off by paying London rents and business rates, are you?' said Sarah scornfully. 'We could go to – I don't know, Ramsgate? Or Brackhampton? There's nothing but a couple of tacky newsagents there, doing bestsellers and puzzle books. And ever since they set up the history trail round the friary and the castle ruin, the town does get the more upmarket trade. House prices are going up too. Bet you anything it'll be quite smart down there in a year or so. And the Channel tunnel's going to help, I bet.'

'But your job?'

'I could commute. Intertech's only three minutes from Waterloo. And I'm pretty sure they're not going to ask me to relocate.'

Leo thought for a moment or two then said slowly, '*Brackhampton*. Near your mother.'

'Well, we wouldn't live out on the Brackley estate, obviously. But would you mind? Being near Mum, I mean?'

'No,' he said. 'Not really. I suppose she can't actually make you pregnant just by sending out rays of magic 'fluence, can she?'

☆   ☆   ☆

But of course, somehow, she did. Leo and Sarah sold the London flat at a gratifying profit and bought a bankrupt butcher's shop on the corner of Friar's Alley and the High Street, with a beetle-ridden cellar for a stockroom and a one-bedroom flat over half of it.

'Which we can open up for a children's department – or a coffee shop – when we can afford to move out to a house,' said Sarah. 'The next generation of bookshops will be hangouts. Places people want to spend time in.' She was a great reader of lifestyle pages.

The premises smelt unpleasantly of meat, but there was nothing wrong with them that energy, paint and a bit of plaster would not cure. They resolved to use Sarah's last fortnight of holiday entitlement for a pre-Christmas blitz on the old cream gloss paint.

Within a week of the move, though, the smell of paint itself was too much for Sarah.

'Tummy bug,' she said, groaning as she knelt to stir the leaf-green paint. 'I've been feeling queasy all morning.'

'You felt queasy all yesterday morning too,' said Leo. 'You don't think—'

She looked up. On the top of the stepladder, scraper in hand, her husband stood frozen in horror, looking down. Sarah stood up slowly, one hand on the small of her back, and gazed at him. After a moment contemplating his pale, wretched wife among the dustsheets and tea chests, Leo said emphatically, 'No. No, you can't be!'

But she was. Putting down their tools, the two of them fled along the High Street to Boots, bought a pregnancy testing kit and ran shakily back to their chilly shop. Together they read the instructions. Sarah vanished into the butcher's bleak lavatory, then together they stared at the test tube and watched the brown ring of sediment form, clear and un-mistakable.

The shock of that moment never left them. It was, Sarah told

Maggie many months later, like being hit with a hammer. 'Or hijacked at gunpoint.'

'Should bloody think so,' said her sister. In contrast to Sarah's pale, nauseous, eight-month bulk she was thin and brown, fresh back from a spell of illegal work and makeshift travel in the USA. 'What are you thinking of? I turn my back for a few weeks—'

'Months!' said Sarah miserably.

'Well, a few months then, and first of all you decide to support Leo's business with your salary, tying yourself down to Intertech for the foreseeable future, then you get up the spout. You shouldn't be let *out* alone. It's madness! You aren't even twenty-five!'

'It's my baby!' said Sarah angrily. The child was moving now, with little popping kicks in her belly; she had become reconciled to it. The doctor had signed her off work, so the sweaty hell of commuting on crowded trains to an unsympathetic office was over for a while at least. 'It's my baby, even if I didn't want it just yet.'

'OK,' said Maggie equably. 'But a shop and a baby – a ball and chain. Talk about being tied down. I'm glad you're happy, but bloody glad it isn't me.'

Nancy, of course, was delighted; her metaphors were different from Maggie's, reflected Sarah, but they meant much the same thing.

'You've got your anchor now. You can put down roots. *You* won't go drifting through life like your sister. Did you hear this harebrained scheme of hers about Australia? We don't even have *family* in Australia.'

To Nancy and her friends on the estate, the only valid excuse for going abroad for longer than a fortnight was to visit colonial branches of the family. Anything else was dubious, probably dangerous, and vaguely upsetting. She had stopped worrying about Maggie becoming pregnant; her younger daughter seemed, these days, to be hardly a daughter at all. She was more like a son: high-spirited, evasive, always off on some mystifying expedition. There had been no boyfriends either; at least, none brought home for approval. Forgetting Maggie's gender, the mother got along with her a little better.

Leo was reconciled to the baby too. Sarah remained resolute about returning early to work, so he thought they could cope financially; the shop had had a surprisingly good launch and he faced its first Christmas with optimism. He had a good knowledge of the trade. Once he was over the shock of the publishers' robust credit terms for independent bookshops, he worked out a way of balancing the books. He quickly grasped – by way of a few disastrously quixotic mistakes – what books the denizens of Brackhampton would actually buy, and when they would buy them in profitable hardback. He rapidly learned that there was no point despising the rock music biographies, celebrity froth and sumptuously gimmicky cookbooks; yet his gentle, scholarly diffidence of manner and wide enthusiasm for his wares won him friends among those who thought of themselves as Brackhampton's intelligentsia. Two months after the opening he managed to persuade one of the TV celebrity authors of the moment, a handsome firebrand of a Cambridge don whom he had slightly known in their youth, to come and deliver a talk. The little bookshop was packed that evening, the local radio station came, and his reputation shot up. He had plans to start a specialist service finding rare books on military and naval history and sending them out by post. There was profit in that, if you were organized. Leo was always organized.

On the strength of all this and Sarah's maternity pay, the young couple decided with some trepidation to rent a little house behind the High Street rather than try and live in the flat with the baby. When she got back to work they would be able to afford a local girl to help out – the father shied away from the word 'nanny'. Babies, he had heard, grew up very fast these days.

In no time it would be at school, and the difficult bit would be over.

Despite his many talents, Leo, at thirty-four, was still in many ways an innocent.

Samantha Margaret Penn was born in February 1985, two weeks late, red-faced and howling after a long and difficult labour. Her aunt and prospective godmother got the news on a sweltering desert morning in Western Australia, over a crackling radio-telephone link. She had been called out from a tin-roofed classroom where she was imparting the basics of world geography to a dozen tanned and inattentive children.

'I want to come home and see it!' yelled Maggie over ocean waves of static. 'But I can't leave this job till the term's over. I'm only doing it because Kathy got ill. No, a different Kathy. Never mind. And I haven't got the fare together yet anyway. Long to see the baby! Give it my love!'

'Not *it*!' shouted Sarah. It had taken her three days to get through, three days of being kept under observation in a grimy ward, waiting her turn impatiently for the telephone trolley. 'Not *it*. Her!'

'Sorree!!' said the distant voice from down under. 'Look, I have to go. They wander off outside if I turn my back. Write! Tell me about her. Photos. All that. I'm here for at least two more months, then I'll go down to the coast and see if I can work a passage on a ship pointing north.'

'Mags, why can't you FLY home like everyone else?'

'There speaks a yuppie. Intertech executives fly. Me, I know my place. I earn peanuts here, Sarah, less than peanuts. I'll try and fly part of the way, perhaps.'

'I want to see you!' Sarah twisted the cable of the telephone between her fingers, and tears pricked her eyes. Maggie's strong, happy, careless voice tormented her like the singing of a bird outside a prison cell.

'I want to see you too. But I have to finish term. I'm not a free agent till I draw my last Wooroo paycheck. Honestly. Look, I can't talk now, they're going outside, any minute now it'll be a full-scale white man's walkabout, *Hoy! In!* Sare, I really do have to go and shout at them. 'Bye. Take care.'

Leo, who was walking up and down with his baby in his arms, saw his wife's face twitch as she put the phone down. Gently he laid Samantha down in the cot, where she waved her small arms and looked up at nothing with blue, unfocused eyes. He went to Sarah and put his arm round her.

'Tired? Did she keep you up a lot last night? You're doing so, so well. I'm proud of you. Both.'

Sarah did not relax into his arm at once. She pressed her lips together, and glanced at the cot.

'It's for ever now, isn't it?' she said. 'That's the thing that never sinks in till it happens. She's actually here. She's real. This is it.'

Leo, carefully, kept his arm round her and said, 'It? What do you mean exactly by it?'

'A lifetime contract,' said Sarah. 'The anchor. The ball, the chain, the root. I'll never be a free woman again.' And she wept, with great tearing sobs.

'Fourth day blues,' said the consultant next morning, after he had checked Sarah's difficult stitches and signed her off as fit to go home. Leo had intercepted him on the way into the ward, drawing him insistently aside to ask about the evening's desperate bout of weeping. 'Fourth day blues. Sometimes we call it fifth day blues, depending when it turns up. Psychology is an inexact branch of medicine.' The consultant smiled, a hasty professional smile. Leo was silent.

'But fourth or fifth, it nearly always does happen, according to the nurses. Your wife had a hard time. In the old days we'd have kept her in for eight days, but you know how it is. You've got help at home, I suppose?'

They had Nancy. She came to sleep in the spare bedroom,

not even complaining at having to share it with boxes of unsold books. Adept and delighted, she doted on baby Samantha, would not let her whimper even for a moment, cuddled and cooed and very soon took over the job of feeding her. Sarah had tried, but her breasts ached and bled.

'Not every woman can manage it,' said Nancy with happy confidence, holding the baby to her. 'It's all to do with the shape of your nipples. Better a bottle than a hungry baby, izzen't dat so, precious popkin?'

Sarah retreated into a sullen dreamworld, and did not much care about the alienation of Samantha from her breast. The suckling hurt, anyway; and sitting anchored to the sofa with the child latched to her bosom made her feel powerless, bloated and irritable. The doctor told her to get gentle exercise; she took to walking aimlessly round the town centre during the periods when her mother would be feeding and caring for the baby. She slept badly at night and dozed during the day; but the sound of Samantha's coughing cry as she woke from her midday sleep was Sarah's signal to get up and leave the house while her mother fussed with bottles and baby talk.

The alleyway to the main street took her past the bookshop. Leo, watchful behind his desk in the corner, saw his wife pass almost every day, and guessed that she was escaping. In the evening he would nurse the baby and try to create an affectionate circle of the three of them; but his mother-in-law would chatter excitedly about vests and colic, and Sarah would go early to bed with a book, silent and morose. Then Nancy would take the baby from him and cluck off upstairs, leaving him alone and dismayed.

At first Leo filled the void by pulling out his stock records and account books and working late into the night, finally going to bed with a pile of catalogues in which he sought to divine and predict local taste. He did not yet feel confident enough to hire a proper assistant, and was learning the hard way that not every sixth-former in search of a Saturday job was capable even of opening a box without defacing half the stock inside it. He was overstretched in those early days, and not a little frightened of what he had taken on.

But after a fortnight of this life he could no longer bear the dark, cold feeling in the pit of his stomach. Halfway through a working day, when Nancy had just wheeled the baby past the shop window in her buggy, he abruptly got up from his desk, eased his aching shoulders, breathed deeply, then locked the shop door and went up the alley to the little house. It was silent. Cautiously, he climbed to the bedroom and found Sarah lying on her back on the bed, staring at the ceiling. For once he did not speak gently to her.

'This,' he said, 'has got to stop. Either you are ill with that post-natal depression thing, and you've got to get treatment. Or else you're angry with me, or the baby, or something. I don't know what it is, I don't know about women and babies, it's all Greek to me. But it's not going to go on. It's got to stop.'

Sarah sat up and stared at him, her face unreadable.

'The baby's all right,' she said defensively. 'Mum's got her.'

'Shall we offer to let your mother adopt her, then?' said Leo with studied callousness. 'Or perhaps hand her over to someone younger. There's a shortage of babies for adoption, they say. If her own mother doesn't want her, obviously that's the answer.'

He had hardly ever spoken to anybody so cruelly; a kind of bewilderment seized him at his ability to draw up so much unkindness from himself. All he knew was that he must get a reaction from his wife, whatever it took. She was thin in the face during those months, and wide of eye; for a moment as he looked at her his mind flashed back confusedly to the day in the Canadian forest when he had brutally told Maggie that if she did not go home now she would never again see her father alive.

The shock worked. Sarah's face crumpled, and she began to cry. 'My baby – how dare you—you don't care . . .'

Leo crossed the room, took her in his arms and let her cry.

After a while he said, 'Your mother had better move out. We've got to do this properly. Samantha is ours. Not hers.'

'But the shop – you can't help – I can't cope alone – I don't know how to do any of it – oh, Christ, Leo! We aren't ready, we weren't expecting any of this.'

'Don't be such a control freak,' said her husband kindly, stroking her hair. 'We'll cope. People cope. People always have. The pill is a recent accident of history. Babies by tradition turn up when they feel like it. And people cope.'

Fifteen years later, Sarah the mother of three baked her cake in a sunny kitchen, remembered these things and shook her head in tolerant wonder. What a pathetic, panic-stricken child she had been! It was rare in life to be able to look back and identify a moment of truth, a corner turned, but that day had proved one of them. Everything had gone better after Leo's remonstrance. Nancy had been persuaded back into her proper grandmotherly place, Sarah had learned her way round the problematical baby ways of Samantha, and suddenly one afternoon, between a windy smile and a small flailing fist, the baby made herself beloved. As the child patted her cheek, Sarah felt an almost physical sense of dissolution and relaxation; her hard-edged dreams of liberty and control melted into a warm nurturing broth. 'I'm your mummy,' she whispered to the wriggling creature in her arms. 'For always and always.'

Going back to work was a torment, even though Nancy jealously and vigilantly monitored the baby's successive au pairs; but after two short hectic years commuting up to Intertech, the birth of Jamie put an end to Sarah's progress up the executive ladder. The shop was doing fine, and so was the rare-book catalogue, administered largely now by two unspeakably enthusiastic part-timers, General Madson and Rear-Admiral Havelock. This time, Sarah accepted severance pay and a boisterous farewell party in the tapas bar behind Waterloo Station.

'We'll really miss you,' said her colleagues, and, 'We'll stay in touch!' But of course neither was strictly true and Sarah knew it, and did not care. When she did at last return to earning, it was as a part-time clerical assistant to Samuel Miller, senior partner at the local veterinary practice.

When they could be bothered to come all the way down to Brackhampton for the weekend, more ambitious women friends looked askance at her having left the corporate world with no plan to return. But: 'I hated it, really,' said Sarah. 'Marketing meetings, non-drip brand identity reinforcement seminars – bleaagh!' She reached down to straighten the handlebars of small Jamie's pushalong trike before his notorious temper exploded in frustration. 'Besides, I think I'm pregnant again.'

'But a *vet!*' said Jeanette, who worked for a magazine publisher. 'There's just no future. No ladder. Why don't you try for flexitime, in a big company? Intertech would have you back. I bet.'

Sarah merely smiled.

Seven months later Maggie, who had by now finished her Antipodean travels and based herself rather loosely in Spain, came home to see the newest baby and was far more understanding.

'I couldn't have worked in that paint place for six months,' she said, 'let alone three years. At least working for a vet you must get some laughs.' She had Jamie on her knee, playing with her ropes of carved amber beads, and addressed him with a confidential air. 'I'll tell you a thing about life, boy – the crap jobs are far more fun than the good ones.'

'*You* couldn't work *anywhere* for more than a few months,' said Leo. 'How many jobs did it take you to get round Australia?'

'Six,' said Maggie. 'Schoolteaching, cooking, washing cars, packing fleeces, grape-picking, and mending smelly wet-suits in the dive centre at Cairns. That was the worst. Gluing up salty old neoprene crotches. And all so that I could get the fare back every two years to see what you'd sprogged. I've had to stick to Spain

lately, just so I can afford to commute to your milky and ever-
fertile bedside.'

'I would have thought the fleeces were the worst of your
jobs,' said Sarah, who was nursing the newborn Teddy beneath a
shawl in the warm kitchen, light-headed with the hormones of
lactation and the pleasure of having her sister home. 'All full of
fleas and sheep shit, I should think.'

'Nah,' said Maggie. 'Lovely, they were. Lots of lanolin, my
hands have never been so soft.'

'When are you going to settle down and get a real job?' asked
Leo, from the sink. Maggie's visits always made him a little
stiffer and more pompous than usual, which in turn made the
two women playfully gang up against him. The joke of this grew
imperceptibly less funny every time. He wiped the draining
board deliberately. 'I've heard of gap years, but you seem to be
taking a gap decade.'

Maggie looked at him, her dark brows arching satirically.
'Were you offering me a job, brother-in-law? Do you want me to
step into Miss Mountjoy's cardigan when she resigns again?'

Nearly five years after founding the business Leo had at long
last hired a full-time assistant: an angular, Anglican churchwar-
den who had twice handed in her notice on grounds of principle,
the principle usually involving books about what she referred to
as 'unnatural practices'.

'I wouldn't hire you with a ten-foot pole,' said Leo. 'But
you'll have to decide what you're going to do some time, won't
you?'

'No,' said Maggie. 'No, I don't think so. In my increasingly
global experience of life, people are always deciding things with
great solemnity, and then events come along and change their
direction. Companies vanish, countries vanish, careers and trades
become extinct overnight. I thought I'd just cut out the middle
bit and let fate have its way.'

'Drift, you mean?'

'No, no, no. There's an art to it.' As the child scrambled

down from her lap, Maggie looked across at Leo, who now had his back to her and was fiddling with the sink plug with a lofty, householderly air. 'The strategy is this. The more places I put myself, the more interesting and different will be the things that happen. That's why I'm learning Spanish so hard. There are three hundred and fifty million Spanish speakers in the world, so that's three hundred and fifty million new conversations I can have. Good, eh?'

'If you don't mind the prospect of still being a chambermaid when you're knocking thirty,' said Leo repressively.

'Temporary chambermaid,' said Maggie cheerfully. 'And windsurfing instructor, and very nearly TEFL. Multiskilled, that's me.'

'What's TEFL?' asked small Samantha, who was colouring at the kitchen table.

'Teaching of English as a Foreign Language,' said her father automatically.

'English isn't a fowwen language, silly.'

'It is when you're not English,' said Maggie. 'Most people in the whole world think you're a foreigner, Sammy.'

'Well, I aren't,' said the child. 'Where's my red pencil?'

'I looked in my old diary the other day,' said Sarah with apparent irrelevance, propping the baby upright and rubbing his back. 'And you know, it seemed really weird, and wild, that there used to be a time when I had absolutely bugger-all to do apart from earn a living and keep myself amused. It seemed unimaginable. An impossible concept. I don't know how I filled the time. But I suppose you're still in that phase, Mags. Stay alive, stay roughly solvent, stay amused, and that's your day's work done.'

'Correct,' said Maggie. 'Except for the solvent bit. I'm better than solvent. If nobody will lend you any money, it follows you don't have any debts. In Australia once I ran out of everything — money, food, clean clothes. Technically, I suppose I was destitute. So I went to the petrol station, just on the way into

Canberra from the desert road, and that's when I started the car-washing. It was a breeze. One day and I had a big steak dinner and a night in the hostel. Two more days and I had enough to buy some new boots and a bus ticket to the coast.'

'And what did you do on the coast?' asked Leo, with a small air of triumph.

'Err . . . stuck new crotches in skanky wet-suits for fat tourists,' said his sister-in law, who was good-natured enough not to grudge him his victories. 'OK, I give in. I'm a bum. I need to be rescued from my pathetic life. I'll take over from Miss Mountjoy tomorrow. Just give me half an hour to buy a nice grey cardigan.'

This time Leo laughed properly, and threw the tea towel at her.

That baby Teddy was eleven now. Even Sarah, who knew Maggie best, had not really believed back in 1989 that her sister would still be rootless in the new century; but she was. Slotting the last cake into the oven, she washed and dried her hands and then picked up the postcard from the table again. It was a bigger house now, further up the High Street with a more comfortable kitchen. Samantha was a clever, tricky, high-strung adolescent; Jamie's voice was beginning to break. Sarah herself was softer and rounder in the face and body; the pretty, sharp young marketing executive had vanished for ever, swallowed up in the plump blandness of a nice efficient motherly lady who did accounts for a small-town vet.

Leo was a little heavier too, almost jowly, and even more anxious for his evening drink. He had every excuse: he was still running the shop with only Miss Mountjoy and an ever-changing cast of part-time sixth-formers. Attempts to bring the General and the Rear-Admiral in to man the shop for the odd hour had foundered; after gamely trying it, they found themselves too irritated by the browsing, handling, indecisive ways of the public. Both stated firmly that they preferred to work at home, sending out book lists and parcelling up orders. As for Nancy, she had grown quite suddenly into an old woman, with parchment skin and sunken cheeks.

Maggie, on the other hand, came home once or twice a year and seemed at first glance unchanged: merry, unattached, always full of adventures. Sarah read the card:

'*Got a free lift . . . Under sail . . . Evangelina . . . am assistant cook but German cook is mainly pissed . . .*'

Ten days to the canal, it said. Sarah pulled from among the cookbooks the school atlas she kept for this purpose. She checked the postmark on the card, with some difficulty, and began to calculate. Ten days, then the Atlantic – four weeks? Five?

It would be July then, the start of the summer holidays. That would be nice for the children. They always looked forward to Auntie Maggie.

Chapter Four

Captain Lopez shaded his eyes and looked aloft. He ran his eye over the clean obedient curves of his squaresails, the crazy logic of his web of rigging, and saw that it was good. On the upper foretopsail yard two figures worked, small black silhouettes against the sky: his bo'sun and one of the Chilean boys left over from the film job. There were ten or eleven of them on board, including a few American students, and he was glad enough to have them. They paid for their food and skivvied at any job going. But he would be glad to have a proper payload again: either sail trainees on whom he could impose proper discipline, or else a paid crew and paying passengers.

His eye swept down the foremast, found it satisfactory, and rested on the figure which sat lightly astride the lower yard, steadying itself on a footrope and looking out at the eastern horizon. Captain Lopez smiled; his assistant cook, too, was good. Of all the riffraff crew he had assembled to bring his ship back, late on schedule after the irritating delays of filming, she was the treasure. Gunther was drunk and dirty in his habits; the film crew had refused to eat in the galley and brought their own supplies in hampers each day. When they docked in Spain Gunther would have to go, and he knew it, but to abandon him in Chile in his present state was unthinkable.

At least, it was unthinkable to a decent man like Joaquim

Lopez. They had sailed together two years earlier from Kiel, and Gunther had been a good enough cook then, if prone to bitter ranting about his wife and child. What further harm had come to him in the hot Americas and made him the useless liability he now was, Captain Lopez did not know. However, he felt responsible. A woman, probably. Women were terrible trouble.

But this one, perched neatly in his rigging, was no trouble, and he approved very much of her. So much that now he raised an arm aloft and cried, '*Hola, Maggi!*' and returned her wave with an almost boyish glee. '*Esta pasando bien?*'

The wind took her words, but he heard '. . . *muy bien!*' and cocked his head at her, with a wink. Not so bad-looking, but thin. Thin, however, was good in the circumstances. With so many men together on the sea, and no other women aboard, it was good not to have breasts constantly forced into the crew's notice. This woman was friendly, kind even, but neither scoldingly maternal nor flirtatious. Perfect!

Joaquim Lopez shuddered at the thought of how nearly he had missed capturing this treasure. The first he had seen of her was a pair of long, ragged denim legs, dangling over the side of the quay in Acapulco. An insistent voice had called his name; hot and irritable, he snapped at her for a tourist before he took in what she was asking.

'You need a cook?' she was saying in easy Spanish. 'No pay, just the passage to Europa. You are going to Europa, *si?*'

'*Si,*' he said crossly. 'And I have a cook.'

'I do not think he is a good cook. I have been drinking with some of your crew all last evening, and I think this cook is a man who needs help if he is to make good food for sailors.'

'Is that what they say?' The captain bristled, his professional pride wounded by the notion that every bartender in Acapulco knew by now how badly managed was the galley of the *Evangelina*. 'Ignorant men will always talk when they are drinking.'

'OK,' said the girl on the quay. 'But I have a UK passport, I can land in Spain with no trouble, I won't upset your cook, and I don't want any pay. I have also worked on deck before in a *barco*, with sails. It is a pity that you do not want me. I am sorry to waste your time. To show my sorrow I will do a penance. Now.'

She swung down from the quay and before he could stop her had invaded the dark, rancid space of the galley and begun to run water into a kettle and ferret energetically for mops and cloths. He made as if to stop her but could not bear to; although he regularly sent seamen in to clean out Gunther's horrible domain, it remained the sole source of shame on his otherwise excellent little ship. An hour later she reappeared, pouring the last bucket of evil black water into the dock and wringing out the last cloth. She looked at him where he hovered near the galley door and said, 'OK. And now adios, Captain.'

So of course it had not been adios, and he had taken her on for the passage to Santander. And there she was, blithely aloft, no trouble at all and a very great deal of help, on deck as well as in the galley.

'Maggi!' he said softly as he padded back to his own quarters beneath the bridge. 'Maggi-Reava!' He shook his head sadly. The night before, offering her a ceremonial liqueur after supper, he had formally asked her to sail on as paid cook for the winter and the following spring. 'Even the French will eat your food,' he said. 'Come. My owners will pay you well, and your insurance.'

She had turned him down, smiling all the while. 'No. With regret, Captain, I must go home to see my family.'

'You have a husband?' he said, fixing her with eyes of brown doglike devotion.

'*Nunca!* Never!' she said. 'Husband? No, no, no. You know what bad things marriage does to a cook. Look at Gunther. If he had not married the famous devil-woman from Bremen, there would not have been black beetles and hard *patatas* for your crew.'

Captain Lopez had never particularly thought about Maggie Reave's sexuality before, but at that moment, looking at her bright, spare, tanned face against the velvet darkness of the porthole, he said with a conviction so strong that it made him vehement, 'It is not a joke! You should marry!'

She had laughed at him. She generally did.

'Yes, but *when* is she coming?' asked Teddy for the third time that meal. 'When is Auntie Maggie coming? Is it tomorrow, or *when?*'

'I don't know,' said Sarah patiently. 'Teddy, you know what it's like. She's coming on a ship. A sailing ship to Spain, which should be nearly there by now – then she's got to get back to England. It could be weeks.'

'It only takes 'n hour and a bit from Spain,' insisted the small boy. 'It's less far than Greece, and that wasn't even two hours when we went, was it?'

'She doesn't always use aeroplanes,' said his father drily.

'She hates aeroplanes,' added Samantha firmly, 'unless they're really, really small, with propellers, like in the jungle.' Her recent veneer of fifteen-year-old cynicism was, her mother silently noted, breached by the prospect of Maggie's arrival. Her eyes were sparkling nearly as much as the boys'.

'She goes on planes that are really, really old and dangerous, like in Russia,' added Jamie. 'She went on terrible aeroplanes there. She told me that on some of them you could decompress the cabin by taking off the top of the lavvy cistern.'

'So you see,' said Leo, emptying his glass and reaching for the wine box, 'your aunt cannot possibly be expected to travel like a normal twenty-first-century human being on a fast and comfortable aeroplane. If there's a truly frightful way to get here, that's the one she'll choose.'

'It's not *fair*,' said Teddy. 'I want to see Auntie Maggie.'

Samantha shrieked suddenly, her sophistication finally deserting her. 'Mum!' she said. 'At the *window!* I *saw* her!'

The whole family turned together to follow Samantha's pointing finger. Sure enough, in the autumn evening gloom a familiar face was grimacing through the panes above the sink. A fist rose and tapped, then uncurled to give a flippant little wave of the fingers towards Samantha. Then the eyes swivelled towards the entranced, staring Teddy, and Maggie stuck her tongue out at him. His own shot out in reply. Sarah scraped her chair back and went to the window. Leo, more practical, went out of the kitchen door and addressed his sister-in-law's back as she perched on top of the dustbin, still grimacing at her sister and the children.

'Don't you *ever* just ring the bell?' he asked.

She turned and looked at him in the dusk, surprised at the genuine irritation in his voice.

'Well, of course I do,' she said. 'I just couldn't resist, that's all. It was so ghostly, walking up from the bus station in this mist. And then when I saw you've got these wheelie bins with rubber lids that don't even clank, how could I do anything else?'

By now the other four Penns were outside, shivering slightly, reaching up hands to haul her down and into the warmth of the kitchen.

'Hello, friends!' said Maggie. 'Oh, this is nice. Teddy, you have grown a foot. Jamie, you're virtually adult. Samantha – you look amazing. I mean, shit, I'd forgotten about how big you all were. I've brought you the most unsuitably kiddie presents, I could kick myself.'

An extra plate was found, and family supper continued in agreeable uproar as Maggie produced from her vast backpack a series of sugar skulls and coffins from Mexico.

'For Christ's sake don't eat them! They could have any kind of germs on them.'

'Mainly from your aunt's rucksack, by the look of it!'

There were glass beads and bracelets too, carefully wrapped in layers of newspaper so garishly redolent of another continent that Samantha and Jamie were almost equally fascinated by them, and spelled their way by guesswork through the lurid news of murders and *ladrones*. They spread out these exotic treasures between the plates, crowding the table and making Sarah worry even more about germs on the food (*O God, I am turning into my mother*, she thought in sudden horror). They fired questions at their aunt who answered, her mouth often full of pasta, in terms which raised even more questions.

'Why was it a sailing ship?'

'People like sailing ships. There are lots of them, here and there in different countries. *Evangelina* came out in spring as part of a race from Europe, then she was chartered for some pirate film, and after that Spanish and French schoolchildren were going to have lessons on her.'

'Cool. Was it ever so slow?'

'Well, not very fast. Especially with the wind against us, at the end.'

'Did you climb the mast? Did it lean over? Is it scary?'

'Lots of times. No, not scary at all. Very nice up there. Like being a monkey up in the jungle canopy, friendlier than you'd think. There's always a rope or a wire to hold on to. And it was a good way to get away from Gunther the cook.' She went into an impression of Gunther, drunk, which Teddy in coming days was to reproduce frequently in the playground for the benefit of his friends.

When he had recovered from his hilarity he asked, with the bluntness available only to the very young, 'Did you have a boyfriend on the ship?'

Leo and Sarah both pricked up their ears, watching Maggie's response. It was, however, disappointingly debonair.

'Nope. If you'd seen the crew, you'd know why.'

'You shouldn't ASK those things,' said Samantha crossly to her brothers. 'It's not polite.'

'Samantha's got a boyfriend,' said Jamie smugly. 'He's called Duane and he's from the council estate and he's a really, really rough biker yob.' He ducked as his sister aimed a swipe at his head, almost falling off the chair.

As he clutched at his little brother, Teddy too dissolved in fits of laughter, adding, 'He's a biker but he hasn't actually got a *motorbike!*'

Sarah intervened swiftly. 'Behave yourselves. Jamie, you can shut up about Sam's private life. Or go to bed now. I mean that.'

Samantha's face burned red, and her eyes were hot, with a risk of shameful tears. She stood up, her droopy wide jeans flapping over her toes, swayed tall and awkward across the room and ran water noisily into the sink, bringing back a glass of water which she then pushed across the table and ignored. Sarah smiled at her daughter and was met with a ferocious scowl.

Leo looked uncomfortable. Although he might not have used precisely the same words, he too was of the view that Duane was indeed a really, really rough biker yob. He felt that Sarah's strategy was all wrong ('Make him welcome, let her make her own judgements as to how this new friend fits into the world she knows'). He suspected it of coming straight from one of the glutinously sensible family self-help books which he so resented having to stock in the shop. He frowned at Jamie, endorsing Sarah's rebuke; it was easier than looking at the sullen, beautiful face of his daughter. He did not like to think of her being anywhere near Duane, let alone – He reined in his thoughts, sharply.

Maggie had assumed an air of serene unconcern at this family ruction, and was winding spaghetti round her fork. Teddy recovered himself and continued the questioning. Of the three, he had the haziest idea of Auntie Maggie; it had, after all, been three years since her last fleeting visit to England.

'Daddy says you never take planes like a modern lady. He says you always do things in the difficultest way, just to be contrary. How did you get here from the harbour that the ship went to?'

'British Airways standby from Bilbao,' said Maggie demurely, throwing a sidelong glance at Leo, who pressed his lips together in real annoyance. She smiled, relenting. 'But I did hitch a lift from Santander to Bilbao on a cheese lorry. Mountain goat cheese, Cabrales. Cor, it did smell.' The boys were beginning to crack up again, and soon even Samantha was smiling. 'Smelt like a waggonload of dirty old feet.'

The children giggled, delighted.

After a suitably dramatic pause, Maggie said, 'And I can prove it!'

'How?' – 'What do you mean?' – 'Go on, then!' The three spoke at once, children together once more. Maggie twisted on her chair, lugged her rucksack over, and unzipped a front pocket. From it she drew a plastic packet fastened with rubber bands; inside that was another plastic bag, tied in a tight knot.

'Pass the parcel!' said Jamie. 'Who gets the prize?'

'Go on then,' said his aunt. She handed him the packet, barely bigger than a fist, and watched him tear the plastic away. As soon as he had done so a ripe, overpowering odour filled the kitchen. She took the wedge of blue-veined cheese back from him and broke it open. The smell intensified.

'See? Imagine a great big lorry all full of cheeses – this was one of the *weakest*-smelling. Go on, taste it.'

With noses pinched and a gleeful pantomime of disgust, the children gathered round, daring one another to taste the strong cheese.

Later, in bed, Leo laid down his book and said to Sarah, 'I can still smell that damn cheese.'

Sarah sniffed. 'Hmm. Possibly. Even for goat, it's pretty ripe.' Then, tacitly accepting responsibility for the cheese and its giver alike, she said meekly, 'Shall I go and put it in the yard?'

He considered, sniffed again and then said resignedly, 'No. Not for my sake. It's very faint. Probably just molecules still stuck on the hairs in my nose.'

They lay together in silence for a while, then Leo said in a different tone, studiedly casual, 'How long is Maggie staying, this time?'

'Here, you mean?' She knew perfectly well what he meant. Now that the boys had separate bedrooms, there was only one guest room. Leo had taken to setting up his laptop computer and files there, so that he could come home to a glass of wine and the comforting sounds of home rather than work on in the shop after closing time.

They had vaguely talked of building an extension, making the kitchen bigger and a study on top, but balked at the cost. Leo had ridden well through the brief crisis of 1996 and the change in book pricing, but the sense of danger never left him. A small bookseller, he always said, could not afford unnecessary debt. So he worked on in the spare room, and with Maggie and her rucksack ensconced there now, his books and files were back downstairs, piled higgledy-piggledy on the cluttered escritoire in the living room. It was not satisfactory.

None of this was said, but after a pause Sarah continued, 'She's learning Chinese, apparently. She says it's best to do it in the UK. So it might be a few months.'

'That wouldn't be local, would it?' said Leo in a tone of careful neutrality, pretending to look at his book. 'She'd have to go to London, to the School of Oriental and African Studies, or wherever.'

'She might go to Mum for a bit,' said Sarah feebly. She was a bad liar. While Leo had been out of the room after supper, Maggie had mentioned that it might be worth her trying some of the websites of colleges in East Kent. Sarah, stretching out in rapture on the shabby sofa with her shoes kicked off, had said, 'Then you could stay here – oh Mags, do!'

Leo now turned sharply to look at his wife, half-moon glasses slipping down his nose. He hated the reading glasses; they seemed a mark of decrepitude, reminding him daily that he was over fifty and his wife was nowhere near it. He pushed them back, irritably.

'Come off it. She's never stayed with Nancy. They'd drive each other insane.'

Sarah acknowledged the fact with a dip of her head, and then said with a new firmness, 'Sweetheart, I haven't seen her for years. The way she lives, the odds are that I might not see her for years more. You know what she's like. She'll vanish off with some camel train and then get hooked up with some project or other, and never notice time going by. She's my sister. I think it would be really lovely to have her here for a couple of months.'

'How?' said Leo, dangerously bleak.

'Well, I've often thought – why don't we move your desk and the shop files into the alcove in here?' She pointed at the space beside the chimney breast, currently occupied by a curly Edwardian coat stand on which hung various brightly coloured garments of her own. 'It's got lots of light, we could have a neat little filing cabinet. Nobody's ever up here till bedtime. Bedroom offices really make sense, these days. We could run a phone point up if you wanted to get online. It could come straight up through the floor from the downstairs one, and we could cable-clip it neatly along that skirting.'

Leo understood that she had thought this through, all of it, right down to the cable clips. He hunched his shoulders in his striped cotton nightshirt, pushed his glasses back up his nose again and said, 'Right. I see.' He looked down at his book, and after a moment or two, without apology or concealment, let out a loud and vinous burp. Burping men were one of Sarah's small phobias; she flinched, threw aside her book, and lay down with her back to him.

They never slept on a quarrel, the Penns. Or never had, until that night when no further word passed between them. In the morning, though, while Maggie was entertaining the children with traveller's tales at breakfast, Leo carried the spare-room table and a kitchen chair up to the marital bedroom and made three further trips with files and boxes, devising himself an office. Two velvet jackets and a floppy hat of Sarah's, which had been hanging on the curly coat stand, somehow got thrown without ceremony on the floor, and may have been trodden on as he worked.

✢   ✢   ✢

44

'It's the half-and-half places that are so interesting,' Maggie was saying to Samantha and Jamie, for all the world as if they were adults. 'If you follow the great silk road, you find countries which were part of the USSR, but actually if you look at the people and listen to them you see that they're basically Chinese. It looks like fabulous country. Mountains. I'm hoping to get into the Taklamakan Desert, too.'

'Jamie,' said his mother, 'it's gym day, isn't it? Have you got your kit together?'

The child grimaced, busily carving map shapes in the margarine tub with his knife. 'Uh.'

'Do you ever get scared, travelling round on your own?' Samantha asked her aunt, intently. 'I mean, bandits and rapists and that.'

'Not really,' said Maggie. 'You stay alert, and you cover up in a long cotton skirt in some countries so as not to offend people. If it's really dodgy you generally hook up with someone else for a week or so. But honestly, if you dress unobtrusively you're safer than you'd think. Most men in most countries have some kind of code of respecting women.'

'More than they do at my school,' said Samantha feelingly.

'Jamie, *gym kit!*' said Sarah. 'Come on, I'll help you.'

When they had left the room, Maggie grinned at her niece and said, 'I never had a brother. Let alone two.'

'Brothers suck,' said Sam bitterly. 'Jamie's a spy and a peeping Tom and an arsehole.'

The aunt remained silent, head cocked, dark brows arched in sympathy. She liked this thin, dark, spiky, uncertain girl. It was difficult to connect her, as yet, with the chattering rosy-cheeked Girl Guide she remembered from last time home, but this was part of the fascination of watching her sister's family. 'It's like a film,' she said sometimes, 'with frames missing. You all move forward in sudden jerks.'

After a moment Samantha added, 'He spies on me and Duane.'

'Arsehole behaviour,' agreed Maggie.

There was a silence, during which Samantha pressed her lips together and stared down at the table, as if angry at having offered a cue and not had it taken up. After a moment her aunt, who preferred more directness in her dealings, emitted an imperceptible sigh and gave her what she wanted.

'So, Duane,' she said. 'Is it going well?'

There was another silence, in which Maggie carefully regarded her niece. Samantha, she thought, looked more preoccupied and depressed than a girl in love ought to do. Clearly there was something she wanted to say. She made an effort and summoned an air of sympathetic interrogation, but hearing Sarah and Jamie arguing beyond the door she changed to a grimace of warning.

But even with her mother at the door Samantha finally answered with a little rush, 'Boys don't think about anything 'cept doing it. Do they?'

The question hung on the air; before Maggie could answer it, the door opened and Sarah came in, flushed, followed by Jamie and his sports bag, and Teddy wearing a furry spider backpack, a rubber alien puppet on each fist.

'School!' she said. 'Sam, you coming? Dad says he'll drive you.'

Samantha stood up and shucked on her school blazer over untucked blouse and abbreviated grey skirt.

'See you, anyway,' she said casually.

'Yeah, right,' said Maggie. 'Don't let the bastards grind you down.' She raised a fist in a rather dated Black Power salute.

When the children had gone, Sarah spooned coffee into the machine and said, 'What was that all about? Who's grinding Sam down? I can't get a word out of her about anything these days.'

The answer was a question.

'What's the boyfriend like?'

'Nightmare,' said Sarah briefly, pouring in cold water and clapping the machine shut. 'Thick, sneering, stupid, sexist. One of those bloody irritating white boys who pretend to be black rappers. Insecure. Dodgy family. With an earring. And another ring in his nose, like a pig.'

'How old?'

'Same class as Sam. Fifteen, I suppose. Real yob. Leo goes purple at the sight of him. People go tut-tut when fifteen-year-old girls step out with much older boys, but I'd prefer it. Some civilized chap of twenty would be a lot nicer to her than Duane.'

'Have you spoken to her about it?'

'She'd only dig in her heels if I did. So I try to be cunning, and welcome him to family meals so that she can compare him with normal people. He's come twice now, and both times it has been ap-pall-ing. Leo starts coming on like he's the Duke of Edinburgh, and the little boys just stare. But you're supposed to bring the dodgy boyfriend or girlfriend into the family circle. I read it in a parenting book.'

Sarah jiggled the coffee machine's switch, which was loose. She rattled on, as if, her sister thought, she was trying to convince herself.

'Everyone agrees that you have to hang loose, these days. Remember how Mum used to go on and on about us getting in what she called "trouble"? I couldn't bring myself to lay that stuff on Sam, she'd go ballistic. Anyway, they're totally sussed by the time they're twelve these days. Sex education seems to start at about seven years old at Brackhampton. The boys know more about condoms than I do.'

'Not working, though, is it?' said Maggie. 'The magazine technique, I mean. Sam's still stepping out with the sexist pig with the ring in its nose.'

'Well, I suppose the flaw in the theory is that the only men she can actually compare him with are a bright purple harrumph-ing father and two annoying little brothers,' Sarah conceded. 'I can see that Duane might look mildly attractive as a sort of contrast, when Leo's glowering into his drink and the boys are having a belching competition. He does have a touch of James Dean about him.'

The coffee machine was working now, hissing and bubbling with promise. She clattered mugs, and drew a firm line under the subject with, 'But it's all part of growing up. My theory is you have to stay cool. Not interfere.'

Maggie thought of the troubled look on Samantha's face a few minutes earlier, and wondered.

Chapter Five

———•———

Sarah left for the vet's after breakfast with a bundle of invoices stuffed into Samantha's old schoolbag. When the house was quiet, Maggie washed, dried and stowed the remaining breakfast things with a camper's finicky tidiness. She paused to admire a large Spanish bowl brought back from the Penns' last holiday; it was green, with oranges in it and a single apple which, in her view, clashed. She moved the apple, and nodded in satisfaction.

Then she spent a few moments standing, eyebrows raised, in front of the jumble of family notices and timetables on the kitchen board. Dentists, doctors, scout camp schedules for Jamie, maths coaching for Teddy, an under-14s football programme for the autumn season, kit lists, shopping lists, imperious notes from Samantha, a pair of unused tickets for a long-past amateur production of *Annie*, and a homework diary pinned carelessly to the corner of the board by its back cover, as if picked up from the floor in some rushed attempt at cleaning the kitchen.

There were photographs too, put up with more care, four pins apiece pressed well in to discourage impatient pilfering fingers. The little boys with surfboards, grinning against a Cornish rock face; Leo with an infant Teddy on his shoulders doing look-no-hands, juxtaposed with an older image of Jamie in the same position only with an anxious hand twined in his father's hair. There were two pictures of Samantha: one baby shot, all fluffy hair and toothy smile, and one formal picture of her at the head of a Guide patrol. Maggie paid particular attention to this one. By the date on the photographer's mount, it could not be much more than a year old, but the buxom, beaming fourteen-year-old Samantha looked years younger than the nervy, scowling, skinnily elegant creature now on her way to school. Maggie shook her head slightly, and glanced around the board. No Guide schedules or camps in sight. That would figure. Given it up, but only lately.

She thought back to the long, uneasy boredom of her own adolescence, lit by sporadic and troublesome escapes, and conceived a very good idea of the form Samantha's escape was taking. 'Blind alley,' she said aloud. 'Hiding to nothing.'

She left the board, poured the dregs of the coffee into her mug and took it upstairs. The house felt strange around her: solid, unchanging, British. It was a kind of carapace, she thought; a bricky garment smelling faintly of shoes and damp and soap powder and warm towels, a whitewashed costume which her sister and brother-in-law wore like a crinoline, with their children tucked under its skirts. To be alone inside it felt unnervingly intimate. She stood for a moment or two at her bedroom window, absently picking flakes of old paint off the sill and watching a cat negotiating the flat roof and parapets of the house over the street. It was a stout tabby, well beyond its first youth, yet its sleek tiger grace mocked the fussy Victorian skyline. It slipped onto the slope of the roof and ran up to perch on the apex of a dormer window, silhouetted against nothingness. Pushing back her loose dark hair, Maggie looked through and above the chimneys at the flat plastic greyness of the English sky.

Then she turned to the bed and began to unpack her rucksack with deliberation, sorting the clothes into categories – T-shirts, jeans and shorts, fleece and sweater, two rolled-up long cotton skirts, carefully paired socks, one bra, and a rabble of tangled knickers. Personal decoration was represented by two large, very beautiful silk squares, one red and gold, the other green and silver. In the attic at Nancy's house there would still be a trunk containing the rest of her meagre wardrobe, and a wicker hamper into which she was prone to throw any souvenirs which had, in a brief acquisitive mood, retained her fancy for long enough to prevent her giving them away. The hamper also contained a dozen fat, closely written notebooks of various sizes, detailing her travels since the first Australian adventure.

'You should write a book,' Sarah had urged her. 'Loads of people who do much feebler journeys write travel books.'

'I might,' said Maggie. 'Only the book wouldn't ever be as good as the life, would it? So you'd always be annoyed at it. I'm not a poet.'

'You don't have to be a poet,' began Sarah, but her sister cut her off.

'Yes you do. Yes, you would. If you really wanted to do it right, a poem or a song would be best. I know the kind of travel book you mean, and I can't be bothered. Lists of places, and grumbles about boots, and undigested chunks of history to show they did research, and badly remembered conversations with locals to show that they're real people. Oh, and all that shit about their *feelings*. Nope. Can't be bothered even trying.'

Now Maggie turned over in her hands the cotton-covered notebook she had kept aboard the *Evangelina*. She supposed that it would end up in the hamper with the rest, never to be read. The thought filled her with a reluctance she had never felt before. The ship had stirred something new in her. Although she had often cooked and cleaned aboard charter yachts, and once served for three months as a stewardess on a Caribbean cruise liner, something about the old brig and the long, slow Atlantic crossing tugged at her heart in a new and troubling way. It was a ship, she thought, which demanded that you belong. It had been harder to leave *Evangelina* than any job, any country, any journey she could remember.

'You do not have to go, Maggi,' Captain Lopez had said, his

brown eyes sorrowful. They were together in a harbour-front bar in the confused days before their farewell. 'You can sail on with us. Chief cook, real pay. We go to Cadiz and the Canarias.'

But of course she had said no. She had gone, because going was what she did best. The day after that last drink she was off aboard the cheese lorry in the dawn, craning back to see the tracery of tall masts and rigging against the sky. *Evangelina* became no more than a postcard of a ship, a hackneyed image from a tea towel. The thick familiar ropes which had calloused her hands were reduced to spiders' webs, then vanished. *Adios.*

When she had organized her few possessions to her satisfaction, Maggie Reave locked up her sister's house and set off, with long loping strides, towards her mother's. It was never her favourite part of a homecoming, but it had to be done. She left the notebook, though, tucked carefully into the front pocket of her pack. It was not yet time to relegate it to the hamper of history.

'My aunt,' said Teddy impressively to his cronies at break, 'has come home from the Americas.'

'Whatchoo mean, Americas?' said Colin Byfleet derisively. ' 'S only one America, right?'

'Wouldn't be room for two,' said Adrian, who regarded himself as something of a wag. 'It'd fill up half the ocean.'

'That's stupid,' said Joanne from behind Adrian's ear. She was a stout, confident child who had not yet learned that in secondary school a girl did well to retreat to the company of her own gender; at least for a couple of years, while everyone sorted out the troubling mystery of their identity. Joanne was stolid and clever and had known Colin and Teddy since playgroup. She did not see why they should be so sniffy with her now. She elaborated on her point.

'There's North America and there's South America. And

Central America, like Mexico. So Ted's right, OK? You *can* say the Americas.'

Teddy, with breathtaking ingratitude, switched sides to line up with the boys. 'Yeah,' he said. 'But nobody ever does, really. Just people like my aunt. She doesn't live in England much. She brought us sugar skulls from Mexico.'

'Eugh! Gross!' The boys moved away together in a tight little flock, pointedly excluding the furious Joanne. 'Did she bring you anything else?'

'No,' said Teddy. 'She's only got a rucksack. She goes all round the world with just that, in canoes, and on a bike, and hitching, and dangerous Russian planes and stuff.'

Little Joanne hovered, agonized. She was torn between a wish to walk away from these scornful boys to prove she didn't care, and an urgent need to know more about this captivating new model of adult female life. Sugar skulls! Canoes! Russian planes! Just a rucksack! She was not a pretty child, nor domestically useful enough to be very highly regarded within her own large family. Already at eleven she felt a pressing need to explore more options in life than had so far been presented to her.

She blurted out, 'Does she have a job? Is she, like, a journalist? 'Cos Kate Adie—'

'What's her job?' asked Adrian, as if the girl had not spoken.

'Doesn't have one,' said Teddy uncertainly. 'But she does all sorts of jobs for a bit, then stops and goes somewhere else. She was a cook on a sailing ship.'

As he said it, the enormity of his aunt's way of life abruptly struck him in turn, and he fell silent. He remembered Jamie in the car that morning, pushing it as usual a bit too far with their father, saying that he didn't see why he had to do all those stupid GCSEs when he was going to go round the world later and learn stuff that way, like Auntie Maggie.

Leo had snapped, 'Your aunt happens to have a degree. Even if she is a professional homeless bum on a permanent gap year.'

Then he had thrown a glance back at his sons, almost a half-scared look.

And Jamie had read the glance with insolent accuracy, and said, 'Presumably you'd rather we didn't tell Mum you said that.'

Leo avoided confrontations; he stayed silent and pinched for the rest of the school run, offering only a brief. 'Have a good day' as they tumbled out at the gate. But now, remembering that line about a professional homeless bum, Teddy marvelled: his aunt, his mother's sister, had no house or job or habits or permanent neighbourhood. Just a rucksack. Yet she seemed perfectly content and cheerful; indeed, rather more so than most of the grown-ups around him who led proper grown-up lives. It was intriguing. Unsettling.

Colin Byfleet broke into his thoughts with a new question. 'So she's like, on holiday all the time? Just going to new places?'

'And doing jobs,' said Teddy primly. 'Like being a cook.'

'On a *ship!*' said Colin. 'Like, with sails?'

'Yep,' said the proud nephew. 'She went up the mast a lot.'

'I'm going on the Tall Ships Race when I'm fifteen, like my cousin did,' announced Colin. 'We saw them at Southampton.'

'I'm prob'ly going when I'm *fourteen,*' said Teddy.

'Can't. S'not allowed.'

'Might be for me. My aunt could fix it.'

'Dickhead.'

The boys began to scuffle. Eventually a football, strayed from a game across the playground, bounced between them and set them running and kicking until the bell went. Joanne watched, eyes narrowed in her chubby face, then walked alone towards the school doors. If Miss March didn't see her, she could sneak into the library and spend the rest of break looking at Mexico and stuff, in the atlas.

Samantha was, thought her geography teacher, unusually quiet even for her. It was a big class, and not all of the pupils even in her GCSE set were truly individuals to Mrs Ellerman; but she had taught Samantha Penn for two years at primary school, and this earlier acquaintance gave her a fair sense of the girl's hinterland. As she looked down consideringly at the dark, bowed head in the third row, without effort Sue Ellerman could call up the images of Samantha's parents: bright chatty Sarah and thin, quiet, studious Leo, whose bookshop everybody knew. Although, of course, the school library did not use it, preferring to negotiate large discounts with the cut-price chains.

Mrs Ellerman had thought Samantha to be a scholar like her father. Until this term the child had been consistent, careful, and apparently interested. The staffroom saw her as one of the brighter hopes for the exam season. She was no trouble, gave no cheek, and had a real flair for some of her subjects, notably history. Yet two weeks ago Mrs Ellerman had found herself remarking tentatively to the head of Year 11, 'Sam Penn's very quiet. I think there might be something going on there.'

Nobody else had picked it up, but now the teacher's unease sharpened into real concern. From the dark head, with its corkscrew trails of hair escaping the regulation ponytail, a single tear could be seen to fall on the photocopied map which she had just told the class to study. She frowned, uncertain what to do. While she stood thinking about it, twiddling her board marker between her fingers, her eye travelled automatically to the back of the classroom where the bad boys sat. There they were, the awful triumvirate of Andy, Duane and Paulie, hulking in a sullen row with their lesser jackal Tyrone looking hopefully sideways for cues. As she watched, Andy nudged Duane in the ribs, jerking his head forward. Duane's thick mouth formed into an unappealing sneer, and with the elbow and arm which rested on his desk he achieved an almost imperceptible but unmistakably obscene gesture. The other boys sniggered.

When Mrs Ellerman followed the gesture's direction, she found without much surprise that it was aimed at Samantha Penn's back.

Chapter Six

———•———

'I went to the internet cafe,' said Maggie at suppertime. 'On the way back from Mum's.'

'How was Mum?' asked Sarah, clattering plates. 'I haven't seen her for weeks, I'm ashamed to say.'

'Fine. The same. Older. Fussy. Officially glad to greet roving child, but telly nonetheless kept permanently on,' said Maggie. 'Anyway, I went to that internet cafe that's opened, and did a surf. Guess where they're doing external courses in Mandarin?'

'Pass.' Sarah dug her big spoon into the cauliflower cheese, and began ladling it onto the six plates.

'Southwick Community College! They got a grant for it, from the Ethnic Diversity Board or something.'

Sarah flipped some crisped bacon onto the first pair of plates, but said nothing. The boys listened, interested. Samantha was still up in her room, despite having been called three times.

'You'll have missed part of the first term,' said Leo, accepting his supper. 'You'd have trouble catching up.'

'Only missed two weeks,' said Maggie. 'Anyway, I clicked for availability. There are still places. It's a one-year course but the summer term is mostly placements in China, which I don't need. Three places left. So I clicked again. And I rang. And I'm booked in. It's amazingly cheap.'

'All *year?*' said Teddy, dismayed. 'You're going to go to college for a whole year like normal people?'

'Aren't you going back to the ship?' said Jamie accusingly.

'Where are you going to live?' said Leo, hardly less accusingly. But before he could finish the sentence Sarah had cut in smoothly.

'You'll stay with us for the winter, then? That'll be lovely!'

She had finished filling the plates now and, avoiding her husband's eye with practised ease, made a great show of looking around for her daughter. She began a maternal shout towards the stairwell, '*Saaam!*' but stopped when she heard the front door slamming. Quick on her feet, she was out of the back and down the side of the house in time to catch Samantha on the path.

'And where do you think you're going?'

'Out,' said the girl economically. She made as if to push past Sarah.

'It's suppertime!' her mother remonstrated.

'Not hungry. Feel sick. School dinner poisoning probably. It's, like, full of listeria, that cottage cheese on the salad bar.'

'Where are you going?' demanded Sarah.

'Nadine's. We're working on a project, all right?'

'Where's your bag then? Your folders?'

'She's got the stuff. Get outta my face. I'll be *late.*'

Sarah returned to the house, her step heavy. Maggie was entertaining the boys with stories about poisonous tropical fish. Under the hubbub, Leo said to his wife in a low, angry voice, 'I wish you wouldn't let her just roam around on her own. She's only just fifteen, you treat her as if she was a university student.'

'She's got to have her freedom. I remember what it was like at that age, and how we hated Mum fussing. We have to keep lines of communication open, and you don't do that by confrontation.'

Recognizing again the voice of the self-help family book, Leo gave an angry, hissing sigh. 'And it's rude, anyway,' he persisted, 'while we're all eating. And I bet she's gone to meet that boy—'

'She's gone to Nadine's.'

'Huh!'

In the diversion of the low, tense argument, the issue of Maggie's staying all winter was forgotten; or rather, went by default. By the end of supper it seemed generally accepted that the guest room was, for the duration of her studies, 'Auntie Maggie's room'. It was only when Sarah had gone upstairs to help Jamie with his maths that Maggie turned to her brother-in-law and said without preamble, 'Leo, I won't stay if I'm in the way. Sarah's very insistent, and very sweet, but it's a bit steep to expect you to put up with a lodger.'

'You hardly count as a lodger,' said Leo politely, but without warmth.

'Yes, I do. What's the proverb? Guests and fish stink on the third day. If I do stay, I am going to pay board and lodging. I'll be getting a part-time job, obviously. And I'll be away in June at the latest.'

'As you wish,' said Leo. 'But Sarah's delighted. We all are.'

His welcome rang hollowly on the air.

Samantha dug her hands deep in the pockets of her jacket and hunched her thin shoulders against the cutting autumn wind. It was a wild night, and growing dark; along the High Street, windows rattled. Litter bowled down the road, pattering like an unclean snowfall against the lit, dead shop windows. A knot of boys lounged outside the Wimpy Bar, among them a silhouette she knew very well. She walked towards them, tentative but defiant, the thin glow of the streetlights making her face even paler.

Andy Moss greeted her first, with a raised fist and a yell of, 'Hey! Duane — it's your ho'!'

The others joined in.

'Gi's a blow job, darlin'!'

'Hot bitch!'

She ignored them and spoke directly to her lover.

'Duane, come on. I want to talk to you about something.' Her voice had tightened with tension, and slid treacherously up the social scale from the normal slouchy, classless patois of the school day. The three boys mimicked her with glee, while Duane stayed silent.

'*Ay wawnt to talk to yew abeyout some-theeng*,' they jeered. 'Oh, oh, oh. Orf to Benenden in the maw-ning, are we?'

'Duane,' said Samantha, squeaky and breathy now. '*Pleeeease.* Just let's go for a walk.'

The boys erupted in obscene babble.

'She wants you, man!'

'Hey, hot bitch!'

'Man, do we get a share? She've got plenty for everyone!'

Samantha instinctively backed away from them, glancing through the lighted window of the burger house to make sure of the safety of witnesses.

'Come on!' she said again, with diminishing hope. Duane looked uneasy, and glanced at his companions. Then one of them played into Samantha's hands by taunting the boy.

'You shagged out already, man? No stamina. You wanna come to the gym with me 'n'Andy.'

'Fuck off!' said Duane, but moved towards Samantha and roughly took her hand, half dragging her off along the road away from his friends. When they were out of sight, however, he dropped her hand and said ungraciously, 'You wannna make me look stupid, or what?'

'I wanted to talk to you,' said Samantha. Her voice was shaking now, a vein jumping in her thin neck. 'You used to talk to me. I don't know what's wrong with you. It's two weeks now you've been avoiding me. Why've you gone horrible? What've I done wrong, anyway?'

He looked her up and down, and lust stirred mindless within him. He took her arm, not gently.

'Le's go to the railway hut, then.'

'No, it's cold,' said Samantha. She pulled her arm away; it felt bruised. 'I didn't mean that. Let's get a coffee. Not at the Wimpy. The Costa's still open. I want to talk to you.'

'Oh, fuckit!' said the boy angrily. 'Teaser! You winding me up? Serve you right if I call the boys over. Give them all a go.'

'That's a horrible thing to say,' said Samantha, fighting back tears. 'Just because I, just because we—'

'Slag!' said Duane. 'Posh fucking slag!' With a lightning twist and stab he slammed an open hand between her legs, as if to force his fingers inside her. She wrenched his arm aside and threw a kick at him; it landed harmlessly on the ankle of his boot, but almost unbalanced her. With a sob she turned and fled.

'And where have you been, young lady?' asked her mother angrily when the child arrived, trembling, inside her own front door. 'I rang Nadine, and you certainly weren't there.'

'Decided to go for a walk,' said Samantha with all the surly confidence she could muster. 'Do the project tomorrow. It's only half past nine.' Sarah's face made her momentarily hesitate, but the sound of Leo's laughter from the sitting room hardened the girl again. She wasn't fooled by all that tolerant stuff. They both thought she'd been stupid to go near Duane. Not middle-class enough. And now he and his friends mocked her as well, so now everyone on both sides thought she was stupid. Well, fuck it. Samantha summoned all her hauteur. 'I got homework. G'night.'

When Maggie went upstairs to fetch something from her bag, she heard sobbing from the room next door to hers. Without a moment's hesitation she walked in on her niece without knocking.

'Hello,' she said. 'You hungry? Did you get a burger or something?'

Samantha was face down on the narrow bed. Her aunt sat down by her feet, and regarded them gravely.

'Throw me out if you like,' she said conversationally, 'but are you sure that this Duane bloke is worth all the trouble?'

There was a snort, then a just audible, 'No. He's an arsehole.

I thought he was really nice, different, but nice. But he's just as horrible as all his mates.'

'So dump him.'

Samantha twisted over and sat up, propped on stiff arms. She sniffed. 'Yeah, but I already . . .'

'You already had sex,' said Maggie, unruffled. 'I guessed.'

'Do you think Mum . . .' The girl was horrified now.

'Nope. Hasn't a clue. It takes a bad girl like me to spot something like that. Promise.'

Samantha looked carefully at her aunt, and decided after a moment to trust her. She rolled onto one elbow, dragged a tissue from the box on her untidy bedside table, and blew her nose. As she did it, Maggie thought with a pang of unfamiliar tenderness, Sam suddenly seemed to drop the burden of her years and look again like the child she remembered.

'So what's the main problem?' she prompted.

Samantha stared at her in amazement. 'Well, like, how can I dump him?'

'Oh, come on!' said Maggie, derisive and, her niece felt, comfortingly bracing. 'It wasn't that good, surely?'

'It was *horrible*.' There was savage relief in her tone, as if it was the first time she had admitted it even to herself. 'He said it would get better, but *six times*, and it didn't at all. Then he tells all his mates, and they tell the girls, and half the school starts giggling about me, and my friends give me funny looks, like they're thinking "gross". And then tonight he says, he says . . .'

She stopped, close to tears, and Maggie saw how thin and drawn her face had become. She laid a hand on the girl's ankle and said without emphasis, 'There's nothing special about being a virgin, you know. One minute you are, one minute you aren't, so what? You're still you. It's just an incident. Good if it's a good incident, but if it isn't, you move on. Think of it as a seriously bad kebab.'

Samantha sniffed, childish again. Then morosely she said,

'It's not going to be easy at school, though. I wish I didn't have to go back now.'

'Well, you do,' said Maggie. 'But you can always leave and go to Southwick College for A levels, can't you? I'll suss it out for you while I'm learning my Chinese. It's a big world, Sammy. It's all out there waiting for you. Stuff Duane.'

'He'll tell people I'm no good at it,' said the child mournfully.

'So? Tell them he's even worse. Blokes are more scared of that than girls, trust me.'

'His mates call me a whore and a slag and stuff.'

'So call them dickheads! Sticks and stones may break my bones, but names will never hurt me.'

'Oh, Maggie!' said Samantha, who had decided she was too old to give her the honorific title of Auntie. 'I'm glad you're here. I couldn't talk to Mum about it. I'd die.'

'You should,' murmured Maggie dutifully. 'She'd be broad-minded, you know.'

'But I can't,' said Samantha firmly. 'Apart from everything else, she'd tell Dad. Oh shit, what a thought. Then I *would* die. Ssh, shit again, that's her coming down from Jamie's room.'

By the time Sarah poked her head round the door for a conciliatory word with her daughter, Maggie was nowhere in sight. She had swung her long legs out of the window and eased herself down the cast-iron Victorian drainpipe onto the convenient lid of the wheelie bin. As she jumped off it, Leo glanced up from loading the dishwasher, puzzled at the slight sound; he saw nothing in the dark square of the window. Maggie hesitated by the back door, then decided to take a walk around the windy empty town.

As she passed the Wimpy Bar she looked speculatively at a knot of scruffy, big-booted louts, barely more than children, who hunched around emitting occasional shouts of 'Oy oy!' and 'Wooor!' She shook her head and smiled, but then the smile faded. A small memory was nagging at her.

While she was in the bedroom with Samantha she had been

driven wholly by an instinct to minimize what had happened, and help the girl to find the proper pride to shrug it off. Being Nancy Reave's daughter, she had a wholesome hatred of the notion that a girl could be 'ruined' by one mistake.

But now the small, sniffing voice came back to her. '*He said it would get better, but six times . . .*' Maggie found herself hoping, very much, that the ring-nosed sexist pig had taken every precaution in the book. She was fairly certain that her niece would not have. Looked too skinny to be on the pill, for one thing.

'Hell,' she said aloud into the dimmed window of Woolworth's. 'I really am turning into my mother now, aren't I?'

Chapter Seven

Autumn wore on, under damp leaden skies. Maggie lived with the Penns but in a parallel world. Her energies flowed from a different source to theirs; her interests were volatile and passionate. Sometimes Sarah thought that it was like having an older teenager in the house, and had to remind herself that there were barely five years between them.

Maggie seemed to feel none of the plodding weariness that the adult Penns accepted as a normal state. Nothing about her suggested that she was anywhere near mid-life; she did not share the rather cosy, manageable tiredness which both Sarah and Leo now realized was the defining quality of their lives. They sank into their routines as into a feather bed, watched the news together, desultorily discussed their day, read a chapter of their books at bedtime and turned the light out early. Maggie, on the other hand, could barely watch television for five minutes without growing bored. When she started a book she became engrossed, and read for most of the night; or else threw it aside and plunged into a game of table football or Snap with the boys.

Her day was her own creation. She rose at dark, incredible hours of the morning to go loping through the town and round the park, not in the careful sports kit of other Brackhampton joggers but in thin shorts and a torn old T-shirt, her hair wound up carelessly with a child's hairband donated by Samantha. Back home for breakfast she ate a couple of pieces of toast, teased the children, and then changed rapidly into jeans and a sweatshirt to catch the bus to Southwick. By mid-afternoon she was back in town for a three-hour shift chopping vegetables and laying tables at the Blue Lady Restaurant, then she brought her books home and sprawled on her bed, making notes and practising her Chinese intonations with strange chiming cries which, inevitably, drew Teddy to sit on the end of her bed copying her.

In the evenings she either worked relief bar shifts at the Black Lion or went out in search of music. Almost any music would do; she slipped into the back of school concerts, made friends with a teenage rock band who practised in the back room of the Black Lion at weekends, and even persuaded Leo – once – to join her and Sarah at a folk pub in Southwick. Maggie herself led a set with great confidence on tin whistle and mouth organ, neither of which her sister had even known she could play. 'Well, I can't really,' she said modestly. 'One bluffs.'

On Saturdays she went back to the Blue Lady in a demure black dress and apron provided by its proprietress, and a pair of black shoes borrowed from Sarah, to serve lunches. It seemed incredible to Sarah and Leo that the pay she got for twenty hours at the cafe and a few at the pub somehow stretched to cover her bus fares, lunches, occasional cinemas and the fifty pounds a week which she insisted on paying for her keep. 'Look, you're cheaper than a hostel and you feed me. Take it, take it!' But then, they had to admit that Maggie's only luxury was melons, which she bought at the market – 'Can't live without them. Too long in the tropics. God knows what I'll do in the Taklamakan Desert.' Her clothes never cost more than fifty pence at the charity shop, and in any case Sarah had given her two pairs of jeans and some white shirts which no longer fitted her plumper frame, and probably never would again.

'I'm really fine,' said Maggie one Saturday night when Sarah as usual disputed the need for the fifty pounds. 'This minimum wage they've brought in is brilliant. It's years since I earned so much hard currency. I'm actually saving. If I need more, the Blue Lady's hinting about doing Saturday nights. Double money, see?'

'But you ought to have real savings. Pension fund, that sort of thing,' protested Sarah. 'At least let me invest your rent money for you. In an ISA or something.'

'If you do, I shall go and live with Mum,' said Maggie threateningly. 'And if I do that there will be bloodshed, sooner rather than later. Look, Sare,' she shook her shaggy hair, and pushed it back, 'Leo doesn't much like me being here. Face it, he doesn't. The least I can do is pay for my food.'

'He *loves* you being here. We all do,' said Sarah stoutly. 'And so does Mum. She was saying just last week how nice it was us all being together for Sunday lunch.'

'Leo – well, never mind,' said Maggie. 'Anyway, you keep the damn money.'

'All right,' said Sarah, folding it into her purse. 'I'll put it in the account with the child benefit. It's their university fund. OK?'

'Fine.'

Samantha, after the first burst of confidence, withdrew slightly from Maggie, who in turn decided not to intrude by asking for bulletins on the Duane situation. The boys just artlessly revelled in their aunt. She read their bedside books voraciously, discussing Harry Potter plots with as much impassioned argument as they did. She listened to their music, head on one side, frowning, and told them about other music she had heard, from the breathy pipes of Peru to the strange vibrations of the outback. She taught Jamie to play the harmonica. She passed on what she learned day by day from the patient Professor Chang at Southwick College. As her learning intensified, whole musical Chinese sentences floated from her room each morning as she changed, and lulled the household to sleep last thing at night as she yawned into the outsized T-shirt which served her as a nightdress.

The boys were enthralled, and copied her with care. At

school, Teddy developed quite a following for his tales of the
eccentric house guest. 'My aunt says,' he informed a knot of
respectful Year 7 listeners in the playground, 'that if you want to
speak Chinese right, you have to watch Chinese people, what
they do with their faces when they say words. You have to stand
like a Chinese, and put your neck like a Chinese, because it's like
singing. You have to get the note right. *Aha-ching-wa!*

'You look more like sunnink in *Star Trek*,' said Adrian
witheringly. 'An' I bet that's not a proper word anyway. So
who's she going to talk Chinese to, then?'

'She's going there in the summer. To the *borders*,' said Teddy
with an insouciant air. 'The mountains. I will probably go with
her, as a porter on her expotition.'

'You won't,' said Joanne, who was still hanging around the
boys, despite their wounding lack of interest. She had little
choice at playtime; she had lately become a shade unpopular
among the girls for expressing her new-found contempt for
domesticity, designer clothes and possessions in general. Pretty
Anthea Harding had even ventured the view that Joanne was a
dyke for spending her savings on a rucksack. But the child stood
four square on her admiration for the Penns' mysterious Aunt
Maggie. With all her heart she wished to know this marvellous
woman. Now she said:

'She won't take a stoopid little boy along. She's a free spirit. I
heard your mum say that to Miss March.'

Free spirit! Joanne had hugged the expression to her ever
since she first heard it. It warmed her. You did not have to do
what all the other girls wanted to do! You did not have to like
Steps or even the Spice Girls! You did not have to have a
boyfriend. Or a baby. You could go round the world on
adventures instead. Even if you were a girl.

Teddy rose to the barb, as she had intended, and turned to
glare at the square, dark, stubborn child.

'She *is* taking me, so. That's why I have to learn Chinese too.
Ahha! Ching chaa cheng!

'That is *so* not real Chinese,' said Joanne. 'Will you tell us again the story about the snake in the wall?'

Teddy could not resist this, and nor could the others.

Nor, indeed, could Jamie, who at that very moment was telling it at the other end of the playground to his gruffer-voiced peers.

'She was at this place once, right, in Australia, called Cape Tribulation or something – anyway she was working in a hostel where the backpackers go. And there was this awful smell for days and days, and nobody could find out what it was. Then someone had a fight, 'cos they do that in Australia, and the guy kicked the wall, and the wood had gone all soft and rotten so it got a hole in it, right?'

Entranced, Jamie's audience nodded. He, too, had told the story more than once, and they were accustomed to the dramatic pause at this stage. They would have thought the less of his storytelling if he had not put it in.

'So anyway, out of this hole the smell got really, really worse. Like the worst rotting thing you ever smelt. And something began to slide out.'

Another dramatic pause, even longer this time.

'It was a dead snake. A huge dead rotting boa constrictor, twelve feet long from its rotting head to its putrefying tail. Gone in there to die.' He was quoting now. 'And it lay there and nobody would touch it, even with a shovel, except this one big guy called Spewt. And he picked it up in his bare hands and said they were all a load of wusses, and he'd known whores smell worse' an that and still do good business.'

The listeners relieved the tension of the story with guffaws of indecorous laughter. Jamie smiled with due modesty.

One of the bigger boys said gruffly, 'Wanna smoke?'

'Yeah, all right then,' said Jamie, and with a glance around accepted the proffered cigarette and dexterously slipped it into his shirt pocket beneath the grey uniform sweater. His standing, like Teddy's, had risen greatly since Maggie's arrival in the house.

Of the three children, the only one who did not talk much about the exotic aunt was Samantha. But then, she did not talk to anybody very much in that autumn term.

Down at the bookshop, meanwhile, Leo was being confronted by Miss Mountjoy. She was sixty-nine now, and after eleven years he supposed that he should have been expecting her retirement. All the same, it came as a shock. During the first few turbulent months in his employ she had spiritedly handed in her notice several times over the obscene, violent or blasphemous content of modern novels on the shelves, not to mention the novelty titles involving talking penises. After a while, however, she had reached a personal accommodation with the spirit of the age. Instead of refusing any contact with the more distressing works, she resolved to intercede with heaven for their authors.

'I am *praying* for Will Self,' she would say serenely. 'I made a special intention for him this morning at Communion. Such a sad person he must be, to imagine such dreadful things as he does. I have also prayed for Mr Jeffrey Archer since his tribulation.' It was not always tied down to one individual writer: she made a whole novena once, before the statue of the Virgin in her favoured High Anglican church, for the intention of immodest young female novelists 'who all seem so unhappy with this shag life they talk about, poor dears'.

Leo soon found that provided he listened with apparent respect to her bulletins on the relationship between prayer and modern literature, she would work on, contentedly and efficiently, for the very modest salary the bookshop was able to pay her. She had been doing accounts all her life, and once she was asked to do so she made an impressive transition from neat crabbed handwriting to the computer ('I have prayed about these unmapped memory exemptions, and I think I have found Guidance'). She was capable of surprising firmness, even asperity, with the credit controllers of publishing houses when they rang up trying to chase their money days before it was due. 'I don't think Mr Penn has ever defaulted, and nor would he. We are rather busy here. Good morning.'

Miss Mountjoy had become an affectionate, reliable standing joke among Leo's friends and family. She had been, he sometimes thought privately, a kind of surrogate mother to him. Or, at least, a surrogate maiden aunt. Her brisk, unbending, kindly presence had steadied him through bad Christmases, the collapse of the Net Book Agreement, through panic shortages of hot titles and disastrous misjudgements which left his shelves full of dross. Miss Mountjoy had been at his side through all the times when he felt that nobody in his family really cared about the dreadful precariousness of his chosen trade.

And now here she was, resigning. He stared at her angular honest old face in dismay.

'I have not decided this lightly, Mr Penn,' she said, still formal after all these years. 'It is time that I retired into private life. My friend Louise is not well, and needs more daily help than the council will give her. I no longer need a salary. My duty is plain.'

'Oh dear,' said Leo. 'You're part of the shop now. I hardly know how I shall cope.'

'Would you like me to investigate a successor?' asked Miss Mountjoy. 'Nobody comes immediately to mind, but clearly you need somebody local, with an ability both for paperwork and for meeting the public. I shall pray about it also.'

'That would be kind,' said Leo. 'But when must you go?'

'On the eighth of December, which is a Saturday. Louise will be out of the nursing home that afternoon. I shall work Saturday morning as usual. This gives you over a month, although I am, as you know, weekly paid. I hope that is satisfactory?'

So with less than a month to Christmas, Leo's permanent staff of one would leave him. Hot books would be flowing in, re-orders would become critical for the season's important titles, customers would be rushed and impatient, sales either rocketing – if he had the right stock – or plunging to nothing as the bookbuyers flounced off to snap up seasonal discounts at the chain newsagents. He swallowed. But it was, he knew quite well, useless to argue with her.

'Well, thank you for the generous period of notice. I know it hasn't been as highly paid a post as your talents deserve, but—'

'Heavens, Mr Penn,' said Miss Mountjoy. 'It has been a privilege to plough this furrow with you.' She smiled graciously, and returned to check a delivery of pictorial biographies of the Queen Mother. Leo watched her with real affection, glad that on this momentous day she had a box to open which could give her only pleasure.

That night, he told Sarah. Maggie had taken Samantha to the cinema, and the boys were at friends' houses; unusually, the couple were alone together, and to celebrate the quiet they opened a bottle of wine. Leo drank three-quarters of it, and said for the fifth time, 'I don't know what to do really. I can't believe I'll get anybody for what I've paid her. Not anybody I can leave in sole charge. And the shop won't stand much of a hike in the payroll. The Saturday kids are all right, but not on their own.' He poured the dregs of the bottle into his glass, shaking out the last drops with more agitation than finesse. 'God, what a nightmare. With Christmas coming.' He looked across the glass at Sarah, suddenly foxy.

'I don't suppose you . . . ?'

'No,' said his wife firmly. The question had occasionally arisen of her giving up the job with the vet Sam Miller and working in the bookshop, making it a true family business. Leo favoured the idea very strongly, more and more as the years went by. He had been ready to dispense with Miss Mountjoy in the event of his wife's saying yes.

'Apart from the financial advantage,' he would say plaintively, 'I'd like the company.'

Sarah always refused. She had a deep, warning sense that if she agreed she would compromise her freedom more gravely than either of them understood. She had no particular understanding of the book trade, and in the shop Leo would always be the boss. Her wage would be compounded with his. They would spend all day together, every day. The business would inevitably come home and be discussed between them over the family table. There would be no place of refuge. There would be no acid-tongued elderly vet to talk to when she needed to let off steam. She tried to explain these things to him, but her refusal remained a bleak grey area between them.

'I just thought,' said Leo now, 'with Miss Mountjoy going, it gives us a chance to rationalize things.'

'Leo, it wouldn't be rational. It would be awful. I would be bad at it, and spill things on books or get things wrong, and you would get annoyed with me, and then how do you sack your own wife?'

Samantha had recently said much the same when he asked her to be a Saturday assistant. 'How would you sack me, if I was pants at it?' She was, to his annoyance, thinking of applying to Boots the Chemist for weekend work instead.

Leo sighed. He felt a great deal of bitterness over this. The bookshop paid the family's way, for God's sake, yet none of them seemed to care about it. He had nursed it through good times and bad, and extracted a useful extra income from his rare booklist, using only part-timers like the General and the Admiral. Yet his achievements seemed to mean nothing to his family. As far as they were concerned he just 'went to work' each day, as if he were some pensionable cog in a corporate machine.

All he said, though, was, 'All right. I get the message. I'll look around.'

'God,' said Sarah, looking out of the window into the night. 'It's raining again. That's four days now it's hardly stopped.'

Chapter Eight

Maggie's morning runs always took her up to the top of the town, along a bare track round the park, then down to the slow-moving River Brack and over the bridge to rejoin the High Street. So for five minutes or so in each dim morning she ran alongside the Brack, under the dull sodium glow of the park's few lights.

She had always loved rivers, although this one, in its concrete gutter, was unattractive. In the first days of a rainy October she noted with pleased interest that it was taking on a livelier aspect than usual: rising higher, moving faster, curling and swirling brown in the dull wet dawns. Now that it was nearer to its cement brim the high winds even whipped up some tiny wavelets. She thought of the wake of the *Evangelina*, of the slope of the deck and the rip of the sea winds; at such moments she was raked by a small, treacherous pang of loss.

Maggie's life had made her into an observant stranger in all lands, including her own. Besides, she had once been a geographer. After a few mornings of running beside the newly extrovert river, old instincts stirred in her. She began to take a different route, staying longer beside the water to survey its relationship with the town, hopping on parapets and squinting along sight lines before finally doubling up the High Street as usual and heading to her temporary home for breakfast. One morning, fielding the toast which always sprang too energetically from the machine, she said to her sister and brother-in-law, 'Do you have an Ordnance Survey map with the town on it? With contour lines?'

'Somewhere,' said Sarah vaguely. 'Sammy, weren't you doing a project last year?'

Samantha looked up from the plate on which she was crumbling toast.

'Dunno,' she said.

'Of course you know, young lady. Answer your mother's quite reasonable question,' said Leo, who was riffling through the coat pegs in the kitchen lobby in search of something more waterproof than his usual tweed. 'And you should be on the way to school by now. Coat, coat, coat . . . oh, I am sick of this rain.'

'That's why I want the map, really,' said Maggie. 'I want to look at the flood profile.'

'Major Harding and Miss Mountjoy both say there hasn't been a flood in Brackhampton since the war,' said Leo. 'It's not like the Medway towns. They built up the town embankment pretty well, according to the locals.'

'Mmm,' said his sister-in-law, taking her plate to the sink. 'But suppose it broke through farther upstream than the town. In the park, where there's just that sort of concrete v-section, and then grass. That's why I wanted to look at the map. I reckon Abelard Street is a kind of gully. A natural conduit.'

Leo frowned. He had come back into the kitchen wearing a green anorak of Jamie's. Incongruous beneath his thinning hair and spare, lined features it said YOUTH VOLUNTEERS on the left sleeve.

'What do you mean, if it broke through in the park? Near the oaks?'

'Yup.'

'It'd soak into the grass, surely.'

'Only the first inch or so. It's clay soil, I tested it.'

Sarah, quietly wiping the worktop, ignored the subject matter but registered pleasure in the fact that Leo and Maggie were having a co-operative conversation, neither spiky nor unnaturally polite. This was a novelty. Although the slight chill of their relationship was usually camouflaged by the noisy flow of family life, there had been some uneasy moments in the past month. Once or twice she had thought the pair seemed almost overtly hostile. She was not sure that Leo had forgiven Maggie for causing the loss of his spare-room office. At a further goad from her father about the map, Samantha heaved herself up from the table and said ungraciously, 'Prob'ly in the geo file from last year. Hangon. Gettit.' She vanished.

Maggie was moving things round on the kitchen table now, like an admiral deploying battleships, building a street out of butter dish and milk bottle and flowing the river down it with her finger.

'So this is the oaks – if it broke through *here*, see, there's nothing to stop it creating a quite deep stream along that sort of trench that the path runs in, right to the bottom of Abelard Street. And there are slopes either side, and terraced houses. So everyone's looking at the main river by the bridge and thinking it's fine because the embankment is nice and high, when sloosh! Up comes the floodwater from behind.'

'You seem very expert at all this,' said Leo with a touch of the old dryness.

'Seen it happen. Floods don't always come from where everyone thinks. The lie of the land gets camouflaged by familiar buildings.'

'Where'd you see it?'

'Guatemala.'

Leo snorted. 'Yes, but it didn't happen here in nineteen fifty-three, or that other time in the seventies. Or in all that rain last month either. If the river broke out there—' he, in turn, tapped the milk bottle – 'it would just soak away in the meadows. Even if it lay, it would just lie in the park. It's happened once or twice, I remember people skating on it in the really cold winters in the eighties when we first opened the shop.'

'Yes, but look—' She broke off. Samantha had brought the map in and slapped it down on the table before slouching out of the room. Maggie pushed aside her makeshift objects, unfolded the map and spread it flat with strong capable hands.

'Look. It can't soak away there now because there's the new estate with the embankment and the wall to protect it. It can't go *that* way, because there's the bypass embankment. Neither of those lumps of concrete was there in nineteen fifty-three. Or even when I left, in the eighties. I reckon the new development has created a lovely alternative river bed, just waiting to be used by any spare water.'

'Only with incredible rainfall all the way upriver,' said Leo. 'And they'll have allowed for that. The builders. The planners. The council. This isn't Mozambique.'

'Hmm,' said Maggie. 'That's probably what they said in Guatemala.'

That day at college she spent her lunch hour in the library with more maps. And when she had finished her afternoon shift at the Blue Lady, she walked down in the rain to the closed, silent bookshop and stood outside it, looking carefully up the street in each direction. She squatted down to peer through a wall grating by her feet and frowned, then with swift strides walked to the bridge and the brown river pockmarked with raindrops.

She stared for a while at sliding water, focusing on the structure of the bridge at the point where water met air. When she had first come home and leaned again on this bridge of her childhood, that line had been as she remembered it, green with river ooze. Today the water lapped against clean, mellow red brick: brick more used to sunlight than to slime and darkness. The dark arches were shallower too, thin slivers of space rather than the mysterious glinting tunnels she remembered.

It was eight o'clock when she reached the house; the rain still fell in great sheets, turning her black hair to rats' tails. The seams of her thin plastic jacket had leaked, leaving stripes of soaked darkness over her shoulders.

'Look at you!' said Sarah. 'Get changed, supper's nearly ready. You've been in the tropics half your life, you ought to keep warm.'

'Where's Leo?' asked Maggie. 'Only it's urgent. The shop.'

'Oh, *not* a break-in!' said Sarah agitatedly. There had been a spate of minor but irritating High Street vandalism. The Blue Lady had had its plate glass cracked. By the fuss Mrs Pritt had made, you would have thought widespread rioting had broken out in Brackhampton.

'Oh, shit,' Sarah continued. 'I thought bookshops at least would be reasonably safe. Bloody little yobs can't read. Leo!'

'No, not a break-in,' reassured Maggie. 'But could be worse than a break-in. Leo—' he had appeared in the doorway, holding a glass of whisky – 'I'm really sorry, but what we talked about this morning, the flooding, I think it could be tonight. I seriously do. Your shop is at one of the lowest points of the High Street. And if water did come down Abelard Street it would get into your basement. At least.'

'There haven't been any warnings for Brackhampton,' said Leo, for it had been a season of flood warnings and television pictures of unfortunate towns with dinghies paddling up the street. 'The Brack isn't a big river, like the Medway or the Ouse. We aren't even on the list.'

'Fuck the list!' said Maggie roughly. 'Lists are a really bad idea, they just make everyone else feel smug. Leo. Listen. Please. It won't be people canoeing through the town, not here, because of the hill. But I just want to ask you, what is in your shop basement? What?'

'Books,' said Leo. 'It's a bookshop. Stock.'

'Insured to full value? Including labour for clearing out the pulp, loss of profits, all that stuff?'

'Ummm . . . there's an excess,' said Leo, wavering. He thought for a moment. 'And I did agree to a cap on the profit compensation so it doesn't include fluctuations like Christmas.'

Maggie said sharply, 'Kiss your excess goodbye, then. Either that, or let's all get down there and shift stuff up higher. Truly. I mean it.'

Leo hesitated, then glanced at his wife.

Sarah said, 'Might as well check anyway. See if there's any sign of trouble. Supper can wait ten minutes.'

'There won't *be* any sign,' said Maggie. 'It'll be really, really quick when it happens. And we'll need everybody. And for more than ten minutes.'

Her generalship carried the day. Leo took the shop keys down from their hook, Samantha was summoned from her bedroom and the boys from the television, and in the pelting rain the family skittered down the alleyway to Brackhampton Books. Leo unlocked the shop then glanced up and down the dull, peaceful provincial street. The tarmac and the pavement flags shone wetly back at the streetlights, and nothing stirred beyond the bouncing rain.

'Come on then.'

There was a steep flight of wooden steps to the stockroom, put in by Leo to replace an old ladder. They were glad of it. With Sarah at the bottom, pulling boxes from shelves and towers, they made a human chain: Sarah passed her load to Samantha on the first step, Samantha gave it to Maggie, who twisted and reached with strong agile movements on the precarious middle step, passing boxes up to Jamie on the top one, hence to Teddy struggling manfully to and fro across the main floor, finally to Leo. After a moment's hesitation he had constructed a plinth of upended plastic milk crates in the middle of the shop, and on this he began building a tower of cardboard boxes. When it was too high for further progress, he began carrying boxes up the few steps to the children's department, and stacking them there.

'It's going to be a pig mess,' he said. 'God knows what Miss

Mountjoy will say.' But there was an edge of enjoyment in his voice. The children caught it, and began singing catches from *Noye's Fludde*, which the school choir had done last year, and then 'One More River'. Outside, the rain pattered on the plate-glass window and a chill, cutting wind began to howl around the chimney pots. Sarah, down in the basement looking round at dusty, empty shelves, heard the note of buzzing cheerfulness above her and smiled. It was an absurd manoeuvre, it was probably unnecessary, but it had created a Blitz spirit among the family and for that she was grateful. Even Samantha's clear soprano, unheard (she now realized) for many months, rose joyfully above the rest as she sang, 'Oh, River! Keep 'way from ma door!'

'Can we have supper now?' said Teddy, tiring. 'I've got homework.'

'I'll walk you back and get it hotted up,' said Sarah comfortingly, emerging from the trap door. 'Come on, Jamie, Samantha. Job done, I think.'

'Shall Leo and I follow on?' asked her sister. 'Only since we've built an ark, we might as well finish the job. Just clear the bottom shelves, anyway?'

'If Brackhampton is not visited by flood and pestilence tonight,' said the bookseller, 'I am going to look bloody silly in the morning.'

'We can make the shop look OK,' said Maggie. 'You don't use the tops of the bookcases, we can move all this low stuff up there.'

'Right . . . oh God, sheep as a lamb and all that. Ten minutes, Sarah, and we'll be up.'

They worked in silence. After a while Maggie, stretching up with an armful of dictionaries, grew uncomfortable with the silence and said with a rare note of pleading in her voice, 'Leo, if it doesn't happen, it doesn't. You can blame me for all this. I'll round up some volunteers from college to put it all back if you like.'

'No,' he said, answering the tone rather than the words. 'I am truly grateful. For you thinking of the shop. You took trouble.' He smiled. His smiles were rare these days; it lit his face, and eased her mind.

'It's just that I've seen floods,' she said more conversationally. 'More than once. They're horrible even in simple countries, and here . . . well, in overdeveloped countries you do always get the sewage thing. The drains overflow.'

'You're right. It'd be horrible, especially with all this paper. The damp. If it does come in, I daresay we'll still lose a fair bit of stock to wrinkled pages, all that. I had a roof leak in the children's department last year, that was bad enough. Makes you wish you sold something a bit more robust.'

'Like, um, ironmongery?'

'That'd go rusty,' said Leo.

'Garden statues?'

'Do me a favour. They're so cheap and porous these days you'd have muddy watermarks halfway up all your Three Graces.'

'Well, rubber goods. Beach toys. Inflatable women . . .'

They began to laugh, easy now and comradely. Leo went round the shop checking windows, then turned off the spotlights and made his way to the door in the dim security lighting. As he reached it Maggie, who had pushed it open, abruptly froze.

'Sh!' she said. 'Listen.'

It was not the sound but the smell that Leo caught first: a dank, graveyard, drainpipe breath. It was a moment or two before his ear, attuned to the thuds and laughter of the work, caught the stealthy lapping.

'Flaming Norah!' he said fervently. 'You were only fucking *right*.' His hand went up to Maggie's shoulder as she stood, looking out into the thinning rain and up at the sky where high ragged cloud tore dark patterns round a crescent moon. 'I do believe . . .'

It was only a shallow, chuckling current, not high enough to mount the pavement in front of the shop. But as their eyes grew accustomed to the dimness they saw that it was flowing, down from Abelard Street and towards the row of shops where they stood. As they watched, a fat gout of water broke over the pavement's edge and joined the slick of rainwater already weeping over the flagstones. Another came from further along and joined it. Leo watched with fascinated horror as the main water level rose unhurriedly over the pavement to become a glittering, moving glaze on the flagstones, reflecting the white crescent of the moon. Then his eyes widened at the unmistakable sound as water poured down the ventilator into the basement beneath them.

'It's a *waterfall!*' he said with horror. 'Christ, half an hour back . . .'

'I didn't really think it would be tonight,' said Maggie in a faint voice. 'To be honest, I thought it would take two days to talk you into it, so I just thought I'd make a start with the propaganda campaign. Jee-sus!'

They stepped back and peered down the trap door, shining the shop torch onto the water. 'Almost knee-deep down there already,' said Leo. 'What's the physics of this? Does it come up under us and through the floor?'

'It finds its own level,' said Maggie. 'Remember? Everyone does that at school. Physics. Geo. You know. I reckon it won't quite reach the basement ceiling, unless it comes up much higher outside.'

'Is it going to come over the doorstep?' He sounded childlike, wondering and afraid.

'Yes. Probably. Look.' She pointed down at the first horrid trickle creeping through the cracked corner of the door. 'Got any sandbags?'

'Of course I haven't got any sandbags!' said Leo, suddenly explosive. 'Until this morning not one living soul had, to my knowledge, predicted that the River Brack would bloody creep up from behind and flood Brackhampton.' He turned to her. 'What are you, psychic or something?'

'The stranger's eye,' said Maggie. 'It's a well-documented phenomenon. Like the Emperor's new clothes. And anyway, I'm probably just more used to being in the kind of place that has natural disasters. People don't expect undignified, disrupting things to happen among familiar buildings. We all close down our primitive fear mechanisms most of the time. You have to. Otherwise you'd never drive, or go in a plane. Or even a lift.'

Leo considered this for a moment, taking comfort in fleeing from the present into the realms of theory.

'You mean,' he said, 'if there's a building society fascia that you recognize, you feel reassured and assume that Godzilla won't rear up and smash it?'

'Right.'

'So that's why horror films with a familiar setting are so effective?'

'Yup. Because we know it won't happen, so we play happily with the idea. Like a child safe on its mother's lap, hearing stories about giants and witches.'

There was a silence while they watched the trickle of water pushing its way through the cracks around the doorframe. Then, 'Oh God, my *floor!*' said Leo helplessly, staring down at the blond wood at their feet. 'It'll be wrecked.'

'Veneer strips, laid on concrete?' said Maggie.

'Yes, blast you. I like to think it looks real.'

'Well, concrete dries faster. Better than if it was planks. This stuff'll curl up and die, and you can just lay it again in a fortnight. Look.' Now it was Maggie who laid a hand on Leo's shoulder. He had begun to shiver, shocked. 'You go home, tell Sarah what's happening, bring us a thermos of soup. I've had an idea that might help with this sill.'

'Will you be safe?' He sounded childlike again.

'Never happier!' said Maggie, with a grin that spread from ear to ear.

And indeed, she was suddenly happy. Although she did not show it, the weeks in Brackhampton had been oppressing her.

Arriving from the *Evangelina*, planning the Chinese course, she had reasoned with herself that it could be no worse staying in England for a few months than staying anywhere else. Although more than anything she loved to be on the road from day to day, her travels had often kept her in one country for a year or more. She had lived for two years almost constantly in Guatemala City once, helping with a social project for street children.

But she had not reckoned with the steady deadness of Brackhampton, nor the autumn darkness of British skies, nor the troubling echoes, on every street corner, of her frustrated youth. Although she dearly loved Sarah and enjoyed her nephews and niece, the town itself possessed a quite unexpected ability to get her down. Southwick and the Further Education College were not very much better. She had fought the feeling; the purpose of the morning runs was as much to preserve her optimism as to keep up her traveller's fitness. If she hurled herself physically through the dark dawns, made herself pant and palpitate with effort, the day began as well as a Brackhampton day ever could. Yet it was harder with each passing day; it would have surprised her sister very much to know that on recent mornings Maggie had been waking up as reluctant as any of them to get out of her warm bed.

But this crisis, this dark flood and disrupted evening, brought a renewal of her habitual mood: the surge of joy in action which had marked most of her adult life. She stood frowning for a moment, looking down at the seeping water, then grinned again and ran over to the trap door, which was still open. She climbed down into the basement, ignoring the cold water welling round her knees, and waded to the corner under the grating. Water poured steadily, unhurriedly down in a torrent beside her. She bent, plunging arms and shoulders into the flood, grasped something, made a wrenching movement that pulled her face almost underwater, then straightened up. In her hands was what she had been looking for: a solid laminated board, the base of a discarded set of shelves. She let it float alongside her while she groped again, and wrenched out two more planks. The shelving, as she had foreseen, was only slotted together; now that she had removed the first piece, the remains came away easily, and bobbed around her.

Dripping, her jeans flapping nastily round her ankles, she took the three best boards up the ladder with her, closed the trap, went to the sales desk and pulled out the lowest filing drawer. To her delight there was a hammer and some tacks, left over from some display job. The tacks were too short for her purpose but the hammer had a claw, with which she swiftly drew a series of nails out from the skirting board in the children's section. Before more than a few pints of water had found its way into the ground floor of the shop, she had nailed the boards securely across the bottom of the doorway and reduced the flow to a trickle.

She talked aloud to herself as she worked. 'Sandbags,' she said. 'Sandbags. There are no sandbags, so think of something like sandbags. What do sandbags actually do? They absorb water. They lie still. They shape themselves to where they are, and make it difficult for more water to seep in. Hmmm . . .' Straightening up, steadying herself on the island of book boxes, she looked around. Forgotten in the haste and half-dark were the copies of the pictorial tome on the Queen Mother, which Miss Mountjoy had been unpacking. The first of the water had ruined them, wicking upwards through expensive cloth covers and glossy paper. Even the top few copies were beginning to wrinkle.

'OK, Queen Mum! Time to save the nation!' Grinning, Maggie began to take them out and stack them behind her barricade of boards, sometimes pulling out handfuls of pages to stuff tightly into the cracks where the angle was not true. Outside, in the darkness, the water rose. It pushed against her planks and their backing of glossy monarchism, gave up, and turned to swirl on down the street towards the Blue Lady and the Wimpy Bar. There was little force in it now. Maggie roamed around until she found the cleaning cupboard, pulled out some cloths and a mop, and began to deal with the water which had puddled across the floor.

By the time Leo got back with the soup, almost tripping over the barricade in his confusion, his ground floor was dry and his sister-in-law posing in comedic triumph, leaning on her mop.

Chapter Nine

It was a famous autumn for floods, a season of deluge all across England. Night after night the rescue helicopters and the news photographers hovered over towns and villages which had turned to vast brown lakes with islets of red brick and slate, and the television news showed streets that were canals, and hitherto quiet brooks enjoying a brief period of celebrity as waterfalls and rapids. From Yorkshire to Kent, haggard householders waded helpless through a rank, stinking sea of wrecked possessions. Violent arguments raged in the media concerning the practice of building on flood plains and the evils of global warming. Government ministers, royal princes, bishops, and commentators of every political colour weighed in joyfully. On *Thought for the Day*, amateur theologians drew trite little morals from the deluge, causing numerous radios to be flung from windows into puddles.

The Brackhampton flood, everybody agreed, was slight in comparison. The Brack never burst its embankment in the town centre, despite two anxious nights when citizens stayed up to watch it. The Penn boys had one of the most memorable nights of their young lives, sleeping out in a bivouac in the park with their Auntie Maggie. The floodwater, in the event, only made one major incursion into the town and that was just deep enough to affect a dozen houses, and the lowest shops of the High Street. The next belt of rain dealt lightly with them, and the waters subsided rapidly. Despite the wild predictions of Teddy and Jamie, nobody had the satisfaction of canoeing a slalom course through the parking meters or being removed from a rooftop by the inshore lifeboat. Sarah had a brief moment of glory when she waded knee-deep up Abelard Street on the first day, to rescue a ginger kitten miaowing on a garden wall. Samantha, who after the exhilarating rescue of the bookshop had subsided back into a torpid, sullen world of her own, merely shuddered and picked her way delicately through the muddy streets to school to sit through classes as listlessly as before.

Maggie's shop-door barricade held good through the worst two days, reinforced with extra nails and the five old pillowcases which Sarah filled with builder's sand to replace the pulp which was all that remained of the Queen Mother books. The flood defence was, the children agreed, a 'wicked' feat of instant civil engineering on the part of their aunt.

It also cost Maggie her jobs at the Blue Lady and the Black Lion.

At school, on the morning after the first flooding, Teddy gathered his usual group at playtime. They were indoors, in the echoing gymnasium, with rain sluicing down the high windows.

'My dad's shop didn't get trashed by the river,' he began, 'because my aunt warned him to get stuff up high, and we all worked in the night, movin' books.'

The boys were incredulous.

'How did she know to warn him?' asked Colin. ''Cos it wasn't on the radio or anything. My dad says—'

'She must've been in lots of floods,' Joanne, hovering entranced, interrupted him: 'We never had a flood before, did we?'

'She just knew,' said Teddy smugly. 'She got maps, and worked it out. In our kitchen. Even the *police* didn't know, but my aunt did.'

'Like in the Bible,' said Adrian piously. 'Only Noah knew what to do, 'cos God told him, and all the rest drowned.'

'That's just a story,' said Adrian, crushingly. 'My dad says the Bible's bollocks.'

A theological debate ensued, involving much scuffling of trainers on the faded block floor of the gym; but the marvellousness of this auntly prescience made such an impression on Joanne that later on, under cover of a joint science project, she told Louise Pritt. Whereon Louise told her mother, Marion, who owned the Blue Lady Restaurant in an acrimonious and unsatisfactory partnership with her divorced husband Tim. When her daughter related the miracle of Leo Penn's early warning, Marion exploded.

'What? You mean Margaret Reave, Sarah Penn's sister? *She* told Mr Penn the floodwater was coming?'

'Yes,' said Louise proudly. 'She worked it all out on a map. She's a world traveller, Joanne says. A free spirit. She knows stuff about floods and disasters.'

Marion Pritt's small mouth closed with angry force. The Blue Lady, four doors along from the bookshop and a few inches lower, was still an inch deep in foul water. It had welled up from the drain alongside as it flooded; the kitchen would be unusable for months, the flooring and much plaster in the restaurant would have to be replaced. Moreover, it was far from certain that Tim Pritt had remembered – blast him!—to upgrade the insurance after the new stove and fridges went in. Too busy with his bloody bimbo, thought the ex-wife bitterly.

When Maggie arrived, gumbooted, at her usual shift time to offer assistance, Mrs Pritt said sourly, 'I gather you warned your brother-in-law about this flood. Family first, I suppose.'

'It wasn't that,' said Maggie. 'I wasn't sure. I just thought that his basement might flood, and it was full of books.'

Marion Pritt gestured at the wrecked interior behind her. 'Well,' she said. 'I'm sure he'll be anxious to employ you, if only as a soothsayer. There's no work here, as you can see. We shall be closed for weeks.'

'Can I at least help sort out the mess?' offered Maggie. 'Just as a volunteer, you understand.'

'No, thank you,' said Mrs Pritt repressively. 'That won't be necessary.'

Up at the Black Lion, which had merely had its garden flooded, her chickens did not come home to roost until two days later. The landlord, mildly embarrassed, told her that following the flooding in the town they were 'downscaling' the bar staff. Shortly, however, it was to be observed that an eighteen-year-old boy was working Maggie's accustomed Wednesday to Friday shifts.

'Your sister's name,' said Leo to his wife in bed, 'appears to be mud in the town. It's funny, you'd think they would blame me for being the only one with a dry floor. But the word I'm getting through Miss Mountjoy is that people blame Maggie more. They think it wasn't cricket for her only to warn me.'

'What could she have done?' demanded Sarah heatedly. 'Run through Brackhampton with a bell, shouting "Doom, doooom, prepare to meet your God"? Who'd have paid any attention? I can understand Marion Pritt, perhaps; she's having an awful time, after the divorce and everything – but the Black Lion wasn't even flooded.'

'It's the customers,' said Leo. 'The General says there really is a lot of ill feeling. It's all rather atavistic. Do you know,' he said, hauling up the duvet against the dank night air, 'I reckon they think she's a witch. In the sixteenth century, if a fox copped everyone's chickens except yours, and you were a woman, you were straight onto that ducking stool.'

'Poor Mags!' said Sarah, amused in spite of herself. 'No, really, it's terrible. Leo, I wondered . . .'

Leo turned off his light and rolled over, his back to Sarah. 'Yeah, so did I. You mean, p'raps I should see if she wants to work in the bookshop?' He was addressing his words to the dark square of wallpaper near his head, and made no attempt to look at his wife and gauge her reaction.

'Well, it's logical,' said Sarah slowly. She was still sitting up, causing a chilly draught to get beneath the duvet. Leo hunched against it. 'She could only do afternoons, obviously. Till term ends. But it might help with the run-up to Christmas. Maybe Sam could do a bit in the holidays. Then you could get someone permanent later, when you've time to interview.'

'Mmm,' said Leo. 'G'night. Lie down, you're making me cold. Love you.'

'Love you,' said Sarah, flopping down, but making no move towards him. And a few minutes later, she said to Leo's back, 'People wouldn't be as prejudiced in a bookshop, would they? It's not like a pub.'

'You don't have to employ me,' said Maggie, astonished, when Leo made the suggestion at breakfast time. 'I can get pub or café work in Southwick easily. There's never a shortage of jobs. Not the kind of jobs I do, anyway.'

'There's people on the dole,' said Jamie, who had joined the debating society at school and taken to frowning his way through the newspapers. 'You know, unemployment. Mum, where's my maths book? And I have to have games kit for cycle club.' And to Maggie again, 'There *is* a shortage of jobs. We did it in Citizenship with Mr Glover. People get redundancied for *years*.'

'Not me,' said his aunt. 'You're right about the unemployment thing, I suppose. But what that probably means is there aren't enough proper decent jobs for people who've got families and houses to keep up. There are always lots of jobs for casuals, and students, and underpaid bums like me.'

'You could do a proper job,' said Teddy. 'You could be a meeter-meety-meeteryologist. You could tell people about floods.'

'P'raps,' said Maggie. 'But I don't want to stay put and have a career. Never did. Take each day as it comes, I say.'

'It wouldn't suit everybody,' said Sarah, handing Jamie his sports bag. 'Come on, you'll be late. And don't you start thinking that the way your Auntie Maggie lives is easy, either. She works jolly hard, for not much money and no security whatsoever. That's the price of freedom.'

'God, you sound like Mum,' said her sister with kindly scorn, capturing and eating a raisin that had strayed onto the tabletop from somebody's cereal. 'Sam, since the sun is at last shining, I'm going to get the bus from the top of town today. D'you want to walk up with me, if the boys are taking their bikes? Get some fresh air, ultraviolet light, all that good stuff?'

Leo was growing impatient. Somehow, between his question and any coherent answer from Maggie, the whole topic had been hijacked and driven away in several directions by his family. He had never quite taken to the loose unstructured nature of family conversation. It annoyed him.

'So what do you think?' He tried to regain control: 'It'd be doing me a favour, not you. It was Sarah's idea. It would just be to fill in for the Christmas period. I can only pay pretty casual wages, but probably the same as you were getting from Mrs Pritt, and you wouldn't have to peel carrots.'

Maggie glanced at Sarah, who was trying to brush crumbs off her younger son.

'Go on,' said Sarah encouragingly. 'Solve Leo's problem, solve your problem, and you can both re-think at New Year.'

'I'll walk with you,' said Samantha abruptly, answering Maggie's last question and ignoring the ongoing topic of the bookshop. 'Lemme just get my bag.'

'Oh, all right,' said Maggie to Leo. 'But I've never worked in a bookshop. Don't know anything about it.'

'Can read, can't you? How about today? Half past two?' said Leo, pressing home the advantage. 'Miss Mountjoy can show you round.'

'Two, if you like. I'll take the one o'clock bus. They're cutting afternoon classes anyway. Library time. C'mon, Sam.'

Maggie began looking around vaguely for her canvas sack of books; Sarah passed it to her, thinking with fleeting amusement that it was as if she had another schoolchild to see off. Samantha abandoned her uneaten toast and, schoolbag hanging from one hunched shoulder, began searching through the kitchen bowl of rubber bands and paperclips for something to tie back her barely brushed hair. Maggie, seeing her dilemma, yanked a green cloth scrunchie from her own hair and proffered it, silently.

'Bye, darling. Have a good day,' said Sarah to her daughter, brightly.

'Bye,' said Samantha, not brightly at all.

'Well, there you are then,' said Leo when they had gone, and the boys were outside unlocking their bikes. 'Christmas reasonably solved, anyway. She can work with Miss Mountjoy for a couple of weeks. Learn the ropes.'

'She'll be invaluable,' said Sarah. 'Perhaps . . .'

Leo threw her a sharp glance. He knew what she was thinking. *Perhaps she'll settle down, get a little flat, stay in Brackhampton, start a personal pension, always be there for family gatherings.*

'Don't count your chickens,' he said with unaccustomed gentleness.

Chapter Ten

Maggie and Samantha walked up the road together. Neither spoke until they had left the old town and were on the wider, emptier pavements of the suburban street that led up to Brackhampton High School.

Then Maggie said casually, 'How's the work going?'

'Pants,' said Samantha briefly. Her aunt glanced sideways at her. Too thin, she thought, not wirily and actively thin but starveling, scrawny and pale.

'Yup, I remember the feeling,' she said. 'It gets better. After filthy GCSEs it gets better.' Then, her voice neutral, 'That's not the problem, though, is it?'

Samantha stopped in her tracks.

'You being nosy?' she challenged. 'Like Mum?'

Maggie paused as if considering the charge. She rubbed her nose, apparently perplexed. They were both standing still now, in the middle of the empty pavement with the morning cars flowing past them. Eventually Maggie began to walk again, slowly, and Samantha fell into step beside her.

'No,' she said. 'Sorry. I used to hate people being nosy about me. My mum – your granny, you know – was always convinced that we were going to get pregnant and ruin our lives. So we got into the habit of being a bit secret about things. It made sense.'

'Still does,' said Samantha curtly.

'I was just worried – no, not worried,' Maggie amended hastily. 'Just, you know, concerned, because I like you. And despite your recent sphinx-like silence on the subject, I seem to remember that we did have a conversation once about your Duane . . .'

'He is NOT my Duane!' burst out Samantha. 'He is a stupid yob, he's just a little boy, he's disgusting – it's been weeks since we even spoke to each other.' There were tears in her eyes.

'Ha! So you did dump him, as I advised,' said Maggie. 'Well done. And has it given you problems? Are people being vile to you at school?'

'N-no,' said the girl, kicking a stone neatly off the pavement 'Not nearly 'smuch as I expected. To be honest.'

'You reckon he didn't talk about it?'

'I reckon he did,' said Samantha reluctantly, 'only not many people like him any more 'cos he and his mates beat someone up quite badly by the Wimpy Bar and two of them got excluded, and Duane nearly did. Most of my class think he's well out of order. Even Tyrone's a bit funny about him now.'

Maggie noticed, in passing, that whereas her brothers always sounded much the same, Samantha's argot and accent were subject to quite violent changes. Once away from the gentility of home and the town centre, her manner dropped by several social classes. Leo, she reflected, would not like it at all; she herself rather approved of the child's chameleon versatility. The ability to adapt to her surroundings would stand her in good stead when one day she trekked out into the wider world. Aloud she merely said with studied lightness, 'Well, that's fine. They do like you, and they don't like him, so they'll be all right to you. So all's well. But you say it's not?'

Samantha stopped again as if to turn to her aunt, but then changed her mind, speeded up, and fired the killer question at the beech hedge instead.

'I wanna know something. Do people, I mean women, always know, like, straightaway, if they're, you know . . .'

Maggie's heart skipped and a horrible dread came on her. Since the night in Samantha's room she had tried not to allow herself to entertain this particular fear. The child's thinness made it easy to discount. With an effort, she said levelly, 'You mean, do women always know if they're pregnant?'

Samantha flinched. Maggie wished she had found a euphemism in time. Expecting? Up the duff? Knocked up? No, none of them would have done. Hell! The girl was nodding, speechless, her dark hair falling from its elastic to hide her face.

'Well,' said Maggie. 'Things happen. Your periods stop.'

Samantha walked on, silent and alert. Every line of her thin body said, scornfully, *I know that.*

Into the emptiness the older woman continued, 'But lots of other things can stop your periods. Stress. Being too thin. That sort of thing. I didn't have any during the hardest bit of the South American bike trip. Working too hard. So it's not a sure sign.'

The girl grimaced. 'What other signs d'you get?'

The child should be asking her mother these things, thought Maggie in a panic. Sarah should cope with this. But how ironic, how beautifully and horribly ironic, that after all those years she and Sarah had spent fending off Nancy's morbid dread of teenage pregnancy, it should now be a granddaughter who pulled the pin from that particular grenade. Even more ironic that it should be Maggie who reeled and trembled at the awful possibility.

She took a grip on herself. Samantha was asking again, 'What other things? I mean, like, without doing a test?'

'Oh, I don't know, feeling sick and not wanting coffee and things. Your Mum always said, anyway. Look, it's best to do a test. There are kits. You buy them at the chemist.'

Samantha strode on, her thin back eloquent.

After a few paces Maggie asked tentatively, 'Do you want me to buy you a kit? From the chemist in Southwick, where nobody knows any of us?'

The dark head nodded. Of course, thought Maggie. How on

earth could a schoolgirl buy a kit in Boots in Brackhampton High Street? A schoolgirl, moreover, who was the daughter of a leading citizen and shopkeeper? A wave of protective pity swept over her, and echoes of confused feelings from her own secretive adolescence. Poor bloody kid!

She said, as comfortingly as she knew how, 'Tonight, then. I'll go past the chemist near college.'

'Mum,' began the girl pleadingly, 'you won't tell Mum . . .'

'I won't tell her. But Sam, look, if it turns out that you—'

'I'm not. I'm not. I'm not. I just want to be sure,' said Samantha. 'Like, bloody sure.'

'Yes,' said Maggie. 'I can see that you would.'

When she had left Samantha at the school gate, she walked on to the bus stop in a daze. Looking down, she saw that her hands were trembling. When had they ever trembled? When had she ever felt the ground so treacherous beneath her feet? Not in the desert, not in the jungle, not on the ocean, not in the slum hostels of the American tropics. Only once, in a time she rarely thought about these days.

'Christ,' she muttered aloud. 'Oh Christ Almighty, fuck, fuck, fuck! Why did I have to come back to bloody England?'

Panic tightened in her breast. The octopus of family life was throwing tentacles round her, one after the other, and it was not a Dear Octopus to her, not at all. She should have been more wary. She should have seen it coming, and made her usual brief convivial visit before going off to lodge somewhere alone and anonymous. She should never have let the creepers grow over her, or allowed herself to be furred by the soft insidious moss of family. She should have kept on rolling, and kept to her lifetime habit of making her human contacts in bars and at roadsides. It was enough, it had always been enough, merely to link herself with the human race through tales and laughter, songs in the night, brief strenuous assistance in crises and passing easy kindnesses in the good times.

Staying with the Penns had dangerously enchained her. First

there had been Sarah's unspoken, dependent relief at having her company in the house. Then the seductive devotion of the boys, then the rescue of Leo's claustrophobic little shop, and now the unwanted confidence of this poor child, enmeshed in the stickiest, sickliest of female dilemmas.

She shuddered, staring out of the bus window at the fleeting countryside. For despite the college course, despite her unflagging air of cheerful insouciance and her enjoyment of Sarah's children, Maggie's inner equilibrium had depended for fourteen years on the fact that she was tied to nobody and to no place. It was an article of faith to her that wherever she was, whatever she was doing, whatever friendships she had made, she could leave any time at half an hour's notice without reproach. Twice in those years she had come close to commitment, even to domesticity; twice she had, with implacable rigour, disconnected herself from the encroaching tendrils. Once, she had wept as she left. Yet always, deep within her, lay the certainty that she was right.

So how had she let this happen? How had she not seen how sticky were the fingers of the Penn family? Her fear, when she arrived from Spain, had been focused entirely on the possibility that her mother might try to claim her; but old Nancy had proved vague, and even slightly bored by her younger daughter. Her mother had presented no challenge at all to her escapological skills. Why had she not feared Sarah and Leo?

Swinging off the bus at the stop before the college, suddenly Maggie understood why. It was because things had been so different last time she had been in England. Four years ago, the Penns had been a perfect, complete, almost hermetically sealed unit. Samantha was eleven, proud of her Patrol Leader uniform and big-school status. Jamie was nine, Teddy a romping small child who still climbed on his mother's knee. The little ones still had bedtime stories, often from Leo. Neighbours with children of the same age were for ever popping in and out. Leo and Sarah themselves were, she remembered, always yawning, always rushed, but given to hugging one another and leaning together exhaustedly in the kitchen like a pair of bookends, moaning humorously about their busy-ness. In 1996 the house was relatively new to them after years of renting, and still a source of pride and constant discussion about shower fitments and carpet bargains. On that visit Maggie had stayed for three weeks but never once felt at the slightest risk of being entrapped by her relatives' needs. They had no needs, frankly; they were a snug, functional, little city-state all on their own.

Now they were not. Now, thought Maggie with a spurt of anger, the cracks were showing. Leo was harassed, and drank too much in the evenings. Sarah seemed impatient with her husband, quick to mock and openly bored by his complaints about the book trade. The children were as much fun as ever – more fun, thought Maggie, who had little taste for mewling infancy. But the family was – yes, definitely cracking open, she thought. The obvious symptom was that, with the exception of Leo, they had been just a little bit too keen to see her. They needed to be distracted from themselves. Sarah wanted a companion, the boys wanted fun, Samantha wanted a confidante in her awful dilemma. And now even Leo had decided that there was, after all, a place for her. In his shop. Selling books. Instead of Miss Mountjoy . . .

And here she was, standing outside a chemist's shop on Southwick High Street preparing to buy, in secret, a pregnancy test for Leo and Sarah's only daughter. She was the sole adult confidante of Nancy's granddaughter, a child who had every reason to suspect that she was up the spout at fifteen. I did not want this, thought Maggie, I did not want this kind of life at all. I ran halfway round the world to escape it.

The shop oppressed her, with its cloying discreet sweetness, its ranks of scented creams and soaps and lotions. She was never ill, and had not spent much time in chemist's shops even as a teenager. She associated them mostly with buying first-aid kits for journeys, and with her brief visits to each new baby and the

temporarily enfeebled Sarah. Leo was brave enough to buy
nappies and wipes, but had an old-fashioned diffidence about
standing at a counter with a basket of sanitary towels, nipple
creams, remedies for cystitis and worryingly shaped pieces of
rubberware. So Maggie ran all the errands during her visits, and
tried not to make comparisons between what a new Western
mother needed and what most of the world's women got.

Now she looked wildly around the shop for what she had to
buy. Christ, but it was a female kingdom! Single men, she
supposed, came in and turned directly to the more austere
medical counter, or snatched a suitably virile deodorant and
scuttled to the till. But by and large the married men of
Southwick let their wives buy their shampoo and deodorant,
for such shops were surely the province of women.

A woman's whole captivity, thought Maggie with an edge of
panic, was arrayed on these shelves of glass and plastic: the
agonized discretion, the lifetime of coping daintily with effluence
and seepage. Biology was destiny and Boots was its instrument.
You smoothed and painted and shaved and scented and con-
ditioned and slimmed yourself until you caught a man's attention
and he (or, more likely, you) felt the need for the contraceptive
counter. Then came the moment for your pregnancy test (where
the hell *were* they?) and from then on, the chemist was your life-
support system, source of all things elasticated and antiseptic,
jellied and homeopathic and vitamin-enriched. Its wares rattled
behind you like Marley's ghost all the way to the baby wipes,
zinc and castor oil cream, Calpol and disposable nappies. Soon
you were back as your children grew, for Elastoplast and arnica
and gumshields for games. And then, God help us, it was your
daughter who wanted the creams and lip glosses and black tights
and conditioners and razors.

And as night follows day, the pregnancy test. Maggie
shuddered as if a thousand female ghosts were crossing her
grave: provocative, voluptuous, doomed ghosts on phantom
kitten heels.

Squaring her shoulders, she marched through the shop, spotted what she needed more by luck than judgement, and stood for a moment irresolute. There were four different kinds where she remembered only one. They were unbelievably expensive in her eyes: over ten pounds each. How did girls manage? Schoolgirls? Only one was cheaper and that, she noticed, was also marked '2 TEST PACK.' Her eyes filled unaccountably with tears and, with a half-blind, embarrassed grab which did not go unnoticed by the assistant, she laid her hand on a discreet little blue-and-white box and handed over £7.95.

Poor Sam, she thought, poor bloody Sam.

Chapter Eleven

'These all need signing,' said Sarah, putting down a sheaf of letters on the vet's desk. She was in the small office behind the surgery, in the faint familiar smell of antiseptic. 'I could get them to the post tonight if you like.'

Privately, she thought that Mr Miller's habit of personally signing all the practice invoices was daft. But he had been doing it for all of the twelve years she had worked for him, and there seemed little chance of his changing now.

'Did you ring Mrs Pritt about her dog?' he asked, flipping over a set of notes on his battered desk. 'I really have to take those stitches out. You'd think people would remember.'

'The flood probably drove it out of her mind,' said Sarah. 'It's going to be months before the Blue Lady's dried out properly.'

'The flood,' said Samuel Miller irritably, 'makes the dog all the more susceptible to infections. If people won't take proper responsibility for their animals—'

'Anyway, I did ring her,' said Sarah. She grimaced, remembering that the conversation had mainly consisted of herself listening resignedly, with the phone held an inch from her ear, to a tirade on the subject of Maggie's lack of loyalty in the matter of flood warnings. Sometimes the neighbourliness of a small town was a distinct drawback. 'I put her straight through to the desk, when she'd finished going on about my sister, and Louise has made her an appointment.'

'Yes, how *is* that sister of yours? Saw her running by the river,' said Miller, beginning to sign the invoices with a rapid, jerky action. 'She's an active creature. Wish half the dogs I see were as fit to run through the park.'

Sarah perched on the end of his desk, as she often did when he was in a conversational mood. She enjoyed talking to the old vet. His acerbic, cynical view of the world provided a bracing counterpoint to her own soft-hearted optimism.

'Maggie's fine,' she said, idly admiring the silver wings of hair which swept up with senatorial elegance behind the old man's ears. 'She's even going to help Leo in the shop over Christmas. We're loving having her home, it's a real treat.'

Samuel Miller looked up sharply, his pen poised to sign the next sheet.

'She's going into the *bookshop*?' he said incredulously. 'What'll all the old tabbies make of that? Bit of a change from Mountjoy. Like replacing a chicken with a kestrel.'

'She worked in the Blue Lady, and the pub. That went fine, till they all decided she was a witch for warning Leo about the flood.'

'Pub's different. People like something a bit wild behind the bar, they know they're safe, it can't get at them, and it makes a man feel like a gay dog, having a barmaid with a bit of danger about her. But in that little shop – hell, she'll drive poor old Leo insane.' He bent to his task again.

'They've always got on really well,' protested Sarah, then with a guilty twinge modified the statement. '*Now* they do, anyway. Leo was very grateful to her for all the work she did that night. She built a sort of dam out of planks and tacks and books that got spoiled, and saved a lot of mess.'

'Crisis management, fine. Some people are made for shipwrecks and emergencies. Not shop life.'

'She's keen to do it.'

The vet snorted. 'Not a restful girl. She never was. My wife taught her, you know, at the High School. Never there, always off with the circus or whatever. Not like you. You got all the steadiness in the family genes, she got all the Vikings and pirates and troublemakers.'

'Well, I know,' said Sarah, laughing and climbing off the desk to smooth down her sensible dark wool skirt. 'But people calm down as they get older.'

'Hah!' said the vet, who had not stopped his manic, jerky signing of invoices through the whole conversation. 'That's what they say about dogs, but in my view it's once a biter, always a biter. Here you are, that's the lot. I'll tell my wife that Maggie Reave is going to be a bookshop assistant. She'll bust a gusset laughing.'

'I think it's a great idea,' said his employee stoutly. 'Who knows, she might even stay in Brackhampton and settle down. Be lovely for all of us.'

The vet glanced up, his blue eyes fixing her from their nest of wrinkles so sharply that she hesitated, standing with her bundle of papers held in front of her like a shield.

'Can't believe you're saying that,' he said. 'Butter her paws, like a kitten, to stop it running away? Think you can do that? I doubt it.'

'She's my sister,' said Sarah defensively. 'I was only thinking—'

'I suppose that somewhere in the world,' said the vet, 'there's some idiot following a Bengal tiger around with a tub of butter and a spatula, thinking he'll eventually succeed in making it lie down and purr by the fire. One born every minute.' He laughed, but there was kindness in it. 'Sarah, dear, don't count your chickens.'

'Leo said that,' replied Sarah, glumly.

While this conversation was going on at the veterinary surgery at one end of Brackhampton High Street, Maggie was meekly undergoing her first session of training with Miss Mountjoy at the bookshop. She received praise for her facility with the computer and the till, and nodded keenly through a lecture on the proper handling of books and the need to prevent customers from using their covers to rest on when they signed credit card chits or wrote out cheques.

'It marks them terribly,' said the old lady. 'And another thing. There are certain people you have to watch: they'll clip over a page or dent a spine in order to ask for a discount. If you've any suspicion at all, even if you didn't actually see them do it, you must always insist they have a perfect copy from the stockroom, at the full price. If we have any *at all*. That discourages them from being so dishonest again.'

'Why's it so important that books are spotless?' asked Maggie, before she could stop herself. 'It's the words that matter. Some of the best reading I've ever had was terrible, yellow, brittle, bloated old paperbacks with the backs falling off. Stuff you find under bunks in grotty hostels.'

'That's true, dear,' said Miss Mountjoy surprisingly. 'Indeed, philosophically, I would say that is a very Christian attitude.' She settled her spectacles and smiled, and Maggie saw that she could once have been a handsome woman. 'But in this imperfect world, we sell a lot of books to people who never actually read the words. They either give them away as presents, or just look at the illustrations. Or they get them signed by the author and put them away as an investment.' A delicate little shrug of disdain. 'And on these customers relies the prosperity of the shop. Books,' she concluded, 'partake not only of the divine spark of the under-standing, but of the crudity of materialism. That is why they are so very fascinating to work with.'

Maggie looked at the old lady with new, amused respect. Directly she asked, 'Is it true that you pray for authors who write dirty books?'

'Not only dirty books,' said Miss Mountjoy tranquilly. 'I have progressed from what was, I must confess, a rather naïve and panicky response to the modern trade. I have perhaps refined my sensitivities. I now also pray for those who write gratuitously bad and lazy books, in the hope of making easy money. I even pray for their publishers, who lead them so grievously astray. I am,' she continued reflectively, 'kept very busy, sometimes.'

'She's *wonderful*,' said Maggie to Leo later, when Mountjoy had gone out to replenish the shop's stock of coffee and biscuits. 'You *can't* let her go. She's a national treasure. I know Americans who would cross half the world to do business with her. Eighty-four Charing Cross Road would have nothing on the Mountjoy Experience.'

'I have no kind of control over her,' said Leo. 'You'll have to do, for the moment, until fate throws me another real assistant.'

'Not fate,' said Maggie. 'God, surely. Isn't Miss Mountjoy praying for someone?'

Leo grinned. 'I shouldn't tell you . . .' he said, tantalizingly.

'But what?'

'She told me she already had prayed. And . . .'

'And?'

'The answer has come already. You're it.'

'I totally am *not*! I'm going to China in May!'

'I'm only telling you what she said. You've been sent.'

Maggie stared at him, amused and horrified. 'But you know better, huh? A dog is not only for Christmas, but I bloody well am. Leo. You know that? Leo? Hello?'

'Well, she could be wrong,' said Leo, turning back to the cardboard dumpbin he was filling with paperback editions of a saucy political diary. 'But she's never been wrong yet.'

His new temporary assistant was, he was pleased to note, rendered for once entirely speechless.

During the hours in the bookshop, Maggie briefly forgot about the blue-and-white box in her bag, the one that contained Samantha's pregnancy testing kit. It was a blessed relief not to think about it, or at least to push it firmly to the back of her mind while she grappled with tills and stock control systems. When she did remember it, she kicked her bag further under the desk, as if Leo might have X-ray vision and guess everything. Leo, whose grandchild—

The thought made her unwontedly sick and faint. She did not want this confidence, this involvement in the stickiness of family life. Yet she had it, and must be faithful to it. But dismay rose in her, chill and murky as the floodwater, at the thought of giving this cold clinical test to the child and standing by while she did it. It was obvious that she would have to stand by. As confidante she must be there, to share the guilty relief or the cold shock of disaster.

She had darted to the college library after her morning classes, and there discovered that it was generally thought that the tests on sale in chemist's shops were of a higher, more sensitive quality than any that a GP would be likely to do. This discovery filled her with foreboding. She had hoped very much to find a consensus that they were useless, and thus an excuse to pass the buck, belittle her purchase and persuade Samantha to go to the surgery. It would be best, she told herself, for a child of fifteen to hear such momentous news from a neutral and responsible medical source, some doctor who could counsel her from a standpoint of experience and wisdom. Failing that, she still hoped to persuade Sam to confide in her mother. Walking home, the reluctant aunt rehearsed her speech. 'Better all round if you talk to her first . . . she'll understand . . . it's her responsibility, you being under age . . . I'm sure she won't tell your father unless it's absolutely necessary . . .'

Samantha was already home. The boys were not, and Sarah had left a message to say that she was dropping in on her friend Nita Syal, who was recovering from a hysterectomy. Leo had closed the shop door and said he needed an hour to look through catalogues. So when Maggie turned her key in the lock,

Samantha heard the sound echoing through the empty house and was in the hall to meet her.

'Well? Did you get it?'

'Yes,' said her aunt, heavily. 'But look, I think we should talk before you do it.'

'Why? Mum'll be home soon, and the boys, and Dad, and – look, give it here. I'll pay you later.'

'I don't want paying,' said Maggie patiently. 'Call it a really depressing early Christmas present. But the point is, honeybunch, if this test is positive it's going to mean a lot of thinking. And it might be sensible to do some of the thinking first. Like, about who you'd tell.'

'It's not going to be positive. I am not preg— No, I truly am not. I just need to be sure, OK?'

Still Maggie kept her hand on her canvas bag, holding it shut. She opened her mouth to speak again but Samantha – dishevelled, pale, angry now – looked at the bag and jerked forward as if planning a snatch.

'Give it me! Please!'

So Maggie did, and silently followed Samantha upstairs. She stood irresolute on the landing outside the bathroom, listening to Samantha stabbing and swearing over the slippery cellophane packaging. After a few minutes her niece burst out again and said, 'I can't read the fucking thing! My eyes just go – fuzzy. It does my head in. What the fuck do I do? You read it!'

Maggie sat on the top of the stairs and began reading the leaflet, while Samantha leaned in the bathroom doorway fiddling distractedly with a little clear plastic tub she had taken from the box.

'There's two stick things in sort of paper packaging,' she began, but her aunt hushed her.

'Do shut up. And don't undo anything else. I'm trying to get the idea, it's different from when I—'

'Have you done one before, then?'

'I said shut up!'

Maggie knew, as the print swam before her eyes, that she was not handling this very well at all. She took deep breaths, muttered something, then screwed up her eyes and read. '*Human chorionic gonadotropin . . . present in increasing amounts as the pregnancy progresses . . . excessive fluid intake before testing may dilute the hormone and invalidate the testing process . . .*'

'You're reading the wrong side,' said Samantha in an exasperated tone. 'The stuff about dipsticks and swim rings is all on the other side.' She snatched for the paper. 'Look!' She dropped the little plastic trough, which bounced and skittered down the top two stairs.

'You have to understand what it is before you do it,' said Maggie, snatching back the leaflet. 'And I bet you've been drinking.'

'Have not, so! I don't drink, since, since . . .'

'Not alcohol, dummy. It's your PE day, you drink your sports bottle, then you come in and drink all the fridge water. You always do.' Indeed, Samantha was a prodigious drinker of water, believing that it prevented spots.

'So? What's water got to do with it?'

'Everything. Look, it's best to do it first thing in the morning. It says here. It's more accurate.' Maggie looked down at the leaflet again and now it was her head which was swimming, blood pulsing in her temples, panic grasping at her throat. Oh, this woman's world! '*. . . hCG. . . Clomiphine Citrate Tablets do not affect the result . . . The Health Education Authority recommends that you start taking a daily 400 microgram supplement of folic acid as soon as you start trying for a baby . . . freephone number 0800 665544 . . .*'

Samantha wailed, a baby herself. 'I want to do it now!'

Maggie breathed carefully, regaining control with an effort. She folded the leaflet with care.

'No,' she said. 'You can't do it now, you're all diluted. So it's quite likely to give you a negative result. And you'll have a sneaky suspicion it's a false negative, and you'll still be worried. What's the point of that? Do it in the morning!'

Suddenly Samantha crumpled, her defiance melting. Through seeping tears she muttered, 'If I do, will you walk to school with me again?'

'Yes, of course.' Maggie looked at the pale face and red eyes beneath the tangle of dark hair so like her own, and felt a treacherous tug at her heart. 'Of course I will. We'll leave early. Say we want to look at something in a shop window. I'll fix it.'

'Even if it's raining?'

'Yup. What's a bit of rain?'

The front door opened, crashing back against the cracked plaster of the hallway in a manner which signalled the arrival of the two boys. Shrill and gruff voices, arguing, floated up the stairs. Quick as a flash, Maggie stuffed the leaflet back and slipped the box into the sleeve of her sweater. Samantha gave her a brief, almost grateful glance and went into her room. As Teddy thundered upstairs he trod heavily on the little clear plastic trough, invisible on the stairs.

'Whassat?' he said, picking up the crumpled plastic and flicking it disdainfully. 'Looks like a Barbie's rain hat.'

Maggie took it. 'Mine,' she said. 'God, though, it does, doesn't it?' She put it on her head and grinned at the child, then when he had clumped onward to his bedroom, studied it with care. It would go back into shape, she thought. A bit of Sellotape round the edge to stop it leaking. Or might the sticky side of Sellotape have some ingredient which mimicked human chorionic gonadotropin and would seep into the tub to give a false positive? 'O God, O God,' she muttered under her breath. 'I fought so hard not to live like this . . .'

'Auntie Mag!' shouted Jamie from downstairs. 'D'you wanna see the new Eminem single video? It's coming up after the break.'

Chapter Twelve

Maggie woke abruptly in the darkness before dawn. Sleep always left her quickly. Shaking her head, she rolled out of bed and was upright, reaching for the sweatshirt and jeans in which she took her morning run. Before she could do more than pull on the ragged top, however, a low scratching sound at the door made her pause. Stealthily, creaking on the old boards, she moved over to open it.

Samantha stood there, her hair a maniac's tousle, her eyes bleared with uneasy sleep. She was wearing a nightshirt with a fluffy cat appliquéd on the front, and looked about ten years old.

'I heard you,' she said. 'I can't go back to sleep. Anyway I need a wee.'

Maggie put her finger on her lips. Crossing to the chest of drawers, she pulled open the top one; its handle came off.

'Christ, we can't do anything right,' she whispered. 'Here it is. I read the proper instructions in bed. It's quite easy. You've got to collect some wee in this trough thing. Then you push the cardboard stick through the floating ring thing, and float it, and leave it for ten minutes until you see whether there's a faint blue line under the other blue line.'

'And if there is, you're . . . ?'

'Yup.'

Samantha took the box and shook out its contents on the

bed, grimacing at the crumpled and mended plastic trough. She peered into the bottom. 'There's another,' she said. 'Look. There's two tests.'

'Well, you can have a trough without Teddy's footprint on it, then. That'll be nice.'

Samantha sat on the bed and shivered. 'Oh God,' she said, the whispered tone adding an eerie quality to her throbbing worry. 'I know I'm not going to believe the result anyway. How do I know whether it's the right kind of blue stripe? You can't ever quite tell, my friend once said. You need to see an unpregnant one as well.' She looked sidelong at Maggie and said, 'Suppose you do the other one? Then we'd know. We could compare them.'

'You ought to save the other one, in case you want to do it again to be sure.'

'But I *would* be sure, if I had a control. Like in chemistry at school. I could look at your unpregnant one and see if mine was different.'

'Oh, all right.' Maggie picked up the crumpled plastic container. 'Let's for God's sake get on with it. Or we'll both go mad. All this *faffing*. I bet they're both exactly the same anyway, which is negative, so this whole nightmare is about nothing.'

A few minutes later the girl and the woman were both back, each holding her specimen, oddly shamefaced at the intimate banality of it. Silently, each assembled her testing kit.

'Don't muddle them up, for God's sake,' said Maggie. She placed hers carefully on the bedside table. 'Put yours on the windowsill.'

'We can't muddle them up because you've got the crumply tub.'

The whispering was beginning to get both of them down, and Maggie said, 'Right. Ten minutes. No looking. Get your shoes and jeans on, we're going for a run round the block.'

'I can't!'

'Bloody can. Come on.'

'I wish we'd got the quick sort of test. Where you just wee on a stick and you know straightaway.'

'They cost pounds and pounds more. I'm a cheapskate.'

Together they crept downstairs, put the door on the latch and went out into the dank morning. Jogging slowly, Maggie led the way down the alley towards the bookshop and turned left. Shafts of fog lay across the silent High Street; only the newsagent was outside her shop, hauling in heavy bundles of papers and sawing through the flat plastic tapes that bound them. In silence they ran past the Blue Lady, the beauty salon, the estate agent, Woolworth's, the shining brass plaques of vet and dentist, the whole crooked jigsaw of Tudor and Victorian, Georgian and 1930s brickwork. Maggie felt an unaccustomed pang of affection for Brackhampton. It was the essence of bourgeois small-town England – dull and reliable, kindly and dated, as distant in atmosphere from Britain's own big cities as from any foreign land. Brackhampton was even distant from parts of itself; near the children's school and on the outlying concrete estates, daily lives were led which were not dull, reliable, dated or remotely kind. The centre of Brackhampton was a stage set, a wistful Ealing comedy version of Disney's Main Street USA.

But all the same, thought Maggie, the story it told was not a dishonourable one. The shops and businesses it nurtured, and the window boxes in the flats above them, were evidence that in an age of superstores and howling bypasses, enough people still wanted a small-town High Street in their lives to make it viable. If Brackhampton were an endangered species of puma or flying fox, environmentalists would applaud its tenacity and demand its protection. If it were in Russia or Andalucia or the Western Desert, strangers like her would arrive there from the open country, dusty and weary with their backpacks, and look around with sharp, interested eyes, understanding that they were in a real place, a place with its own flavour. There was, at the end of the day, not all that much to choose between Alice Springs, Seville and Brackhampton. They were what they were. Lives and deaths happened there, babies were conceived and bred . . .

'We should go *back*,' puffed Samantha at her elbow, breaking into the reverie. 'If it's more than ten minutes it might go *funny*.'

'Be fine,' said Maggie briefly. 'Stop worrying.' But she turned and led the way back up the High Street, throwing over her shoulder a provocative, 'You ought to run more, child. You're unfit.'

Samantha had not the breath to snap at her. Together, calmed by the exercise, they slipped back into the house and crept upstairs. The peace of the morning affected Maggie strangely. Entering the silent house, it seemed to her that she felt its quiet, sleepy breathing; the vulnerability of it struck her to the heart. She remembered her sister years ago, dozy and contented, nodding off with an equally somnolent baby at the breast, to have it gently taken away by Leo. She remembered the younger Leo, entranced, wiping the dribble of sweet milk from his child's mouth and laying it down in the cot. The first of those babies was the same Samantha who now stood beside her, all too mature, shivering on the threshold of some awesome, horrid revelation.

Sarah, decided Maggie, should not be rudely woken to such a shock. There must be no cries, no hysterics or histrionics. The quiet home, made peaceful by her sister's acceptance of dull routine, must not wake up to crisis. It would be time enough for that later.

On the landing, she turned to Samantha and said, seriously, 'Whatever the result says, no hysterics. Either way. No noise. We'll look, and think, then you and I will get properly dressed. *Without talking about it*, right? Then we'll leave a note and nip out to the Costarica for coffee and a bun. We can talk there. Out of the house.'

'Come *on*,' said Samantha impatiently. Maggie reached out and pulled her hand from the doorknob.

'Agreed? What I said? Stay cool, whatever? Until we're safe out of the house?'

'Yesss!'

They walked into the room. Maggie hung back; Samantha went straight to the windowsill where the little cardboard stick still bobbed serenely on its yellow sea, buoyed up by the foam float. She picked it out, shook it, and stared. Then she turned and said, 'Give me yours. I need to see if they're the same.'

Maggie sat on the bed, watching her warily. 'So?'

'It's positive,' said Samantha, in a low choked voice. She had taken Maggie's stick out of the tub, looked at it, and after a moment's hesitation, unwilling even in her anguish to lay it on the varnished tabletop, put it back in the tub. She turned. Maggie saw that she was white round the mouth, shaking violently. 'They're different. Two blue lines there, one thick blue line there.' She held her stick out to her aunt. 'What am I going to do?' Tears started in her eyes.

Maggie pulled her down to sit beside her on the bed, and threw an arm over her shoulders.

'Steady. Steady. It's all right. Whatever happens, it's all right.' Her own eyes blurred with tears as she looked down at the nasty little paper stick with its smug stripe and ludicrously, daintily, medically pink foam collar. She blinked. 'It's all right, sweetie.'

Samantha choked out something which her aunt did not quite catch. After a moment she said it again. 'Don't wanna kill a baby. S'wrong.'

'It isn't exactly like——' began Maggie, but the child cut across her.

'Oh, don't worry. I'll have to do it, I'll have to have an ab—— a termination. S'just I don't want to. But I'll have to, won't I?'

'You don't have to do anything. You're free. You make your own choices,' said Maggie. 'But look, we promised not to talk here. Your parents will be up soon. And the boys. Go and get dressed for school, and we'll get out of here.'

Tears coursing down her face, Samantha obeyed, absently

laying the stick back on the windowsill as she went. Maggie stood up, shuddered, and pulled on her college clothes with careless haste. Then she looked with intense dislike at the paraphernalia and prepared to clear it up and tie it away in a plastic carrier bag she had thoughtfully brought up from the kitchen. Sarah must know the awful news, clearly; but they must tell her properly at a good time, not leave her to stumble on sordid evidence. She reached out a hand for the control test, then froze.

Moments later, with the instruction leaflet in her hand, she knocked cautiously on Samantha's bedroom door.

'Did you switch the sticks?'

'What do you mean?' Samantha had regained a little of her fragile poise.

'Did you put your stick in my wee?'

'No. Obviously. I put yours back, so it didn't mess up the bedside table. Once I saw they were different. I've got one thick blue pregnant stripe, you've got two thin ones. They're, like, totally different. That's how I knew.'

'And you didn't switch them over?'

'No. What're you on about?'

'You're not pregnant.'

'What?'

'One blue stripe means you're not pregnant. Two stripes means you are. *Look!*' She held up her own testing stick, and with her other hand brandished the leaflet, stabbing at the diagram with the strip of cardboard. 'Two stripes. Pregnant. See your doctor. One stripe. Negative.'

'What?' Samantha stared at her, not understanding.

'You – are – not – pregnant.' Maggie spat the words at her.

'But then that means . . .' The girl stared.

'Right. Yes. It means that I am.'

Deafening, apocalyptic in the silence between them, Sarah's tinplate alarm-clock sounded high and strident as a fire alarm.

Aunt and niece, of one accord, fled downstairs in silence. Maggie had the presence of mind to scribble a note and stick it to the kitchen table.

'Gone to watch the sun rise, walking to school, Mag & Sam.'

Chapter Thirteen

Miscreants together, silent in stunned acknowledgement of their new and unspeakable bond, aunt and niece walked rapidly down the alleyway. When Maggie spoke, it was to say, 'The Costarica? Will there be anyone you know?'

'No. Not this time of day.'

The coffeehouse lay in a side street just beyond the vet's office. Glancing at the brass plaque Maggie said nervously, 'Your mother wouldn't come down early – see us?'

'After nine. Got ages yet.' Samantha smoothed her hair, distractedly. As they sat down she began a question, but Maggie frowned a warning until the waitress had moved away. At last, with an impatient wriggle, Samantha began.

'So you're saying it's the two blue stripes that mean yes?'

'Yes, yes, yes. It's in the leaflet. You read it, didn't you?'

'Yes. No. Sort of. My brain must have sort of switched things. I just never thought—'

'You just thought it couldn't be that way round.' Maggie tried to smile, with little success.

'You aren't – I mean, I didn't know—'

'You mean, I'm not married.' Her hand, Maggie saw to her annoyance, was shaking so much that black coffee spilt hot over her fingers and sleeve. She put it down, sharply. Samantha was hurriedly correcting herself, stumbling over the words:

'No, not that. I mean lots of people aren't married, and that's cool, but I just didn't know . . . I didn't think you had a boyfriend. I mean, at the moment.'

'I don't.'

'But how . . . ?'

'Not a virgin birth,' said Maggie. She tried to pick up her cup again, but thought better of it. 'Not a miracle. Miss Mountjoy need not roll out the red carpet for the Second Coming.'

Samantha wriggled unhappily in her chair, although Maggie saw that she, at least, was steady-handed enough to continue sipping her coffee. After a moment's silence the girl spoke again, awkwardly.

'Auntie Maggie.' After the morning's events, the renewal of this childish appellation hung oddly between them. 'I'm really, really sorry, but the thing is I have to be sure. To know what's what.' She took a deep breath. 'And if it's sort of, you know, impossible that it's you that's pregnant, and one of us in that room *was* pregnant . . .' Maggie noticed that her inhibition against saying the word appeared to have evaporated. 'Then it's me, isn't it? So if you tell me it's impossible that you are . . .'

She suddenly looked childlike, as earnest in her supplication as a little girl petitioning for a party frock. Maggie found her hand becoming steadier, and took a draught of black coffee, shuddering a little at its sour, metallic taste.

'No,' she said. 'It isn't you. For one thing, you didn't switch the sticks round. I'd have seen you. And anyway . . .'

She did not know how to put it, but in the past few minutes, like shadows crowding into a solid darkness, a dozen memories, perceptions and doubts had come to her. Her breasts ached as they had never ached; her coffee was each morning less welcome, and at odd times of day in college she had felt passing nausea. Her monthly cycle, never regular, had last manifested itself in mid-Atlantic aboard the *Evangelina*. To none of these things had she paid any attention, for reasons which had always been good enough before. But every arrow pointed the same way, towards the accusing blue stripes.

'Oh, I'm pregnant,' she said. 'And I'm a complete fool not to have suspected it earlier. Therefore you are not pregnant. Rejoice! I would, if it was me. Go, and sin no more, as Mountjoy would say.'

The child struggled not to smile, but her face split at last into a grin. 'Sorry. It's just – oh God, it's like being let off death row.' She finished her cup of coffee and looked round 'I'm starving. Do you mind if I ask for a croissant?'

'Go and get one.' Maggie shivered. 'I need a minute.'

When Samantha returned, Maggie was sitting with her head in her hands, almost as if she were crying. 'Are you . . . ?'

'No. It's just a shock. I have to deal with it. I was counting how long.'

'How long?'

'Has to be three months.' She looked up, and saw the anxious pale face opposite. The girl's tact and worry touched her, and resolutely she said, 'I'll tell you about it. If you want.'

'You don't have to. You've been ace to me, honestly. I don't know what I'd have done. But it's your business.'

'No, we're in it together. And I suppose I'm better off than you would have been. He may have been a one-night stand, but he was a lot nicer than your Duane, and I enjoyed it more than you did. And he was a good man.' She gave a watery smile. 'A dear, good man.'

'Are you in touch? Now?'

'No. He's married with children, thousands of miles away. Like I say, it was a bit of an impulse thing. I don't do it often, hardly ever in fact.' She drummed her fingers on the table. 'But this was a sort of celebration. Home is the sailor, home from the sea. That sort of thing.'

'What was his name?'

'I mainly called him Captain.' Maggie tried to smile. 'But Joaquim – Joaquim Lopez.'

'Are you going to tell him about the baby?'

Maggie frowned. 'I never asked *you* that,' she said. 'And I never said the b-word, either. I wouldn't have rubbed your nose in it like that.'

'Sorry.' An awkward silence. 'What are you going to do, then?'

'I don't know. You'd better get to school. Start over again. Don't worry about me. I'll have to think it over. Do you mind walking up on your own? I might not go to college.'

When Samantha had gone, lighter of step than she had been for weeks, Maggie rose slowly and emerged into the High Street, where once again it was beginning to rain. Sarah, she knew, would still be at home. The impulse to run to her was intense. But first she had to think. She would walk, that was it; she would do her old student walk to the sea, along the verges of the bypass and the bleak dual carriageway.

She would not, she realized as she strode rapidly towards the edge of town, be back in time to go to the bookshop for another afternoon's training with Miss Mountjoy. Leo would wonder where she was. At the thought of Leo a hot, unexpected surge of fury overtook her, and with it came a wave of nausea stronger than any before. The tinny taste of black coffee rose in her throat, making her gag. Leaning on a garden wall, coughing her discomfort, she suddenly felt a weakness in her legs and fought to stop their trembling. Passers-by in cars glanced at her, curious, as she struggled for control of her suddenly unruly body.

'Panic attack,' she said aloud. 'Breathe.' She cupped her hands over her face, but the treachery of her body put her feelings beyond such easy control. She remembered Sarah when she was expecting Samantha. '*Like being hit with a hammer. Or hijacked at gunpoint.*' Oh yes, indeed. She thought of Samantha's artless question – 'Are you going to tell him about the baby?' Baby! What baby? No, impossible.

But then she remembered something else: the child's thin, frightened voice earlier, saying, 'Don't wanna killa baby.

S'wrong,' and how she had honoured Samantha for that, for saying the word 'baby' when she had hardly been able to bring herself to say the word 'pregnant'.

She breathed deeply, leaning on the wall, head back against the safe brick, her knees locked straight in case they should betray her. What did words matter? Action mattered. Action this day! Movement, energy, a journey . . . if she could walk to the sea, stride the beach, clear her head . . .

She would ring the shop when she got to the coast, tell Leo she was held up. Against the driving rain, in her thin, light waterproof and on shaking legs, Maggie Reave walked out of the grey town and took the bleak road to the sea.

'Heaven knows what my sister and my daughter were up to this morning,' said Sarah to Nita Syal. 'They were stumping around the house at crack of dawn, then left a note about watching the sun rise. And look at it.' She gestured towards the window, the leaden sky and weeping rain. 'Sunrise, my foot.'

She was sitting on a high hospital bed, sharing a bunch of white grapes with its occupant. In the last two years the soft-spoken Nita had become her closest female confidante; she was the mother of a twin girl and boy in Teddy's class and a gentle, dark-eyed daughter of fifteen who had stayed in the Guide troop, amassing badges, when Samantha left. Now Nita lay in a side ward at the nursing home, recovering from a hysterectomy.

'Recovering from daily life, too,' she had said lightly when Sarah tiptoed in. 'Truly, it is wonderful to lie in clean sheets, and quietness, with flowers, and no need to cook.' She seemed genuinely happy and comfortable, so the women rapidly exhausted the subject of her operation and moved on to family matters. Nita had always been intensely interested in Maggie and her life.

'It must be an excitement for Samantha, to have a bachelor auntie,' she said wistfully. 'All that my girls ever see within the family is the life of a good Asian wife. Me, my mother, their aunties – all of us running so nicely on the rails and doing our duty.'

'Well, yes. I'm not sure Maggie's exactly a role model,' said Sarah thoughtfully. 'I mean, I don't think I am, either. But it isn't as if Mags was a whizzy professional or a scientist or anything sort of – solid. She does rather doss around the world.'

'But she is free!' said Nita. 'She is not defined by the sons she bears, or by serving a man and a family. She works, her work earns money, and she can spend or keep it according to her own judgement. Or she can give work and money to others, but freely.'

'She does give,' agreed Sarah. 'She's worked on charity projects and social things here and there. But she's not consistent. She doesn't progress things. She helps a bit, or has a bit of fun, and moves on. I'm not sure I'd want any of my children to live the way she does.'

Nita looked at her, her big dark eyes alight with amused intelligence. Sarah thought, not for the first time, that this deceptively submissive housewife was brighter than a great many harder-edged women she had worked with in the old days at Intertech.

'I think,' said Nita, 'that in a few years' time it will not matter how you think your children ought to live.'

Sarah grimaced. 'Suppose not. They'll go their own way. But it frightens me a bit.'

'The important thing is to show them many different ways,' said Nita. 'So they can choose, and not follow rails. I am hopeful for Uma, who is clever and asks the world many questions. But I wish we could arrange for Maggie to meet my Leela and shake her up a bit. My youngest daughter is too fond of taking instructions. I think these Guides and Brownies are very good, but I was a little envious when Samantha left.'

'I was furious,' said Sarah. 'She was really rude to Mrs Turner.'

'But she *chose*,' said Nita. 'She chose her own way. I know Mrs Turner. She is very bossy. Uma argues with her, but Leela likes instructions. I sometimes think she is practising to be a bride bossed around by a good Indian mother-in-law, as I was. I tell you one thing clearly, whatever Ravi says, no daughter of mine will have a husband found for her by family. Or be made to have one at all.'

'You're a bit of a rebel, in your way, aren't you, Nita?' said Sarah admiringly. 'Do you know, I think I'm more suitable to be an Asian wife than you are.'

'So your parents arranged your marriage, hey?'

'N-no,' said Sarah. 'But they approved very much. If Mum had been looking, she'd have chosen Leo. And as soon as he was set to join the family, they seized on him as an instrument of discipline to bring Maggie back under control.'

'No! Tell me.' Their friendship was still fresh enough for each to enjoy exploring new stories from the other's past. Nita had told Sarah about her childhood in Birmingham, her father's shop, her enthusiasm for the wider worlds opened to her at school, and the heart-stopping day when they had informed her that her husband-to-be was arriving from Lahore and that all was agreed between the families. 'But against all sense and modernity,' she would ruefully say, 'we were happy from the start!'

'But you could have been a doctor! Your school thought so.'

'Well, well. Perhaps Uma will be one instead. Or Leela.' They laughed. 'OK, no chance. The child asked Ravi the other day about an arrangement. Imagine! My retro daughter! I should be thankful that Uma is more modern!'

In return Sarah had told about her life: about Intertech, and Samantha's unexpected arrival, the struggle of commuting in the early years and the sheer relief of settling down with the dead-end job and the school run and the family. But she had not told the story of Maggie's escape to the Canadian forest and Leo's pursuit.

'Tell me!' said Nita again, agog and amused, leaning forwards in the bed, wincing slightly, arms round her blanketed knees.

'Well, Maggie was on a field trip, in Iceland. Geography. Geysers and things.' Nita nodded, delighted at the thought of such travels. 'And she was meant to come back to university, but she decided to travel on instead, so she got a job on a tugboat and landed in Newfoundland, and sort of vanished into Canada as cook for a camp of scientists. She sent us teasing postcards.'

'So your parents made Leo this — what did you say? Instrument of family discipline? Oh, very Asian!'

'Well, he offered to go out and persuade her to come back and finish the course. Dad was usually on Mags' side when she ran away as a kid, but he had this superstitious reverence for degrees. Thought it would all be over if she didn't graduate. So Leo went, and found her in the forest. I've often wondered . . .'

'What?'

'What he said to her to make her come back. I think it might have been about Dad being ill. He died, you know. The next year.'

'So was that good, or bad, to tell her?'

'I don't *know*,' said Sarah. 'I just know that when they got back, and for years afterwards, and even now, if I'm honest, there's been something not quite right between them. I'm amazed Leo's having her in the shop, actually. He's desperate for an assistant for Christmas, and he's grateful about the flood thing, but all the same — I dunno.'

'You think, as a good chemist, that they are a dangerous mixture?'

'Yes,' said Sarah. 'Yes, I do. Thank you for helping me put that into words. I do.'

The rain did not stop all morning, as Maggie walked the nine miles to the coast. The wind eased a little, though, and she grew hot; by the time she saw the line of beach huts and bungalows that marked the low, dull seafront, she had taken off her plastic jacket and was letting the rain soak into her sweatshirt to cool her. Her head was clearer now, her step steadier. The old route reminded her of her youthful pacings, and of nights in the tent by a driftwood fire, trying to forget the overheated little house that held her anxious mother and dying father. She had walked away once, she thought, and could walk away again from the cloying, sticky domestic traps that nature and culture laid for women.

Eschewing the track, she clambered over the rain-pocked dunes and stood between two faded beach huts to stare at the ocean. The wind was at her back, and her face was whipped and stung by tendrils of black hair. The last of the rain was passing now, scudding away eastward across the grey North Sea in a distant line of black. She thought of other seas and oceans: Atlantic and Pacific, Tasman and Caribbean, the hot weird waterlane of Panama. From babyhood, it seemed to her, she had known that there was a world out there to be discovered. From childhood she had understood that if she was to see it, taste it, smell and feel its strangeness and its riches, then she must labour to make herself strong and free and resolute. She had struggled, and was still struggling, to be at all costs quite unlike her parents.

Or her sister. Dear Sarah: kind and thoughtful, welcoming and smiling, still with an edge of the old dry wit which reminded her of their father. Poor Sarah, devoting her whole life to the needs and whims of children, and to Leo and his shop. Sarah, who had worked so hard at school, begun a career and a life of her own and then smilingly renounced both when Samantha was born.

Smilingly? Maybe not. Maggie had an idea, from odd things her mother said from time to time, that Sarah had not immediately become a natural mother. And it was Sarah who had spoken of a hammer blow, a hijack. Had she, too, struggled as she was bundled over the threshold of pregnancy? Despite Leo, had the moment of the two-blue-stripes been a horror to her, too?

Yes, a horror. Leaning on the hut's side, staring at the grey waves that broke on the beach before her, Maggie chewed her lower lip, uncomfortable and uncertain as she had rarely been in her adult life. What kind of diabolical ill luck did it take, for Christ's sake, for a woman long accustomed to infertility to be undone by one carefree night with Joe Lopez in an upper room at the Bar Europa?

It was true, she reflected bitterly, that she had not often put to the test the verdict of that snake-faced college doctor in Coventry. All those years ago, on being told by the unsympathetic cow that infertility was the price she paid for having managed a private crisis badly, the young Maggie had responded with characteristic bravado, irritating the woman with a crisp, 'Good. Excellent. Maternity is not my scene.'

Only one man had ever made her waver, and that was Adam. 'Caribbean magic,' he had said when they parted, and added diffidently, 'But it doesn't have to end there, does it?' She had told him that it did, not least because she could never bear him children for his family dynasty. Judging by their meeting two years later on the afterdeck of the *Blue Bayou* at Cape Cod, he was far better off with his preppy little blonde. She had loved Adam the student in his bare chest and frayed shorts on the beach, but she would have been a poor sort of partner for Adam the rising realtor, chatting up the clients in a Ralph Lauren blazer and monogrammed shirt.

There had been a long blank time after Adam, and a long time before him, too; but all the same, she thought now, she had taken enough risks over the years to be pretty certain that Doctor Snake-face was right in what she said. On the night with Joaquim, drinking sour Spanish cider and revelling in the knowledge of an ocean well-crossed, it had never occurred to her to take the slightest precaution. Nor to him, apparently. Ah well, he was a Hispanic and a Catholic, and probably assumed that all foreign Protestant women were on the pill.

She smiled at the blank grey sea, remembering. *Is that an order, Captain? Are you sure?* How flippant, how happy, how heady it had been. A night could only be taken in that spirit if you knew for certain it was the only one there would ever be. Like—

No, not like that. The smile faded on her lips. She turned back, facing the wind; now her hair stopped whipping her and streamed out behind, the roots tingling. She glanced at her watch: two o'clock. She had better go back. Winter darkness would fall at four. She should hitch a ride, perhaps. At the thought, the memory of Samantha swam back into her mind, for one of the few things her sister expressly forbade her to do was to mention hitch-hiking to any of her children as a norm.

'It's hellish dangerous, Mags. You can make your own mind up, and ride around on all the lorries you like when you're abroad. But I will not have you putting the idea into the kids' heads that it's all right. The culture's moved on here. We all have a lot of new terrors.'

Maggie had acquiesced meekly enough, referring in all her traveller's tales to 'a lift from a friend' or 'the local transport'. Samantha, she thought, would be wary of all men and boys for a while now anyway. Just as she herself had been, back in the eighties after the abortion. Thank God the kid didn't have that particular road to tread. Samantha was free again now. Samantha, at fifteen, did not have to make that hardest of choices.

But she did. Again! The physical release of the long walk had eased her anxiety, but now it returned in an overwhelming, choking torrent. She had been managing in the last few minutes to think about the pregnancy as something which had happened, as a stroke of ill luck like having your money stolen or missing a boat – something bad, and burdensome, but safely in the past tense. Now it came home to her with sickening force that the moment of discovery was the smallest part of it. Pregnancy was a continuum, a roller coaster, a conveyor belt leading into the flames. Even during the morning, even as she fled along the familiar route of physical exertion, this thing had been growing within her. On the way back to Brackhampton she would become more pregnant still, and lose another half-day on the way to her decision. She turned her head, hair slapping across her face, as if she were looking for an abortion clinic that could free her here, now, quickly . . .

But as the word came to her, so did memories: of invasion, instruments, masked faces, pain, ignominy, the horror of a certain covered bowl, the glimpse of a barred sluice as she turned her groggy head. She had made a death happen. Long ago, to be sure, and for the very, very best and kindest of reasons. Christ, yes. Better reasons than anybody would ever know. And it was a small death, a debatable death, a socially permitted and legally sanctioned death.

All the same, there were tears on Maggie's face as she turned her back on the sea and began slowly to walk towards the long road home.

Chapter Fourteen

'Where *is* she?' asked Leo, rhetorically. It was not the first time he had said it.

Miss Mountjoy looked up from the shelf she was arranging and said sharply; 'Don't keep *on*, Mr Penn. She's probably delayed. The buses have been dreadful ever since this rail crisis. I can't imagine why. Perhaps some of the drivers arrive by train.'

'Well, it can't go on,' said Leo with a petulant slap of his folder on the table. 'You're leaving us next week, and she did accept the job. It's too bad! Unprofessional!'

Miss Mountjoy indulged herself in a facial expression which, in anybody who was not a perfect lady, might have been interpreted as a sneer. Mr Penn's mood was very fragile at the moment, she thought. The slightest thing set him off grumbling and fretting. He was turning into a bit of an old woman.

When the absurdity of this thought struck her, a moment or two later, the real old woman began to laugh aloud. This annoyed Leo still more, as she was not even working on the Humour shelf. He hated to be mocked. For a while relationships in the bookshop were distinctly strained.

The afternoon wore on, and still Maggie did not appear. Nor was Leo's temper improved when his daughter came in after school, accompanied by Uma Syal, and he saw that both of them had studs in their noses. Uma had always had one, accepted by school and Guides alike as a legitimate part of her commitment to her ethnic roots. Pink and white Anglo-Saxon Samantha, on the other hand, had been specifically banned from any form of body piercing beyond her sleeper earrings. Leo exploded in fatherly rage, which turned to fleeting horror and then to irritation as Sam reached up and casually pulled the gilt stud from the outside of her nose and a magnet from the inside, saying,

'Chill, Dad. It's the temp'ry kind.'

'Well, if you've nothing better to spend your money on—'

'One pound eighty-five for two. Get a *life*, Dad.'

'It's still money.'

'Anyway, sad-Dad, can we have some Christmas catalogues to cut up, for the art club collage?'

He gestured towards Miss Mountjoy, who rose stiffly and led the way to the catalogue drawers at the back of the shop. Even through his irritation and continuing concern about the missing Maggie, Leo dimly noticed that his daughter was more cheerful, and cheekier, than he had seen her for months.

Maggie was cold in her damp clothes, and her legs ached. When she reached the main road to Brackhampton she hesitated, wondering whether to hitch a lift. She had always disliked standing still with her thumb or placard out like some helpless petitioner; she preferred to walk in her chosen direction, only making a casual thumbing gesture when she heard a vehicle approaching from behind. But it was a long time since she had hitched on a fast UK road, and the tight flow of traffic made her realize that she would do better on the grass by the slip road, catching the eyes of drivers before they got up to cruising speed.

A sudden sense of vulnerability made her hesitate. She, who was rarely tired, felt a dragging physical weariness. It was as if the heaviness of late pregnancy were being prefigured, a ghostly bump impeding her. The poise and balance of her body were obscurely disrupted, leaving her listing and awkward. Maggie had, in her travels, experienced a few brushes with real risk but had always maintained a sense that if danger came, her reflexes would be fast and hard and her body fit to respond to the moment with a sharpened ability to hit, twist, jump and dodge. This essential sense of safety had rarely left her, and combined happily with her generally sunny view of the human race. 'Most people in the world would rather have a laugh with you than hurt you,' she would say. 'Unless you hang out anywhere really, really stupid. And even if you do, you're more likely to be scolded by some old lady for being there, and dragged into her house, than attacked.'

But now she felt awkward, unbalanced and vulnerable. The cars that pelted down the bypass wailed on the wet road like demons; the light, feeble all day, was perceptibly dying. She stood for a moment irresolute, arms by her sides, and was startled when a black car, unbidden, pulled into the lay-by beside her. Its electric window hummed open and an elbow emerged, in a white shirt sleeve, followed by part of a man's head.

'Hoy! You OK? Wanting a lift?'

Maggie hesitated, miserably aware as she did so that hesitating was not one of her normal habits. Where had she gone, that clear, determined, happy woman of yesterday? She took a step towards the car to answer the man's offer, still uncertain as to what she would say, but as she approached the open window she suddenly felt an emanation of warm air from the car's heated interior. The dank chill of her clothes made her shiver, and she made up her mind. With a parody of her old cheerful manner, she said, 'Thanks. I wouldn't mind. It's got a bit wet out here. But,' she paused, with all the delicacy of the seasoned favour-taker, 'my clothes are wet. Even if I take off the jacket, I'm worried about your upholstery.'

'Dog blanket,' said the man economically, twisting and

hauling something from the back seat. 'Sit on that. Not that it matters. Company car.'

'Well, if you're sure,' said Maggie.

She went round to the passenger side while the man hummed the window up again and observed, as his guest sat down and kicked her wet jacket into the passenger footwell, 'Bloody freezing. Bollocks off a brass monkey.'

She saw that his suit jacket swung on a hanger inside the back door of the car, in the immemorial fashion of the travelling sales rep. A briefcase lay on the back seat, and a black squat case bearing the logo of a computer firm.

'Brackhampton? Or beyond?' he asked, letting in the clutch and sidling the car out of the lay-by into a gap in the traffic. He accelerated with the fast, sure touch of the professional driver. 'I'm going right on to Maidstone, if it's any help.'

'Only Brackhampton, thanks. Bypass will do,' said Maggie. She looked ahead at the wet road and the red rear lights of the traffic. The man was silent for a moment as he changed up through the gears, but she sensed in the silence that he, like many drivers in her hitch-hiking experience, had picked her up at least partly in the hope of conversation. She would have preferred to be alone and quiet with her dilemma, but the questioning silence defeated her. Wriggling a crease out of the blanket she sat on, she took a safe option.

'You got a dog, then?' she said with all the brightness she could muster.

'Nope,' said the man. 'Wife got the dog. I got the blanket. Christ knows why. Story of my life.'

Hell, thought Maggie, hell and damnation, an embittered divorcee. Still, it was only nine miles. She had once spent eight hours bumping across the Western Desert in the cab of a refrigerated lorry with a driver whose wife had run off with a male nurse in the hospital where she had her baby. A half-Aboriginal male nurse. At times during his peroration she had wondered whether it would not be more agreeable to get out of the lorry and die in blessed silence by the desert roadside.

But this man showed no sign of wanting to pursue the subject, asking instead, 'Where you travelling from, then?'

'Mexico,' said Maggie, thankfully identifying an escape route. She could go onto autopilot with a traveller's tale or two, and that would easily fill the quarter-hour to the Brackhampton bypass.

She began to explain about her journey up through South America, but after a moment he broke in with, 'In Mexico. Go to Cancun?'

'Nope. Tourists, very expensive. Very crowded, too, they say.'

'Good,' said the man, grinning ahead into the darkness. 'The more money flows in there, the better. I was there in February last year. Sold a whole lot of computer peripherals to the biggest American hotel complex. Great business, nothing but the best. I love selling things to Yanks.'

Maggie was momentarily nonplussed, then the man said teasingly, 'See? I tear off my false moustache and stand revealed as the filthy enemy. I'm the capitalist West. I fly in, sell hard, piss off. *Veni, vidi, vici.*'

'Why do you think you're *my* enemy, in particular?' said Maggie. 'How do you know what I think?'

''Cos I've got your number. You're a nice, caring, respectful, cultural traveller, right? Leave only footprints, take only memories, like it says on the Greenpeace T-shirts. Aren't you?'

'Well, I try.' There was, Maggie thought unexpectedly, something oddly enjoyable about having to defend herself. His aggression, in any case, was delivered so lightly that there was no sting in it. 'Yes, I try. I don't think Westerners should impact—'

'Ah, but I do. Memories are no good to people like me. I take contracts, and leave thousands and thousands of inkjet cartridges and office consumables. You are a tourist, and tourism is decadent. I am part of world history. I am a merchant traveller, in the tradition of Marco Polo.'

Maggie smiled, for the first time since early morning. 'Maidstone next stop, was it?' she asked sweetly, and the man turned his head towards her momentarily and laughed aloud.

'Nice one,' he said. 'Yup, you got me bang to rights. I'm grounded now. Gave up most of the travelling job last Christmas. Flying a desk in head office for a spell.'

'Where else did you travel?' Generous now, she wanted to give him back the upper hand.

He began to rattle off names and countries. 'St Petersburg, Moscow, Belgrade before the war, Tokyo, Seattle, Santiago, Brisbane . . .' and she rose excitedly to match him, comparing notes. 'Hellhole, isn't it? . . . Fabulous mountains . . . were you there in summer or winter . . . ?'

As they approached the Brackhampton turn-off, there was a tiny pause in their flow of reminiscence. Impulsively, liking this glib, cheerful man in spite of herself, Maggie offered him a small tribute.

'You know, actually, there is an argument for saying that guys like you are the real travellers now. You're not tourists, you can't be sentimental, you have to get right down into the commercial nitty-gritty of a place.'

'And you have to meet the people,' he said, with a shudder. 'Whether you bloody want to or not. You dippy-hippy back-packers can hang out with shepherds and share weird brews with nomads. Me, I have to go to hideous karaoke nights in Kodo with bonsai chief executives who get rat-arsed on sake and cry all over you. I have to make small talk on balconies with trophy wives while sinister Panamanians in white suits decide whether to give you a quarter-mill contract or shoot you in the kneecap.'

Maggie laughed now, a proper open laugh. 'So you'd rather hang out with the nomads?' she said.

'Probably not,' he conceded. 'If I wanted to get covered in animal turds I'd get a job in the elephant house at London Zoo.'

'I was an elephant keeper once,' said Maggie, before she could stop herself. 'When I was fourteen, I ran away to be one.'

'Excellent,' he said. The car was slowing, close to the Brackhampton sign.

'Here would do,' said Maggie, 'on the hard shoulder. I can walk into town.'

'Ah, bollocks,' said the man, turning left. 'It's still bloody raining. I'll drop you further down. It's all right.' He turned his face to her, glimmering white in the pale neon streetlights, and she saw that he was younger than she had thought. Younger than her, certainly. 'Don't panic. I'm not going to insist on taking you home and then spend the next six months hanging round outside the house committing a public nuisance.'

'I didn't think—'

'Yes, you did. All women do. Very wise, too.'

Silence fell between them once more. When he dropped her at the top of the High Street, in the mournful damp glimmer of early Christmas fairy lights, Maggie got out of the car and leaned into the open door to thank him, suddenly formal. 'Really, really kind of you. Much obliged.'

'I'm called Steve,' he said. 'And I know *your* name.'

She was nonplussed, and began to stammer in confusion.

He grinned. 'The old gag. Gets 'em every time,' he said. 'Vera. Mavis. Rumpelstiltskin. Lorna Doone. Mopsa. Any or all of the above. 'Bye 'bye, Rumpelstiltskin. Hope you get dry soon.'

She watched his red lights vanish, heard his tyres squish down the road. She was halfway up the alley to the Penn house when she remembered that her waterproof jacket was still on the car floor.

Chapter Fifteen

Sarah was all solicitude when Maggie came in, her hair and clothes bearing every mark of having been soaked through and only partially dried. She gesticulated with the kitchen knife across a pile of onions.

'God! You haven't got as wet as that just coming up from the shop, have you? This weather!'

'Well, no,' said Maggie. 'I'm afraid I bunked off college and the shop today. Went for a walk.'

Sarah glanced sharply at her. 'The old walk? To the sea?'

'Yes. No tent, though. See, I'm growing up, gradually.'

'Pacing the cage again, though,' said Sarah, in a sad voice. 'Oh, Mags, I've been having stupid delusions that you might put off China and settle down with us for a bit. I do miss you, you know. When you go away. It takes me weeks to cheer up, every time.'

Maggie looked at her feet, unwontedly abashed. Their affection was rarely made so explicit by either of them. Then she said, 'I wasn't pacing the cage, actually. Not the way you think. I just had something to think through.' It would be a blessing, a mercy, an unutterable relief to tell her sister. Together they could face the horror of it, and she would not be alone. *Sarah, I'm pregnant, I'm three months gone, what in hell's name can I do . . .*

But even as she opened her mouth, an unshared fragment of

their history came between them, so solid that she put up her hand as if to fend it off. With a small gasp she clawed down her pale cheek, and only said, 'So I took a thinking walk. S'good. S'fine.'

'Well, go and have a bath,' said Sarah, turning back to the chopping board. 'You can have a good long soak. The boys are at Scouts, and Sam's doing some art project. She's brought Uma Syal home to help, and I couldn't be more thrilled. Now *there's* a nice girl.'

'You sound like Mum,' said Maggie, trying hard for her normal bantering manner. 'Remember how keen she always was for us to have Nice Girls as friends?'

'Well, I always did. All the keen swots and patrol leaders. You were the one with the dodgy friends.'

'Remember when I brought home Tracey Jones?'

'Do I not! First navel ring ever to cross Mum's threshold. Poor Dad, didn't know where to look.'

'Duh! Pull your vest down, child!'

'He didn't say that, did he?'

'Course not. But you could see that he was dying to.'

'I miss Dad,' said Sarah. 'I still miss him.'

'So do I,' said Maggie.

Upstairs, in the bath, she looked down at her body and immediately the hollow, sick panic returned. How could she not have suspected earlier? Three months! Samantha, hardly more than a child, had been more sophisticated.

Perhaps, she thought sourly, it was because Sam took baths like a good decadent wallowing Westerner, rather than her own swift economical showers. Perhaps having baths made women think more critically and obsessively about what was going on in their central zone. She never gave hers much thought, frankly. Even when she fondly remembered the *Evangelina* and its mournful-eyed captain, her thoughts had always gone to the weeks of slow, beautiful progress across the ocean rather than to that one aberrant night of over-enthusiastic friendship in the Bar Europa.

Now, gazing down at the slight swelling of her belly, Maggie remembered the morning after, when she had woken at Captain Lopez' side and seen him, innocently asleep in his stubble, by the light that filtered through the dusty shutters.

He had stirred, and thrown out an arm. She stroked it briefly, then with infinite stealth slid from the bed and pulled on her clothes. It was early, and the street outside was empty; with her pack on her back she walked to the main road and almost immediately found the cheese lorry, pulled in at the roadside while its driver urinated against the rear wheel.

She supposed that Joaquim Lopez would wake and be disconcerted by her absence, but doubted that he would be surprised. It was only after she had made it utterly clear that she was leaving the ship that they had grown so rapidly, instinctively, lustfully close. Lopez would not, she felt sure, have deluded himself that one intimate encounter would change her mind about leaving. He would have taken it for what it was: a traditional harbour celebration. She grinned, in spite of herself. She could not regret it. He was a dear man, and they had gone through gales together.

Nor would he have thought for one moment about pregnancy. She did not blame him in the slightest. In her experience, men of Latino Catholic cultures never gave a thought to the consequences of affairs with Englishwomen of loose morals: they serenely assumed that the Pill was universal.

And she, with equal serenity, had assumed that the college doctor was right. It had been made perfectly clear to her in 1985 that any girl so stubborn and secretive that she fixed herself an ill-managed, dubiously legal abortion in an unregistered clinic had only herself to blame for infection and permanent infertility. After that time it had been five years before Maggie slept with another man, and then she had done it without precautions, still obscurely angry enough to dare the consequences. There had been none, though. Nor ever again, not even in the six months with Andy. Thenceforth, she took her infertility for granted.

'The ultimate natural contraception,' she said once, in a bout of girl talk in a Missouri hostel. 'Who needs Norplant?'

She breathed in, a deep shuddering breath, and her newly rounded belly broke the surface of the bathwater. She leaned forward and turned on the hot tap to cover it. 'Gin and hot baths,' she said aloud, under her breath, as the water rose. 'And jumping off tables. Hunting used to do it for the Mitford generation, didn't it?'

Her eyes filled with tears. Outside the bathroom she could hear some altercation beginning. Leo's voice rose in petulant complaint.

'. . . never turned up at all. I don't know, we might have made a mistake.' A lower voice, probably Sarah's, shushed him, and she could imagine her pointing at the bathroom door. Leo began to mutter. Then Samantha's door slammed open and her higher voice broke in.

'Are you blaming Auntie Maggie, Dad? 'Cos it's my fault she didn't make it to the bookshop, right? So yell at me, not her.'

Maggie stiffened in horror. Samantha wouldn't betray herself, would she? After all that troubled secrecy, all that relief?

'What do you mean?' asked Leo. 'How can it have anything to do with you? And take that revolting stud out of your nose.'

'I asked her to pick up some stuff for our collage, from the Southwick Art Gallery shop. So she very kindly said she would, because *some* people care about my coursework. It must have made her miss the bus.'

Maggie relaxed into the hot water. The child was a born white-liar, she thought. Do well in the diplomatic service one day. Sarah, of course, knew perfectly well that her sister had not even been in to college. Would she too, collude in deceiving Leo? Better all round if she did. This, presumably, was how families worked.

Maggie hauled herself out of the bath, and padded through to her room to find dry clothes. At supper, when she had made her peace with Leo and promised to be more efficient about the bus, Samantha threw her a troubled, inquiring look under cover of a spirited argument between the boys and their parents.

'OK?' she mouthed. Maggie gave her a slight nod. Aloud, Samantha said, 'I liked walking up the town early with you, Mags. Can we do it tomorrow?'

'Yep,' said Maggie, smiling. 'We might have better luck with the sunrise.'

'Great,' said Samantha. But her troubled eyes continued to rest on her aunt until the family meal was over.

Maggie slept badly that night. After an hour of turning over her situation in her mind, she threw off the bedclothes and went to the window. She never closed her curtains; leaning on the sill, looking out at the intricate roofscape of the little town, she saw that the rain had stopped and the clouds lay broken into pale fragments around a misty moon. They were still moving in some high-altitude wind, and she watched them for a while and thought about the *Evangelina*.

'That's what I love,' she said aloud, noting that this habit of talking audibly to herself would have to be watched. It helped, though; standing up in the cold, hearing the words aloud, gave the thoughts behind them a clarity and reality which they never achieved during the silent, kicking, sweating battles with the duvet. Quietly she said it again. 'That's what I love. The open road, the open sea, the ship, the journey. That's what I love. I wouldn't love a baby, I couldn't. It would choke me. I would hate it for tying me down.'

Her hand, treacherous, moved down to her stomach, and a silent voice inside her said, 'It already has. So what'cha going to do about it? Kill it? Again?'

She opened her mouth to say 'It's not the same' but could not. The light intensified as the moon trailed through between the clouds. But I love what I love, she thought, silently this time. I have to be free. Sarah wanted all this stuff. I don't. I never will.

She went slowly back to bed, and rolled herself in the duvet. The pillow had gone flat, and she punched the feathers hard. She closed her eyes defiantly but the moon, the sky, the memory of the ship pressed in on her, making it impossible to take a solution involving death – even a small, allowable death.

There was a third option, she thought. She could let the creature live, but give it away instantly. New babies for adoption were, so the newspapers said, the scarcest of commodities. She could go away, she thought sleepily, have it somewhere quietly, hand it over and carry on.

Go *away*? The thought jolted her back into wakefulness. Why? Was she ashamed of Sarah and Leo and the children knowing she was pregnant? What hideous hangover from her mother's terrors was this? Nobody got turned out into the snow with a shameful bundle these days. Every kind of woman had babies outside wedlock – stars, politicians, powerful women executives, schoolgirls, sportswomen. Why did she think she had to go away?

Not because of the baby. Obviously not. Where Sarah was concerned, the shame would lie not in the fornication or the pregnancy, but in the adoption. Your first child at nearly thirty-six, and you give it away! You might as well get a T-shirt with SELFISH UNNATURAL BITCH printed across the breast. Whereas if you had an abortion, some would dislike you for it but most would understand and few would know.

But the baby would still be dead.

Maggie curled up into a ball of concentrated fear and self-disgust. After a time of suffering, she slept.

Leo slept badly too. He kept waking, squirming with irritation, aggrieved and full of formless dread. More and more often in the past months he had felt a sense of impending doom, of something just out of sight flapping dark wings. Middle-aged depression, he thought. Existential angst. *Weltschmerz*. Any number of German words. Nothing worth paying attention to. The shop was fine, Sarah as serene and comfortable as ever, the children healthy and, apparently, happy. He was not, he knew, getting enough exercise; the presence in his household of Maggie's rangy, restless energy had borne that truth in upon him. He should walk at weekends, maybe frequent the soupy chlorinated warmth of Southwick Pools.

Next to him Sarah lay, beautiful and calm, fast asleep. He edged towards her, hoping that her serenity would seep into him. But the black wings flapped at the edge of his mind. There was something nearby, something bad and dangerous. Leo shuddered and a single, unmanly tear rolled down his cheek.

Chapter Sixteen

Maggie was woken from a heavy dawn sleep by a soft scratching at the door. She sat up, and saw the door edging open. Samantha, fully dressed, put her head into the room.

'Sorry,' she said. 'Only, if we're to get out before breakfast . . .'

'Right,' said her aunt. She spent a few moments longer than usual finding clothes; yesterday's jeans were still wet through, and the other pair inherited from Sarah were in the wash. She pulled out some white trousers from her pack, unworn since Mexico; they were too summery to be sensible, she thought, but put them on anyway.

They were too tight. Dismay overcame her, and she sat down on the bed with a bump. Her waist size had not changed in twenty years, not until now. The truth of her situation almost overwhelmed her and tears pricked behind her eyes. Eventually she put on a pair of tracksuit bottoms and a sweater, which would just pass muster at college, and grabbed her folder.

'You going to college, then?' asked Sam in a low voice as they crept out of the front door.

'Well, obviously,' said Maggie. 'I've got to get notes on yesterday. It's a very intensive course.'

Samantha digested this information, with all its implications. Still going to China, then, she thought. They walked down the road to the Costarica coffee shop, and settled at their table in the corner.

When Sam's coffee and Maggie's tea had come, the niece said, 'I told Dad it was my fault you didn't come to the shop.'

'I heard. Thanks. Very tactful. For a moment I thought you were going to tell him everything.'

Samantha shuddered and made a sign as if to ward off the evil eye. 'Anyway,' she said, 'I don't want to be nosy, but I was wondering all day whether you were all right. 'Cos I know I wouldn't have been, if it had been me.' She shuddered again. When Maggie remained silent, touched almost to tears, Samantha added, 'But I'm sorry if it's a cheek. You're probably, like, totally sussed about it. It's only 'cos I'm a kid really that I'd panic like that.'

Maggie recovered herself, and gave her a fond, watery smile. 'No, it's sweet of you. And as it happened I'm not sussed. To be honest, I'm floundering. You see, I thought I couldn't have children.' She looked down at her hands, playing with a spoon. 'I was *told*, once, that I couldn't.'

Samantha's eyes widened. A whole romantic understanding came to her: this, of course, was the reason why her aunt stayed on the road! Never settling, never having a home, never becoming like her mum or all the other women. It was like a really sad song, or a novel.

She said, a little breathless, 'Well, gosh, then – are you, like, I mean – thrilled?'

Maggie threw the spoon down with a little clatter which made heads turn at nearby tables. 'No!' she said vehemently. Then in a lower voice, 'And I shouldn't be troubling you with any of it. I wish you didn't know. I don't want the – the thing at all. It's a disaster.'

Samantha looked down at the table, but finding it too blank, neatly and deliberately poured some sugar off her spoon and began to make precise little patterns in it. She did not want to hear what her aunt would say next. Her schoolfriends talked sagely enough about the options confronting girls with un-wanted pregnancies, and it came up often in the weekly, highly popular period of 'Personal and Social Education' (highly popular because, leading to no formal examination, it provided an enjoyable sense of leisure and freedom from consequences. Whether this sense of relaxed laissez-faire was entirely suitable to the subject matter was something which the more thoughtful PSE teachers worried about a lot).

But although in theory Samantha knew all about the law on abortion, the sources of termination advice and the moral rationale of a Woman's Right to Choose, a darker thread of intelligence also reached her. Girls told stories about friends of friends. Pro-life pamphlets circulated, full of horrid pictures of small twisted red arms with miniature hands and threadlike fingers. A girl at Southwick had cut her wrists, unsuccessfully, six months after a termination, and Sarah had shaken her head over the local paper and said, 'It's never as easy as they think, poor lambs. We're not made for it.' Gentle Uma Syal, in rare impassioned moments, inveighed against the wickedness of some Asian men who forced their wives to have amniocentesis and terminate girls merely for the crime of being female.

Samantha, freed herself from having to contemplate the horrid need, felt profoundly unwilling to contemplate the fact that her aunt was clearly about to do it. Yet Maggie had been good to her, had bought the pregnancy tests and not judged her or scolded her, or even asked about contraception and called her a fool. So it was her duty to help, to become an accessory to the unspeakable business.

She summoned up all her chivalry and said, 'D'you need any phone numbers? You wouldn't have to go to our doctor. There're some in the library at school.'

'For terminations, you mean?' Maggie looked at her directly. 'I don't know that I want to do that.'

A great wave of relief swept over Samantha, but she still did not understand.

'You mean you *do* want to have it?'

'I mean, I can't terminate it. When it's born . . .' She shrugged. 'There's other ways. A lot of people want babies to adopt.'

Samantha stared at her in open, childish dismay. Before she could control her tongue she said, 'But suppose it looked like you? Or like Mum, or Gran, or one of the boys? I mean, once it's there, it's family!'

Maggie sighed, and sipped her tea. She made a face; even tea tasted nasty now. She would have to go herbal. It was a relief to talk about it to Samantha, but at the same time she felt achingly guilty that it was not Sarah, her faithful, adult, experienced sister, to whom she was turning. Thinking about this, she said, 'Sam, you won't *ever* tell your mum that you knew first, will you?'

'Cross my heart.' Another pause, more scraping at the sugar pattern on the table, then, 'So you really reckon to have it adopted?'

'Maybe. I've got no money, remember. I don't live anywhere. It wouldn't have a father. I don't know which way up to hold a baby. Kindest thing, don't you think? Someone would give the kid a really good life.'

'Mum might—' began Samantha, but her aunt cut her off with a frown. Maggie had thought about this herself, in the night. After all, the child would only be eleven years younger than Teddy. She could send home money regularly for its keep, like some shamed Victorian chambermaid. It would keep it in the family, and answer the instinctive revulsion which Samantha had voiced at the idea of handing over a small relative to strangers. In one of her troubled half-dreams, the child had been born, a boy with her father's eyes. It had looked at her as it was taken away, and the scene of the dream had changed to Ted's funeral, and to nightmare.

But it could not be considered. Certainly it could not be asked of Sarah. She had given fifteen years of her life to motherhood, and had another decade in front of her if you counted universities, which Maggie vaguely supposed you did. A new baby would double her sentence. Impossible.

Samantha, however, was not giving up.

'She might really, really love it,' she said stubbornly. 'She was joking with Mrs Syal the other day about how broody she gets round Uma's big brother Sanjay's new baby, which I have to say is totally gorgeous, and they were giggling about how appalled Dad looks when she says it—' She stopped, crestfallen. 'Oh, yeah. I see. You think Dad wouldn't want us to keep it, even if Mum did.'

'I think,' said Maggie sadly, 'that it's my responsibility, not theirs.'

'So when are you going to tell them?'

'Before the bump does, I suppose.'

'Well, whatever Dad says,' concluded Samantha, 'once it's born, I reckon you'll have a struggle to stop Mum wanting to keep it. Unless you keep it yourself.' She stood up, took the empty cups to the counter and came back with a cloth to clear up the mess she had made with the sugar.

Maggie watched her. The kid was, she thought, slightly enjoying the situation now. Well, so might she have done at fifteen. The young Sarah certainly would have. Adult confidence, an exclusive ringside seat at an adult soap opera, a host of equally dramatic possibilities stretching before you – pure fun, really.

She grimaced, stretched and got to her feet. *A struggle to stop Mum wanting to keep it, if you don't* . . . It might be, she thought. It might be a struggle to stop Sarah from making Leo angry and resentful, from endangering her marriage and her family. *Once it's born* . . . Well, it didn't have to be born, did it? Three months, perfectly legal.

But she did not want to choose between killing an unborn child and torpedoing her sister's happiness. Not again.

Unless you keep it yourself. And be a single mother, broke and grounded, slowed to baby pace and enslaved into decades of living vicariously, always a step back from life?

With an effort, she wrenched her mind away from all three horrible possibilities. She must send Samantha off to school with some sense of normality.

'You'd better go. What have you got on first today?' she asked with an air of idle interest.

'History. Drama project work, on exploration. Me and Uma have got to do a duologue about Marco Polo.'

Maggie smiled, a real smile this time, transforming her drawn face. 'Oh, I know about him,' she said. 'He sells a lot of inkjet cartridges to the Mexicans.'

'She's crazy, my aunt,' said Samantha to Uma later. 'But she's cool.'

At playtime, Teddy was in the gym as usual, surrounded by a gratifyingly large ring of admirers. Crouched down, resting his palm on the ground, he was demonstrating how he could twist his hand round three hundred and sixty degrees without breaking his wrist. It was one of Maggie's street-magic tricks, which she had learned during half a year as cook on a Mississippi towboat. The boys were entranced.

'Ugh, gross!'

'It's gonna break, euuugh!'

Adrian, though, leaned forward and said, 'You sort of flipped your wrist. You did. When you were trying to make us not look.'

Teddy stood up, grinning. 'I gotta practise,' he said. 'Tomorrow, I'm gonna push a ciggie through a one pound coin.'

'A fake coin!'

'A fake ciggie!'

'Nope. Both real.'

'I'll bring the coin, then,' said Jimmie Brind.

'I'll bring the cigs,' said Adrian.

'You'll get suspended,' said Joanne, who had eased her way into the group as usual.

'Shut-uuurp! Only if some *girlie* tells on us.'

'He learnt all those tricks from a *girlie*, so there,' said Joanne. 'Little boys don't know anything unless *women* show them.'

The resulting fracas was broken up, mercifully, by the school bell.

Meek and punctual, Maggie turned up at the bookshop that afternoon and worked steadily, unpacking Christmas stock and reorganizing the shelves and the big square table near the door where the most popular gift books were temptingly placed. Leo was busy with the insurance loss adjuster, displaying soggy boxes and crinkled Queen Mother books in a corner of the children's library. Miss Mountjoy, seeing that Maggie was competent enough on her own, slipped off down the road early to help her sick friend Louise choose an electric wheelchair. Maggie stacked books neatly, propping up a copy of each on top of the stack in a metal holder, but showing little interest in the contents. She arranged gardening, cooking and decorating books, books on how to be vibrant on carrot juice, identify valuable antiques, draw up your family tree, and be fit, fabulous and fifty. She yawned, sleepy in the warm little shop, but worked on steadily until the table was finished. At last Leo came down from the children's section and saw off the insurance man with great cordiality. Turning to Maggie, who had moved over to the desk and begun ticking off stock, he said, 'He was amazed by how little we lost. We've got great Brownie points there, I shall probably be invited to the loss adjusters' annual dinner-dance at this rate. It's all down to you, you know. You saved our bacon that night.'

'The insurance would have paid,' said Maggie, dismissing the compliment.

'They'd have paid wholesale value. Any loss-of-profit payment would just be based on an ordinary month. I know a lot of shops that got flooded are finding that they can't replace lost stock before Christmas, so they're going to lose the peak trade of the year. Honestly, Maggie, if I'd lost my Christmas profit we might have been in quite a lot of trouble.'

The door pinged, and two women, one large and one small, bustled in with capacious shopping bags that meant business. Leo looked at them, then at Maggie.

'You OK to serve on your own?'

'Yes, of course.'

He went back up the steps and watched unobtrusively from behind a pile of Harry Potter books.

Maggie smiled at the women. 'Can I help you, or are you just browsing?'

The larger, more commanding of the women beamed back at her, and pulled from her handbag a Sunday newspaper review page with some red circles on it. Maggie took it and made an encouraging remark about the selection; together, with the small pale woman trailing astern, they went over to the Biography shelf.

You would think, thought Leo contentedly, that she had been a bookshop assistant all her life.

Chapter Seventeen

It was, in the event, hardly more than a week before the rest of the Penns heard about Maggie's condition. Samantha hated keeping secrets but drew on all her reserves of heroic discretion, only sometimes darting anguished glances at her aunt when related subjects came up during family supper.

'Adrian's sister's up the duff,' announced Teddy one night, through a mouthful of spaghetti. 'She's at Southwick College but she's going to keep the baby, only her boyfriend doesn't want to pay for it, Adrian says.'

Jamie squirmed on his chair, darting his brother an irritable glance. With his newly gruff voice and growing awkwardness around girls, he found such subjects unfit for mealtimes. Leo would normally have been inclined to agree but was too engrossed in his catalogue of spring books to bother.

Sarah, on the other hand, had read a great many articles about the importance of taking natural opportunities to discuss sex and procreation in an open manner with your growing children. She plunged in now with enthusiasm – starting, as per instructions, with a question.

'Well, what do you all think?' she said. 'It's a terribly difficult decision for a girl to make.'

Jamie stared at his plate and twirled spaghetti.

Teddy, always ready with an opinion, said, 'I think she ought to have the baby born, and give it to one those test-tube ladies that have to have babies grown in a bottle. 'Cos that's really expensive, innit? And Suzy's baby's, like, free.'

'It's very *hard* to give away your own child,' said Sarah. 'I wouldn't have wanted to give any of you away.' She smiled fondly. Reinforce their own sense of being secure and wanted, the books said. Teddy betrayed his loss of interest with a yawn, and Jamie concentrated fiercely on his food. Sarah turned to Samantha – who, after all, was the one most likely in the future (God forbid!) to face such a choice. Brightly she asked, 'What do you think, Sam? Do you suppose it's best to struggle with a baby on your own when you're not ready for it, or have it adopted, or – well, the other thing.'

Samantha could bear it no longer. 'Don't say "the other thing" as if it was a piece of poo!' she snarled. 'Termination. Some people have terminations, Mum. Live with it. Move on.'

Sarah stared in astonishment. They had never actually discussed the subject, that she could remember; she was not aware of being particularly mealy-mouthed. As the emotional temperature in the room rose, she noticed through the corner of her eye Leo starting to glance up from his catalogue and pay attention. It was true that she had not wanted to use the ugly word 'abortion', and had genuinely forgotten the euphemism for a moment. Why was Samantha so savage all of a sudden? Surely . . .

A horrid suspicion came over her. Duane was not a nice boy or a responsible one, not at all. Samantha had been morose of late.

No, surely not. A veil seemed to fall over Sarah's eyes, blurring the room; her stomach sank with unfamiliar terror. She blinked, then looked closely at her daughter. But Sam, unaccountably, was looking at Maggie. Maggie's lips were pressed together, and her habitual slight smile was absent, but she did not look upset. Determined, rather, as if she were contemplating a difficult decision.

'Mum,' said Jamie, 'can I go out? I said I'd go down to the Scout Room.'

'You're not *in* the scouts,' said Sarah, surprised.

'No, but there's a meeting. About some stuff. Helping the Sally Army, Christmas stuff, collecting toys and cleaning them up an' that.'

'Oh, I remember! That's nice, I thought you weren't going to do it.'

'He is now,' said Teddy, 'because Toyah Robinson's going to do it.' He snickered. 'Fancies her.'

'Piss off, moron,' said his brother angrily. 'So I'm going, right?'

'Can I come?' said Teddy.

'No. It's Year Nine and upward. Not stupid, pant-wetting babies.'

'Teddy, you've got homework,' said Sarah swiftly, to head off aggression. Or, at least, to direct it safely towards herself. 'Go upstairs *now*, and get on with it, and let your brother get on with his evening.'

Teddy dragged his feet out of the room, sniffing as irritatingly as he knew how, but once out of sight he accelerated to thunder noisily up the stairs. Jamie selected an anorak from the lobby and slipped out through the kitchen door.

Leo put down his catalogue. 'I dunno,' he said to nobody in particular. 'Do you reckon Jeffrey Archer's finished now? I suppose the market—'

Maggie cut across him. 'Leo. Sarah. Sam. While we grown-ups are together, there's something I have to tell you all.'

Samantha sat stock still, nervous. Inclusion in the circle of 'we grown-ups' was not, at this moment, a welcome promotion.

Maggie shot her a tiny smile of reassurance. 'And what I have to say may come as a bit of a shock. Certainly did to me.'

She had their full attention, and did not draw out her narrative.

'I'm pregnant. Just over three months. And no, nobody in

England, nobody I can contact. And I wouldn't want to. This is a solo expedition, I'm afraid.'

Sarah's mouth hung open, foolishly. 'Darling, are you all right?' It was the wrong question, but rightly intended.

Maggie put a hand on her arm, fondly. 'Yes,' she said. 'I am now. It was a shock at first.'

Leo was silent, stunned. This was out of context, and he liked context. Maggie and pregnancy did not go together. It was Sarah who had babies. Maggie had rucksacks instead. He needed a drink. The wine box was nearly empty, but he reached for it and began to concentrate very hard on getting out the last drop, tipping and squeezing and pumping the little plastic tap. Samantha, too, was silent.

'What are you going to do?' asked Sarah. 'Have you decided? Three months . . .'

'I'm not going to have an abortion,' said Maggie. 'That's now definite.'

There was a discernible relaxation of muscles around the table. Maggie thought with brief bitterness that this was clearly the deal: if you had an abortion you were private about it, kept all the sadness and sordidness to yourself and did not burden your family with vicarious guilt. They had suspected that she was going to announce her fell intent and force them to know about it, and now they were pleased at being let off. She, however, was sentenced to carry on down this grotesque roller coaster, all the way to childbirth and what lay beyond.

'Do you have plans?' asked Leo and Sarah together.

Maggie avoided Leo's eye and answered her sister. 'I've been thinking about how to play it. Obviously. And, obviously, I can't bring it up.'

'Why not?' It was torn from Sarah. 'You could, you're perfectly – I mean, I never expected Sam so early, but it was bliss, truly. Anyone can—'

'Not me,' said Maggie sadly. 'I really can't do it. I don't want to, I don't know how to, I never meant to. One might as well be honest. I'm no more fit to be a mother than all those fallen fourteen-year-olds Mum used to go on and on about.'

Samantha began to jab the tabletop viciously with her fork. Sarah, normally protective of her scrubbed pine, ignored her.

'So you're thinking of – ummm – adoption, then?'

'Probably.'

'But it's so difficult – I mean, for a new mother. Let's talk about it . . .' Sarah was floundering. What she meant was, 'Let's talk about it without Leo in the room.'

Leo, however, had every air of being thoroughly engaged and involved in the conversation. Sarah's last words had irritated him. He felt unreasonably needled and sidelined by the cavalier assumption that only women had feelings for new babies. It stirred half-buried memories of his own struggle with Sarah and Samantha.

'It's not just difficult for a new mother,' he said. 'I think a father has some right to know if his child is to be given away to strangers.' As he said it, he heard the words fall on the warm kitchen air and knew that they were unforgivable.

Maggie looked directly at him for the first time since she had delivered her news.

She never knew, in all the after years, why at this precise moment she chose to destroy at a blow a safe and ancient structure of decorative falsehood. Why do it? Malice, pique, hormones?

She never understood. It was not planned. When she had first spoken, only moments earlier, she had not thought of herself as being unstable or hysterical. She was convinced that she was back in control of her own life after long days and nights of working out what would produce the best result for all the wide family. She had concluded that the child must be adopted, and had made the first tentative inquiries in Southwick. Soon she was going to sign on with a doctor, and had steeled herself to endure the horrible months of bloating and slackening. She would give birth under anaesthetic, sign every necessary paper renouncing the baby, and leave for China to forget it.

Meanwhile she needed shelter for a while with Leo and Sarah, but was planning financially how she could spend the last two months elsewhere, to avoid distressing her sister with the sight of a fruitless pregnancy. Her plan was not ideal; she dimly saw that there would be more than one kind of pain involved. But she had made her map of the future with care, and reason, and concern to cause the least violence and suffering all round. It was a tough plan but she was dully, staunchly proud of having made it.

And now Leo, patriarchal and pompous, looking every year of his age, had the nerve to lecture her on fathers' rights – her, whose body was suffering and stretching and aching, her who wept at nights alone, a bound, trussed captive of biology. '*I think a father has some right to know if his child is being given away to strangers.*'

Ignorant, bloody, snotty bastard! As if poor Lopez would even want to know, him with his good Catholic wife back home in Chile! The unforgivable words hung on the air, and before Sarah could intervene with some soothing protest, Maggie said in a hard, shaking voice, 'Yes. I'm sure a man worries about these things. Dreadful people, strangers. I knew you wouldn't like that sort of thing, Leo. That's why I got rid of your baby instead.'

Chapter Eighteen

Three pairs of eyes stared at Maggie. Leo spoke first.

'What do you mean?'

'I got rid of it. Your baby. After Boston.'

Samantha knew the story. From early childhood she had been told, as part of family lore, how poor Daddy was sent out to persuade Auntie Maggie to come back to college and not to live in the woods, and how he had to walk through a forest which might have bears in. He had had the wrong kind of shoes, and got bitten by mosquitoes, and found her at a log cabin. It was part of the Maggie legend, an early precursor of all the delightful and treasurable ways in which she would disrupt the dullness of family life over the decades.

She understood immediately. White, shocked, the girl stumbled to her feet. Her chair scraped on the tiled floor; it was a sound which none of the four people round the table could hear in comfort for several years. She was staring at her father, and in his face she read, through the naked shock of it, the truth.

'You bastard! You bloody – you didn't –' Tears overcame her. She did not have to wait for his answer. It was there in Maggie's white impassive face. 'You did! You got her pregnant! You were engaged to *Mum!*'

Sarah put out a restraining hand towards her daughter, an instinctive gesture of protection which made Samantha's tears run even faster. In a flash she had realized many things; absurdly, some of the hurt came from knowing that she was not, after all, her father's firstborn. She flinched away from her mother, unable to bear contact with anybody so grievously betrayed. Small relief came from turning on her aunt.

'And how *could* you? You slept with Dad and then you killed his baby. You killed my big brother!' Confusion overcame her. It could have been a sister, she knew that, but she had often dreamed when she was small of having a big brother like Uma had. Perhaps the dream had come because somewhere, inside her, she *knew*. Perhaps you were sort of programmed to know if a brother or sister was missing . . .

She heard whimpering, fast breathing, a cry in the room, and did not know it was her own.

'Sammy,' said Sarah in an odd voice. 'Sammy, I think the three of us need to talk about this quietly, by ourselves. Sweetheart, don't cry. Shall I take you up to bed?' She talked as if the tall young woman was a baby. 'Shall Mummy tuck you up?'

'Ess!' said Samantha, running a sleeve across her nose. ''S'please.'

Sarah turned to her husband and her sister. 'Don't move,' she said. 'Don't move, either of you. Maggie, don't go out. I'm asking you. Five minutes.'

Upstairs, she helped Samantha out of her clothes as if she were five, not fifteen, handed her a nightshirt and in silence pulled back the bedclothes. Samantha slid in, still shaking. Sarah bent and kissed her forehead.

'I'll be back later,' she said. 'Good girl. Sweetheart. Breathe deep. Read your book. Forget it for a while.'

Samantha clung to her for a few moments, then fell back on the pillow. Her thumb stole to her mouth, as it had not done for years. Sarah kissed her again. On her way downstairs she looked in on Teddy and said quite brightly, 'How's it going?'

'Nearly finished. Mum, can I watch *The Vicar of Dibley*?'

'Yes. Use Jamie's television, lie on his bed, he'll be out for another hour at least.'

Teddy grinned. Telly-on-a-bed was a luxury not permitted to under-thirteens in the Penn household. He gave his mother a bear hug. All in all, it was nearly ten minutes before she rejoined the adults in the kitchen.

Leo could get nothing more out of the wine box. He threw it on the floor after trying, and glared across at his sister-in-law, who sat pale and still, elbows on the table, her face framed between thin hands.

'What the hell did you mean by that?' he asked, his voice brittle with anger. 'What baby?'

'I was pregnant. After Boston.'

'And you say it was mine? I mean, it's not as if we—'

Maggie slapped her palms down on the table and sat upright, glaring at him. It unnerved Leo sometimes, the way this lean, feral creature looked so like his plump and gentle wife.

'Of course it was bloody well yours! And yes, with extra bad luck it does only take one time to do it. Think of Tess of the D'Urbervilles, Mr Bookseller! How dare you ask whether it was yours! What do you think I am, some kind of slapper?'

'Well, why didn't you tell me?'

'At the wedding, perhaps?'

'You could have said something!'

'And you'd have said what, exactly? "Oh yes, go on, have the baby, Sarah'll be thrilled to have a nephew or niece, especially if it's her husband's child too, keeps it in the family"? Grow up, Leo. You'd have wanted me to do exactly what I did do. And I did you and Sarah a favour by not telling you.'

Leo was silent. Next to the horror of the present moment, he weighed the alternative, hypothetical horror of having Sarah told this thing before their wedding. Maggie was right. Yes, it probably had been best for her to neutralize their terrible, culpable mistake in the swiftest possible way, however brutal. And yes, she was probably right not to tell him. In that moment, with a sick feeling in his stomach, he acknowledged his own weakness. He would not have coped as well as she had with the knowledge of what they had done. Perhaps women were stronger in that way.

They heard Sarah's footsteps upstairs, and the soft closing of Samantha's door. It reminded both of them of the present moment, and what Sarah knew. They stared at one another, appalled.

'Why now?' said Leo, his voice cracking. 'I can see that you were right. Yes, you were. But why'd you do this to Sarah?'

Maggie dropped her eyes, and rubbed her forehead again in a gesture so like her sister's that the husband could hardly bear to look at her.

'I don't know,' she said miserably. 'Bloody hormones. And you being so pompous and snotty about fathers' rights.'

'But I didn't *know!*' Leo almost howled it. 'I had no idea, no idea. You don't think of a stupid one-night stand as being—'

'As being full of eternal consequences? No,' said Maggie sadly, 'I suppose men don't think that. And I suppose I always thought more like a man than a woman myself. Which is probably why I'm pregnant now.'

'Oh Christ. That,' said Leo, who had forgotten how this all began. He looked around wildly for the wine box, then saw it on the floor and aimed a kick at it. It skittered easily in its disappointing lightness and came to rest against the fridge door. 'Yes. Well. That's another thing.'

'The main thing,' said Maggie, hearing Teddy's door shut, in turn, and the footsteps moving towards the stairs, 'is what to say to Sarah.'

Leo hunched in his chair. 'Well . . . the truth,' he said.

'The truth,' said Maggie. And with a flash of her old spirit, 'I'll drink to that.' To Leo's irritated envy, she still had quite a lot of wine in her glass. She raised it and gulped it down. 'To the truth.'

The door opened and Sarah came in, quiet and composed. She had been working on her composure all the way down the stairs, and had indeed stopped in the hallway and practised the old deep-breathing tricks remembered from childbirth. *In . . . one, two, three . . . out, one, two, three, four . . . in . . . and out . . .* It reminded her of Samantha's coming, and her mixed feelings about the pain, and the worry and the first wailing weeks of infancy. It reminded her of Leo's devotion to the baby and his banishing of Nancy's interference. She remembered Jamie's more joyful birth, and Teddy's, when she had been so expert that she was almost absent-minded, staying at home tidying rooms and cooking until labour was well advanced, and ticking off home tasks in her head even as she gave the baby his first feed. *In . . . one, two, three . . . out, one, two, three, four . . . in . . . and out . . .*

She stepped into the kitchen remembering these things, and almost laughed aloud at the sight of the guilty pair, sitting as far away from one another as possible across the table, looking terrified at the sight of her. Nobody, not even her children at their naughtiest, had ever presented such a scared visage to Sarah Penn. She had a fleeting instinct to reassure them. It passed.

She sat down, and looked first at Leo.

'OK. Now you tell me. What was it? How long did it go on for?'

'Once. Just a stupid, stupid . . .' Leo could not go on. 'I've only ever loved you, since we first met. I don't know what happened.'

His sheepish, pleading face was new to her. Unaccustomed to this sort of power, Sarah found to her horror that she quite liked it. The pain, she suspected, would kick in later. Harshly she said, 'Well, I suppose I can work out what happened. Since it resulted in my sister –' Maggie flinched. Could Sarah not say her name, even? '– getting pregnant and needing the services of an abortionist, I can make a pretty good guess about what happened.'

'I mean I don't know why I was so stupid and vile,' said Leo.

'I was shaken up, we both were, it was a long way from home, nothing felt real.'

'That's true,' said Maggie. 'And I was upset. He'd told me about Dad, how ill he was. And the plane got delayed and we had to stay over at an airport hotel. It was all just a muddle.'

'So he put a brotherly arm round you, and you carried on from there, huh?' said Sarah. 'And you never thought to mention it when the two of you got back home. Do you think I'm stupid? Were you at it for very long? Or did you stop after the wedding? Just so I know, you understand. Just so I get the picture.'

'No!' They almost shouted it, together. From Leo, 'Once, I swear it. And we felt terrible, terrible . . .'

'Terrible,' said Maggie. 'So we said to each other that we'd scrub it out, never remember it, never talk about it. We said that it just didn't happen.'

'But then you found you were pregnant? And that it was Leo's?'

'I didn't have anybody else it could be. You know how I was about men, you know how I am. I was determined not to get tied down. Leo was the only possibility. But I never, ever told him. He never knew anything.'

'And you just did it, just like that? Aborted it?'

'It was hard to get the two doctors. I took some short cuts. It had to be done quickly, because I was coming home every week to see Dad.'

'It was illegal, then?'

'Sort of.'

Sarah was silent. Waves of outrage kept rising in her, and then subsiding to reveal to her that she still loved her little sister. Leo was another matter, one she did not yet dare think about. Unwillingly she muttered. 'Were you all right? It didn't harm you? The termination?'

'I got an infection. They reckoned I was infertile. That suited me fine. As you know.'

'And now you're pregnant again. Bit of a coincidence.' The

rage was rising once more, and she wanted to lash out and do harm. 'I don't suppose by any chance it's the same father. One-take Charlie, Mr Miracle Sperm here?'

Maggie and Leo stared at her aghast. 'Ker-rist!' said Maggie, her voice running up an octave at the end, so that she sounded almost Australian. 'Jeezus Christ Almighty, I hope you're joking!'

Leo was looking at her with wide, spaniel eyes, too shocked to speak. Sarah felt suddenly weary, remembering Samantha shivering upstairs, Jamie needing to be seen back home safely, and Teddy who must be chased to bed after his programme.

'Yes,' she said wearily, 'I was joking. God knows why. Leo, I've got to get Sam and Ted settled. Then I'm going to bed. You stay up and make sure Jamie's back from the Scout Room by ten. Maggie . . .'

Her practicality deserted her. There was nothing she could say to Maggie now. She shrugged, and left the room.

Chapter Nineteen

For Maggie, there was no question of going to her room. She was too dangerous a substance, too toxic an influence to remain under the same roof as these people she had so grievously harmed. When Sarah left the kitchen she got up from the table, went into the lobby and pulled on an old waxed jacket. It was one of a collection, belonging to nobody in particular, which she had adopted since losing her own. It had a rip across the sleeve, which let in water. Leo still sat, motionless, at the table.

'I'm going for a walk,' she said in a flat, expressionless voice. 'I've got my key.'

'Fine,' he said.

She walked out into the drizzle, glanced at her watch and saw to her amazement that it was still only nine o'clock. The rapid walking and the night air began to revive her, cutting through the stupefaction of the scene in the warm kitchen. With only one sentence, a sentence she need never have uttered, she had brought the whole security of a family crashing down in ruins. She could not bear to think about Samantha. She could not begin to let herself envisage the grief and confusion of the two boys if their parents were sundered because of this moment of mad wickedness. It seemed to her that this would surely happen; such a long and ancient lie must carry additional destructive power, smelling ever worse as the years went by. It was the dead python in the wall, the unsuspected festering foulness that flopped out hideously into the room and could not be ignored.

She had done this to them, by coming home. After carrying her private and unwholesome burden alone for years until she hardly noticed it any more, she had brought it home and cast it stinking and dangerous at the feet of this kind, steady, dutiful, secretless family. She should never have stayed more than a fortnight, never allowed herself to grow so close and unguarded. She should have kept away from Leo, kept him at the usual teasing distance which had served them well enough for sixteen years. She should have moved on, because moving on was what she did best.

It was what she had to do now; as soon as she was confident that Sarah truly believed in the absurdity and unimportance of those short hours with Leo in the blank airport hotel. She had sworn at him, she remembered, straight after it was over.

'*Sod* you, you stupid bugger! What have we done? You ought to have known better, you're older than me.' And so he was, she told herself angrily: thirty-five to her twenty. And he was in a kind of authority over her during those days: he was the envoy sent by a trusting sister to persuade her home from the freedom of the forest.

He knew perfectly well that he was in the wrong. When she shouted at him he had been meek, appalled by his own behaviour. Maggie had dressed and gone back to her own room, and lain sleepless till the early morning flight. Leo, on the other hand, had slept so heavily that she had to hammer on his door to wake him. On the way to the plane she had railed at him again, woken to a new rage by his determination to pretend that nothing had happened.

She must leave town, very soon. She walked swiftly down the High Street, intending to go out into the darkness of the park and seek comfort from the river. After a few steps, though, she saw the warm lights of the Costarica cafe. A few shops were open late for Christmas shopping and the cafe had risen to the challenge. 'OPEN STRICTLY TO 9.45 ONLY, TILL 22 DECEMBER.' Even through her distress Maggie smiled at Brackhampton's grudging version of nightlife.

Her legs ached unwontedly, and a phantom pain darted around her lower back. More than that, she found herself longing for casual, uninvolved human contact: for the breath of others misting the window with hers and the silently potent comfort of strangers. She glanced in: there was nobody she recognized from Sarah and Leo's circle. Well, obviously not; they would all be indoors with their families, discussing whether to put up the Christmas decorations yet.

She pushed the heavy glass door and went in; the waitress motioned her to a table in the corner. On her way to it, however, she was stopped by a familiar voice.

'Rumpelstiltskin! Mavis! Minerva-Louise!'

She looked down. The man from the car was sitting at a table alone, his back to the wall on a velveteen bench, with a newspaper and the wreckage of a chicken Kiev spread before him. 'Boudicca! Esmeralda! Remember me, Marco Polo from Maidstone? I've got your coat here. Look!' He pulled her rain jacket from the bench beside him. 'See? All yours.'

Maggie took it, wonderingly. 'Oh, that is kind. How did you . . .?'

'I have to get my supper somewhere, on my way from here to there. So whenever it makes sense, each evening I come and have it here, with the coat beside me like a faithful dog. See? Persistence pays off in the end. All the world flows through the Brackhampton Costarica.'

'That's extraordinarily kind. This one leaks,' said Maggie, showing him the torn sleeve. 'I have to remember to roll up the sleeve of my sweater underneath, or it trails around like a wet rag all day.'

'Do you suppose it'll ever stop raining?' asked the man. He kicked the chair opposite him so that it scraped back, inviting her to sit down. 'Go on, join me. Humour me. I can amuse myself guessing your name for the next half-hour.'

'Maggie,' she said firmly. 'Margaret Minerva Louise Reave.'

His light, wild eyes widened, and a grin of pure delight spread across his face.

'You mean I was right about Minerva-Louise? Wowwwww!'

She allowed him his moment of satisfaction, then said tiredly, 'No. I lied.'

'Well, thank you. It was a quality moment. You lie beautifully. Coffee?'

'I can't. I'm—' She nearly said 'pregnant,' so great was the relief of talking once more to somebody wholly disengaged from her life. 'I'm off it at the moment.'

His eyes appraised her with a new sharpness. 'Yes,' he said. 'My ex-wife went right off it, I remember. It was the first sign.'

Maggie felt invaded, but the chair was comfortable and his face was, she thought, not unkind. She sighed, and said resignedly, 'That obvious, is it?'

'You could say I'm sensitised to it,' he said. 'Anyway, my name is Stephen Arundel. A noble old name, you might say, except that it came to me by way of a grandfather in County Cork. In Ireland, Arundel is a name you find on small flyblown bars, not medieval tombs.'

He ordered herbal tea for her, and they talked, calmingly, of Ireland and the Hebrides and Brittany and Asturias, and the curious similarities between the western fringes of Europe. They compared notes on the lilting music of Ushant and Nova Scotia, the world migration of the bagpipes, and the politics of the Boston Irish. He knew more about western Britain and the near Continent, she about eastern America. The travel talk was balm to her.

After a while he asked, 'Where are you off to next?'

She was grateful for his assumption that she was, despite the pregnancy, off on her travels again.

'China,' she said. 'I want to get into Hunan Province. I was going for the borders, but I think not quite yet.'

'Language?' he asked. 'Speak much?'

'I'm doing a course at Southwick. It's not bad.' She looked at her watch and saw that it was ten to ten. They were alone in the cafe now, and the waitress was clearing the tables in a huffy manner. 'We'd better get out.'

'Bugger,' said Steve. 'Don't you just hate middle England, the way everything bloody shuts just as you're settling down?'

'People go home,' said Maggie. The edge of bitterness in her tone was not lost on him, she saw, and regretted letting it show. For all his jokey glibness, this man had efficient antennae.

But he said nothing, merely paying at the counter and turning back towards her with an easy grin.

'Would you,' he asked, 'tell me something?'

'Probably,' said Maggie. 'Come on outside though. She's hating us.' And indeed the waitress was wiping tables now with sharp, vicious strokes, glancing at them meaningly. 'I've done that job,' Maggie said in a low voice as they pushed the door open. 'I know how much you detest the customers who hang around.'

The damp air struck them as they left the fuggy, warm-lit room. The coloured Christmas bulbs, which had spread further along the street each recent day, only gave it an air of dank desperation. Three boys lounged outside the Wimpy, but otherwise the street was empty. Steve Arundel turned to face her and for the first time she saw his height: six foot four or five, he cast a long, gangling shadow under the streetlight. Noticing her reaction, he stepped smartly off the pavement into the gutter, and became at once a more manageable size. 'Sorry,' he said. 'Sorry to loom.'

'You wanted to ask me something,' said Maggie, as much from politeness as curiosity. He had, after all, paid for her herb tea.

'Yes.' He hesitated, weighing her up, an almost crafty look coming over his thin, constantly amused face. 'You won't hit me, though, will you?'

'No,' said Maggie resignedly. Oh God, a proposition. All she needed.

'All it is,' said Steve, 'is to ask you whether this, er, expectant state of which you speak – or rather of which you don't speak—'

'My pregnancy,' said Maggie flatly. 'Nearly four months now. What about it?'

'Well,' he said, 'whoever it is that the condition, er, emanates from . . .' He squirmed, polishing a shoe on the back of his trouser leg like a schoolboy; it was deliberately arch and theatrical. Maggie watched him, silent, amused despite herself.

'This guy,' he said. 'Is he by any chance a) local, b) bigger than me, and c) of an aggressive and territorial temperament?'

Maggie smiled, and ticked off points on her fingers. 'No, no, and no. Well, he may be territorial, but his territory is in Chile.'

'So he could be back any minute? Chile doesn't seem very far away to me. Not if he's a knife-throwing psychopath. I would prefer Antarctica.'

'No,' said Maggie. 'He is out of the frame, and far in the past.' Suddenly an image of *Evangelina* came to her, the ship bending to the wind and shuddering with its power, and tears sprang to her eyes. She tightened her lips and said as lightly as she could, 'So he will not reappear. I am a fallen woman, since you ask so nicely.'

'So he's definitely far enough away for me to ask you out to dinner? This big Chilean with the knife? He won't come and do me *grievous* bodily harm?'

'You're not terribly chivalrous, are you?' said Maggie. 'If you want to ask me out you're supposed to say that you would kill dragons for me, dare any torrent and face any hardship just for one single rose from my hair.'

'Well, I wouldn't,' said Steve. 'But I'd buy you dinner.'

'I don't know,' she said, flat again. 'I'm tired, and life has just taken an unfortunate turn. I can't take on anything new.'

'I'm not new,' he said. 'I am very definitely second-hand.'

She said nothing.

'Someone has to make the decisions,' he said with a sigh. 'First law of business. So, Friday, then. I'll meet you outside the

Costarica at seven. We'll go to a pub. If you don't come, I'll just go into the Costa, order another of their undercooked Chicken Kievs and die of salmonella. And it'll be your fault.'

She was on the verge of refusing, but something about him stopped her. The jokes kept coming, fast and brittle, but beneath them lay something she recognized: a yawning uncertainty, not quite loneliness but not far from it.

'Just be friends?' she said suddenly. 'Just friends?'

'Possibly not even that,' said the tall man, smooth again now. 'You have to remember that I am an insensitive capitalist bastard.'

'Not friend material at all,' agreed Maggie gravely. He raised a hand in salute and strode off towards the car park. She stood watching him, then shook her shoulders and headed down into the riverside park.

The rain had stopped. She hid both coats under a bush and ran for almost an hour under the dreary glimmer of the park lights. When she stopped she was perspiring, but her limbs were less stiff and heavy. She pulled the coats out from under the damp leaves of the bush, and put on her own familiar jacket. There was ease in it, for it had travelled a long way with her. Besides, she did not want to wear anything of the Penns' any longer, not now that she had lost the right to take the smallest favour from them. With a heavy heart she walked back towards her sister's house.

Everything was quiet. Jamie, she thought, must have got back in time. Leo would be upstairs with Sarah. She hung up the torn jacket, tiptoed to her room and closed the door very quietly.

When Leo had seen Jamie upstairs he closed the doors and windows and climbed the stairs, his stomach icy, to face his wife. He undressed in the bathroom and crept into their room without switching on a light; for a wild moment of hope he thought she was already asleep. But as he sat carefully on his side of the bed, the hunched shape opposite reared up, and he saw a glimmer of white face turned towards him beneath the loose dark hair.

'Did you love her?' came the hoarse, exhausted whisper. She must have been crying for over an hour. 'Were you in love with *her?*'

'Christ, no!' said Leo, his voice shaky. 'I was in love with you. Always. I still am.'

'No, you're not,' said Sarah into the darkness. 'In-love doesn't last. Not for anybody. You graduate from that, into properly loving each other, which is better.'

'And I love you.'

She continued, as if he had not spoken. 'But the long-term love has to grow out of the other thing. The in-love thing. And now I don't know if that was ever real. If the root was a fake, the whole thing could be a fake.'

'Of course it was real. I only ever loved you.'

'You slept with her. You went to Canada for a week, only a week away from me, and you had to sleep with her. Men in love don't do that.'

Leo could have said 'Yes, they do' but he dared not. He could not explain, if only because he had so completely lost touch with the younger man he used to be. Why had he done it? His memory was hazy. He remembered Maggie's defiance, her shock about Ted's illness, her capitulation to common sense, her anger at his having bought her ticket home. He remembered how young she had looked and how like Sarah, and how instinctive was his move to comfort her when the airline announced that agonizing delay.

He remembered little else. It seemed absurd to him, looking at the lean, assured, mocking, weatherbeaten Maggie of today, that he had ever had the slightest inclination to take her in his arms. Even when they had stood together in that incredible moment watching the floodwater rise in the moonlight, his hand on her shoulder, there had been no squeak or tremor of sexuality between them.

He said, 'There isn't an excuse. But it was you I wanted, always. And I truly never had the slightest idea she was pregnant. Till tonight. It was one mistake, just one. Before we made our vows. It's always been you.'

Sarah forgot to whisper. Her voice rasped with unhappy sarcasm. 'You thought of me while you screwed *her*, I suppose.'

'No! Yes! Look, a man doesn't always think *anything*.'

Sarah sat up properly, shaking her head as if to free herself from nightmare. Whispering again, she asked, 'Were you drunk?'

Leo grasped at the lifeline. 'Yes.' He lied, and knew that she knew he was lying. But it was enough for the present. She lay back, exhausted, on the pillow. Her back was to him; Leo rolled over until he was facing it, but not touching. They had begun. They had put into place the first brick of the new edifice that would shelter the family. He would persevere in telling her that he was drunk that night. Made a drunken mistake. For the moment, that would have to do.

Two doors away, Samantha lay sleepless, hot-eyed, staring at the ceiling. She longed to suck her thumb again, but lay on her hands instead, summoning all her willpower not to be a baby. There was a yawning hole in the roof of her life, a jagged gap ripped through the overarching branches of her parents' lives and family legend. Beyond it stretched illimitable blackness. But if it had to be faced, she would face it. Plenty of other kids had divorce happen to them. It was part of modern life.

It was only when she heard the stealthy footfall of Maggie in the passage, and the soft closing of her door, that she began to cry again.

Chapter Twenty

When Maggie woke, she saw to her horror that it was gone eight o'clock; the family was on the move downstairs. She lay beneath the duvet, afraid to get up and face them. But Teddy came to her rescue, bursting in without knocking to say, 'Dad says anybody who wants a lift uptown has to be ready in five minutes flat, or no lift. Are you coming with us? Sam's walking but she went *ages* ago.'

'Oh, uh, I must have overslept.'

'You'll miss your bus then if you don't come in the car with us. And Mum won't drive you because she's having a headache day at home.'

Maggie had been considering skipping college again, but the fear of being alone in the house with Sarah galvanized her. The time would come for a reckoning between them, but it was not yet. She justified her cowardice to herself by reasoning that she ought to leave Leo time to give his wife an account of it all. She must give them a chance. What lay between a married couple was theirs alone.

Smiling with some difficulty, she said to the little boy, 'OK. Scram, I'll get up quick and join you at the car. I can get coffee at college.'

The drive was silent, or as silent as any drive could be with Teddy among the passengers. Jamie sat in the front and kept glancing at his father, puzzled by his passivity. After a while he turned on Radio 1, and turned it up, little by little. Still Leo did not react, driving on in a dream. In the back, Teddy started rapping along to the music and laughing uproariously at the woman disc jockey's crude innuendos. Both boys kept glancing at their father with fascination. Usually it took only ninety seconds from the switching on of Radio 1 to his eruption. His silence almost worried them. In the end it was Maggie who startled them by snapping abruptly, 'Look, turn it down, we'll go insane.'

So Jamie did, and they rode on to the school gate with only a low, breathy rhythm seeping out of the speakers.

When the boys jumped out, Maggie made as if to follow them, but Leo said, 'Stay put, I'll take you to the bus stop.'

'I can walk. I've got ten minutes before the bus.'

'Stay put!'

She closed the door obediently.

Half twisting his head round as he pulled away, Leo said, 'I haven't spoken to Sarah yet about the bookshop. About you carrying on working there.'

'Oh,' said Maggie. 'I did wonder. I was going away quite soon anyway, I can't face being pregnant in the same town as Mum.'

'You won't go before Christmas?'

'I'm not sure you'll all want me in the house at Christmas. You and Sarah and Sam, anyway.'

'I meant, in the shop. Look, I know it's crass, and I couldn't say it to her, but I really do have to have an assistant. And I'm not going to find another.'

'Well,' said Maggie, 'it's between you two. But I don't imagine she'll really suspect us of falling on each other lustfully in the shop, will she?'

'Don't joke. Don't make jokes about it. We're fighting for our lives here.' He stepped on the brake, jolting the car to a halt by the bus stop. 'She was talking in her sleep last night, going on about how you mustn't have the abortion.'

'I'm not.'

'She meant, back then. I assume so, anyway. She was worrying about her little sister, for Christ's sake. In her sleep. How does *that* make you feel?'

Maggie pressed her lips together. It would not help anything if she fell out with Leo now, dearly as she longed to slap him.

'What shall I do then? Today?'

'Just come into the shop. I'll nip up at lunchtime and have a word with her. I told her I was drunk that night. It's the best thing for her to think.'

Maggie got out of the car, pulling her coat round her. Enjoying the familiar settling of the old waterproof on her shoulders, she thought of the tall, dry, oddly kind Steve and how he had kept vigil in the cafe for her. She turned back towards Leo as he prepared to drive away.

'Is today Friday?'

'No. Tomorrow. Don't forget, late night opening till eight.'

'Oh, bugg—Well, OK.' She could, she supposed, nip out to the Costarica at seven and tell Steve she would be late. He didn't have to wait, obviously, but perhaps he would . . .

She hoped he would.

'Bye, then. I'll be in the shop. But not at supper. I'll go out somewhere tonight, and I'm out tomorrow too.'

'Good.'

As Leo drove back into town he saw Samantha walking the last few hundred yards to the school gate. She would be late for school. He slowed down to signal to his daughter, but she looked straight through him and clipped on along the pavement, chin high. Leo, who had not wept for years, found himself sniffing, awash with self-pity. The boys, he thought, the boys must never know.

When the house was empty, Sarah got up straightaway. She did not have a headache. Of all the family, she had spoken only to Samantha, when she woke in the dawn to hear her in the bathroom. She had put her head round the door to find her daughter sitting on the edge of the bath, stirring the fluffy bathmat around with one bare foot.

'All right, sweetheart?'

'Are *you* all right, Mum?' The blue eyes looked up at her, swimming.

'Yes. Don't worry. It was all a long time ago.'

'Mum, shall I stay at home today? With you?'

'Absolutely not. Go to school. Be normal. Just tell Dad and the boys I've got a headache, and I'll stay in bed and get myself organized later. Do that for me, and that's all I need.' And, seeing the tears welling in Samantha's eyes again, she added with a gentle sharpness, 'Brave girl. No fussing. I'll sort it all out.'

'Will you leave Dad?' said Samantha, standing up and leaning on the basin, which creaked alarmingly away from its mountings on the wall. She straightened up hastily.

'Darling, I am not up for questions like that. Not now,' said Sarah. 'Don't ask. But we both love you, all of you, and we'll do what's best for everyone.'

'The *best* would have been for none of it to have *happened*,' said Samantha. '*Bloody* Auntie Maggie.'

'She only told the truth,' said Sarah sadly. 'It was only the truth.'

She went back to bed, lay down on the edge furthest from the still-sleeping Leo, and closed her eyes.

Now, rising in the quiet house, she moved around automatically, straightening curtains and cushions and rinsing the breakfast mugs and plates. When her coffee had brewed, she sat down and pulled the morning paper towards her. She could not concentrate, though, and after a while stood up, scrabbled in her folder of papers and set off for the vet's. His grumpy presence was what she needed. She would not tell him anything about the crisis. Of course she would not. That was obvious.

Sam Miller was scrubbing his hands at the basin in the

consulting room when she arrived, and raised his eyebrows at the sight of her.

'You don't come in till two on Thursday, woman,' he said. 'Are you going to tell me you can't do this afternoon? Because I've got a long, long letter to the Royal College about micro-chipping—'

'I'll be here all day,' said Sarah. 'I don't want to be at home.' And she burst into tears and told him everything in the short time between his kicking the door shut and the young veterinary nurse pushing it open again to bring in a drooping Shi-Tzu with a pink, lolling tongue.

Sarah turned her head aside and pretended to check the notices on the wall while the girl flopped the dog on the table and said. 'He's due to go home today, post-op, but I don't think he looks right, Mr Miller, do you?'

'Hmmph. Look, Mrs Penn can hold him if need be. You'd better go and check the other night kennels. The Siamese is supposed to go home today as well, isn't it? The one with the mangled ear?'

'Righty-ho,' said the girl amiably, and vanished in a whiff of antiseptic.

Sarah looked at Samuel Miller across the recumbent, panting pile of fur and said, 'I'm sorry to burst out at you like that.'

'No, you're not. You feel much better for it. People always do, when they've told you about their lives. That's why I decided not to be a doctor. Animals don't relate long atrocious sagas about their love lives while you're stitching them up.' He rolled the dog's eye open and grimaced. 'Bloody thing. I knew he'd do this to me.'

Sarah wondered, not for the first time, how the old vet got away with it, and why she was so stubbornly fond of him.

'I said I'm sorry,' she insisted. 'But I've had an awful shock. It just came over me.'

The vet reached for a syringe, holding the dog down with his free hand. 'Just hang on to him for me a sec,' he said, and filled the syringe to plunge its needle deftly into the little dog's hindquarters. 'There you are, boy. No, I do see it was a shock. You've never quite grasped that your sister is designed by nature to give people shocks, it still surprises you every time.'

Sarah stroked the little dog's head. 'Sweet,' she said, playing for time.

'You know whose he is, don't you?' said Miller, throwing the syringe into the bin. Sarah was momentarily distracted from her own troubles by a professional misgiving.

'Oh no, not Mrs Harrison!' she said.

'Oh yes, Mrs Harrison,' said the vet. 'So I can cut you a deal, if you like.'

'What?'

'The deal is this. You ring the old bat and tell her that Muffy-Poo or whatever its name is has had a slight allergic reaction and has to stay here for another night. Remember to say "slight", which is a lie, but I don't think he'll die. Then you listen to her squawking for half an hour, and tell her I'm tied up with a dying pussycat or something and on no account put her through. And in return—'

'This deal had better be good,' said Sarah, with an attempt at spirit.

'In return,' said the old man, 'I will give you wise counsel as to what a woman should do when she discovers that her husband slept with her sister sixteen years ago before the wedding.'

'OK,' said Sarah. 'Shoot.'

'The wise woman's best course of action is . . .' He paused impressively. 'Forget it.' He held up three fingers and ticked off the syllables. 'For – get – it.'

'Why?'

'Because it doesn't matter. Because it's in the past and can never happen again. Your sister is a wandering albatross. She'll be off again soon, baby or no baby. Leo is a backyard chicken. The two never mate for long.'

'But I just feel so—'

'Hysterical and irrational,' completed the vet. He reached over to the buzzer, and before Sarah could gather her wits to reply to this insult, the nurse came in.

'Come on, darling!' she cooed to the dog. 'Back to the ward for tonight, then?'

'Yes. Mrs Penn will ring Mrs Harrison,' said the vet. When the nurse had gone, he washed his hands and said over his shoulder, 'You know I'm right. Oblivion, that's the answer. Just forget it. Women have no idea how little sex can mean to young men. Bet you fifty quid that Leo had virtually forgotten he did it.'

'But what about my sister?'

'I told you. She's a pirate. A Viking. Different rules. Get treated rougher, treat other people rougher. Is she still working in the bookshop?'

Sarah stared at him in wide-eyed dismay. 'I'd forgotten that,' she said.

'See?' He tossed the paper towel in the bin and looked around. 'Forgetting's quite easy, when you get the hang of it.'

Leo went through the morning like a sleepwalker. At lunchtime he went up to the house to speak to Sarah, but found it locked and empty. Unreasonably disconsolate, he made himself an untidy cheese sandwich and mooched around the kitchen taking bites of it, dropping shards of Cheddar on the floor, and trying not to imagine how it would be if Sarah were never there at all.

Except, of course, that it would be him who had to move out, if anyone did. That was how it worked when there were children in the case, and he supposed that was the right thing. He, Leo Penn, could be imminently thrown out of his house just for something he did more than fifteen years earlier, on another continent, for no motive that he could remember. It was ludicrous, it was terrifying, it was unthinkable but – he convinced himself – it was probable.

Where had she gone? To a solicitor?

At two he dragged himself back down to the shop, and unlocked it. Two indignant women were standing outside. One was stout and wore a furry jacket too short for her figure; the other was stooping and nondescript in a grey coat with a bit of hem coming down.

'I didn't think you closed for lunch,' said the big one accusingly. He half recognized her as a regular at his quarterly bookshop events, and forced himself to smile.

'Well, not for much longer,' he said heartily. 'When term ends, I'm happy to say, I once again will have a full-time assistant. She's a scholar in Chinese, very interesting person, very well-travelled. Doing afternoons at the moment. Taking a sabbatical.' God, he thought, what a pompous arse he sounded. But it was better than kicking the furry woman sharply on the shins, as was his deepest instinct. Had he spent all his life, Leo wondered gloomily, suppressing his natural urges and veiling them in false politeness? Was the moment with Maggie at the airport hotel the only time that he had ever acted without thinking of the consequences?

Leaning on the counter, he frowned. No. That was not true. His desire had been all for Sarah, from the first day he saw her. The tough, wiry little sister was nothing to him. If Sarah had been standing beside her on that night there could have been no contest. He had slept with Maggie because she was the nearest thing to his Sarah, and because he was lonely and shaken up after the excursion into the wild alien forest world, and because she was afraid for her father, and powerfully frustrated by the plane's delay, and because he was moved by her savage despair. That was all. Nothing to it, really. A million couplings every day must happen for less good reasons. It was the way the world wagged. The Victorian whimsy of the expression made him smile momentarily despite himself; goodness, he was becoming a fogey. Then he realized that the furry woman was asking him about the Booker shortlist.

'You *used* to have a special display,' she said crossly.

'Only before the announcement of the winner,' said Leo.

'Why? The books are just as good after the announcement,' she said crushingly, and turned away to peer at the fiction shelves. Leo went to the desk.

At two, Maggie arrived, and without a word went up to the children's department to unpack a delivery.

Leo called up to her, 'Since you're here, can you man the barricades while I go out for twenty minutes?'

'Course,' she said, glaring at him over a pile of Grinch books.

He went back to the house, found it still empty, and wandered along to the vet's surgery. The nurse glanced up at him as he came in.

'Mr Penn. You looking for your wife? She's taking some letters from Mr Miller before afternoon surgery.'

'Can I see her?'

'All righty! You sit down-io and I'll grab her.' The girl was really insufferably cheerful, he thought.

Sarah appeared a moment later, looking annoyed, and found him deep in a leaflet about mange.

'What d'you want? I'm working.'

'Had to ask you something.'

'Ask.' The nurse was pretending to tidy up prescription forms but eyeing them with interest.

He lowered his voice. 'Maggie. Her working in the shop. Is it OK with you? For the moment?'

'Course.' She turned away, leaving him faintly shocked and not knowing why. Then he realized.

It was what Maggie had said, and in the same contemptuous voice, and with the same glare.

Chapter Twenty-one

You always go home, thought Maggie, you always have to go back to the place where you left your toothbrush and clean pants. Dislocated, exhausted, at the end of the afternoon in the bookshop she muttered something to Leo and walked up towards the house. She longed to lie down. Her legs ached, her head was swimming, and she yearned for sleep. Teddy and some freckled friend waylaid her at the door, with demands for instruction in street magic.

'Will you show us how you do the one where you sort of burn the name on your arm?'

'Is it with wax? Only Adrian says—'

'He saw it on Channel Four.'

'We could do it for the school revue. Hardly any Year Sevens ever get to be in it.'

Maggie shivered. It was not just that she was tired. Her whole view of the world and her place in it was knocked askew. She did not know how to behave. After what she had done it seemed unfitting for her to frolic as she used to with her sister's child, the youngest and cleanest-hearted of them all. Had she stripped herself even of aunthood? Behind the boys, she could see Sarah's back view in the kitchen, deliberately not turning to greet her.

'Look,' she said, 'I can't do the arm trick now because I need special stuff. It isn't ordinary candlewax you use, it has to be soft.

But if you like, you can get the magic coin trick out. It's in the bedside table drawer in my room, in the red velvet bag. OK?'

'Wicked!' said Teddy, and to his friend, 'I'm going to be a street magician when I'm fourteen. I'm not doing GCSEs, I'm going to be a busker.'

Sarah still did not turn.

When the boys had gone, Maggie went up to her and said with all the force she could muster, 'Talk to me. Sare, talk to me. I'm leaving town pretty soon, it's best with the pregnancy and everything. But Leo wants me to work over Christmas in the shop. Is that all right, if I stay in the house till then?'

Sarah turned, her eyes hard but unfocused, not really looking at her sister.

'I don't see that it makes the slightest difference,' she said coldly. 'Not to me, anyway. To Samantha, perhaps. She's very upset. It's a difficult age for a girl, just coming to terms with her own puberty. Not the time you want to drop this kind of bombshell on her.'

'I wish I could tell you how sorry . . .' began Maggie miserably. But Sarah snapped.

'You keep out of her way. I'll explain to her that you're needed for the shop.' She slapped a wedge of pizza dough down hard, and ground her knuckles into it.

'Well, I'll keep out of everyone's way,' said Maggie with sad finality. 'I'll go out tomorrow, and perhaps take a walk at the weekend. Right now, I'm going to bed.'

'No. Mum's coming to supper,' said Sarah levelly, still not looking at her. 'So it would be better if you were there. She says she's hardly seen you.'

'You asked her?'

'I saw her in the supermarket after work,' said Sarah. 'And guilt kicked in. *Some* of us have to think about other members of the family, sometimes.'

'I'll change into a skirt,' said Maggie dully. 'Then perhaps I should lay the table.'

'Do that,' said Sarah, and turned her back squarely. 'Cloth napkins. You know what Mum's like.'

Nancy talked nonstop through supper; about her friend Emily, about Miss Mountjoy being so wonderful with her bedridden crony Louise, about the church and the flowers and how nice it was that the scouts and the Salvation Army were working together this year on the Toys for Children project. Jamie, after a little coaxing from his father, launched into a long account of how he and Adrian and Toyah Robinson were renovating a wooden garage set, with ramps, and going to put all their old Dinky cars into it. Samantha spoke little, but gave her grandmother some satisfaction at least by admitting that she was thinking of rejoining the Brackhampton Ranger Guides, because Uma Syal reckoned it was pretty cool these days since Mrs Turner retired and the new PSE teacher took over. Teddy talked about his future career as a busker. Sarah pressed food on others but ate little herself. Maggie answered her mother's few questions politely but briefly, and sat fiddling with her food until she could decently absent herself.

Leo drove Nancy back to the Brackley estate and was heartily glad to be out of the house. At least his mother-in-law did not appear to have noticed the atmosphere among the three adults. But as they swung into the cul-de-sac where Maggie and Sarah had grown up, she said, 'Margaret looks very peaky. I hope she hasn't picked up some foreign disease.'

'She seems all right,' said Leo evasively 'Lots of energy. Goes out running.'

'She's lost her looks,' said Nancy triumphantly. 'Thirty-six, and she looks quite the old maid.'

Leo wondered, not for the first time, at the curious depths of malice which could lurk in a maternal soul.

✷   ✷   ✷

On Friday morning Maggie, by a great effort of will, hauled herself out of bed before first light. As she looked in the bathroom mirror under its harsh neon light, she saw what Nancy had seen: she looked suddenly older, the lines on her temples more pronounced, her skin yellow as its old tan faded in the Kentish rain. Her hair was wet from the shower; her wide reflected eyes looked out at her from a thin face. Like a wet cat, she thought. Wet old stray cat. Mirrors had played less part in Maggie's life than in the lives of most women, but all the same the vision in front of her brought faint dismay; it was as if a long-disregarded possession had been stolen and suddenly missed.

She pulled on Sarah's old jeans and white shirt with the ache of guilt which had, over the past thirty-six hours, become as familar a pain as the dull pregnant ache of her back and the constant faint nausea. It was colder today under the clear skies, and with a faint pricking of dismay she realized that she owned virtually no clothes suitable for a proper British winter. So far the season had been inordinately wet, but mild. Now she realized that her one fleece and store of tattered sweaters might not take her far into the cold season. She must go to the charity shop, but most of the stuff there was either hopelessly teenage, or else capacious enough for the matrons of Brackhampton, and would hang like sacks on her . . .

Not for much longer. The thought halted her, frozen in the act of combing her long hair. Jesus Christ, but she was pregnant! She would *need* huge clothes soon. Already the old jeans she wore leaving *Evangelina* did not fit. Sarah's were still fine, but for how long? Tears pricked her eyes. Imagine buying maternity clothes, wearing them, having her bump remarked on, all for a baby she would never even see. It was pathetic. Not because she wanted the baby, but because of the lumbering figure she would cut when pregnant, all the more lumbering and ludicrous for not intending to be a mother. But there was no alternative. Not now. She must endure what was coming.

She felt sick, and knew she would have to eat. She could not take any more of the Penns' food, not just now, even as a paying lodger. From Leo and Sarah's room as she tiptoed past it came a faint creak of someone turning over, and a sleepy grunt. Maggie hurried down the stairs, pocketed her key, grabbed her jacket and bag and stepped out into the frosty air. She must watch every penny now; there was no question of seeking the cafe's expensive warmth. From the shop on the corner she bought a waxed carton of fruit juice and a pallid sugary Danish pastry, and ate this dreary breakfast as she walked up to the bus stop. If she got the earlier bus, she could at least have a subsidised cup of hot coffee at college.

'If I tell you something awful,' said Samantha to Uma Syal, 'will you promise to keep it, like, totally secret?'

Her guilt at even considering this confidence was lessened by the knowledge that of all the girls in the school, this quiet, dark-eyed, self-possessed creature was the most likely to keep such a promise. They had been inseparable friends at primary school and the first years at the High School, only losing one another during Samantha's defection to the fast set and to Duane. When the dust of recent alarms had settled, it was with relief and a certain humility that she looked round and saw the dark, kind eyes still willing to look in her direction. They had renewed the friendship with careful casualness, but the warmth of it comforted them both equally. Nita, Uma's mother and Sarah's friend, watched with satisfaction. Unlike her husband, she liked to see her daughter robustly friendly with the modern girls, the rebels, the dangerous ones. She was glad also when Uma talked with the boys. Ravi preferred to praise the ways of little Leela, who never spoke to the boys or the rowdier girls in her class, preferring to cast her eyes down modestly, giggle if addressed by a male, and play dolls and cook-stoves with her equally prim small cousin Shyama.

'I can keep secrets,' said Uma calmly, 'if it is not

dangerous or wicked to keep them. If you tell me you have murdered Mrs Harvey or put secret poison in the head-master's tube of wine gums then I will tell the police.' She grinned. 'Go on then. Tell. What is it? You've looked so pissed off these two days!'

Samantha sighed, and stretched her long legs. They were sitting together on a bench in the gym, waiting for Mrs Randall the PE teacher to come back from answering the phone. They knew, from experience, that it would be five minutes at least. Mrs Randall had a pregnant daughter who rang her in a panic every time some new symptom surfaced.

'Well,' she said. 'Basically – you know my aunt?'

'The famous Aunt Maggie? My mother talks about her. The other day she was teasing Leela, saying she should grow up to be a proud spirit with a rucksack like Maggie Reave, and travel the world alone. Leela was horrified. So was Dad.'

'Yes. Anyway . . .' Samantha hesitated. One secret she had not told her friend was the story of the pregnancy test. She was not yet quite sure how Uma would react to the information that she had actually got that far with Duane. She decided to cut to the chase. 'Well, my Aunt Maggie – she's pregnant.'

'Aie, aie! Difficult. No husband. Will she have the baby at your house?'

'It's not that. She says she's moving out of town anyway, and it'll be adopted. But it's not that.'

Uma looked at her friend, surprised by her dismissal of Maggie's momentous and – to her – appalling decision. 'There's something even more secret than that?'

'Yes. The other night Dad was being a bit pompous about her having it adopted, saying fathers had rights, all that. Which I do believe, actually, because, well, they do. I suppose.' Confusion overcame her for a moment; she had not thought about Duane when she thought she was pregnant, had she? Perhaps she should have. 'But anyway . . .'

'What?' Uma was impatient now. Mrs Randall would be

back, they would have to hop over the vaulting horse and somersault on the mats, and there would be no more talking. 'Anyway what?'

'It was awful. Maggie burst out and said that, huh, when she was pregnant by Dad she got rid of it. It turns out that just before Mum and Dad got married, he slept with her — my aunt.'

'Aie, aie, aie!' said Uma again. 'Oh, that's terrible!'

'Yes. It made me go all weird, and I had to go to bed, and I keep crying when I don't mean to.' Samantha's eyes filled with tears. 'Mum says it's all right, they'll sort it all out. But! I mean, it's awful, why did he do it?' She shook her head violently as if to dislodge the images. 'And then just to let her kill the baby, which if you *think* about it was my big brother. Or sister.'

'Did he know?'

'He must have known! Mustn't he?' Samantha looked briefly happier as the doubt occurred to her. She, after all, had never had the slightest impulse to tell Duane.

'What about your Aunt Maggie? What does she say?'

'I'm never going to *speak* to her again. Bitch!'

'And your father?'

Samantha stared at her in horror. 'Oh, come on. If it was *your* father, would you ask him? I mean!'

Uma shook her head in shared dismay at the dreadful prospect of knowing anything, anything at all, about a father's sex life.

'Oh, poor Sammy!' Then, frowning, she asked, 'Do the boys know?'

'No. Unless Mum's told them, and she wouldn't.'

'That's good.'

'Yes. That's something.'

They brooded together, then the gym door swung open violently and Mrs Randall reappeared, pink-faced from hurrying.

'Right, girls! Sorry! Now, warming up — round the walls, jog!'

As they jolted obediently off past the battered wall bars, Uma turned to whisper to her friend.

'Will your aunt go away now?'

'I hope so,' said Samantha, but there were tears in her eyes again.

Chapter Twenty-two

When Maggie stepped into the bookshop she hardly recognized it. Leo was wrestling with a trestle table, assisted by two elderly men in tweed jackets, battered trousers and highly polished shoes. Another table already dominated the centre of the room. Cardboard boxes, trussed up with flat plastic tape in the manner she had come to recognize as the mark of book wholesalers, were stacked against the wall on the left. A large, wobbling cardboard effigy of Raymond Briggs's cartoon Father Christmas was propped on the right, obscuring the travel shelf. As she watched, a gust blew through the door behind her and the creature began to topple sideways towards the desk, where three half-drunk mugs of coffee were balanced on a pile of glossy, slippery catalogues.

With a lightning reaction that surprised her as much as the three men, Maggie dived forward and caught the collapsing Santa. For a moment it seemed as if her elbow might send the mugs and catalogues flying in the general direction of a pile of pale-jacketed hardbacks, but she twisted round and righted herself, ending up slightly breathless with one arm round the cardboard figure's waist and the other clutching the desk.

'Oh, well saved!' said one of the two men. 'That's the sort of customer you need, Leo.'

Leo flickered a smile and said, 'Not a customer, General.

This is my sister-in-law Maggie Reave, who is helping out over the Christmas rush. Maggie, you haven't met General Madson and Rear-Admiral Havelock. You've heard me talk about them, they run the rare-book catalogue. This is the only time of year I manage to get them in the shop for an hour or two.' He beamed nervously at the old men, not meeting Maggie's eye at all.

'Bobby Madson,' said the one who had first spoken, putting the table down and extending a polite hand.

'Tim Havelock,' said the other. 'Don't for Christ's sake call me Admiral. These days they're just a kind of butterfly as far as I'm concerned. Leo here likes to use the ranks. Gives him credibility among collectors of militaria.'

'Also makes him feel less guilty about forcing poor old men with dodgy hips to help him move heavy tables. He feels as if he's got troops, not dupes.' They laughed, a bluff, wrinkled Tweedledum and Dee. Leo looked even more awkward than before. Maggie, unspeakably relieved to see that there would be company in the shop for a while, gave the old men a smile which, had she known it, brought back almost all her beauty.

'Let me help with the tables,' she said. 'How do they go?'

Leo explained that during the Christmas rush, he always abandoned the spacious, peaceful layout of the bookshop in favour of narrower aisles and higher heaps. It was not to his taste, and every year he loathed the process of destroying the calm, academic browsers' privacy of the place and transforming it into a bustling souk. But experience, backed by conclaves with other small booksellers, revealed that it was not only a practical measure to keep fast-moving star books on display. It actually attracted a different class of customer. For these crucial weeks the shop became more welcoming to those who liked bustle and garishness, and eschewed the library atmosphere that Leo preferred.

So the long tables dominated the centre of the room, and soon Maggie was at work with the Stanley knife, ripping tape and easing open boxes, while the two old men tacked up the

Santa in the children's library, wound tinsel along the spotlight tracks and climbed down into the damp storeroom, with much badinage about submarines, to collect extra metal display stands. The afternoon customers who drifted in and out looked approvingly at the bustle and the sparkle; Maggie sold a good number of books, and Leo took orders which, trying not to cross his fingers, he assured the buyers would arrive by Christmas Eve.

'Nothing like a deadline,' said Bobby Madson, shrugging on his coat at five o'clock. 'Main point about Christmas, I always think. It sharpens you up, knowing that if things aren't done by Christmas Eve you're finished. No procrastination.' The old servicemen made their exit at five onto an increasingly busy pavement, and soon the shop was filled with late-night shoppers. Maggie was kept busy, for these were the hurriers rather than the browsers, anxious people who would pounce on a book as a quick, easily wrapped way of ticking off another family duty.

'It'll do nicely for Harry . . . oh, look, the *Pressed Fairy Book*, Lorna would love that . . . now, which is the Bryson that George *hasn't* got? Darling, is it Harry Enfield that Sheila likes, or Rory Bremner?' Sometimes they asked Maggie or Leo for advice, but mainly they plucked books, carted them to the desk, paid with their rectangles of plastic and made for the next glittering shop window. At six, a brass band struck up carols outside the Market Hall, instruments gleaming golden in the coloured lights. A hot-chestnut cart appeared and sent warm smells down the street. For once, the town teemed with life. At six thirty the Mayor appeared and made a short speech before switching on the overhead lights outside the town council office, golden stars with several bulbs missing.

At five past seven Maggie finished a transaction and turned to Leo, who stood momentarily idle, rubbing his lower back. 'Do you mind if I nip out for five minutes?' she said. 'I need to speak to someone. I'll be right back.'

Leo frowned, but to argue with her would be too much like a

conversation. They had avoided conversation successfully now for two days. 'OK. Be quick.'

She slipped out of the shop and half-ran down the road to the Costarica. Peering through the clouded windows she saw a dozen resting shoppers in there, carrier bags piled around them. None was the tall, familiar shape. She was surprised at the treacherous power of her disappointment. But turning resignedly away, almost cannoning into a shopper on the pavement, she found herself staring up at Steve Arundel, and gasped.

'Oh! I thought—'

'Sorry. Couldn't park. Forgot about Christmas shopping.' He gestured at the festive street. 'Merry mayhem.'

'The thing is, I'm working in a shop down the road. The bookshop. And I forgot too – it's open till eight tonight. I'm terribly sorry. Perhaps another evening . . .'

'Why?' he said. 'Do you need a couple of hours to go home and run up a dress out of the green velvet curtains before you can face a gentleman? Why, Scarlett!'

'No! I can come straight from the shop at eight, if you don't mind the jeans – but you don't want to wait around in this lot.'

In fact she longed for him to wait, yearned for an evening's easy company. But she would not say so. If he had asked her, flirtatiously, 'Do you want me to wait?' she would have said no. She could not do the slightest thing which might be construed as Leading A Man On. Not now, perhaps not ever again.

She sniffed, glanced away, held her breath. Steve looked at her, consideringly.

'I'm not bloody well going into the Costarica,' he said, finally. 'Can't face it. Actually, I'm not sure we can eat in this town at all, tonight.' He watched her.

Maggie began, with all the brightness she could muster, 'Well, another day perhaps . . .' She was suddenly conscious, as if the bathroom mirror had reared up accusingly in front of her, of her lank hair and tired countenance. But smoothly the watcher cut in, as if to prove to her that his hesitation had another root.

'No, I was going to ask, would you consider driving off somewhere else? My dad always said it was rude and inconsiderate to ask a strange woman to go in a car with you on the first date, in case she thought you were a kidnapper. But seeing how we met . . .'

Maggie looked up at him again and smiled. 'Which car park?' she asked.

'Top. Near the cinema. Black Saab. I'll be in it, singing along to Radio Two like all the other sad divorced sales reps.'

Before she could assent and leave him, he pulled out his wallet and handed her a card. It bore his company's name embossed with a logo, his own name printed in severe capitals with 'Senior Representative' under it, and a photograph of Steve himself looking as stern as the typeface, with his hair slicked down and an unnaturally direct stare.

'Yes, yes, very naff. I'll tell you about my company later. It was sixteen tries before they accepted a mug shot as being dynamic enough. Any sign of a goofy Tony Blair grin and my boss vetoes it. But just give that card to someone you work with. Then if you're found dismembered in a trunk tomorrow, they can pull me in, and I can explain, with shifty rolling eyes, that it was a very determined and tidy-minded suicide.'

She hesitated, not quite knowing whether to laugh. He pressed the card on her, suddenly very serious.

'No, take it. It's a wicked world. Women have to be suspicious. Men have to be cool about being suspects. Go on, do yourself a favour, give it to your workmates, feel safe.'

She looked at him wonderingly, then took the card. There was no point explaining the impossibility of her giving it to Leo just now. But she saw that he was trying to reassure her. Maggie was not accustomed to having people think about her protectively, and something in her was touched. She smiled up at him, and nodded.

Steve melted rapidly away in the crowds; she walked more slowly back towards the shop, and on the way met Miss

Mountjoy, flushed from the cold, hurrying along with a carrier bag. They had not met for a week, and again Maggie was touched, this time by the enthusiasm with which the old woman greeted her. 'Maggie dear!' Soon, she thought, soon her visible pregnancy would throw a barrier of awkwardness between her and such kind, pious old ladies. On an impulse she handed her the card.

'That's a man I'm going out with tonight,' she said. 'I don't know him very well, and he thought it would be a good idea if I made sure someone knew who he was. So that I felt safe.' She blushed.

Miss Mountjoy beamed and examined the glowering face on the slip of card. 'How very considerate. He must be a gentleman. Funny stare he's got, though, hasn't he? Caught unawares by the camera, perhaps. I'll pop into the shop tomorrow to make sure you're safe. Have a lovely evening.'

When Maggie joined him in the car park, Steve was not singing along but listening, intent, to a soprano singing Verdi; a simple aria, unadorned, yearning, tragic. *Vergine dell' angeli . . . pieta, pieta de me!* The car window was slightly open, and she heard the singing and waited a little behind the car until it ended in a troubled, emotional mush of swelling orchestra. When it did, he reached forward, turned the radio off and got out of the car to face her. Blushing again, she realized that she had been clearly in view of his rear mirror. He said nothing about the music or her patience, but only, 'Hop in. Mystery tour begins. Anywhere but Christmasland.'

'Mmm. It has been a bit overpowering,' she said. 'I never knew the Sally Army played "Jingle Bells".'

'It wasn't the Sallies, it was the British Legion,' he said. 'Not a bonnet in sight.'

They fell silent in the car for a few minutes, while Steve made his way to the bypass and put his foot down. Then:

'Where are we going?' she asked.

'Sea,' he said briefly. And indeed, for a few minutes they

followed the same road they had first travelled, the road Maggie used to walk on her youthful escapes from Brackhampton. It was the shortest way to the coast, but led only to bungalows and beach huts and a few summer cafes. She sat back, waiting to see what he meant. Moments later he took the left fork, off to the north.

'Where *are* we going? Which sea?'

'North Sea. Well, Thames Estuary.'

'Do you know, I spent all my childhood here and I don't know that side of the county at all? We always went to Margate, or to Scotland.'

He drove on. Maggie found that she could relax in his silence. It was a novelty to be taken somewhere she had not chosen, on a road she had no map of. She closed her eyes; it had been a long day, her traitorous body was more sluggish than it once had been, and even in the morning's lectures she had found her eyelids drooping. The car was warm, its pace on the clear road smooth.

With a jolt she woke. They had come to a halt, heaven knew how long ago, and through the windscreen she could see a bright moon shining a hole in dark, ragged cloud. Again the memory of nights on *Evangelina* came to her, so powerfully that she gasped. She turned her head and saw Steve Arundel sitting beside her, reading a book by the tiny map light.

'God, I'm sorry. What——?'

'You fell asleep. Seemed a pity to wake you.'

'How long?'

'Half an hour. We got here twenty minutes ago. I haven't white-slaved you, honestly. Frankly, there's not much of a white slave trade in Whitstable. In spite of all the oysters.'

'Whitstable! Do you know, I've never been here.'

'You have now. Fish restaurant. Very good. Booking's in fifteen minutes. Time for a walk, if you like.'

Maggie tumbled from the car, stretching stiff limbs. Immediately she understood why in her moment of waking she had thought of the ship; apart from the ragged sea-moon, there was salt air all around them and she could hear a faint susurration of waves. They were barely ten feet from a sea wall and a shingle beach. She clambered onto the concrete wall and looked out: distant lights twinkled across the estuary.

'Oh, thank you!' she cried, transported. 'Oh God, you don't know . . .' It was as if she had woken from the whole bad dream to find herself on the edge of freedom. Still mazed with sleep, she forgot all the troubles that were unchanged, and exulted on the seashore. 'Thank you!'

'You haven't had your dinner yet,' protested Steve mildly, amused at this unexpected ecstasy. In his experience, girls who fell asleep in your car with their mouths open spent their first minutes of consciousness looking at the mirror, not the scenery.

Maggie turned, her thin face alight. 'No, it's something else. I'll tell you about it. Come on. There's a harbour!'

'Oooh, a harbour! We might see *mud!*' he mocked, and held out a hand to get her down from the wall. When she had alighted, he kept it.

'Cold hand,' he said. 'C'mon, harbour's this way.' They wandered along to the little dock where dark water lapped at the stones and the still darker shapes of fishing boats tugged gently at their lines. In the outer approach lay a small sailing ship, its sails making paler lumps against black spars, its mast rearing high above the level of the harbour wall.

'Brixham trawler,' said Steve. 'I used to sail weekends on one of those before I was married. Belonged to some club. Don't often see them in here.' There were lights in the boat's cabin, and the faint sound of an accordion playing. They peered down, hand in hand, enjoying the bittersweet sense of being outsiders. After a while, not yet ready for their supper, they walked the other way. It was a silent little town that night, with closed-up holiday cottages and only a few lights along Sea Road. Maggie admired the wooden walls of the old buildings, with their white overlapping planks. She ran her hand over them, lovingly.

'Shiplap, is it called?' said Steve. 'Americans call it clapboard. Or is that different?'

'Built by people who normally built boats, I suppose. I love it,' said Maggie. 'You feel so different in brick.' She kicked the low wall of a Victorian cottage. 'Brick just slowly crumbles. With wood, if a bit rots, you can put a new bit in and get on with your life. And you know that somewhere there's a live forest growing more for the next generation. Wood is optimistic. Brick is fatalistic. It assumes the worst.'

She thought of the Penns' house, the house she must go back to, the brick garment that Sarah's family wore. She halted, suddenly choked with emotion, and found to her dismay that she was crying. A loud sniff in the darkness alerted Steve, who stopped admiring the planking round an old door and turned to her, miraculously unembarrassed.

'Dear oh dear,' he said. 'Blood sugar dropping. Time to eat, I think.' He took her hand again and led her back to the restaurant.

'It's all right,' he said kindly as they approached. 'Look, it's all made of wood. An old oyster shed. Hardly a brick in sight.'

'Sorry,' said Maggie. She sniffed, and grinned.

'*De rien*,' said Arundel, smooth again.

Chapter Twenty-three

'So,' said Steve, when they had ordered. 'You said you'd tell me why you were so pleased to see Whitstable. It can't just be the blissful lack of fairy lights and brass bands. You opened your eyes and looked as if you'd seen into heaven.'

'I felt that way,' said Maggie. 'It was just that when I opened my eyes, and smelt the harbour, and heard the waves, it reminded me of *Evangelina*. And sometimes you have to be forced to remember things you've lost, even if it hurts.'

'Who's Evangelina?' Crikey, thought Steve to himself. A lesbian. I should have guessed. But a pregnant one? Well, that would explain why she's not looking too happy. He looked at Maggie with almost brotherly fondness. Poor kid. Poor, queer, skinny, lit-up, wandering kid. 'So tell me about Evangelina,' he said evenly. 'Sounds Portuguese. Where did you meet her?'

Maggie stared at him. 'She's a *ship*,' she said helplessly. 'Did you think . . . oh my God!' Her mouth fell open.

'Well, how was I to know it was a ship? I thought . . .' He blushed fiery red. 'Oh shit, I thought—'

'You thought it was a girlfriend?' Maggie saw his face change, and he saw her begin to laugh properly for the first time since he had picked her up, bedraggled, on the sea road. 'God, men! Why couldn't you have assumed she was my long-lost sister, or child, or dog, or crippled auntie who died last month?'

He made a noise which sounded like 'Ug!' and drank noisily from his wine glass.

Maggie watched his blush spreading, enjoyed the destruction of his suavity, and remorselessly added, 'And why so politically correct? *Where did I meet her*, indeed? All set to listen understandingly to tales of dyke clubs in Acapulco, huh? What happened to your judgemental right-wing capitalist bastard instincts?'

'Oh, bugger!' said Steve. 'Look, have pity on me. I am so embarrassed I might die. Ooh, look, the United States Marines are coming, the relief column — gimme!' He took his plate of mussels from the surprised waitress's hands, and snipped one out expertly with the double shell of another. 'Mm, delicious! Let's talk about mussels. Did you know they change sex all the time, can't make their minds up, it was probably them that I was thinking of.'

Maggie accepted her scallops and began to eat with equal enjoyment. After a moment she said, 'Can I tell you about *Evangelina*, though?'

'Shoot.'

She told him the story of how she came upon the ship, the rakish masts and piratical rigging drawing her eye across the Acapulco naval basin. 'I thought I might get a passage home. Or somewhere near home. Found out about her from a mate on the base, chatted up some crew in a bar, then talked Captain Lopez round. Actually, I hopped on board and cleaned the totally disgusting galley. That convinced him. They had this pissed German in charge. Divorced and furious.'

'Well, we're like that,' said Steve. 'Divorced men. Take our wives away and we get drunk and throw our food everywhere, just for spite.'

She went on, talking of the passage and her growing sense of wonder on the ocean. 'I'd sailed on quite a few boats, some of them really big yachts, but always faffing about in the Caribbean, with spoilt tourists always wanting to stop and "do scooba". And

I'd never been aloft before, working on yardarms. You know, where you stand on the rope and pull the sails in.'

'Very retro,' said Steve. 'You'd not get me up there. So the view was good?'

'Oh yes. The moon, the sunrise, a pod of whales, eternity all around. I never wanted to arrive, but when we got near Spain, and I saw the Picos de Europa rising out of the sea . . . and all the crew just going wild . . .' She sipped her wine, smiling, and talked on. 'Oh God, Steve, it was amazing. Some of them had never been to Spain, but it's always a sort of mother country to South Americans. I got caught up in it like they did – we jumped around and pointed and climbed up to the royals to see better, and played our whistles and mouth organs in the rigging . . .' She paused. 'Well, it was sad to arrive and leave the ship, but sort of wonderful too.'

'The voyage wouldn't have been a voyage without the landfall?' he said, so quietly that she hardly registered that it was not her own thought.

'That's right. Things have to end.'

They were silent, each with their own thoughts. The waitress cleared away the plates and brought them cod and skate wings. Then Steve said, 'So here you are. And from what you said outside the Costarica, I assume the proposed infant is a sort of farewell present from the voyage. Half Chilean? The sort of baby that's going to climb up ropes to see the Picos?'

Maggie found that she no longer minded talking to Steve about her situation.

'Yes. A reprehensible one-night stand. In my defence I would stress that he *was* the captain. I obviously took my duties that bit too far.'

He did not react to the joke, only asking quietly, 'But you want it?'

She looked him in the eye. 'No.' She paused, and he held her with a questioning look so that she continued, less willingly, 'It's completely impractical. I have no money, I have no fixed home.

My life doesn't suit a baby. Anyway, babies ought to have fathers.'

'Amen,' said Steve, with an edge of bitterness.

She remembered his fleeting mention of his wife, she who hated coffee in her pregnancy, and asked, 'Do you have kids?'

'No. Jill – my wife – was pregnant. It was brilliant. I thought life couldn't get better. But it could definitely get worse. She lost the baby. Seven months. Stillbirth.'

'Oh God . . .' Maggie felt treacherous tears rising again. 'That's terrible. Oh, how awful. I mean, I don't want this baby, it's going to be adopted, but I'd be horrified if it died.'

'We did want ours,' said Steve flatly. 'But when Jill lost it, I handled everything wrong.'

It was her turn to wait for him to continue. Finally she said, 'How?'

'I said the wrong things. Christ knows what wrong things. I was trying to be helpful. And I wasn't sleeping any more than she was, we both had nightmares, but we couldn't share them. Things got confused. So I said wrong things. Blokey things, I suppose. Stuff about going forward, trying for the next time, all that.'

'Well, fair enough. You'd *have* to look forward.'

'Not so soon. I see that, now. Jill – well, it had lived inside her, hadn't it? Moved. She said it used to kick and stuff. Blokes don't get that. Emotional illiterates, they call us. Quite right. I should have gone out and slain a hairy mammoth and kept out of it. Not tried to talk to her.'

'But someone had to talk to her,' objected Maggie.

'Her mother did that. No Men Past This Point.'

Maggie rubbed a piece of bread in the sauce from her cod, and ate it. After a moment she said, 'Was that why you separated?'

'Probably. It was six months later. She left a note, and that was it.'

'Back to her mother?'

'Nope. Off with her fitness coach. An ape, even more boneheadedly macho than me. That's the weird thing. Her mother thinks he's ever such a nice young man.'

'Is she all right now?' Somehow, Maggie felt she had to go on asking, as if the absent, bereaved, unfaithful, unhappy Jill was her concern. The sisterhood of pregnant women, she thought, must be grasping her to its soft bosom already. Eugh. But she could not help herself. She reiterated, 'Is she OK? Over it?'

'Yes,' said Steve. 'I would say so. Fresh start. I heard she's pregnant again. There's no medical reason it shouldn't work out OK. Last time was some sort of one-off poisoning, I don't know, cream cheese or something.'

To her dismay there were tears in his eyes. She put her hand on his, patting it like a mother.

'I'm sorry. Shouldn't have pried.'

He recovered. 'Anyway, I hadn't finished grilling you about *your* mysterious intentions. Come on, spill it all. You're expecting a semi-Chilean baby but you don't want it, you're off to Hunan, and meanwhile you're doing what? Living with family? Did you say you had a sister?'

'Oh, God, you don't want to know. My life at the moment is like an edition of the Jerry Springer Show,' said Maggie bitterly. 'I am totally trailer trash.'

'I *love* Jerry Springer,' said Steve. 'Come on, let's have pudding and tell me all the unspeakable details. It'll cheer me up. Oh, go on.'

'Well,' said Maggie slowly. 'It begins in the year my dad died. Sixteen years ago.'

He called the waitress over, named two puddings, and settled back to listen.

Sarah prowled restlessly round the sitting room, unable to sew or watch television, unwilling to read. Leo sat with a book; the children had retired to their rooms.

'I ought to talk to Samantha,' she said. 'She's obviously in shock. I think the boys are all right.'

Leo looked up. The page was swimming before his eyes anyway. 'Sarah. Sweetheart.'

She looked at him coldly. 'Yes?'

'We have to sort it out between ourselves first. Before Sam, before anything. It's you and me.'

'You and *her*, more like.'

Leo flinched. 'There is no me and her. There never was. There was one night, one confused night.'

'All night?' Sarah could not help herself. It was a wound, a scab, a spot to which she kept returning.

'No,' said Leo, understanding her perfectly. 'Not even all night. We knew what a disaster it was straightaway. She was angry, she went off to her room. I couldn't believe it had happened. We weren't even meant to be in a bloody hotel, but the plane was delayed. I fell asleep, and when I woke up I managed not to believe I'd done it.'

'People don't get pregnant that easily.'

'Maggie did. I swear to you. And I swear, Sarah, that until she said the thing about the baby on Wednesday, I had no idea at all. God, do you think I would have let her do that? She didn't even do it properly, legally. She did herself harm, apparently.'

'So now she's spreading the harm about a bit, messing us up and upsetting Samantha. Oh, great.'

Leo sensed he was being unwise, yet could not prevent himself from slithering to the edge of the unthinkable slope. 'To be fair, love, when it happened Maggie wasn't that much older than Sam is now.'

Sarah turned away from him and left the room. Leo looked down at his book as if he had never seen such an object before. Then he threw it from him with some force, and stared into emptiness. In that moment, for the first time in his life, he wondered how he could most quickly and easily make himself die.

Upstairs, Sarah was saying, 'Are you all right, darling?' to Samantha, who was pretending hard to be asleep.

'So you see,' concluded Maggie as the candle on the table burnt low, 'Jerry Springer would love to have me on. I Secretly Aborted My Brother-In-Law's Love Child The Week Of His Wedding.'

'Not to mention I Did Secret Pregnancy Test With My Teenage Niece,' said Steve. 'And I Don't Want To Bring Up Married Sea Captain's Bastard Child Alone. You could do a whole edition of Jerry Springer all on your own, no trouble.'

'Right,' said Maggie. She turned and smiled at him, and he saw with surprise that she might sometimes be a beauty. 'Look, I *am* grateful. I didn't think there'd be anyone I could tell the whole awful story to. And confession is good for the soul. Such a *string* of crimes against decent society. I haven't even begun to think about Mrs Lopez back in Santiago.'

'Oh, for God's sake,' said Steve bracingly. 'Leave her out of it. What she doesn't know won't kill her.'

'I tried to tell myself that about Sarah, sixteen years ago,' said Maggie bitterly. 'But she knows now, doesn't she?'

'Well, you're not likely to end up at the Lopez kitchen table in sixteen years' time, are you?' he said. 'Talking of terrible house guests, how long are you staying there?'

'I promised to work in the shop until Christmas Eve,' said Maggie. 'It's not just for Leo's sake but because I reckon the family really can't afford to risk the seasonal profits. He can't cope on his own all the time, I know the job now, and pre-Christmas is the vital time.'

'So you stay there till then?'

'Yup. I'll find some way of not being in the house by Christmas Day.' The candle had burnt out and the restaurant was emptying. She glanced around. 'We'd better go.'

Stiffly, she rose from the table; he moved round to help her back with her chair, and followed her outside. The moon was brighter now, the tattered clouds in retreat; a few stars shone over the quiet waterfront. Silently, by common consent, they walked away from the car park and along by the sea, buffeted by the wind, admiring the glimmering track of the moon and the distant house lights on the Isle of Sheppey. Then they went back to the black Saab and climbed in, glad to be out of the rising gale as it brought back the rain. Maggie felt a brief, absurd wish that the journey home was longer. She could sit in this warm car with this dry, comradely man for hours in contentment. It would be like being in suspended animation, between two worlds. She felt a dread of Brackhampton.

'Bricked up,' she said aloud, staring out at the sea. 'Off to get bricked up again.'

He turned to look at her, smiled, then started the car and eased it forwards.

'You're tired,' he said. 'You need some sleep.'

But she didn't go to sleep on the way back to Brackhampton. She stayed awake, mainly silent, watching the dark wet road flow past and the lights of the little town grow clearer.

Chapter Twenty-four

Teddy had stayed overnight with his freckled friend, and on Saturday morning he came in to the bookshop. He crashed against the Christmas table with a cheerful 'Oops!' and announced to Leo and Maggie and the shop in general, 'Hey, hot news. Duane's in *prison*.'

'Who?' said Leo. 'Don't barge around like that.' He gave a professional smile to a thin startled lady by the travel shelf.

'Sam's old boyfriend, remember?' said Teddy. 'He came to supper and then afterwards you said he was a yob, and she got really upset and stamped out, and Mum said you'd better—'

'Yes, yes,' interrupted his father hastily. Teddy's voice had remarkable carrying qualities, and there were half a dozen people up in the children's department. 'But what do you mean, prison?'

'Young offender place. You know. At Normanfield.'

'What for?' asked Maggie, and almost on the same breath, 'Does Sam know?'

'For agg-agger-avated burgling. Remanded in custody, danger to the community. He hit this bloke on the way out, when he was doing the place over. Colin reckons he didn't mean to, he just lost it.'

Leo winced at his young son's fluency on the subject. 'Well,' he said vaguely. He could think of no other comment. It was for Maggie to ask again whether Samantha knew.

'Noooh,' said Teddy. 'S'why I came down here, to tell her, thought she'd be here 'cos she said she had Christmas shopping to do, and Dad gives us discounts here and Sam's mean as shit so she always—'

'Teddy!' said his father warningly.

'Well, she is. She always, always gives books. So if she comes in for mine, I want the Blackadder book. And Jamie wants Terry Pratchett.'

He left to rejoin his friends in the record shop, making a salute to the muscle-bound rapper who adorned the cover of the biggest-selling pop book of the season. 'Wo! Respeck!' His father delivered a sickly grin to the other customers once more, and vanished up the steps.

Samantha did come in, minutes later, and by her calm appearance Maggie assumed that she knew nothing about Duane. Her niece had appeared slightly less frosty when they crossed paths at breakfast time, so when Samantha was ensconced in a quiet bay the aunt came up behind her and said hesitantly, 'Sam. Teddy was in. He had a bit of news about Duane.'

Samantha started, turning to her wide-eyed. Then she composed herself and said indifferently, 'If it's about his new girlfriend, that is *so-oh* old news.'

'Not that,' said Maggie. 'He's in custody. Burglary with violence. He's at Normanfield.'

Samantha stared, open-mouthed. 'Oh shit! Stupid idiot! I always knew—' She stopped. The thin woman had looked round again.

'You knew that he went burgling?' Maggie kept her voice low, and Samantha followed suit.

'I knew his brother did. Jake. He's horrible. Was Dooze with his brother?' It was the first time Maggie had heard Sam use the nickname; she was strangely affected, almost to tears, by the unwilling proof of old affection. This tearfulness, she thought, was happening too often of late. Pregnancy. Must be hormones. With an effort she kept her voice level and light.

'I don't know. Teddy didn't seem to know much.'

'The thing is,' said Samantha, 'he was actually quite scared of his brother. He used to boast about him, how he was well hard. But I reckon he used to threaten him, to make him come out on jobs, 'cos Duane is really good at climbing, and really thin for windows, and Jake and his mates are all quite fat.'

'Right,' said Maggie. Once again, she was being confided in; the warmth it lit within her was astonishing.

'Yeah, 'cos once he was meant to go and help them break into a house, and I made him stay with me at a party instead. That was when he was still really keen on me. But next morning he had this big bruise down the side of his face.'

'His brother?'

'He said he had a fall and hit the cooker at home.'

Leo noticed them talking, kept his distance, and he, too, was inordinately relieved at the apparent truce. His daughter was still cool and uncommunicative with him, but if she was thawing towards her aunt, perhaps he would be next.

He was right. Samantha had been thinking hard for two days, and discussing the matter with the level-headed Uma at school.

'I don't think you should be too angry with your aunt,' Uma had said that very afternoon, as they walked down the broad avenue from school. 'If you stay furious with her, you have to be just as angry with your dad. And that wouldn't help, right? Hating him is, like, no point. You've only got one dad. And he's still there, isn't he? It's not like fathers who run off.'

It was bracing to be treated thus by the cerebral Uma, who seemed to assume that if people used their heads, reason and calm were bound to prevail. It suited Samantha's instincts better than the almost mawkish sympathy which her mother kept offering, late at night in whispering visits to her bedside, or in oversweet gestures of unspoken female empathy at mealtimes. There was always a hand on the shoulder, a finger trailed across her cheek, a sigh. *We are victims, you and I,* said Sarah's manner. *Men stray, women weep.*

By the end of the second day of this, Samantha found a small, hard core of resistance growing within her. Her mother could think what she wanted, do what she wanted. The fear of her parents' separation still struck cold panic into her stomach, but with an effort she quelled it. As for the crime itself she, Samantha, could take her own view. And with Uma's assistance, that view had come to encompass several aspects which had not at first been apparent to her. It happened before she was born, years ago, before they were married. It was, her father had said, a mistake. He clearly loved his wife and children; that much, as she remarked to Uma, could be spotted by a chimpanzee. He was very meek and sorry and putting up with no end of ratty treatment from Mum.

As for Maggie, she too was acting so meek and sorry that she didn't even eat meals with them any more, except for that grisly dinner when Gran came. And she had had a horrible time, thought Samantha, all alone and deciding about the abortion without even an aunt to help her. She, of all people, should sympathize with a situation where whatever you did, something awful and difficult would happen.

All in all, when Maggie spoke to her in the bookshop, Samantha leapt at the chance to be reasonably civil. When she understood the nature of the news about Duane, she reaped the reward: this was one of those moments when she needed to talk to someone more familiar with the rackety world than her parents.

Leaning on her father's bookshelves, she said, frowning slightly, 'I s'pose I'd better go and see him.'

Maggie was taken aback. 'I didn't mean that,' she began. 'I only told you because Teddy was going round saying it, and I thought you had a right to know early. But you're not Duane's girlfriend now.'

Sam stared at her. 'That's got nothing to do with it,' she said simply. 'I *was* his girlfriend, at least I *tried* to be. We were sort of friends, before – all the sex stuff. I sort of liked him. He was funny in class. I even felt sorry for him about his crappy family.'

Maggie raised an eyebrow, almost in her old teasing way.

Sam snapped, 'No, I don't still fancy him. No way. But I *liked* him. I might be able to help.'

'How?' Maggie was impressed, but unwilling to encourage this line of thought; she dimly saw more trouble ahead and did not welcome it.

'Character reference. If I could tell the police, like, that he got beaten up for not going on the robbery the other time, it could be intimidation, or mitigation, or something. And since everyone knows we broke up, they might listen to me more than his new bird.'

Maggie's admiration grew. Since she had been back in Brackhampton, she had seen Samantha first moody and pre-occupied, latterly terrified of pregnancy. There had been little opportunity to appreciate how much the child had grown up.

'That's brave, but don't do anything sudden,' she said slowly. 'Please. Getting mixed up with him has already cost you.'

'I'll ring his mother,' said Sam flatly. 'From my mobile. I'm not a baby.'

When she had gone, bookless, Maggie's hand went down to her stomach and her own fast-growing peanut of a baby. *Miracle!* she thought. Like it or not, it was a bloody miracle that only sixteen years after being a disposable peanut, only a few years after being a garrulous little Brownie, someone could grow a conscience as powerful and troublesome as that. *Respect, Samantha!* she said silently, and turned to take money from the thin lady, who had at last decided which Inspector Morse novel to read next. Outside the window she saw Miss Mountjoy hovering, glancing in at her with a bright, inquiring smile. She did a double thumbs-up, and to her surprise received one in return. Then a posse of customers tumbled down the steps from the children's department and she was busy for the rest of the morning.

Samantha walked home, and in through the kitchen where Sarah sat listlessly turning the pages of the newspaper.

''Lo, Mum,' she said, and made for the hall and the stairs.

'Oh darling, just a minute – while we've got a chance on our own . . .' began Sarah.

Samantha stopped walking, but shifted restlessly. 'Ya?' Her manner implied that this was not to be a long conversation, but she had little hope. 'On our own' could only mean more sticky emotional talk.

Sarah perceived her daughter's reluctance, but did not want to give up her chance. She was particularly low that morning, despondent and afraid. Leo continued meek and silent, Maggie had made no further overtures of peace, and altogether the burden of righteous victimhood laid heavy on Sarah's solitude. But whenever she felt an instinct to draw a line under the whole thing, forgive and carry on, a small raging voice inside her would begin again.

He never loved me, it was a sham, I was just the available one and he was gone thirty, wanted to settle down, wanted a wife who earned enough for him to set up the shop – preferred Maggie, they always go for the youngest they can, even now he's only thinking about how hard it was on her, poor little Maggie, everybody's baby, Dad's pet, always got away with murder, all her bloody life, never taken responsibility but oh yes, we have to think about poor Maggie having her slutty abortion. What about how I feel, what about my wounds, who cares about me? Who's ever cared? I'm the one who has to look after everybody. Who bothers to look after me, what about me, what about me, what about me?

In more rational moments Sarah knew that the voice was twisting truth, but she could not help it. It was as if a whole stretched life of cheerful hard-working endurance and thought for others had sprung back on itself, with every slight and resentment and small exploitation giving energy to the murderous coiling rage within her. It was as if every kind deed she had ever done was festering, feeding a great poisonous ache that must be lanced. *He only wanted the kids and the security, I was never exciting, never what he wanted, just boring old Sarah to fall back on, to cope with the kids,*

*everyone'll want to protect poor Maggie with her baby, but good old Sarah can
lump it . . .*

Her children, beautiful and bright, were her only reward. But
two of them knew nothing about her betrayal, and even in her
worst moments Sarah did not think of telling them. Only
Samantha knew, through no fault of her mother's, and therefore
Samantha was her ally, a younger self. Sarah persuaded herself
that she watched and comforted her daughter because it was
needed. In fact, as the clear-eyed and unsentimental Sam herself
had spotted, it was Sarah who needed these sessions. Now the
child braced herself and her mother made her inevitable pounce.

'Sweetheart, the thing is, Christmas. It's going to be difficult
for you, I know. We ought to talk about how to manage it.'

'Well, the usual,' said Samantha, surprised. 'I s'pose Gran's
coming round, and the family, and the normal stuff.'

Sarah's voice dropped into a low, hurt register. 'It can't be
normal, though, can it?'

Samantha wanted to ask 'Why not?' but thought better of it.
Instead she said, 'Whatever you think. Only the boys would be
surprised if it wasn't the usual stuff.'

Sarah knew perfectly well that this would be the deciding
factor, and that somehow they would conduct Christmas along
normal lines. Leo's rôle in the feast, anyway, was to arrive home
exhausted from the shop on Christmas Eve, sleep in till eleven on
Christmas Day, be impressed by the latest stocking-filler toys,
and then try unsuccessfully to persuade everybody to go on a nice
walk before lunch; after which, he once again slept. Nancy would
talk non-stop until she, too, fell asleep over Christmas tea, and
everybody left awake would watch the big film and go yawning
to bed. There was no particular reason to put a bomb under
Christmas, except for the very pressing reason that she, Sarah,
wanted to detonate something – anything – to ease her own
anguish.

Sulkily she said, 'Well, what about Maggie? It's hard enough
for you, having her still here, but at Christmas!'

Samantha closed her eyes and hunched her shoulders. After the relief of her *rapprochement* with Maggie in the shop, it was only just occurring to her that it would cause more trouble with her mother. She searched for something to say, something safe. She was only fifteen, though, and happened to come up with the least safe thing of all.

'Well, I don't mind,' she said, thinking she was being cautious. 'And she is pregnant, so p'raps we ought to be looking after her at Christmas.'

Her mother had often told them to think of the vulnerable at Christmas. One or two of the vulnerable, indeed, had spent Christmas Days with them. Sam, in her innocence, thought that it would help to portray her aunt not as desirable company but as a charity case. She even felt guilty on Maggie's behalf as she played this card. She did not expect the reaction she got.

'Right!' screamed Sarah, rising from her chair. 'Out of my sight! You, of all people! Go and run the poor-dear-Maggie club with your bloody father! Just FUCK OFF!'

Sarah never swore. Never. Tears misting her eyes, Samantha stumbled from the room and ran upstairs. Bloody Mum. Bloody parents, fucking everything up. Bloody Aunt Maggie, shooting her mouth off. Everything they did was for their own precious stupid feelings, so fuck them!

It did not take long, though, before she dried her eyes, composed herself, and took out her mobile phone to ring Duane's mother.

'Mrs Atherton?' she said. 'Only, it's Sam here. Remember, I went out with Dooze . . . it's just that I'm ever so sorry . . .'

Downstairs, Sarah sobbed on the newspaper, fat tears soaking into the front-page pictures of Prince William.

Chapter Twenty-five

Without spare money, for she was still anxiously hoarding all she could, Maggie was exercised over the best way to spend the two Sundays before Christmas. Leo would not open the shop on a Sunday even for a few hours, though much of the High Street did. 'You have to draw a line somewhere, and that's mine.' So Sunday, yawned empty before her.

In the first week, the day dawned sunny, and it was easy enough to say that she needed a hike and head out of town towards the sea. There was some grumbling from Teddy, who wanted to come too, but Sarah quelled it. So Maggie walked alone, sat for a while on the shingle, then took the afternoon bus back. Another week passed, with Leo reserved and depressed and Sarah maintaining a frosty silence. Maggie persuaded Leo to stay open late each night, and manned the shop alone until eight, eating a cheese sandwich and avoiding the family meal. She also, incidentally, did some very fair business with the evening shoppers.

On the second Sunday it rained, heavy remorseless rain which made the formerly flooded citizens of Brackhampton grow anxious and start heaving sandbags. Maggie thought of using up the day by going to Nancy's house, to combine a duty visit with sorting out some of her possessions in the attic. But when she phoned, her mother informed her with a faintly triumphant air that no, it wasn't convenient, as she would be out all day on a Townswomen's Guild outing to a Christmas fair and turkey dinner. Maggie thought of asking for the key and spending quiet time on her own in the old attic, but a kind of delicacy prevented her. It was her mother's home now, not hers.

Nor did she trust her feelings about being alone and secretly pregnant in that house whose very mortar was imbued with girlhood memories about Nancy's terror of unmarried motherhood. The one thing that was certain, she reflected with a dry twist of her mouth, was that each one of the old newspapers that covered the attic floor would have neat shapes cut out of it: all the stories about pregnant teenagers with which Nancy used to bombard her daughters when they got home from school.

Finally she resolved to stay in her room working on her Chinese until noon, then go out for a long walk in the rain. The inevitable soaking of her jeans bothered her more than anything else. Out of delicacy for Sarah's feelings she was trying to keep her clothes out of the family laundry system. Sarah ran that side of life, and Sarah was always home when Maggie was; but why should Sarah untangle her detested sister's intimate clothing from that of her husband, her children? So, miserably, Maggie tried to manage as best she could. She tidied and cleaned her room meticulously, but the chairs and bedhead were always festooned with drying clothes.

At noon she set out from the house, trying not to smell the fragrance of Sarah's Sunday roast. Glancing back, she saw Leo relaxed in the sitting room, with Teddy for once sitting sedately at his feet, reading aloud from a book. Leo leaned forward and ruffled his small son's hair, laughing at him. In the doorway she could see Jamie, and for once his moody face, too, was alight with the joke.

Cast out of Eden, thought Maggie to herself in the rain, and smiled at the absurdity of the thought. It wasn't Eden, not with Sarah nursing her cold wounded fury, Leo scared sick that she would leave him, and Samantha fretting over her burglarious ex-boyfriend. Not Paradise, then. But it was as close as most people got: it was a home, and it would heal itself. Probably all the faster once she had gone. She had announced to Sarah, or rather to Sarah's back view in the kitchen, that she would definitely pack up and go on the 23rd, which was Saturday. Leo was not planning to open on the Christmas Eve Sunday, so she would have discharged her duty to the bookshop. Sarah had said, 'Suit yourself, you usually do,' in a flat, nasty voice.

Now, walking down the alley to the High Street, her hood pulled up against the rain, Maggie wondered whether to use the afternoon to look for somewhere to stay. After all her years abroad she could barely remember how far Britain closed down over the Christmas holiday; she ought not to leave it too late. But her soul revolted at the thought of lodging in Brackhampton when her job and family ties were gone. If you were going to be an outcast, you might as well cast yourself somewhere you wanted to be. Nor did she much rate her chances of finding another job in the little town. Still, she could get a local freesheet and sit in the library looking through the rooms-to-let page. Or take the train to London and find a YWCA hostel.

She was so preoccupied, her head so bowed against the driving rain, that Steve Arundel had to call her name twice when he stopped his car at the bottom of the alley. The second time he accompanied it with a loud, 'Hoy!'

'Oh – hi,' said Maggie, surprised. She had heard nothing from him since they parted nine days ago, but then she had not given him an address or telephone number. She had vaguely thought that he might look in at the bookshop, and had glanced in the Costarica each morning, but never saw the tall familiar form. So she had deliberately let this new friend slip from her thoughts. She had, after all, done it often enough before as she changed continents. You met someone, you exchanged stories, you had a laugh, you moved on.

But here he was again, leaning out of his sleek black company Saab, grinning. She was immoderately pleased to see him.

'First time lucky!' he said. 'No, truly. I would hate you to think I had been cruising around all week looking for you.'

'Oh yeah?' said Maggie happily.

'Nope, I've been in St Petersburg,' he said. 'Saturday morning, boss rang, said my oppo wouldn't go because his wife's been ill. Boss said in his tactful way, "You can always rely on the gay divorcees to step in," and transferred me the tickets. I just got back from Heathrow this morning, thought I'd taste some decadent Western city life in Brackhampton.'

She was in the passenger seat beside him now, motioned there by expansive welcoming gestures, glad to be out of the rain. 'You think I'm a fantasist, don't you?' he said teasingly. 'You think I haven't been anywhere at all, just couldn't be bothered to stay in touch. Or else gone back to my wife and nine children in Newcastle. Oooh, men! They're awful!'

With a flourish he pulled out the remains of an airline ticket, and a Russian boarding pass.

'*Now*,' said Maggie, 'I really do think you're a suspicious character. No honest man ever hangs on to his alibi like that. Men always chuck bits of paper away as soon as they can. It's women who have bottomless handbags.'

'You don't know many reps, do you, hippie-chick?' said Steve scornfully. 'Expenses claims! Never discard anything! Some of us spent our underpaid youth going round the waste bins in hotels and airport lounges, hoping to pick up other people's receipts.'

Maggie laughed, and settled in her seat. The car was moving now. 'Where are you heading?' she asked. 'You do realize I'm only using this vehicle as an extra raincoat.'

'Fancy lunch?'

'That's kind, but . . .' She was troubled now. 'Look,' she said. 'I may not have made it entirely clear to you the other night, but I really can't spend money. All that Jerry Springer stuff I told you means, basically, that I've got to move out in a week's time and find another job, and pay my way till I can get sorted. So I can't go

Dutch. And in the circumstances I ought to. Couldn't we just – I don't know – drive?'

Steve glanced at her, then back at the road. 'I want my *dinner*,' he said plaintively. 'Oh, go on, let me have lunch. You can eat the bits off the plate that I don't want. Or you could sit under the table, if you like, and beg.'

'I don't want to stop you—' began Maggie primly.

'Shut up. *One*, I'm still on subsistence expenses, travelling home. So you're compromising your honour to Periffatec, not me. *Two*, I've spent the last week's meals negotiating with spivvy Slavs who like to eat their dinner against a backdrop of large friends with flat faces and shoulder holsters. It buggers up your digestion. I just want to eat food and have somebody talk to me about something other than ultraspeed data backup protocols and the best bank to use for backhanders. Is that too bloody much to ask, woman?'

'No,' said Maggie, settling back. 'As long as I can think of it as necessary social work for the victims of capitalism.'

He drove through the rain, up to the sea road and then off to the left again, and after a while she said, 'Whitstable?'

'Where else?'

'Lovely.' And once again they settled into the companionable silence which was becoming as natural to them as their joshing conversations. Maggie glanced at his profile, wondering about Steve Arundel. He liked to amuse and mildly shock; he took life as lightly as he could, yet had not been unwilling to admit his pain about the lost baby and vanished wife. He was a traveller, but not as she had been; drifting and seeing and marvelling was not enough for him. He liked a goal, a project. He must be good at what he does, thought Maggie, to be the kind of operator who was sent to do a deal in a new country without preparation. A troubleshooter, then; a safe pair of hands.

Steve's thoughts were on her, too. She was not at all the kind of girl he generally took out, nothing like his pretty doll of a wife or his silver-blonde secretary Ingrid. It baffled him slightly that each time he had left her he had felt a pang of worry that he might not find her again. She was not pretty, or not all the time; right now she looked both thinner and more pregnant than a week ago. Her face had subtly aged, too, the lines of tension and anxiety more marked even than on the day he picked her up soaking and dishevelled on the sea road, and she had sweetly worried about dripping on his passenger seat.

Suddenly, with a force that surprised and shook him, Steve felt the impulse to solve her problems. Or at least, some of them. It would not be hard. He frowned, looking at the road ahead with fierce concentration. The germ of an idea came to him almost at once, and he smiled into the rain.

Samantha chose that Sunday lunch to drop another bombshell of unwelcome information into her family circle. Sarah laid great store by family meals, and it had been a successful enough policy to make her daughter instinctively feel that the gap between roast pork and apple pudding was the safest forum in which to introduce a dangerous subject. Everyone was there. There were witnesses, and a variety of different points of view. Jamie, she thought, might be an ally. So might her father, who was always so keen on talking about social justice. So she took a deep breath and said, as her mother doled out the pudding, 'I saw Duane. I got a visiting order and went to Normanfield.'

'Isn't he out?' asked Jamie, amazed. 'Only Bill said—'

'No. His mum hasn't got the money for bail, and she's pissed off with him anyway. He's still remanded in custody.' Samantha had learned a great deal about the youth criminal justice system lately. 'It'll come off his sentence if he gets convicted, but I don't think he ought to be, anyway.'

'Why didn't you ask before you went?' said Sarah, her voice as cool as she could make it. 'I don't know what I feel about you going to that place on your own.'

'I went with his cousin,' said Sam stoutly. 'And I went because I want to help, and I knew you'd want to stop me.'

'What sort of help?' asked Leo suspiciously. 'I thought you two broke up months ago.'

'We did. But if people only ever did anything good for their boyfriends and girlfriends, well . . .'

She was twisting the argument against them before it had even properly begun, using their years of vaguely liberal preaching as weapons to defeat them. Leo saw this and inwardly admired her. Aloud he only said, 'So what is it you want to do?'

'Character witness. I know for sure that his brothers beat him up if he didn't help them do burglaries. I know 'cos once I made him stay at a party and not go, and next day he was all bruised.'

'God Almighty!' exploded Sarah. Everyone jumped; although in the past few weeks her temper had been short, it was unusual for her to break out quite so abruptly. 'What sort of school is this? Some sort of thieves' kitchen?'

Leo looked nervous. From time to time, through their family life, the question of private education had come up. It came up when Jamie was slow to read, when Teddy came home swearing, when Samantha was put in for only eight GCSEs compared to London friends' children who did eleven or twelve. Sarah had several times become concerned enough to wonder whether she ought to try going back into a full-time city career to pay for a private day school. Leo, however, had always been of the view that Brackhampton Park was a perfectly good comprehensive and that it did middle-class children no harm at all to mix with all sorts while they were young. Besides, when Sarah talked of going back to London work, he secretly feared humiliation for her. It was a long time since she had been at Intertech; women in their forties were expected to have longer CVs than she had, and he shrewdly guessed that the working world might reject her. Better for her, he thought, to keep the illusion that she could step back instantly into that high-paid world but chose family and community instead.

Now, however, the venom of her irritation was aimed directly at him.

'I suppose now you'll say how wonderful it is that Sam's mixing with a wide social spectrum. Normanfield!'

Samantha was rattled by her mother's reaction, but pressed on. 'He's not that bad, Mum. He shouldn't have to go to prison. He's just got a crap family, right? And his barrister thinks it'd be really helpful if he had my evidence about the brothers threatening him. Kevin's up on the same charge, 'cos they got him too, but Gaz got away. And apparently I have to have parental permission, 'cos it's voluntary my being a witness.'

'Well, I don't think you should be involved,' said Sarah flatly. 'You're too young.'

'Same age as Duane,' muttered her daughter.

'An' *he* might be going to *prison*,' said Teddy.

'He's *in* prison, dork,' said his brother.

'Yeah, but I meant really, with a sentence an' that.'

'Don't *you* think she's too young, Leo?' said Sarah combatively. 'Do you think a courtroom is the right place for a girl who isn't even sixteen yet?'

Leo stared at his plate, then looked at his daughter with a sort of silent appeal. She looked right back, catching his eye, and he understood with a sinking heart what he must do.

'Sam knows the boy,' he said slowly. 'These young offender institutions are really rough. They turn more kids on to crime than off it. If he does get acquitted now, it could make the difference to a whole life. A whole chain of lives. Perhaps it's what she ought to do. Perhaps it's the right thing.'

'And you'd be the moral expert around here?'

Leo dropped his eyes, defeated. Now it was Samantha who shook with rage.

'Mum, that is *so* below the belt!'

Sarah looked warningly towards the boys, but Samantha blundered on. 'Just because Dad goes wrong once, sixteen years ago, you're making him into a – a criminal! And you're virtually throwing Auntie Maggie out of the house when she's *pregnant*, and it's not fair!'

'Is she pregnant?' asked Jamie, and 'What did Dad do wrong?' asked his brother.

'Now look what you've done!' This from Sarah.

'You started it!'

'Now look here, madam—'

'No, you look here!' Samantha, like her mother and aunt, grew dangerously voluble when roused. 'You're being so unfair! Maggie has to go out wandering around in the rain because of you – she has to wash her own clothes in the basin so's not to upset you – she's all miserable and sorry, and it's not fair, when she's pregnant and stuff. Because she was great about Duane, said she respected me for wanting to help, and she was brilliant to me when I thought *I* was preg—'

She stopped, too late.

Chapter Twenty-six

Both parents stared in horror at Samantha's flushed cheeks and dark shaggy hair. Blushing, caught out, she looked for a moment like a naughty six year old. Leo recovered himself first.

'When you *what?*' he said, in a voice unlike his own.

Samantha took a deep breath and stared at the row of hanging pans and ladles on the wall behind her parents.

'I had a scare, right? It's not that big a deal, lots of girls do. But I was really frightened and I didn't want to worry you, and Maggie got me a test and helped me do it. And I wasn't. It was fine. And that's how she found out *she* was, actually, so that was weird for her too. And I think she's really cool and brave, not having an abortion but letting it get adopted. I would've probably got rid of mine because I'm not brave like she is.'

Part of Sarah wanted to hug her daughter, but there was too much anger and unfocused terror in her. Coldly she said, 'And would you, I wonder, have mentioned this abortion to us at all? Or would your experienced Auntie Maggie have arranged everything for you without thinking to consult us?'

'She said I ought to tell you anyway.'

'She should have told me herself.'

'I didn't want her to, and it was my business.'

'You are only *fifteen!*'

Leo broke in. 'I think we ought to talk about this calmly,' he said. He did not like the way that Jamie and Teddy had withdrawn from their usual flow of commentary and begun to concentrate fiercely on their almost empty plates. His soul revolted at having his sons confronted so crudely with these facts of female life – particularly Jamie, whose blush was visible beyond his curtain of hair. Too long, thought the father irrelevantly; too long; it was time that boy had a haircut, it was time this family was got back under control . . .

'Calmly! I'm sure,' said Sarah with venomous sweetness, 'that it's the kind of thing *you* find it *very* easy to be calm about.'

Samantha had recovered herself. She stood up, carefully this time, not scraping her chair as she had on the night of Maggie's outburst. She replaced it squarely and tidily at the table, although her hands were shaking, and said, 'I'm going round to Uma's, right?'

'You are going nowhere!' said her mother. 'And who was responsible for this – what you call this scare of yours, anyway?'

'Duane,' said Samantha flatly. 'He *was* my boyfriend, right? Because whatever you think, I am not a *complete* tart.'

'And now you want to make a show of yourself in court, standing up for this little yob?'

Leo remembered, wonderingly, how often Sarah had rebuked him for referring to Duane as a yob. A line swam in to his head. 'A liberal is somebody whose interests are not, at the moment, threatened.' Something like that. He was alarmed by this new Sarah, and sorrowful at the part he had played in her creation. But his children were around him, and they were troubled, and he must take some kind of lead.

'Let her go,' he said firmly. 'Sam, you go to the Syals. We'll all talk later.' And to Sarah, 'Why don't you go and take some time for yourself, sweetheart. The boys and I will wash up.'

Sarah, startled by the firmness of his tone, hesitated but eventually went upstairs. Samantha grabbed a coat – not hers but the first that came to hand, the leaking jacket Maggie had worn for a while – and went out into the rain. Leo and the boys washed up, and haltingly, kindly, the father tried to put the upheaval into perspective for his sons.

When the car drew up in Whitstable, Maggie and Steve were deep in conversation about the Inca trail. It began teasingly enough, with him mentioning it casually as they overtook some damp determined hikers, and her joshing him for having abandoned his Marco Polo salesmanship in Lima to walk like a useless tourist for four days.

'So I'm not allowed a soul now?'

'You virtually told me you didn't have one. Didn't believe in them. Called me a tree-hugger.'

'Well, all right. I was pressurized into it by a keen guide I met in Lima.'

'Inca trail guides don't hang around in commercial hotels in Lima.'

'This one did.'

'So what did you make of it?'

'Too many tourists. Bloody packed. Like Blackpool.'

'No, it isn't! Those fabulous moonrises! The lost city, in the morning mist!'

'Lost, my foot. Litter all along the way. Touts. Made me angry. I'll tell you what it made me feel – I felt as if there was nowhere to escape to, even if I wanted to. No parallel world after all.'

Maggie looked at him. They had both got out of the car, and stood facing one another across its sleek black roof. The rain had died away here at the coast, and the sky was lightening.

'No parallel world . . .' she said wonderingly. 'God, I know what you mean. I've always had a vague idea that if I stopped travelling, there was another universe I could step into. Happy families and dull solid little houses and washing the car at weekends and everyone quite contented and not wanting to get out.'

'And there wasn't?' He locked the car, came round, and led the way to the restaurant.

'Well, I thought it existed. I suppose I've always used my sister's home as a sort of theme park. Welcome to Familyworld. I visit, I ride the flumes and roundabouts of aunthood, pay my dues, fold up one of the kids' paintings as a souvenir, and go back to my own life.'

'Mmm.' Steve nodded in complete understanding. 'Me too. I visit other people's realities just to check they're there. Sneak away from the corporate entertainment, go to a dive, play that I'm a poor gaucho for the evening.'

'Or play that you're a backpacker on the Inca trail.'

'Never again. It was as bad as the time I was doing a deal on printers with the Venice police, and went in a gondola. I was depressed for a week.'

'I like gondolas,' said Maggie. 'I went out with a lovely young gondolier once or twice.'

'I bet his mother thought you were a horrid foreign prostitute who'd ruin his life and give him VD,' said Steve.

'Well, yes, actually. How did you know?'

'Worked in Italy, haven't I?'

The reached the restaurant, but its doors were unpromisingly closed.

'Bugger!' said Steve. 'Look!'

There was a sign, announcing a seasonal closure until the 3rd of January. He glanced at his watch and said, 'The other good one'll be full, always is. They wouldn't feed us this late anyway. Have to be the pub. Quick.' He reached for her hand with his usual brotherly insouciance and led her running along the seafront towards a faded sign that swung in the wind, depicting seven unlikely-looking fruits attached to a curling vine. Out of breath, they pushed open the door and found a half-empty saloon, its shabbiness only slightly alleviated by some swags of tinsel, its dartboard ancient and pockmarked, its pool table visibly down at one end.

'Lovely,' he said. 'Used to come here with my uncle when he was alive. Watch out, it's the sort of place where your feet stick to the floor.'

So they did; Maggie felt a definite tackiness between the rubber soles of her sneakers and the dingy linoleum. A cadaverous, sullen man with a blue birthmark on his neck stood behind the bar, sniffing. There was, however, a menu on the wall and within fifteen minutes they each had a plateful of hake and chips to go with their beer.

'Good fish,' said Maggie.

'Always is here. Local. And the landlord doesn't cook it himself, gets a woman in from the town.' He glanced around. 'God, I haven't been in here since Uncle Anton died.'

'Mm, meant to ask you about that. You never said you had family connections here.'

'Used to have. That's why I started coming to the restaurant. Anton was a sort of uncle once removed. Half Russian. Don't ask, my family's complicated. I was almost the only one left he was still on speaking terms with. He lived here because he used to be in the navy, in submarines, and he had to be by the sea.'

'Yes, I can see that. Remember how I cheered up when we first came here? Considering it's such a teeny harbour, it feels very shippy.'

'Is that different from boaty?'

'Oh yes. Boaty means little beach dinghies and plastic skimming dishes with striped sails and people in yellow wellies talking about racing rules. Shippy means – well, fishing boats, and maybe tugs, and a sense that real ships might come from a long way off. *Evangelina*.'

'You're a bit fixated about that trip, aren't you?' He said it kindly enough, but she ducked her head and looked away.

'It's just . . .' She found that she could not go on.

'Captain Whatsit? You miss him?'

Her head came up then, and green eyes met his with a stare of astonishment.

'Noooh! Never! Poor old Joaquim – no, no, no. That was a mistake, like – well, like Leo, only more cheerful at the time.' She ate a chip, with self-conscious debonairness, as if to show her utter freedom from romantic regrets. 'No. It's because of this blasted business.' She laid a hand on her stomach. 'Because I panic. I wonder whether I will ever go on a journey like that again, a journey that blows your mind, gives you, I dunno, a direct line to, to . . .'

The sentence tailed off. She did not know what the direct line might lead to. She shrugged, and ate another chip. 'So I panic, and when I have bad dreams it always seems to be about the *Evangelina*, sailing away without me.'

'You said you could have stayed on.'

'Yes, but . . . it's not what I do.'

'If you had stayed on,' said Steve, pushing his plate away from him, then changing his mind and eating the last three chips after all, '*Evangelina* would have become ordinary, and you'd have felt as if you'd married it and settled down in a little brick house to wash its underpants and go to Tesco's in the car with it every Saturday. Am I, or am I not, one of the leading analytical psychologists of the age?'

For an answer she smiled at him, a heart-stopping smile, and his cautious heart turned over.

They finished their meal, paid, and stood up, stretching stiffly from the pub's uncomfortable wooden settles. As they left, Maggie noticed a curling sign in green felt pen tacked untidily to the upright wooden beam which, without much conviction, supported the ceiling over the bar.

'*Due to defection of ungrateful slut*,' it said, '*bar staff wanted from 26 Dec. until student labour reappears in June. Full or part-time, poor pay, depressed landlord, all the damaged crisps you can eat. Experience preferred, no complete morons please.*'

Maggie laughed. 'My kind of job,' she said, pointing. 'If only!'

'If only what?'

'If only it was Whitstable I was looking for a job in.'

He stopped in his tracks, stock still, understanding that by some providence the last piece of his vague, quixotic plan had fallen into place. 'Why isn't it?'

'Nowhere to live. It's not the kind of place for cheap lodgings, is it? From Easter it'll be all ritzy holiday lets.'

'Come with me.' He took her hand again and drew her out into the damp air. Again they hurried together through the drizzle, down the narrow gut between the white shiplap walls of the old oyster sheds, until he pulled her up short, let go of her hand, and fumbled with the flat leather case of keys from his trouser pocket.

'Hang on – oh, here it is. Look!' He was by a peeling door, next to the barred window of a dilapidated chandlery, and when he found the key he put his hand on the door in a practised manner, and unlocked it. Holding the key in the open position he gave a sharp kick to the bottom of the door and a blow of his palm to the centre; it came open with a reluctant 'chunk!' and revealed a dim yawning space and a stairway.

'Where's this?' said Maggie, amused. 'Don't tell me you live here!'

'No. Uncle Anton did. Come and see.' He went up the stairs first, throwing back words of caution about rotten planking and an uneven riser. At the top he took out another key and opened another door on the right, into the space above the chandler's store. Light flooded the dim stairway. Maggie hurried after him, and looked through the door. Steve had turned, and was standing triumphantly in the centre of an attic, or studio, with a great skylight and a high window looking out towards the sea.

Glancing round, Maggie saw a wide mattress on a makeshift wooden platform, with a ragged curtain on a rail pulled half across it, a plastic garden table and two chairs, and a long set of shelves, once neatly made but now bowed and warped with age and the cheapness of the original pine. There was a wooden chest, too, with a stencilled name just visible on the painted lid, and a pile of paper rubbish and broken utensils cast into the corner which, judging by the ancient and rusting cooker, had served the occupant as a kitchenette. There was a yellowing, chipped electric radiator standing unplugged beside it. One corner of the big square space was partitioned off, with a sliding door half falling off its tracks.

'All mod cons,' said Steve as her eye fell on this unpleasing corner. 'Shower and bog. In fact, you can probably shower while sitting on the bog, which would save time in the mornings.'

'Uncle Anton's flat?' asked Maggie.

He nodded. 'Good, isn't it? He left me a twenty-three year lease, much to the disgust of the chandler underneath, who wants to use it as a store. But I haven't been able to bring myself to sell it on to him. It used to have all Anton's model ships, and bits of purloined RN crockery. I've been moving them gradually, but the flat remains a millstone.'

'You could use it for holiday lets.'

'With that bathroom? And kitchenette? In the twenty-first century?'

'You could convert it.' She had guessed his offer before he made it, but a mixture of fear and excitement made her stall.

'Hardly worth it for the length of the lease. My best bet is to let it to someone who isn't fussy,' he said. 'You, for instance. Go for the bar job, hole up in Whitstable, keep away from your Jerry Springer family, look out at the sea every morning. Get it all over with, and make your plans.'

Maggie took a deep breath and gazed around her. The rain that dribbled down the skylight was not coming in; there was no smell of damp, or mildew, or even of lonely old uncle; only the faint, comforting aroma of wood and tar. In the silence, a sudden gust of wind blew, pattering more rain on the roof; the building creaked comfortably, like a sailing ship. Wonderingly, she laid her hand on the doorframe, and stroked it as she might the shoulder of a horse.

'Oh God, that is so, so kind,' she began. 'Oh Steve, but I can't afford anything as wonderful . . .'

He looked from her transported face to the crooked sliding door of the lavatory, and back again, with such a theatrical expression of comic astonishment on his face that she began to laugh, and the laugh banished the tears which she had been perilously, pregnantly about to shed.

'I admit,' he began, in oleaginous imitation of a Knightsbridge estate agent, 'that its many period details and sympathetic architectural originalities command a premium. And indeed we are looking at generating a substantial rental income. Say, fifteen quid a week?'

'That's ridiculous!'

'Ten, then. Seriously, I haven't known what to do with it. I don't want to leave it empty or there'll be squatters, or the chandler will invade it. I had romantic thoughts of moving in myself, but I have to be close to Periffatec because I hate getting up early. Go on. Six months or so. A couple of days with a screwdriver and a mop, and you could be in here for Christmas with nobody to bother you.'

It was irresistible. She did not resist. When Steve dropped her back in Brackhampton High Street that evening, everything was settled. He even sat in on her brief interview with the dour landlord of the Seven Grapes, and refused to let her work more than a thirty-hour week.

'No maternity pay rubbish,' said Ardriss the landlord, a calculatedly morose, cadaverous figure with an unhealthy high colour in his cheeks. 'Don't care what the law says, can't be bothered to read it. Temps ain't got no rights.'

'Fine,' said Maggie. 'Fine by me. I don't want rights. I don't even live here, really.'

'Australian?' asked Mr Ardriss. 'I like Aussies. They don't mind washing floors. No class-consciousness. Bloody English students think it's beneath them.'

'Nothing's beneath Miss Reave,' said Steve loftily. 'Speaking as her pastor and psychiatric social worker, I am happy to say that she has few delusions about her status.'

'You're not a social worker,' said the landlord witheringly, snapping shut the book in which he had written Maggie's proposed bar shifts. 'You're Anton Arundel's nephew. He used to bring you in here and cheat you at poker.'

'Kept him in whisky, didn't it?'

On the way back to Brackhampton, Steve told Maggie more about old Anton and his friends on the fishing boats, about the ill-tempered chandler and the morose pub landlord. When they parted, she felt strangely comfortable and rooted in the raffish little waterfront community she planned to join. Impulsively, as she bent to the driver's window with her farewells, she kissed him on the cheek. He laughed, and gave her a thumbs-up; they had already arranged to meet when the bookshop closed on Saturday evening.

As he pulled away, a spry little figure which had paused to watch them detached itself from the shadows and walked off along the street. Miss Mountjoy was pleased to see that Maggie and her new boyfriend were still getting along. She mentioned as much to nice Mrs Penn outside the vet's office in the morning, thus accidentally hardening Sarah's heart still further against her wayward, ungrateful, infuriatingly buoyant little sister.

Chapter Twenty-seven

'There is such an atmosphere at home,' said Samantha despairingly to Uma, 'that I don't want to live there any more. Can't I come and stay with you?'

'Oh yes, with my mother such best friends with your mother, I can just *see* how well that would work,' said Uma with bracing sarcasm. 'Especially at Christmas, oh yes.' The two girls were leaning against the brick wall of the science block, sharing a Mars Bar out of sight of censorious dieting friends. 'Mumma was only saying yesterday that she hasn't seen your ma since hospital, and she might pop round.'

'I wonder how much Mum's told her,' mused Samantha. 'She'd probably think Nita would be shocked by it all.'

'Well, *you* thought that I would be shocked about you doing that preggy test,' said Uma accusingly. For upon arriving the afternoon before, a tearful Sam had finally unrolled the whole of her story to her friend. 'Like I didn't *guess* anyway! The way you were round Duane at school, the way that you broke up then got more miserable and not less. It was obvious what you were scared about. Then one morning you get in and you're dead cheerful. Doesn't take Inspector Morse to work it out.'

'Well, Mum didn't guess.'

'She knows now, though. So you have to get back and face

her, don't you? Just tell her it was a mistake, and you handled it, end of story.'

'All very well for you, you've never had anything like that.'

'Well, if I did, I would be proud if I coped with it. I wouldn't hide. I'd say hey, look, I'm a free agent, I get things sorted.'

'Easy to say,' said Samantha, but her friend's words gave her hope. Painful though life was at the moment, it seemed to her as if she was being renewed: shedding a skin, leaving behind the useless shreds and rags of childishness that she had, for too long, been trying to patch together for protection. It was colder out in this adult world, but the air was clearer too. 'I s'pose you're right. I'm not a kid.'

'Right!' said Uma. 'And if you wanna give evidence for Duane, you do that too. They can't stop you. Children Act, human rights, free expression, right?' Uma had lately decided to become a barrister. She frowned, and went on, 'But what about your auntie? I think that's sad, about her and your ma.'

'So do I,' said Samantha, her brow clouding over again. 'Maggie's moving out for Christmas. I don't know whether she's even got anywhere to go.'

After Miss Mountjoy had innocently revealed to her the existence of Maggie's supposed boyfriend, Sarah could hardly complete her morning's work for rage. Sam Miller was forced to snap at her once or twice for elementary stupidities, and Sarah passed his snarls on with interest to the young receptionist. Eventually, exasperated beyond endurance at the frosty atmosphere of his surgery, the old vet said, 'For God's sake, Sarah, draw a line under it, for everyone's sake. Forgive the poor bastard and all get on with your lives.'

'It's not *Leo*,' said Sarah scathingly. 'It's *Maggie*, and all she's done, and the nerve of her keeping it secret about little Sam – the bloody nerve, who does she think she is, swanning in to our family and taking over, keeping secrets, turning my children against me—'

Miller's dry, quizzical look arrested her in mid-sentence.

'Good,' he said quietly, squinting at an X-ray film against the light. 'Good girl!'

'What's good?' Flushed and dishevelled with outrage, Sarah was suddenly conscious of her chaotic appearance, and of the fact that the old vet was also a man.

'Good that you've turned it outside the family. If you and Leo gang up on your sister, it gives you common cause. Already you're much less cross with him, aren't you?'

Sarah examined her own feelings and discovered, to her slight astonishment, that this was indeed the case.

Later that day, over a mug of green tea in Nita's tidy kitchen, she admitted as much to her friend, and Nita, too, made approving noises. Privately, Mrs Syal had a strong sense of justice and thought that Sarah was being unduly hard on her sister. But she was a practical woman, and considered it wiser to rip up a sibling relationship than to endanger a marriage with children. With delicate caution, therefore, she let Sarah rant on, blaming all the trouble on the inconsiderate and immoral Maggie. Maggie, after all, would go away soon; she always did. Sarah's marriage must endure. It was the law of survival.

So gradually, as the two women talked, Leo ceased to be a monster of infidelity and became a fellow victim and an admirably caring father, concerned for his daughter. It helped further that the man himself – tipped off by old Sam Miller when he dropped in to buy his wife a gardening book – took the trouble to leave the shop early, buy a side of sliced smoked salmon, and drive round to Nita's house to offer his wife a lift home.

'I could do us scrambled eggs and smoked salmon,' he said. It had been a staple supper in their early, child-free days. 'The boys can have a pizza from the freezer, and Sam says she'll grab a hot dog at the Christmas market with Uma.'

'That would be nice,' said Sarah, and smiled at him.

✻   ✻   ✻

In the blank utilitarian office block where Periffatec had its headquarters, Steve Arundel was smiling too, grinning at the screen as he rapidly deleted unwanted ranks of e-mails.

'You look perky,' said his colleague, Malcolm. 'St Petersburg obviously agreed with you. Get lucky?'

'No I did not!' said Steve, flicking aside an unopened attachment which would, he knew, be the musical Christmas wishes of some cartoon reindeer, animated for his dubious delight by a supplier of printer capsule mouldings and capable of taking two full minutes to download. If time-wasting electronic mail oppressed him, so did the way that all his colleagues expected every divorced and unattached man to lead a life of dissipation and tell them all the details. 'You family men are all the same,' he grunted. 'Desperate for vicarious sex.'

'Doesn't have to be sex,' said Malcolm, turning back to peck at his own keyboard. 'A hot glamorous date would do. You owe it to us. I've got to dress up as Santa tomorrow for the toddler group party.'

'Bollocks, you know you love it,' said Steve unsympathetically.

'Anyway, who's the girl?' persisted Malcolm.

'What girl?'

'The one you're grinning to yourself about.'

'There is no girl,' said Steve firmly, as much to himself as to his interlocutor. 'I'm just pleased that I've got a winter tenant for Uncle Anton's flat. I won't have to be in and out of there checking for burst pipes and vandals.'

'Is this dream tenant by any chance a female girl?' began his colleague, but was distracted from the reply by the appearance on his screen of a florid, slow-growing reindeer singing 'Jingle Bell Rock' in a high tinny voice. 'Did you just forward me this crap? It won't stop opening.'

'Serve you right.'

But Steve was light-hearted, Steve was gay as he had not been since the ending of his marriage. The rest of the small, busy team at Periffatec noticed it all through that last working week before Christmas, and – because by and large they liked the tall, laconic, competent Arundel – they were happy for him. Ingrid, his pale and elegantly groomed secretary, was less happy than most, for Steve was a generous escort. Shrugging, she hid her mild dismay with typical competence. The old Steve would, she thought, be back before long, needing her.

And in the shop Maggie smiled too; more restrainedly, with lines of sorrow and apprehension and backache beginning to shape her mouth into a new set. It would be better, she thought, when she had left the Penns' house and the bookshop. It would be better come Christmas Eve; and greatest of all blessings, at least she had somewhere to go and a job. She would be able to save for the hard time, the time when her body would make her helpless. The thought made her shudder, but she squared her shoulders, set her lips, and resolved to bear it.

She packed her rucksack in advance, and on the last day of trading she brought it in to work and stowed it in the damp basement ready for the promised lift to Whitstable. Steve had telephoned the bookshop to tell her that he would drive her there and fix the lavatory door while he was at it. Fortunately she had been alone at the desk when the call came. She said her light-hearted farewells to the boys the night before, spoke briefly and clandestinely to Samantha, and told Nancy vaguely that she was 'off away again' on Christmas Eve, hoping that her mother would assume a flight to China. In fact, Nancy seemed so little interested that there were no questions.

She had worked it all out to avoid any need for a formal farewell. At lunchtime on that Saturday, however, she finished a transaction and felt a sudden heat, almost a blush, spreading over her face and neck. *Christ!* she thought. I can't leave it like this! 'I go away,' she said aloud, to nobody in particular. 'It's what I do. But I don't *run* away!' There was a lull in trade; just two deep browsers downstairs and Leo re-stacking the table in the children's section. She left the desk and went up to him.

'Can I take half an hour?' she asked. 'Lunch break?' Maggie never took lunch breaks, preferring to eat a roll behind the desk and save money. Leo looked at her nervously; their conversations had not been prolonged, these past weeks.

'OK,' he said. 'Might get busy again around two, though.'

'I'll be back.'

She pulled on her jacket and half ran up the street in the drizzle, noting with sorrow how much harder it was becoming to run anywhere. As she expected, the lights were on in the Penns' kitchen and Sarah was kneading pastry for mince pies. She spurned the ready-made, ready-rolled variety. As her sister's shadow fell across the doorway, she looked round.

'Oh, it's you,' she said coldly, and went back to her pastry. 'I thought it might be Nita.'

'I like Nita,' said Maggie, with an inadequate instinct to say something neutral but pacific. 'She's a very bright woman.'

'She's a good woman,' said Sarah repressively, with the words '*unlike some*' hanging in the air, all the more emphatic for being unheard. 'You forgotten something, then?'

'No. Sarah,' began her sister desperately, 'we can't just leave it like this. You've hardly spoken a word to me since – since all that. I'm going away. I'll be out of your hair. But can't we just mend a bit of the fence? You're my sister.'

'That didn't seem to bother you when you slept with Leo.'

'Sixteen years ago! It was the stupidest mistake—'

'Nor when you conspired to drag my underage daughter into your scummy, immoral, promiscuous subculture of . . . of . . .' Sarah heard herself, and did not like it, and stammered enough to let Maggie break in.

'That isn't fair. I tried to make her tell you. All I did was help her do the test because she was so, so scared, and I remember how awful—'

'Oh, very experienced in these things, you are! Though it isn't exactly the kind of experience I want my daughter to plug into!'

'What should she have done, then?'

'Come to me!'

'But she wanted to know where she was first. Whether you needed to be bothered with it. She'd finished with the boy, she wanted to move on quietly.'

'I really don't want you interfering in Samantha's life. You've been a baleful influence on all of them these past months. Samantha nearly pregnant, Teddy in trouble at school for playing with those magic tricks, and Jamie's been upset over me and his father, and he's at a difficult age to be embarrassed over your being pregnant by some foreigner. You're a menace to this family. The sooner you get out of town the better.'

'I came to say goodbye,' said Maggie sadly. 'And to say thanks for putting me up all these months. I might not see any of you again before I go abroad. Please, Sare, please couldn't we just shake hands? Call it a day? Then I'll go.'

Sarah turned her back and began to roll the lump of pastry flat, with short, vicious strokes. Nothing that Maggie said could make her speak again, and after a few minutes the younger sister took her heavy heart back down to the bookshop.

That evening, in the car towards Whitstable for the last time, she said to Steve Arundel, 'She won't forgive me. It's frightening, it's not like Sarah at all.'

'Mother tiger, defending her cave?'

'Oh, God, I suppose so. I always thought I was the tiger and she was the nice tabby cat.'

'Never mind,' said Steve comfortingly. 'I've got a screwdriver, and some tracking for the bog door, and a gas bottle for the cooker, and two bottles of ready-brewed mulled wine from the Nuremberg Christmas market, which my mate Malcolm gave to my secretary Ingrid, but she only drinks the most expensive kind of vodka.'

'I've got no food,' said Maggie suddenly, surprised that this was the first time she had thought of it.

'I've got some watery ham and half a dozen eggs in the back. I even got some nasty cardboard mince pies from the supermarket. Uncle Anton would have liked to think of a social rejects' Christmas party going on in his flat. We could invite Evan Ardriss from the pub and make it *really* miserable.'

'You're a mate,' said Maggie. 'God knows why. Perhaps you're an angel, like in all those Christmas films.'

He glanced at her. She was staring ahead, her eyes misty, her thoughts not really with him at all. With a small pang he realized how unlike she was to other women he knew. She had no notion of flirtation or conquest; to her he was a crewmate, a fellow backpacker, a chance comrade doing her a favour for a month or two. She had not the slightest notion of anything more than matehood between the two of them.

Not, of course, that he did either.

Chapter Twenty-eight

The sickness began on Christmas Eve. At first she thought it was the effect of Steve's ham and eggs and mulled wine, consumed the night before under the gloomy light of the single bulb which illuminated Anton Arundel's studio. It wore off by noon, to be replaced by a deep lassitude; she slept on the lumpy old mattress all afternoon, waking with a start to find the world dark and cold around her and the wind hissing beyond the wooden walls. On Christmas morning it came again, worse than before. Retching in the bleak lavatory she wondered if this could be that legendary condition of which Nancy had spoken so gloomily through their childhoods: 'morning sickness'.

But wasn't that supposed to happen sooner, and stop at three months? Why should it suddenly start at three months? Was it reaction, after the end of the bookshop job and the last tense weeks at the Penns'? Latterly, after all, she would hardly have dared to be sick in their bathroom. Shuddering back to her sleeping bag and the two old blankets Steve had donated from the back of his car, Maggie reflected that it really was time she saw a doctor. She had cancelled her appointment with the Brackhampton practice after the dreadful night of her revelation; it seemed indelicate even to share a GP with her wronged relatives. So, on her way to the pub the day after Boxing Day, she signed on with the local clinic. The nausea wore off each day before her lunchtime shift started, and she thanked her stars that the job that had fallen her way was one that started late and ran late.

The pub was busier than she had seen it before, its custom swelled by the few hardy holiday-cottage owners and Canterbury people who liked to come to the sea at bleak Christmastime. There was even some dinghy racing off the beach when the gale abated for a day. Between her lunchtime and her evening shift, Maggie liked to watch the striped sails skimming free and bright across the murky water. A Thames barge came into the harbour too, a stately shape with its sails brailed up in dark bundles against the light sky. It had a Christmas tree tied to its topmast, and in the evenings lit fairy lights on its yard. Young people with guitars strummed and sang in the cabin in the evenings, so after the pub had shut Maggie would wander along to the harbour and look down at the warm lights, then go back to her den above the chandler's shop to curl up under Steve's rugs and fall into a troubled sleep until the waves of sickness woke her.

The doctor, when she saw him in the first days of January, was sympathetic but brisk.

'No, it's not abnormal. Sickness takes different mothers at different stages.'

But I'm not a mother! Maggie wanted to say. I'm just temporarily carrying it. It was absured, so she just nodded and said, 'Fine.'

The doctor spoke of taking it easy, of eating a proper balanced diet and going to a hospital clinic to arrange for the birth, which they agreed would probably be in mid-May. She was given a weight card and a diet card and some patronizing pamphlets, which she threw away as she left. She went to the maternity clinic a few days later, on her day off from the pub, and afterwards, rebelling against the overheated room and the pall of vague anxiety which hung over her fellow patients, she tried to go for a long run along the seafront. After a few hundred yards she was exhausted, puffing and wincing with heartburn, her feet aching as if the arches had dropped.

She sat on the sea wall, staring out bleakly at the water, and realized that she could not after all carry on as if nothing was happening. Particularly, she accepted the end of her studies at Southwick. In her first days at Whitstable she had worked out with some care the system of buses and fast walking which would get her there for eight thirty and back to the pub by half past one, and had persuaded Evan Ardriss to let her start her shift late once term began. But there was not a chance, she thought now, not a chance of her being able to complete such a challenge in her present state. The very idea of a bus, of diesel fumes and swaying, brought back her morning nausea. She walked home and looked sadly for a while at her Chinese folders, then put them away in a cavernous drawer she had discovered under the platform bed. That was her fees gone west, then.

It was growing dark now, and without the job to go to she was at a loss for ways to fill the long dark evening. She had a couple of paperbacks with her, both too well read to provide any escape; there was neither television nor radio in the flat. The library, she thought, might be open.

She walked along the front towards the town centre, dismayed at the beginnings of a waddle in her gait and at the unseemly stretching of the stitches of her sweater in front. The library was shut. She wandered back towards the harbour, and stood under the harsh streetlights looking down at it. The tide was out; beneath her lay not the bobbing, shifting gaiety of the community of boats but an expanse of dully gleaming mud, with only rivulets of water through it. The boats hung at crazy, ugly angles in the slime, as helpless as she was herself. Tears sprang to her eyes.

'Beached,' she said aloud. 'Beached!'

She wondered whether Steve would appear, as she had wondered on her last day off; but the long afternoon and evening brought no sign of him. She laid aside his rent each week, in cash in a jam jar under the bed, and hoped to give it to him personally. He had left her cordially enough on her first night in Whitstable, with a joke and a peck on the cheek after their picnic in Anton's studio. She supposed, a little ruefully, that he went to his family for Christmas like everybody else. Perhaps it was an extended break. Perhaps he was ski-ing. She knew little enough about the man, for God's sake. He was just a mate.

She climbed into bed early, reflecting that one of the few perks of pregnancy was the sleepiness. If she could just lie like Rip van Winkle for the next five months, she thought, and wake up to find it all over, that would be good . . .

In her dreams a blue tide came up, covering the dead mud with sparkling life, buoying up the stranded boats, washing away her encumbrance and letting her swim, clean and naked, with dolphins around her in the sunshine. She woke chilly and sick and heavy, and reached to the bottom of the bed to pull on her too-tight sweater and shudder the blankets around her.

Thirty miles away Steve Arundel paced around his bare, anonymous flat in a block on the edges of Maidstone. He had come here when the value of the marital home was split between him and Jill; she had more taste for knick-knacks than he did, and he had no interest in furniture, so the white modern box had been furnished entirely by one trip to the Dartford Bridge IKEA. Every piece of furniture reminded him, with twingeing thumbs and aches in his back, of how much he had disliked the task of putting it together, all alone. Except for the bed, which reminded him only of two evenings spent with the cool, willing and unnervingly expert Ingrid.

Since his travelling had become curtailed by the new desk job, he had vaguely wondered once or twice whether it might be nice to get a more homelike place to live, or at least to hang curtains rather than white Venetian blinds in this one. But he had no heart for it.

'You're a classic example of Hotel Man,' Jill had flung at him during the bad times after the baby died. 'You don't even begin to understand what makes a home. You think everything in life can be replaced with an online order.' He had thought it monstrously unfair and untrue at the time, but all the same he thought of that insult every time he looked around his hotel-like flat. On Christmas Day he visited his father in an old people's home near Hastings, listened sadly to the old man's half-aware ramblings, spoke briefly to the matron and went home to make himself an omelette, alone. It was his own fault. Malcolm had tried to get him to Christmas dinner with his flourishing family, and Ingrid had kept leaving newspaper travel features open at pages about luxurious festive hotel breaks in Paris and Vienna, but he had resisted kindness and rapacity alike. 'You're becoming a monk, then, are you?' Ingrid had teased, with an edge of anxiety in her wide kitten eyes. 'Given up everything for a long Lent?' But he had only smiled, and offered a comradely pat on the shoulder which was met with an angry shrug.

He wanted very much to call on Maggie Reave in old Anton's grimy flat. But at Christmas and New Year, he thought, he could not trust himself. There was too much emotion in the air, and he would only betray himself, step further forward than he truly wanted, and alienate and embarrass her. It hurt him to think of her alone, shut out by her furious relatives in Brack-hampton, and once or twice in insane moments during the dead weeks after Christmas he imagined himself going into the bookshop and confronting this Leo, asking him how he dared allow his sister-in-law to be the lone sacrificial victim of his misdemeanour and his bloody daughter's. Why should he be forgiven for a sexual betrayal but Maggie unforgiven for trying to help a frightened teenager? Maggie had said to him, over their last supper together, that it seemed to her that Leo and Sarah were getting along better thanks to their joint rage at her over the Samantha business. She had made light of it. 'It's an ill wind!' But, thought Steve, nobody liked to be shut out of families at

Christmas. He did not much like it himself, especially since the news of Jill's newborn baby.

The thought of Maggie's baby also filled him with confused unhappiness. She said she would give it up, hand it over and not look back. But how could she? Wasn't that the hardest thing in the world for women? On Christmas Day he had watched a mawkish film with Bette Davis on satellite TV about a woman forced to give up her illegitimate child to her sister, and to play for ever the part of the child's stern martinet aunt. *The Old Maid*, that was it. Granted, this woman was a freer spirit than any could have dreamed of being, back in those vaguely old-tyme days of Hollywood legend. But even so. A baby!

Then his own pain came back, and he paced faster, until the confines of the bland, white, mocking flat were too much for him and he went outside to walk the deserted suburban streets in the rain, wearing himself out before the last half-bottle of whisky, and oblivion.

When term began, Samantha and Uma hatched a plan. They would wait for a morning of free study periods, get a pass to go to the public library, and go to Southwick instead on the mid-morning bus. They would find Maggie, see how she was and ask where she was living.

'It's bound to be Southwick,' said Sam, 'because of college. She's really keen on college, so she'll be round there. All we have to do is find the right lecture room for her course, and hang about outside till they have a break.'

'Mega,' said Uma. She heartily approved of Samantha's determination not to lose her aunt. 'She's as much yours as your parents'. She was your friend, right? You've got a right to choose your own friends. Human rights.'

But when they got to the college, a bespectacled young American told them that Ms Reave had withdrawn from the course 'on health grounds' and made no booking to renew her membership. He seemed to have some official role in the college, and would say no more; but another student, overhearing, chattered on more freely about how surprised they had all been because she was one of the stars of the group, and had serious plans to go to China in the summer.

'Well, bog!' said Samantha dispiritedly as they took the bus back to school. 'Now what?'

'Missing persons? No,' mused Uma. 'Sally Army does missing persons, but I think your ma would have to ask. Or they'd have to know that you weren't allowed to be in touch with her.'

'There's no fucking *allowed* about it,' said Sam indignantly. 'I will be sixteen soon. I could leave *home* legally.'

Her mother's repeated attempts to 'talk things over' with her had been met with frosty silence; once or twice the child within her had yearned to throw herself on Sarah's breast and be reconciled, but her adult heart was hardened by the cruel and obvious banishment of Maggie. Sam had, she thought, forgiven her father for his past misdeed, but she found it far harder to be reconciled to his share in the present unkindness.

'It's too *bad*,' she said to Uma. 'Honestly, it's awful what Mum and Dad are doing. Imagine being *pregnant*, and all on your own.'

'I thought she had a boyfriend.'

'Mum says she has. Mountjoy told her. But she never said anything to me, and she would have. I don't think she's with a boyfriend at all. I think she's in some skanky *hostel!*'

Uma shuddered. 'Yeah, that is grim.' They contemplated it together, as the bus roared round the Brackhampton bypass. 'C'm on, we'd better ring for our stop.'

'You look better,' said Samuel Miller to his secretary, who was once again filling a staffing gap by holding down a groggy terrier. 'Sorted it all out at home, have you?'

'Yes, I think so. Leo and I are *really talking*,' said Sarah.

'Samantha's being difficult, but the boys are back on an even keel.'

'Hmm,' said Miller, reaching for the hind leg of the dog and plunging a hypodermic needle into it. 'And the wildcat sister?'

'Good riddance,' said Sarah viciously. The dog gave a faint protesting kick. Miller's sharp eyes bored into her.

'Careful,' he said. 'These things can kick right back at you.'

Sarah had an uneasy feeling that he was not talking about the dog.

Chapter Twenty-nine

January passed, and February; Maggie's morning sickness grew a little better. Or perhaps, she thought, it was merely that she was growing used to it. Slip out of bed and hold on to the edge of the platform, head down against the faintness; make your way to the bathroom, vomit, drink a long glass of water; sit in the folding chair for a while, then carefully make your way to the kitchenette and eat a slice of dry bread. Sit down, close eyes against the spinning and swaying; wait, and nibble, and wait, and work out the days until your release. When the time comes, make the brave effort to put on clothes and go to work. Fresh air might make it better.

The clothes were, for a while, a serious problem. She dared not spend on anything new, and the town's charity shop had no maternity wear and their only large dresses were so sprigged, so garish, so skin-wincingly artificial that she recoiled from them, nauseous again. In the end she found two outsize, rather ragged, men's blue guernseys and some dark blue tracksuit trousers without the ubiquitous double white stripe of their kind. This uniform just about passed muster down at the pub, though Evan Ardriss would occasionally grumble about her lack of glamour.

'What the fuck's a barmaid for, if not to show a bit of tit?' he demanded.

'For serving and stacking the shelves, you sexist arsehole,' replied Maggie tranquilly.

Their working relationship was satisfactory; he was just nasty enough for her to feel she owed him nothing, and just funny enough in his misanthropy to give her the occasional therapeutic laugh. She longed to tell someone about him, to imitate his curmudgeonly ways and spill the beans about his meanness and small sordid cheatings with bottle ends and rigged optics. She did not, though; an employee's unwilling loyalty prevented her sharing what she knew with the customers, she had no communication at all with the family at Brackhampton, and the only person she could imagine telling just now was Steve. Who was nowhere to be seen. His rent now filled three jam jars, and she began to wonder whether it would not be more prudent to bank it.

There was company, though, of a kind. Although she still woke to sickness for many weeks, her weariness in the evenings had abated a little by mid-March. Sometimes after closing time, when Evan retired upstairs to his bed and switched off the mains power, she would play dominoes or cards for an hour with a couple of the regulars, usually fishermen on their own but sometimes the long-haired, square-faced folksinger girlfriend of the youngest. They were for the most part as bored and as skint as she was, waiting for the spring and summer liveliness of the town, and the extra work brought by ice-cream carts and souvenir shops. A new face at the bar was more than welcome to them. Sometimes Maggie played her whistle or mouth organ while the square-faced girl sang, but not often. Music troubled her too much, stirring up feelings best unexamined.

'It's all right as long as you bloody lock up,' Ardriss would snarl as he retreated to bed. These, after all, were his best winter customers. 'But you're not burning my bulbs out.' Sometimes Maggie's natural high spirits returned momentarily, and a peal of laughter would unite the odd little company which sat round two candles in bottles, with the roar of the winter sea outside and the men's faces turned into a Brueghel painting by the flickering primitive light. Once, one lad was drunk enough to make a heavy pass at Maggie as she finally saw them out at one o'clock. He was slapped away with practised briskness.

'Gerroff. Can't you find anyone who isn't six months bloody pregnant?'

'I like 'em big. You're a booty, girl!'

'Piss off. See you tomorrow.'

It was not a bad life, when she could forget about the pregnancy. Sometimes it was so like the old times on the road that she even wondered whether the travelling had genuinely been what she needed all those years. Maybe, she thought, it was just that when you were a traveller you were at the bottom of the heap: ambitionless, rootless, without status in a strange place. Maybe, after the painfully respectable caution of her upbringing, it was that sense of hand-to-mouth lowliness and casual un-attachedness that she had needed, rather than the exotic places themselves. Sure, she loved them; jungle and mountain and seashore scenes burned vivid in the back of her mind always. Yet in a curious way she was coming to love this wintry Kentish backwater as much as anywhere she had been. The sea consoled her, the grimy pub was a kind of home, its lonely misfits a kind of family.

But the baby leapt and kicked within her. The weeks passed; every time it moved her heart beat faster, unpleasantly, so that whatever she was doing she had to stop. Pouring a drink, fitting an optic, climbing the stairs above the chandlery, she would find herself suddenly paralysed with shock. The heart of the shock, which never seemed to lessen however many times the creature moved, was her own feeling for the curled thing within her. She had foreseen this. Indeed, she had been warned of it by the social worker to whom she had announced her intention of giving the baby up.

'You'll have strong biological feelings of bonding to over-come,' the woman said assuredly. 'It won't be easy, you know.'

Maggie knew with equal assuredness that she could slap down a biological urge as easily as she could a drunken fumbler.

Yet now that the baby was stretching and turning within her with such vitality, she fell constantly victim to this paralysing shock. It was as if her hard, cool, competent core was liquefying. She felt half-melted, as unstable and drooping as the snowmen which had appeared and disappeared during January's snow flurries. Her fight took the form of another visit to social services.

'I want a definite arrangement,' she said. 'I think you should have a family standing by, ready for the baby. I ought to meet them too, as a matter of responsibility.'

She had lain awake for many hours thinking about this: her first instinct, simply to hand the baby to authority, had been weakened by an unwilling attention paid to news headlines and to documentaries which ran on the pub TV during the dull empty early evenings. She still followed newspapers and bulletins like a foreigner, bright-eyed and curious and perplexed. Britain, her impression was, did not at this point in history show very much competence in the matter of children in care. If this interloper, this half-Lopez within her, was to be handed over then she wanted it to go straight to a family pledged to defend it for ever with their lives and their honour. Not into some scabby children's home full of damaged angry teenagers and run by people like the tired, lank-haired, humourless woman across the desk.

'So we need to have a family ready,' she said again. 'Who have you in mind?'

'It isn't that simple,' said the woman. 'Suppose you change your mind? A lot of women do, although usually,' she glanced at Maggie with mild distaste, 'where there is this intention of giving the baby away, we are dealing with far younger girls. Or suppose baby is born with a disability, or something else – unforeseen.'

'Like what?'

'We have policies on interracial adoption,' said the woman smoothly. 'There is talk of a new government guideline, but—'

'It's not black, you know,' said Maggie irritably, her frankness bringing a disapproving blush to the woman's face. 'And anyway, so what if it was? It'll be a bit Latino, perhaps, but nothing very dark.'

'As I say, there are guidelines and procedures and cooling-off periods.' The woman was almost snapping now. 'It would be very unusual indeed for an adoptive family to take the child on immediately from birth these days. Foster families—'

'No,' said Maggie. 'Not fostering. Not pillar-to-post. It ought to know its mother and father straightaway. For Christ's sake, there's a national *shortage* of free babies — I'd be doing someone a major favour here.'

The woman looked at her, and now the dislike was unmistakable. 'I can't do what you ask,' she said dismissively. 'If, after the birth, you opt to put the child voluntarily into the council's care, you will have to leave such judgments about his or her welfare to us, the professionals.'

Maggie stood up, balancing her new bulk in front of her. She wanted to loom over this damned woman, to face her down.

'What about surrogacy?' she snapped. 'Surrogate mothers just hand them over. I heard a radio programme about it. That works.'

'We do not encourage such arrangements, and some of them are illegal. The exchange of money, for example—'

'For Christ's sake, I don't want money,' gabbled Maggie. The baby kicked hard, twice. That moment of shock kicked in again; her chin dropped to her chest and she breathed carefully. Then her head came up resolutely. 'Thank you for your time,' she said. 'I'll be in touch.'

The woman made a note on her annoying pad. 'We are trying,' she said more mildly, 'to take account of the welfare of both mother and child.'

Maggie did not like that phrase, 'mother and child'. It sounded too indissoluble, too iconic. She almost said, as in the doctor's surgery, 'No, no, I'm not a mother,' but instead she smiled mirthlessly and left, saying she would 'give it some more thought'.

It was April when Steve came to see her. She was wiping down the bar counter at three o'clock, ready for her afternoon of freedom, and for a second or two he barely recognized her. The thin mischievous face had filled out, not puffily but enough to make her look more like her sister Sarah than her old self. Indeed, as he looked at her, Steve realized with a start that he must have actually seen Sarah walking past the cafe in Brackhampton once, and idly thought her strikingly pretty, if a bit mumsy. Maggie's wild hair was tied back for work, and the bony grace of her shoulders was blurred and padded by an unwonted layer of female softness. But when she looked directly at him, her eyes were the eyes he remembered, and so was the sudden leaping joy of her smile.

'Hey, stranger!' she said. 'I've got great wads of rent for you! Didn't know where to send it!'

'I feel bad about that. Should've told you. Suppose something had gone wrong in the flat?' he said with an awkwardness that she, in turn, found strange in him. 'What a crap landlord I am.'

'Well, it did go wrong. Bit of rot in the floorboards, so I ripped it out before it could spread, and got Dinksie to nail some old lump of boat there instead. He says it's mahogany, no problem. And the wiring went funny after the snow got in from the broken gutter, fantastic disco effects on the table lamp – and Evan's brother's sorted that. He's a proper electrician, he wired up the *Mary Sue*. I made Evan pay him in beer.'

'You're well dug in, then,' he said admiringly. 'Be getting the freedom of the city any minute, I should think.' He was in his business suit, fresh from a meeting in Canterbury; he made an odd sight in this grimy pub, awkwardly dapper next to Maggie's draggled guernsey and the landlord's wrinkled trousers and shiny corduroy jacket. He wriggled his shoulders as if to disarrange this embarrassing neatness, and Maggie saw the gesture and laughed at him, flicking her grey bar cloth dismissively in his direction.

'Yeah, you're a bit young-executive for us. Must be like dropping in on the Beverley Hillbillies. Or the Munsters,' she added in a lower voice, as Evan Ardriss stumped depressedly back down the rickety stairway from his flat.

'It's me that's the monster,' said Steve. 'I am a corporate robot, the Thing from the Boardroom of Doom. I came to ask if you might come out to supper. It's your night off, isn't it?'

Maggie looked suddenly embarrassed. 'Well, depends where,' she said cautiously. 'Clothes, you see . . .' She laid a hand on her bump, gingerly, as if it might explode, then snatched it away and blushed.

'Kaftan? Poncho? Shower curtain?' he suggested, trying to make a joke of it. 'Rip down the green velvet curtains, Scarlett . . .'

'Scarlett wasn't up the duff, and there is not much you can make out of a broken Venetian blind,' said Maggie more tartly.

'Vivienne Westwood could. She'd put it on the catwalk tomorrow. Go on, come.'

'Yes, of course I will. I would love to go out to supper. But it has to be a low, seedy pub or a burger bar, not one of your smart county watering holes with BMWs outside.'

'All right. Meet you at six o'clock at Anton's. You can give me the rent, and that way the evening might actually show a profit. Every young man's dream.'

They were back on course, thought Maggie happily. Joking, taking nothing seriously, a pair of mates. In recent weeks she had been troubled in her dreams by a different notion of Steve Arundel. This was, she fully recognized, nothing but a matter of hormones. Pregnant women always automatically gravitated to the nearest man who represented strength. It was a primitive reaction, like when Sarah used to fall in love with her obstetrician for the duration of delivery. ('Honest, Mags, you do. It's because he seemed more competent than Leo. It's natural, all vulnerable female animals latch on to the strongest alpha male in sight.')

So what could be more normal in her precarious state than to have irrelevant, meaningless fantasies about one's landlord?

At six o'clock, her hair loose, she was waiting for him in her cleanest blue tracksuit trousers and a bright pink baggy fleece jumper. It was the day's great find: almost new, four pounds in the Oxfam shop, a casually smart style and a colour that made her hair, brushed into a great dark wing, look all the glossier. Nor was she wearing her usual trainers. The shop had also produced a pair of black patent pumps which polished up beautifully with candlewax and a corner of Steve's old dog blanket from her bed. She had tidied the flat meticulously, thrown her big red-and-gold silk shawl over the chipped table and a jumble sale rug over the scruffy chair. There was a candle in a bottle on the table, and one of Dinksie's father's carved fish on the windowsill. With only the standard lamp lit, it did not look too bad at all.

Steve halted in the doorway and looked round with proper admiration. 'Homelike,' he said. 'I remember now. It always looked nice when Anton was here. Messy, but nice. When he died it sort of expired with him. I have to admit, when I first showed it to you I was a bit embarrassed.'

'It's wonderful,' said Maggie with feeling. 'It's private, it's easy to warm up, it's cheap, it's even a bit shippy. It makes me feel less beached than before, and I am incredibly grateful.' She smiled at him, and the disturbing thought flitted through her mind that a few months ago she would, without thinking twice, have kissed him gratefully on the cheek. Now she could not. Her looming belly came between them, and her meaningless dreams.

Steve just said, without much expression, 'I'm glad. And I'm sorry I just abandoned you here without checking things were OK. I've been working quite hard.' He glanced down. He had also, since Christmas, been reviving his old fling with Ingrid at the office, in the hope of extinguishing some confused and dangerous feelings. In a particularly low moment he had confided these to Malcolm in the pub after work. 'I can't risk it,' he said. 'Not after Jill. I should not be getting involved with an unmaternal, pregnant maverick who's leaving for China any minute. For all I know I only fancy her because she's pregnant, like poor Jill was. But it's wrong for me. If I ever trust a woman with all that – emotional stuff – again, it's got to be someone who wants what I want.'

'Like?' said Malcolm, into his beer. 'Like what do you want?'

'A home. A wife and family. Somewhere I can think about when I'm away, and look forward to.'

'A homebody?'

'I suppose so.' Steve sighed, wretchedly. 'You have to make sensible decisions about things like that. Like you did.'

'I was in *love* with Moira,' said Malcolm with dignity. 'If you aren't in love, it's hopeless. It fades a bit after the kids come, but if it was never there in the first place, it's no good at all.'

'Well, you have to make sure you fall in love with someone who wants to be married and have a home. There's got to be some sense applied to it. I wish I was Asian or Jewish, then I could have an arranged marriage.'

'Ingrid?' said Malcolm. 'Perhaps Frank Mortimer in Human Resources could arrange it. Frank was intended by nature to be a Jewish momma.'

Steve laughed, without much mirth. 'No, the thing with Ingrid is that she just likes sex and expensive outings, and she doesn't really like me all that much otherwise.'

But he may have been wrong. It was only days later that Ingrid, after what he thought had been a pleasant and certainly a very expensive evening in the West End, informed him that it was over for good this time.

'I don't care who she bloody is that you think of all the time,' she said crisply, tossing her neat pale hair. 'But I'm not playing substitute for a minute longer.'

'You're not a substitute! I'm not in love with anybody else!' protested Steve.

'What do you mean, else?' said Ingrid bitterly. 'You're not in love with me, that's for sure.'

'I mean I'm not in love,' said Steve, avoiding her eye. 'I'm not ready. Jill and everything.'

'Ha bloody ha,' said Ingrid. 'You haven't given Jill a thought for months.'

He had been planning to sleep with her again that night, as they did once every week or so; but all the same it was a relief when the door slammed, and he knew it was for the last time.

Now, he looked at the heavily pregnant, flushed Maggie in the tiny studio and found himself smiling like an idiot, lurching forward onto dangerous and uncertain ground with all the élan of a small child staggering into a sandpit. Enjoy tonight, he said to himself. Just enjoy tonight, have fun, go for broke.

'Come on then,' he said. 'Canterbury, I think. Bright lights. We might even do the late movie. I think they're showing *Bride of Frankenstein*.'

'Bit near the bone,' said Maggie. 'Bit tactless.'

'You look beautiful,' said Steve, lurching another step forward, joyfully, into the unknown. 'Totally lovely. A big pink party balloon.'

'Some women,' said Maggie happily, 'would be seriously offended at that remark.' And she too smiled, and put her hand in his as they made for the dark stairway.

Chapter Thirty

The winter had passed slowly, healingly, in the Penn family. Leo drank a great deal less than before and was careful of Sarah's feelings, almost wooing her. Unaccustomed to such solicitude in the rough and tumble of family life, she paid him more attention, even at times putting his comfort ahead of the children's. She was extravagantly pleasant to his new assistant, a thin nervous girl on her gap year. Samantha defiantly went to the defence solicitor and offered to be a witness for Duane, but in the event was not called. At the last minute one of his more respectable sisters unexpectedly stepped forward, to give such a spirited account of his persecution by elder brothers that the court let him off with a caution.

Jamie developed a passion for natural history under the tutelage of an enthusiastic new biology teacher, and began making an exhaustive record of the signs of spring in a notebook and on the family camcorder. Teddy carried on with his magic tricks at school, with slightly increasing competence, but took care never to discuss such aunt-engendered skills at the family table. Sometimes at school he was asked about her.

'Where's your auntie gone? She in China already?' asked little Joanne when she could bear the dearth of news no longer.

'Dunno. She moved on,' said Teddy.

'She's pregnant, right?' said Adrian. 'Only my mum said she saw her—'

'Are you getting a microscooter on your birthday?' asked Teddy, with guile beyond his years. The dangerous moment passed. He missed his aunt, but she had come and gone before. Impermanence was part of her nature, even of her charm. He did not want to think about the baby, so he did not. Meanwhile, home was definitely OK at the moment. Even Granny was quite chirpy, and came to lunch every Sunday. It occurred to him for the first time that when Auntie Maggie was around, Granny was much crosser than when she wasn't.

One night at the end of April, with fear in his heart, Leo said to his wife, 'Your sister's baby must be due quite soon.'

They were in bed, reading their books companionably, with Sarah's naked leg lying alongside his and their shoulders touching. They had made love that morning and the warmth of it still lay over them. Maggie's name had been mentioned so rarely since Christmas that Leo could not bring himself to say it aloud. But the thought of her troubled him.

Perhaps, he often told himself, there was no reason to worry. Perhaps she had terminated the pregnancy and taken off for China weeks ago. He tried to visualize her, carefree in a coolie hat on the edge of some great rice-field or pointed mountain range, speaking her high, chiming, new language, moving on with a laugh. But another vision obtruded: of a pale starveling creature in a sordid hostel, alone and friendless and about to give birth without sympathy or support at the age of thirty-six. Leo had attended childbirth courses, cheered on the labour and held each infant in his arms with gloriously fatuous pride; Sarah had always said it would have been hell without him, and that she didn't know how single mothers coped. Unlike some of her friends, she never had the slightest resentment of the man's passive role. 'I like having someone around who has nothing much to do except be thrilled,' she once said. 'It sort of reminds you that babies really are something to be thrilled about. Not just pain and sweat and heartburn.'

Who would be thrilled for Maggie? Who would mop her sweating brow? He knew whose job it was by nature; and raising the subject, he half hoped that Sarah would respond with: 'Oh yes, she must be, we ought to get in touch and see if she needs anything.'

Instead, she said nothing.

Again, almost sweating with his own temerity, he said, 'It should be May, right? Next month?'

At last Sarah spoke. 'Leo,' she said carefully, as if she was addressing an infant class, 'I think we ought to agree about something. It'll be easier for all of us if we just forget about Maggie. She never gives us much of a thought when she's away, and I don't think it's helpful to our family to be for ever hanging on everything she does as if she was some sort of celebrity. The boys are settled now, Sam's fine. You and I are fine. Maggie is just a load of trouble, waiting to drop back on this family if we give her half a chance.'

Now it was Leo who was silent. There were many things he wanted to say, absurdly beginning with 'She saved my shop!' but he had learned the perils of frankness.

Eventually he said, 'Well, if you're sure it doesn't worry you, sweetheart. It was you I was thinking of. I didn't want you worrying and not saying anything because of me.'

Sarah cuddled closer. 'Leo the lion,' she said. 'Furry lion! Love you.'

Later, when they drew apart, she said enigmatically, 'I talked to Mum about it. Maggie, I mean. She thinks the same. Don't trouble trouble.'

Leo found it hard to get to sleep.

After their evening in Canterbury, Steve resolved to call on Maggie twice a week, once on her evening off and once at closing time on Sundays, when the pub defiantly shut its doors at ten. On the first Sunday he found her setting up a game of pontoon with the fishermen Dinksie and Martin, and Nadine the folk-singer; after a rapid calculation he feigned delight and sat down to join them for the evening. He had been half planning to say some new things to Maggie Reave, alone on a moonlit water-front; but a fine judgement told him that it would be safer to go along with her normal routine. Half an hour into the game, he was aware of a slight prickling of shame when he realized that part of what he felt was relief.

The following week, after another cheerful midweek dinner in a bistro in Canterbury, he arrived on the Sunday evening to find no card players, and Maggie putting her jacket on ready to go home. She greeted him with a convincing start of surprise.

'Hey – hello. Would you like some rent at all?'

'Lead me to it. This is all so new, having women give me money just for existing. I could get used to it. You wouldn't consider tucking it into my breast pocket with a lascivious wink, would you?'

He took her hand, drawing it into his elbow as they walked along the seafront. It was a warm dusk still, with the lengthening days of spring.

'Walk by the harbour?' he said carelessly. 'See what's in?'

'OK,' said Maggie. She seemed listless and, he thought, breathless. Was it too late for her to be at work? Jill, he remembered with a pang, had planned to give up at seven months and rest.

When they reached the harbour they saw tall masts and yardarms, and he felt her arm stiffen against his. Glancing round, he saw her looking aloft, with concentrated care, then dropping her eyes as if disappointed.

'Did you think it might be *Evangelina*?' he asked softly.

'My lesbian lover, you mean?' She tried to make a joke of it, but tears were in her eyes. 'It's just that – oh Christ, Steve, it's just that I dream all the time, *all* the time, abut being back on that voyage, back among the sails, one of the boys, out on the ocean.' She stopped. 'And if you don't mind, let's go back. I don't want to look at a ship, not ever again. It hurts too much.'

They had talked a little about her travels on their evenings out, but rarely about the Atlantic crossing. Steve had done some deals in Panama, and they compared notes on the Canal and the countryside; there had been a recent release of hostages from Colombia, a pair of botanists, and they discussed danger and the Darien Gap. Once, Maggie had told him about a plan she had made to get a ride out to the Galapagos as cook on a cruise ship, only the cruise had been cancelled due to a bankruptcy, leaving her beached and frustrated in Ecuador. But of *Evangelina* she hardly ever spoke.

All he could think of to say, as they came to the door beside the chandlery, was, 'You'll go travelling again, you know. It probably feels impossible now, but it's just that your tide's down. It'll come up again. When it's all over.'

'Yeah,' said Maggie, and he had never heard her so bitter. 'When it's all over.' She turned, lumbering heavily along the sea wall, and his heart went out to her graceless vulnerability.

'Careful,' he said. 'Let me give you an arm.'

She turned to him, the tears still in her eyes. 'Why do you do this? Why? Even my sister doesn't want to know me now – did you know I wrote to her? She didn't answer. Why should you bother with me? I am such a fucking, fucking waste of space – and so *much* space. I'm a drag on the whole fucking world.'

'You're not, you're doing brilliantly under the circs,' protested Steve. He did not want to comfort her like this, like a hearty girlfriend, but could not find any other words, even in the darkness, even with a new moon overhead. 'You're doing fine. You've arranged everything, single-handed, saved up, fixed about the adoption—'

'That's just it,' said Maggie flatly. 'I haven't. I've pulled right out. I hate the social services and I don't trust them, and I don't know what to do. When I come out of the hospital it'll be with a sodding, bloody baby in my arms that I don't know what to do with.'

Steve's heart leapt, and hammered so hard that he could hardly answer.

'Why don't you trust social services?' he asked eventually.

'Because they're clearly going to shove it into some foster home, then another, then another, and take months and years to let anybody have it properly as their own, by which time it'll be just as miserable and confused and fucked-up as all the other kids they look after.'

'Is it that bad?'

'Do you watch the news? Read the papers?'

He did; indeed, since the death of his baby he had found himself drawn ever more tearfully towards stories about children in trouble – and he doubted that she was being unreasonable. Her words opened a new vista.

'So you'll bring it up? Yourself?' He thought of Maggie, the old thin wild Maggie, running with a toddler and swimming with a child, and a wave of tenderness shook him so violently that he closed his eyes and steadied himself on the sea wall.

'Christ, I don't know.' She shook herself. 'Sorry, sorry, sorry. Look, forget it. Come and get your rent and have a cup of hot chocolate for the road. I've got no coffee, but some brilliant cocoa and lots of milk.'

He had loathed cocoa ever since childhood, but followed her up the dark stairs with a song in his heart.

In the flat, she lit the candle and the standard lamp, motioned him to one of the white plastic chairs, and clattered her saucepan on the aged stove with swift, efficient movements. She was wearing the pink fleece top, but her dark hair was tied back lankly in a rubber band and the tracksuit trousers stretched uncomfortably across her stomach. He remembered Ingrid's pale slender grace, and marvelled at himself for wanting only Maggie. *I must not*, he told himself sternly, *I must not, not, not fall for a woman just because she is having a baby.* It was natural enough; he had lost the final months of Jill's pregnancy, lost the birth, lost her entirely in the aftermath of their disaster. His growing passion for Maggie Reave might only be a symptom of his orphan desperation to be reconnected to that aspect of life. He must not let it run away with him. Besides, she needed a friend right now, not some importunate suitor.

She turned to him in the lamplight, a mug in each hand, and every resolution crumbled.

He stood up, took both mugs, set them down on the table and said, 'I love you.'

Maggie glanced round for the other plastic chair and sat down, heavy and afraid. The candlelight flickered in a draught, making her still face dance.

'No,' she said. Her hands rested on her knees, elbows framing the ungainly pregnancy. 'No, we aren't like that. Are we?'

'I am,' said Steve. His head was swimming with risk and exhilaration. 'I am. I've been in love with you since I met you.'

Maggie recovered herself a little. 'You have not! You thought I was a dippy tree-hugger. You took the piss out of me.'

'You are, and I did. But Maggie, I love you. Please. I'm serious.'

'I'm having someone else's baby!'

'So?'

'I've got to keep it! I told you, I'm painted into a corner here. It isn't just the social bloody services woman, it's that I can't let it go to some stranger. I can't!' She mistook his expression for disbelief and repeated, 'Look, Steve, I can't! Suppose it was a baby that had the same sort of feelings I do, and got brought up by some *bore*, or some *bigot*! I've tried and tried, but I can't do it!'

'Good.' He smiled at her, so tenderly that she had to look away, in order to hold herself to her resolve.

'It is *not* good! It's the end of everything that I've done, and been, and all the freedom that kept me alive. I've thought and thought, and basically I've just got to accept that I had my fun and my freedom, and it's over! Till I'm about fifty-five, anyway,' she added, with an unfortunate air of anticlimax which made Steve suppress a smile.

'I could look after you,' he said steadily. 'Both of you. I want to. Please, Maggie. I love you. You don't have to love me back as much as I love you, nobody possibly could. But just stay with me, let me look after you.'

Maggie got up, came towards him and gingerly, so that her swollen belly would not touch him, put her arm round him from the side and kissed his cheek.

'You're a dear soft man. But it's impossible. You lost your baby, you lost your wife, you're just convincing yourself you want an instant replacement. But it's not your baby, and you'd resent it. And anyway, I'm not your cup of tea really. You want someone cosy, a proper wife like Sarah. I'm just a piece of chaos.' She stepped away and sat down again.

'Not with a baby. You won't be chaos with a baby. And I bloody *would* love it. I like babies!'

He told himself that he had not expected instant success, but all the same a cold dismay was gripping him. He remembered what he had told Malcolm about the need to marry calmly and sensibly. Did she detect that thought behind his wooing? Had she divined something ineffably cautious and tedious and shallow in him, which she despised?

'I don't care,' he cried, too loud. 'I don't care if you go on being chaos – and you won't be.'

Maggie was looking at him, sadly. 'Of course I won't be bad to the baby,' she said gently. 'I'll buy all the creams and rattles and stuff. I'll sign it on with a doctor. I'll teach it to walk and talk. I'll probably sing to it. It'll be safe with me. But I don't think I can live in England for long, it's a killjoy sort of place for single mothers. So when the baby's strong enough I'll probably go abroad. Find a housekeeping job with a room, somewhere warm.'

'I'll come too!' said Steve desperately, reaching for her hands. 'I'll be the gardener or something!'

Maggie looked at him with great, sad eyes. 'I do, sort of, love you,' she said. 'How couldn't I, after all you've done? And you make me laugh more than anyone. But it's no good, Steve. I don't love you that way. Don't kid yourself.' She winced, and touched her side. 'Please just be friends. If you can bear it.'

'Well, I can't,' he said, his voice odd and harsh. 'I wish I was bloody dead!'

He dropped her hands, picked up the rent she had left on the table, and without another word let himself out of the studio and down the stairs to the cold midnight town.

When he had left, Maggie began to cry.

Chapter Thirty-one

He did not go home. He had no home any more. Instead of taking the road to Maidstone and the sterile flat, he drove – too fast, with tears in his eyes – along the Brackhampton bypass and down into the dark town where she had lived. Parking the Saab carelessly askew across two spaces behind the town hall, he sat and wept through the night until he fell into an uncomfortable sleep. Once, half in a dream, he reached awkwardly for the old dog blanket because he was cold; when he remembered that he had given it to Maggie, he felt a strange sense of comfort. She did not want all he had to give, yet he had not been useless to her. He pulled his coat around him and slept on.

When he woke it was full daylight, and curious passers-by were pausing to peer at him through the misted windows. He did not care. He got out of the car, glanced around him, peed defiantly against its back wheel and stretched his long limbs. Then he walked stiffly to the High Street and stood for a moment or two looking in through the plate glass of the bookshop. It was already a quarter past nine; he could see a grey, stooping, scholarly man in conversation with an early customer. As he watched, the man actually wrung his hands, Heep-like, and nodded enthusiastically at something the buyer said.

Leo Penn! The creep! This dull-looking man was the cause of

Maggie's misfortune sixteen years ago. He was the chief author –
Steve thought savagely – of all the sorrow she had dragged round
the world with bright, brittle gaiety through her travelling years.
No wonder she had never trusted a man! No wonder she could
not trust him now! All because of Leo! Swine, creep, worse than
creep for siding with his self-righteous bloody wife against poor
beloved Maggie.

Tears of rage choked him. He had his hand on the door,
ready to push it open, storm in and tell Brackhampton's favourite
bookseller his fortune with a fist. His other hand rose to his
cheek, though, and felt the uncomely stubble of his bad night.
He had been a salesman all his life, well-presented for every
difficult encounter; he hesitated for a moment. It was in that
moment that a crackling voice spoke behind him.

'Hello! I do believe I know you!' He turned, to see a spry elderly
woman in a purple coat and woolly scarf. She was holding out
something towards him, and through his anger and bewilderment
he saw that it was one of his own business cards. He stared.

'Maggie Reave gave it to me. When you were taking her out
the first time in your car. *Such* a nice gesture, I thought, so I kept
it. Are you still in touch? We miss her.'

Something in the old woman's sharp eye made Steve, a
professional reader of people, aware that she was not merely
waffling in the manner of her kind. She had a purpose. He was
also secretly impressed by the fact that she did not recoil at all
from his darkly unshaven chin.

He said, 'I have her address, if you like.' It seemed to him that
if he could no longer be a friend to Maggie in the coming weeks,
it would be good if someone who wished her well knew where to
find her.

'Thank you. It's her mother, you see.'

He stared blankly.

'She's dead. Old Nancy Reave. Two days ago. It was a heart
attack. She didn't suffer, but nobody was expecting it at all.
Simply taken, just like that.'

Steve rubbed his chin perplexedly. He had forgotten his intention of attacking Leo. Maggie had rarely spoken of old Nancy except with mild exasperation, but all the same a mother was a mother. Doubtfully he said, 'Her relatives here should be the ones to tell her.'

Miss Mountjoy looked at him with scornful sharpness. Her social manner changed to something altogether more formidable.

'Oh, come on, Mr Arundel,' she said. 'You must know as well as I do how things stand. Family rifts are reprehensible, and I have not only prayed about it but *spoken* seriously to Mr Penn, since we have an old acquaintance. He is not being entirely straight with himself, in my view. But I do not think that in her present state Mrs Penn is going to see her duty very clearly. She is extremely upset.'

'Well, *you* could tell Maggie about her mother,' said Steve. He pulled out a pen and another business card, rested it against the wall and began writing the address in Whitstable.

The old woman peered at it over his shoulder, and made a sound like 'Tchuh!'

'What?' he asked.

'I do not drive a car,' she said 'And there is no telephone number, and in any case it is unkind to inform people of bereavements by telephone. Particularly if their – ah – health is precarious.'

Oh, thought Steve. So she knows that too, the canny old virgin.

'Distances are nothing to your generation,' said Miss Mountjoy. 'You go and tell her, gently and kindly. A man friend is very comforting to a woman at times like this.' She threw him something which, in a less mature, pious and respectable woman, he would have taken for a flirtatious glance. 'The funeral is on Thursday. St Chad's, next to the park, two o'clock. You should bring her. It must be divine mercy that we met like this.'

Steve nodded, still speechless.

'Oh, she'll come,' said Miss Mountjoy, answering an un-spoken question. 'She'll come with you, in your nice black car.'

Sarah had wept, on and off, for two days. Her competence deserted her; Leo had to deal with the coroner and the chapel of rest, and Samantha rose magnificently to the occasion, cooking for the boys and keeping track of them over the confusing, troubled weekend. On Monday Sarah woke in a calmer state and said to Leo, 'I want to sort out her things.'

'Not yet,' said Leo. 'We don't need to do anything till after the funeral.'

'I want to,' said Sarah. As the shock abated, she was beginning to see that a powerful ingredient in her sorrow was a sense of unfinished business, unasked questions, unex-pressed emotions.

'It's always like that when a parent dies,' said Leo when she told him this. 'It was with both of mine. You've never said the things you ought to. Almost everyone feels that.'

'Then you see why I have to go and be in her house,' said Sarah flatly.

'OK,' said her husband. 'I'll drive you over. Anna manages quite well in the shop now.' He wondered whether to mention Maggie, but dared not. She was almost certainly abroad by now anyway, he told himself.

Sarah was dry-eyed on the journey to Brackley Park estate, and maintained her composure as she entered the living room. Nancy had died here, alone in her chair, to be found an hour or so later by a neighbour coming to tea. Sarah stared at the empty chair.

Leo said inadequately, 'I doubt she suffered. The doctor said—'

'I know what he said. Look, go for a walk round the block. I want to be on my own for half an hour.'

Obediently, he left her. Sarah sniffed, then went to the roll-top desk which she remembered from childhood. It reminded her of her father. The hardest thing, she thought, would be to see his tidy, banker's handwriting on the old family files. It was as if he had not truly died until this moment.

She shook herself. That was all the more reason to collect the family documents and take them safely home. She found a key on Nancy's ring, unlocked the desk and rolled back the wooden top. The sound took her back to childhood, to her father's fiddling with 'important papers' while she sat on the floor playing with baby Mags and her wooden bricks.

It was a moment before she could pull out the first folder, marked 'Accounts to 1967.' God, did these old people never throw *anything* away? She peered at it: 'Mortgage £24.7s 6d'. She smiled in spite of herself.

She began to fill the folding plastic crate she had brought with her. After a few minutes she reached a cardboard pouch marked 'Certificates'. Flicking open the dusty folder, she pulled out first Ted's birth certificate, then Nancy's. They were so archaic in style that she studied them for a while, fascinated. Clipped behind them was Maggie's – dated 11 April 1965 – and her own, 3 August 1960. She had last seen it when she applied for her first passport, to go on honeymoon just before her father's death. Handling it, she remembered Nancy closing the file jealously, locking the desk and saying, 'You'd better give it back, for safety, the minute they return it.' She had been mildly annoyed – surely a married woman could keep her own birth certificate? – but had given it back after the funeral mainly as a gesture of respect for poor Ted.

She turned over the papers, and came on her parents' marriage certificate, with the mark on it of Maidstone register office. How long had it been? How many years? Would she and Leo make it that far? Sentimentally she gazed down at the paper, and then went rigid. It was hot in the little room, airless, or was it shock that made the sweat break on her brow?

4 June 1960 was the date. No, it must be a mistake. Must be

1959. Yes, of course – she remembered their twentieth anniversary party in September 1979. She had come home from her first term in college for it, and remembered Maggie teasing Ted about how they were jumping the gun, because most people did the party for the silver wedding, not 'Bakelite, or whatever it is at twenty years'. She remembered how insistent Nancy had been to mark the date, and how full of uncharacteristically coquettish reminiscence about her first meeting with Ted in a railway buffet, and how long he had courted her, and how pleased they were to find Sarah on the way soon afterwards, and what a tragedy it was that their wedding pictures had been destroyed in a fire at the photographer's.

She also remembered that Ted did not join in this upwelling of reminiscence. He talked rather about Sarah's childhood, and dwelt on how delighted they had been to have a baby. 'Both of us,' she could hear him saying, oddly. 'Both of us were pretty excited!' She had never given it much thought, but now it was only too clear why the poor man felt he had to say this so emphatically. Nancy, lifelong deplorer of unmarried mothers, had walked up the aisle seven months gone. She, Sarah, had been on the brink of becoming a Shameful Bundle.

There were tears in her eyes as she closed the folder and put it in the box. No wonder Nancy had always fretted so much about her daughters. How had such a disaster happened to such a congenitally careful, neurotic, self-absorbed person as her mother? Had quiet, considerate Ted been an importunate wooer, back in – Sarah frowned – November 1959? Had he left her for half a year before making an honest woman of her? It was hard to imagine.

Very hard. Something else stirred in her mind, and some time later, when Leo returned to the little house, he found the front room empty and a series of scrapings and bangings reverberating from the attic. He climbed the ladder and stood, puzzled, on a top rung. Flushed, her dark hair trailing a cobweb, Sarah looked across at him from the spot where she knelt under a beam and behind a barrage of cardboard boxes and a sea of spilt and curling photographs.

'Darling, you don't have to go through every last thing now,' he said. 'Only the main documents, surely?'

'I was conceived in 1959' said his wife gnomically. 'In November. And do you know what?'

He was afraid for her; there had been more anger and tears in recent months than he could ever remember, and he mistrusted the weird intensity of her look. He could not tell whether she was horrified or exalted.

'What's the matter?' he asked gently.

'*They weren't married then.* It was another seven months.'

'Well,' said Leo. 'By 1959 . . . well, the world was changing, surely? There must have been lots of brides with big bouquets.'

'Yes, but he wasn't the father,' said Sarah flatly. 'I mean, he wasn't my father. Can't have been. Look.'

She shoved a paper at him. It was from one of Ted's old boxes, the ones he had brought with him to the marriage and put straight in the attic. Nothing of Nancy's was near it and the old string, with her father's neat label on it, had been untouched until Sarah ripped it off. Leo frowned. He felt that Sarah's untidy frenzy of investigation had come far too soon for good taste. Nancy still lay unburied in the chapel of rest.

Obediently, though, he read the paper. Under a printed bank heading, it was a letter about a temporary promotion to the Skipton branch from June 1959 to February 1960 'to replace our Assistant Manager Mr Inglebrough during his journey to the Far East'.

'He was there all right,' said Sarah. 'Here's his notebook.' Again the small, neat writing; again the dates.

'So,' said Leo, 'he came down from Skipton to see his girlfriend, and they were glad to be together again, and all that . . .'

'No,' said Sarah. 'Because when Dad was in a reminiscent mood, he used to tell us about his bachelor days. Especially all about Yorkshire. He had a girlfriend there whose father ran a farm. He was a city boy, remember. I think it was a bit of a thrill being involved with cows and things. He talked about it lots. Maisie taught him how to milk. Then he'd laugh and say that when he left the Skipton job and got properly promoted and posted to Maidstone, this Maisie girl told him she'd never come south or live in a town. So he got off the train feeling a bit low, and then he'd always end the story by saying, "And then I met your mother in the station buffet, just like in *Brief Encounter*, and saw her shining black hair, and that was that!"'

Leo was silent.

Sarah concluded, 'See? By the time Mum met Dad, she was three months gone. And he still married her. She'd grown up here but they got married in Maidstone, and only moved back when I was born and he got the manager's job. None of the neighbours or Mum's old Brackhampton friends need have known.'

The silence of the attic lay between them. Sarah knelt, looking across at the top half of her husband protruding through the trap door.

Leo shifted uneasily on his rung of the ladder. After a moment, helpless to stop himself, he said, 'But you're so like Maggie to look at. And you're both so like Samantha.'

Sarah riffled among the photographs, and thrust one at him. 'We're both the spit image of Mum,' she said. 'God knows what she did with men's genes. Suppressed them by force of personality, I suppose.'

Again Leo winced at the thought of Nancy, waiting alone and cold for the gentle, decent ceremonies of the church. Sarah, however, seemed oblivious of the tastelessness of her quest. She continued, 'But there are things that are different between Maggie and Sam. Sam's got a square jaw, with that dimple. She didn't get it from me, and Dad didn't have it, nor Mum. But look who did. It's just skipped a generation, through me. Look.' She delved in her cardigan pocket, and opened a pale, flat, shagreen card case.

'What is it?' He reached his hand out to take the slip she offered him.

'It was right at the back of her bedside table drawer.'

It was a tiny, black-and-white contact print, cut from one of those sheets which studio portraitists used to give to clients. The subject was a handsome man in his mid-thirties or thereabouts, with dark crinkled hair brushed back, a slightly hooked nose and a dimpled jaw which, when he covered the rest of the face with his finger, Leo recognized instantly as belonging to Samantha and also to Teddy.

'Bloody hell!' he said softly. Looking up at Sarah, he saw that she was smiling, glad that he believed her. 'Well, who'd have dreamed it!'

'At least we know that Dad was willing,' said Sarah softly. 'He knew what he was taking on, and he bothered to keep telling me how thrilled he was when I was born. He was my dad. He'll always be my dad. But poor old Mum, with her romantic secret and her pearly little box by the bed.'

'Who is this? I don't suppose we'll ever know,' said Leo, gazing at the photograph of his children's unknown grandfather.

'Oh, I know,' said Sarah. 'I've seen the twin of it. I know perfectly well who it is. Take away his beard and you'd see that dimple down the High Street any day.'

She had got up from her kneeling position among the photographs and was sitting, Leo suddenly noticed, on a trunk labelled MARGARET REAVE. She seemed to be unaware of this, and he closed his eyes for a moment, as too many ironies spun around him.

'Who?' he asked.

'The nice thing,' said Sarah, 'is that he'll be at the funeral, *ex officio* anyway. I hope he has the decency to say a prayer for her.'

For a wild moment Leo thought about the vicar of St Chad's, the Reverend Harman. They were rare church attenders but knew him reasonably well; the vicar could not be a day over fifty, and had a distinctly receding chin. 'Who?' he almost shouted. 'What are you talking about?'

'Samuel Miller,' said Sarah. 'Remember? We were worried about the hymns? Then Mr Harman told you Sam Miller is filling in on the organ for services at the moment and he's able to take the afternoon off work to do Mum's funeral, being his own boss. And this very photograph is also on view in old Mrs Miller's Victorian silver locket, because she showed it to me once. It was taken when they got engaged.'

'The bastard!' said Leo. 'Somehow you don't think about your parents' generation carrying on like that.'

'No,' said Sarah. 'But, do you know, it makes me fonder of Mum and Dad than I've ever been. He loved her, you know. And he loved both of us, though I always had a hunch Maggie was more special to him, and I was more special to Mum. But it's like that in families sometimes. And it wasn't a bad family really.'

That night Sarah did not cry, but slept close and warm with an arm round her husband all night and her breasts against his back. In the morning she was composed, and spent a long quiet time with Samantha and the boys choosing the hymns for her mother and making sausage rolls and quiches for the freezer, because Nancy's friends would expect a proper funeral tea. Nita Syal came too, with small sweet cakes and sympathy. It was a strangely happy afternoon. Sam and the boys were touchingly careful of their mother, hugging her often and washing up her dishes.

'Don't you have to go to work this week, Mum?' asked Teddy solicitously. 'Will Mr Miller be cross?'

'No,' said Sarah, and smiled at the little boy with the dark, crinkling hair and the dimple in his chin. 'Not him!'

Chapter Thirty-two

Steve ran up the rickety stairs two at a time, because of the sound beyond the door. He had gone to the Seven Grapes first, only to find a surly Evan Ardriss behind the counter on his own.

'Bloody unreliable bitches, barmaids, every bleeding one of them,' said the landlord, only to receive a blast of invective before his guest clattered from the room. Ardriss was inclined to mutter about banning Steve and sacking his idle floozie, but Dinksie, who was leaning on the bar, protested. 'She *is* 'avin' a baby, Ev.' And young Martin, arriving for a quick half after a morning working on his engine, opined that the landlord was bloody lucky to have got Maggie in the first place, let alone kept her at work so long in her state. He was vehement on the subject; his own Nadine was at long last expecting, and spent most of the day writing long happy folksongs about her condition.

'Hope Mag's all right, anyway,' he concluded. 'No thanks to you if she ain't. Bloody old slave-driver.'

Ardriss merely snarled, but in what the observant panel at the bar considered a suitably chastened manner, and the talk turned to fishing.

Steve, meanwhile, panting and terrified, was pushing open the unlocked door of his late uncle's flat. Maggie lay on the platform bed, white as chalk, the dog blanket over the mound of her stomach.

'I can't – breathe properly,' she gasped, without greeting or preamble. 'I don't – get this. I thought it was different. Sarah said—' Her voice tailed off into a long, dragging moan, then she gasped again and said, 'Sorry. Don't know what came over me.'

'You're in labour, fool,' said Steve, whose arm was round her shoulder.

'Not for a couple of weeks yet,' she said faintly. 'Not due.'

'It's not a *bus*,' he said. 'We'd better get you to hospital quick. May I?' His hand was on her stomach, and she nodded, speechless, and let it lie there until the next pain gripped her. It came very soon indeed.

'Oh, bloody hell,' said Steve, snatching his hand away as he felt the terrible tightening. 'How long have they been so close together?'

'Half an hour?' said Maggie vaguely. 'It hurt last night, but I thought it was indigestion. I had cod and chips after work and I can hardly eat anything like that now. Feels as if my stomach's gone too shallow for food. I thought labour contractions were something different. Sort of lower down, or something.'

Steve ripped his mobile phone from an inside pocket, and dialled 999. Maggie panted and moaned again twice while he had a tense geographical altercation with a distant Vodafone operator ('Kent! Kent! Not Whitley Bay!'). She hung on to his other hand all the time, hurting it.

When he snapped the phone shut she said, 'Look, the thing is, Steve, it's sort of – aah – coming out!'

'Are you meant to push it out? What position? Do you sit up or lie down? What did they say in the antenatal classes?'

'I only went to one. They were such awful women.'

'You are hopeless! Useless! You're supposed to know by now!' He felt panic and joy at once, panic that she might come to harm and guilty joy at being her helper.

'It is really, seriously coming out. Something is, anyway. Oh God, the mess – oh God, your flat – this mattress will have to go . . .'

They were both prone to say, in after days, that the next few minutes passed in a blur. They both lied: every detail of it was fixed in their minds and replayed often. Steve had the presence of mind to whip away the ancient dog blanket and run for a clean sheet and towel, stumblingly knocking over two chairs as he did so. Maggie, as her gasps declined and the red, waxy, kicking new thing lay between them, reminded him about 'cutting the rope' and tying a shoelace round it.

Sometimes, telling the story, she claimed that he tied the knot first of all in the wrong end, the one attached to the placenta. Steve always denied this. Whatever the truth, when the ambulance crew came they found Maggie cross-legged on the high bed platform with Steve next to her, both of them oblivious to the mess around them and the upturned chairs, a man and a woman close together and gazing down at an alert, beady-eyed infant wrapped in a threadbare towel.

'Looks like you hardly need help,' said the woman paramedic, grinning. 'Except with the clearing up. Is it a boy or a girl?'

The couple exchanged a horrified glance.

'Oh, bloody hell,' said Steve. 'We haven't actually looked.'

'If it's a girl I'm not sure I want to know,' said Maggie, faintly. 'It's altogether too bloody tough to contemplate, this being female.'

The woman gently unwrapped the towel and said, 'It's a boy.'

'That's pretty tough too,' said Steve. He put his arm round Maggie again. 'Never mind. As they say in *Three Men In a Boat*, humankind is born to trouble, as the sparks fly upward. Either way, we're all stuffed.'

The paramedic raised an eyebrow at her colleague, and together – rather against her wishes – they strapped Maggie to a stretcher and carried her to the waiting ambulance.

Inside, Maggie said shyly, 'I didn't think you'd come any more. I thought I blew it,' and Steve remembered with a plummeting heart what it was that he had come to tell her. After some evasion she got the truth from him.

'Miss Mountjoy, from the bookshop, told me. I'm really sorry. It's your mother. She died suddenly. Before the weekend.'

Maggie was quiet for a moment, as the ambulance raced along the impersonal roadway. Then she said, 'Is Sarah OK? She was always Mum's favourite.'

'Don't know. I only know that Miss Mountjoy thought you should be told about the funeral. Nice old trout, I like her.'

'Yes,' said Maggie. 'Well, I'll go, obviously. I'll stay at the back and keep out of Sarah and Leo's way, but I have to go.'

'If you're allowed out of hospital.'

'Oh hell, it's only check-ups. African women give birth in fields.'

'Most fields are a lot more hygienic than Uncle Anton's mattress. And African women don't dick around for twelve hours assuming it's fish and chips.'

'Point taken.'

'Well, anyway, if you're fit enough to go to St Chad's, I'll drive you. Both of you. We can get a baby seat thing.' He looked down at the sleeping boy with shining eyes. 'Hello again, sprog. Welcome. Happy days!'

Maggie watched him, and her heart rose and swelled with irrational, treacherous joy.

He read her face, and said, 'It was all bollocks, that stuff you said yesterday. About being wrong for me. Wasn't it?'

'Complete bollocks,' said Maggie happily. She reached up and stroked his stubbled chin.

'So can I come with you next time you run away?'

'If you don't, I shan't go.'

'You must always go, if you need to,' he said seriously. 'And somehow or other we'll come along too.'

'Always,' said Maggie.

Tentatively, he touched the baby's tiny cheek. 'You're my witness, Lopez junior,' he said. 'Always.'

Chapter Thirty-three

There were white lilies on the altar, and the organ played a soft regretful voluntary as the mourners filed in to their benches beside the coffin. Miss Mountjoy saw the Townswomen's Guild deputation into their allotted benches behind the family, then discreetly met Leo and Sarah and the three dark-suited children by the door and led them forward. Sarah glanced up at the organ loft and the back view of the old vet, with his wings of silver hair. Leo's eye followed hers and he put a steadying hand on her waist, but Sarah was composed, even faintly smiling. The time would come, she thought, when she would inform her acerbic employer of what she knew. Dear Samuel, with his spiky cynical pragmatism and exaggerated respect for the marital art of forgiving and forgetting. She looked at her daughter: a new generation, and by nice coincidence another Sam. One day, she might laugh about that with Sam Miller. But not with his wife, never with Caroline.

As she stepped into the pew, she laid a hand briefly on her mother's coffin. *Goodbye, Mum. We know everything, and we're happy about it. You did all right, considering.* Leo saw the gesture and thought that he understood it. Obedient to the change in the organ's note, he picked up a hymn book and flicked it open. Joyful, lilting, from above them fell Brother James's Air: 'The Lord's my shepherd, I'll not want, he makes me down to lie in pastures green . . .'

Maggie and Steve were very quiet; not one head in the small

congregation turned as they slipped into the back of the church with the small sleeping hump of their new child in a carrier between them. Only later, as they stood a little back from the graveside party, did the two sisters' eyes meet. Across the grave, under the pale green of the spring leaves, Sarah mouthed one word and Maggie read it.

'Sorry.'

Gravely, Maggie nodded. Then she stepped forward, after her sister and her niece and nephews, and stooped to throw her handful of earth, dust to dust, on the coffin. Looking up at Sarah, she in turn mouthed one word.

'Later?'

Sarah inclined her head.

Then, unremarked by any but the interested eye of Miss Mountjoy, Maggie turned back to where Steve Arundel stood with her baby just waking in his arms. The three of them withdrew from the company as silently as they had come.